The Model Wife

JULIA LLEWELLYN

PENGUIN BOOKS

PENGUIN BOOKS

Published by the Penguin Group
Penguin Books Ltd, 80 Strand, London WC2R ORL, England
Penguin Group (USA) Inc., 375 Hudson Street, New York, New York 10014, USA
Penguin Group (Canada), 90 Eglinton Avenue East, Suite 700, Toronto, Ontario, Canada M4P 2Y3
(a division of Pearson Penguin Canada Inc.)
Penguin Ireland, 25 St Stephen's Green, Dublin 2, Ireland
(a division of Penguin Books Ltd)
Penguin Group (Australia), 250 Camberwell Road, Camberwell, Victoria 3124, Australia
(a division of Pearson Australia Group Pty Ltd)
Penguin Books India Pvt Ltd, 11 Community Centre, Panchsheel Park, New Delhi – 110 017, India
Penguin Group (NZ), 67 Apollo Drive, Rosedale, North Shore 0632, New Zealand
(a division of Pearson New Zealand Ltd)
Penguin Books (South Africa) (Pty) Ltd, 24 Sturdee Avenue, Rosebank, Johannesburg 2196, South Africa

Penguin Books Ltd, Registered Offices: 80 Strand, London WC2R ORL, England

www.penguin.com

First published 2008
1

Set in 12.5/14.75 pt Monotype Garamond
Typeset by Rowland Phototypesetting Ltd, Bury St Edmunds, Suffolk
Printed in England by Clays Ltd, St Ives plc

ISBN: 978–0–141–03364–8

www.greenpenguin.co.uk

Penguin Books is committed to a sustainable future
for our business, our readers and our planet.
The book in your hands is made from paper
certified by the Forest Stewardship Council.

For Clemmie

Acknowledgements

The Oscar bit no one reads, but profound thanks as always to Mari Evans and all the wonderful team at Penguin, especially the brilliant Natalie Higgins, Liz Smith and Ruth Spencer. To Lizzy Kremer and all at David Higham. Everyone at Channel 4 News for advice – especially Jon Snow. Victoria Macdonald was a brilliant help as always. Any resemblance to the *SevenThirty News* is purely coincidental and mistakes are all my own. To Michaela Byrne – thank you for your essay! To Jana O'Brien, Hannah Coleman and above all Kate Gawryluk, I couldn't have written this book without you. To my parents, and to the Watkins family for all their love and support.

I

Poppy Price had always dreamt of marrying a handsome prince, of catching his eye across the crowded ballroom floor, of him approaching and asking: 'Shall we dance?' They would swirl round the floor all night to the strains of the 'Blue Danube' and the next morning, on bended knee, he would ask for her hand in marriage.

Things didn't quite turn out that way with Luke Norton. The first time she saw him was on a damp Friday morning in June when she served him a double espresso. Poppy was twenty and working as a waitress in Sal's, a grimy café in King's Cross wedged between a shop selling Japanese comics and another selling organic beauty products. Poppy had recently taken the job because modelling assignments had been few and far between, and the rent needed to be paid on the tiny flat she shared in Kilburn with her old schoolfriend Meena.

Luke was sitting alone at a corner table, talking agitatedly into a mobile phone. When Poppy saw him, her stomach lurched as if she had leant too far over a cliff. Tall, dark with a broad jaw, he looked like the rugged hero of the black-and-white movies Poppy loved to watch: the kind of man who'd rescue you from a burning building or bundle you on his camel and carry you across the desert.

He was old, admittedly, nearer fifty than forty, but that didn't bother her. As a model Poppy came across a lot of young men, handsome young men, but they were such lightweights: panicking if they thought they'd put on half a pound and sucking in their cheekbones when they looked in the mirror. Poppy wanted someone more solid than that, someone who could protect her from a world which seemed to be full of hard elbows and backbiting. Protect her in a way her father might have done, if she'd ever got the chance to know him.

'Christ, Hannah, I don't know if I can . . .' Luke was saying, when a sour-faced woman three tables away bawled, 'Waitress!'

'Yes?' said Poppy through gritted teeth.

'I've been waiting ten minutes for my coffee. Where the hell is it?'

'I'll just check,' Poppy said as serenely as she could. She stuck her head round the kitchen door. 'Hey, Sal, hurry up with that coffee for table ten.'

'You never ask me for a coffee for table ten,' protested Sal, her very patient Portuguese boss, looking up from his copy of *Metro*.

'I did. Ages ago.'

'You didn't. Poppy, you are a terrible waitress.' But he was smiling, because it was hard not to smile at Poppy with her cropped blonde hair and saucer-shaped eyes the colour of the translucent minty cough sweets Sal was so partial to.

'Oh sorry. Well, she'd like a latte.'

'Coming up,' Sal said. Poppy went back into the so-called dining room with its red-and-black laminate floor, Formica tables and framed photographs of the gardens of Madeira.

'It's coming,' she said to the woman. To her disappointment, she saw the perfect man had been joined by an equally perfect woman. Perfect from behind, anyway. Poppy couldn't see her face. She had black hair in a French plait and was wearing a very elegant pinstripe trouser suit. She was about to go and take their order, when a woman with a buggy stopped her.

'Excuse me, do you have high chairs?'

'Hannah's giving me so much grief again,' she heard the perfect man say. 'She doesn't want me to go to Germany for the elections because it's Tilly's sports day.'

The woman sounded exasperated. 'Poor you. Doesn't she realize this is your *career*? I mean it's not like you were a house husband when she met you.'

'Exactly. How does she think we can afford Tilly's bloody ridiculous school? I . . .'

'I *said* do you have high chairs?'

'Oh! Yes. Of course. I'll go and get you one.' Ears straining to pick up more of the conversation, Poppy returned to the kitchen. Their one high chair was covered in smeary mush from the last baby who had sat in it. Poppy had meant to clean it, but she'd forgotten. Hastily, she wiped it down. As she hurried back into the dining room, she saw the perfect woman disappearing through the door. The perfect man was still sitting at the table, looking gloomy.

'At last,' said the woman with the buggy. 'I thought you'd died.' She lifted the baby out of the buggy. 'Come on, darling. Now you can have some breakfast.' Just then Mrs Angry yelled. 'Waitress! This is getting ridiculous. Next time I'm going to Starbucks.'

3

'Sorry,' Poppy gasped. She hurried back to the kitchen and emerged with the latte.

'About time,' Mrs Angry snapped, 'and if you're expecting a tip, you've got another think coming.'

'Sorry,' Poppy repeated, her face flamingo.

'And I'd like to order too,' chirruped the woman with the buggy. 'Two croissants, please, and a latte.'

She heard Luke clear his throat.

'And if it's not too much trouble, I'd love another double espresso.'

'Oh, OK. Sorry. Sorry.' She rushed into the kitchen, shouted the orders to Sal and rushed out again.

'I'm so sorry. I thought I'd taken your order already,' she said to the woman with the baby, who rolled her eyes and said nothing. Poppy turned to Luke. 'I do apologize.'

He smiled so the corners of his eyes crinkled. 'It's fine. You're cheering me up. I think you're having an even worse day than me.'

The line she'd been daring herself to say rolled off her tongue: 'Want to talk about it?'

'You know I really wouldn't mind.'

Buttoning her green mac, Mrs Angry approached them. Poppy braced herself for a bollocking, but she was smiling.

'Excuse me, I'm so sorry to interrupt. But I've just realized, you're Luke Norton. I had to let you know I love the programme. Only intelligent thing on television these days.'

'Thank you,' Luke said.

'Er. So.' The gorgon had transformed into a simpering southern belle. 'Good luck. Sorry to bother you. I'm just such a fan.'

She bustled out. Luke ran a hand through his hair.

'God, I hate it when that happens. So embarrassing.'

'Are you on TV?' Poppy asked.

'I am.' He smiled. Then he patted the chair vacated by the perfect woman.

'Do you want to sit down?'

'In a minute,' Poppy said, flustered. 'I'll just serve this lady.'

So she served the croissants and – with no other customers in sight – sat down and talked to Luke for nearly an hour. He told her how he'd once been a war correspondent, reporting on conflicts from all over the world. How he was now the anchorman for the *Seven Thirty News*, which sounded extremely glamorous, though Poppy couldn't say she'd ever watched it, and how he was writing a book about the history of the Balkans, which he hoped would be seen as 'definitive'.

'I'm sure it will be.' Poppy nodded, not quite understanding what he was on about.

The woman with the buggy left, leaving no tip. Luke continued talking about his family, his three children, the way he was growing apart from his wife.

Poppy's heart sank temporarily when she heard the word 'wife', but like a cork in water it immediately popped up again because their marriage was so clearly on the rocks.

'It's so difficult,' he said. 'I want to be a good father, but we married too young and we're just not making each other happy any more.'

'That's so sad,' said Poppy, thanking the Lord that Sal's was such a terrible café they'd probably get no more customers until the lunchtime trickle, meaning she could carry on talking to Luke all morning.

He smiled at her. 'You're very sweet. What are you doing working in a dump like this?'

'Well, actually,' Poppy confided, 'I'm a model. I just do this between jobs.'

She hated telling people what her job was, because they immediately looked her up and down, clearly thinking 'too fat, too small, nose too squodgy' – all the things booking agents muttered when she stood in front of them. Women made a sneery, scornful face; men eyed her like an expert from the *Antiques Roadshow* evaluating a Victorian dining table. Both sexes were clearly thinking 'thick as a plank'.

But Luke simply smiled again. 'I thought as much. It can't be long before someone as beautiful as you hits the big time.' He looked at his watch. He had big, competent-looking hands. 'Damn. I've got to go. Conference in five minutes. But it was lovely talking to you . . . ?'

'Poppy.'

'Poppy. See you again, I hope. If you're not strutting down a catwalk in Milan.'

'I hope so,' Poppy said. 'I mean I hope I'm not strutting down a catwalk in Milan, I hope I'm here.'

He laughed and she smiled all morning and not just because he'd left a five-pound tip.

After that, Luke came in regularly and they talked. In the meantime, Poppy started watching the *SevenThirty News* on Channel 6. She was stunned and impressed to discover her new friend presented it on average four nights out of

6

six. Poppy couldn't believe she knew such an important man. She made notes on the news stories of the day and plied Luke with questions. Did he think there would ever be a solution to the Israel problem? What was the answer to teenage crime? How could the government sort out the NHS?

'You're very sweet,' Luke said every time. Poppy knew he was being patronizing, but she didn't much care, though it would have been nice if he'd bothered to answer her properly.

After a couple of weeks Luke asked her if she was free for dinner. She met him at half past eight in a slightly scuzzy Korean place near Channel 6's headquarters in Pentonville Road.

'I'd love to take you to the Ritz,' he said, 'but someone might recognize me.'

She didn't care about the Ritz, but she was a bit upset afterwards when, walking up the road, she tried to slip her arm through his and he shook her off.

'Sorry. But someone might see us.'

Before she could dwell on that, he asked her if she'd like to have dinner again. That happened twice more and after the third meal, they went to bed back at her place, which was happily empty because Meena was visiting family in Bangalore. Then began the most wonderful twelve months of Poppy's life: twelve months of tangled limbs, sweaty bodies and garbled shouts of 'I want you!'; of giggly meals in out-of-the-way candlelit restaurants; meals which were far more about alcohol than food; of expensive lingerie and picnics in hotel bedrooms.

Of course Poppy had had boyfriends before, but very

few. She'd attended a smart girls' boarding school in Oxfordshire called Brettenden House and only met boys twice a term when they were bussed in for what the teachers called a 'bop'. It was at one of these that Poppy, aged fifteen, had met Mark from Radley College. They'd slow-danced all night, kissed in an alley outside the kitchens where the bins were kept and after that had met on alternate weekends in Henley, spending most of the time smooching on a bench by the river. But after three months Mark dumped her because she wouldn't go all the way. Propelled by a mixture of confusion and spite, the following week she lost her virginity to Mark's best friend, Niall, under an elm tree in the far corner of the playing fields. The next day he dumped her, telling everyone she was a 'lousy lay'.

After that humiliation, Poppy avoided all men for a few years. The one to recapture her trust was Alex, who worked in the food department at Harvey Nichols, where she had her first job. Alex cuddled and kissed her a bit, but to Poppy's great relief he didn't pressure her into sex. Then she discovered he was gay and they went their amicable but separate ways.

And that was it. Meaning at the grand age of twenty, Poppy was practically a virgin. She had certainly never been in love before. So when it hit her, it hit hard.

A lot of it was the sex. Luke was very gentle with her the first time and very encouraging. He kept moaning 'Oh God, you're so beautiful' which was an improvement on Mark's 'Can I put it in now?' or Niall's 'I . . . uh . . . awaaargh!' He showed her what he liked and he asked what she liked and the result was so unexpectedly fabulous that every time Poppy thought about him she felt goose pimples explode across her arms like thousands of tiny fireworks and she forgot even more of Sal's customers' orders than usual.

But it was more than just the physical stuff. Luke was a real man. He picked up the tab. He asked her what wine she'd like and, when she admitted she hadn't a clue, said he'd like to teach her all about varieties of grapes and vineyard soils. He took her to the opera which she pretended to love, even though she spent most of it in a fantasy borrowed from a coffee advert involving her and Luke waking up in some sunny loft apartment and feeding each other croissants. Best of all, after one session on her narrow single bed, he lay back on the pillow and said, 'How long has that pipe been leaking in the bathroom?'

He was talking about a pipe under the basin that dripped into a bucket like an unsophisticated form of torture. Meena and Poppy had to empty it regularly into the bath. Once they had both gone away for the weekend and the bathroom carpet had got drenched so it smelt like a mangy dog in the monsoon.

'Months,' Poppy replied. 'Meena and I keep asking Mrs Papadopolous to fix it, but she just says, "Yeah, yeah." I suppose we should call a plumber but he'd just rip us off. Again.' The last plumber had charged two hundred and eighty-nine pounds plus VAT to fix a dripping kitchen tap and – with some justification – Mrs Papadopolous had refused to reimburse them.

'I can't stand it any more,' Luke said. 'I'll bloody do it now. Have you got a tool kit?'

He might as well have asked if Poppy had a guide to

9

quantum physics hidden under the bed. When she said no, he just smiled.

'Hang on there. I'll go and get one.'

He returned twenty minutes later, then lay under the grubby bathroom sink grunting and groaning. By midnight the pipe was fixed. Poppy gazed at him with adoration.

'Thank you, Luke,' she breathed.

It was such a relief. Poppy had always had to fend for herself. Mum had never been the sort to do her cooking or cleaning or laundry. At an early age Poppy had learnt that if she wanted to eat she had to find something to put in the microwave and if all her clothes were dirty she had to switch on the washing machine, though she never was quite sure how to add powder and what temperature you were meant to set it at, meaning her underwear was perpetually limp and grey until Meena explained about whites and colours. When something broke down, Poppy either called a repair man who usually made a pass at her, then ripped her off, or she just threw it out.

It wasn't like that for Meena. When she wanted some TLC she just went home to Wembley where her mum did her laundry – even ironing her knickers – and stuffed her with curries and her dad mended the dodgy gearbox on her car. Poppy found it very tiring being all alone, but with Luke by her side, she wasn't. Not any more.

'Thank you,' she said again.

Luke smiled, only a little smugly. 'Nice to get my hands dirty,' he said. 'It makes a change.' He paused. 'And nice to be appreciated. For once. With everyone else it's just take, take, take. "Why can't you make it to the school play?" "What do you mean you can't take two weeks off at Christmas to join me in Barbados?" "I want a pony." "Can I go skiing?" You're the only one who just lets me be.'

The domestic references set faint alarm bells ringing, but the overall message was what she'd been waiting to hear. Poppy stroked his face. 'I love you,' she breathed.

He smiled at her. 'I love you too, my Poppy.'

In Poppy's short life it was the first moment of true perfection. Perfection only slightly marred when five seconds later Luke's mobile rang and he looked at it, frowned, switched it off and said, 'Oh shit, I'd better be off.'

He began pulling off his clothes for the shower he always took before heading home. Sometimes Poppy felt insulted that he had to wash off all trace of her, but tonight she didn't mind. She sat on the edge of the bath and watched him, liquid joy coursing through her veins. *He loved her. He loved her!* They were going to live happily ever after.

Only after he left in a minicab did Poppy focus again on that pesky matter of the wife. And the three children. Poppy knew they lived in North London, that there were two teenage girls and a younger boy, that the wife was called Hannah and had been a journalist but was now a full-time mother. She wondered if Hannah wondered where her husband was these late nights and for just a millisecond felt a shiver of guilt. But then she shrugged it off. Luke never talked much about his family, then only to complain, so he couldn't care for them that much. It wasn't Poppy's fault if he preferred being with her. It didn't occur to her that Hannah could stand in the way of her long-term happiness. After all, men left wives and children all the time. Look at what had happened to Mum.

Poppy had met her handsome prince. And somehow or another, she would get him to the altar, because that was how all good fairy tales ended.

2

You didn't exactly have to be Sigmund Freud to see why Poppy might be searching for a handsome prince. Her dad had walked out on her mum, Louise, when she was only twenty-two and seven months pregnant. Poppy knew virtually nothing about him except that his name was Charles, and that Louise had met him in the South of France where she was spending a summer selling ice cream on the beaches. Poppy found the idea of her nervy mother behaving in such a carefree fashion rather hard to believe, but there was evidence in the form of a photo of her laughing on a pebbly beach in white shorts and an acid-green T-shirt that read 'Frankie Says . . . Relax', with a floppy black blow in her permed hair and a tray of ice creams round her neck.

Anyway, Charles and Mum had had a brief fling. Then he disappeared and never responded to any of Louise's letters telling him she was pregnant. That was all Poppy knew. If she tried to find out more about him – what he looked like, where he was from, his favourite music – her mother would snap: 'You don't need to know anything about that bastard, we've managed fine without him, haven't we?' So when very young, Poppy had stopped asking questions.

And in a way, they had done fine without him, very well in fact. Obviously Louise had had to work extremely hard to support herself and her baby daughter. She'd found a job with a recruitment agency, so Poppy's early years had been spent either in a nursery or with her gran who came to live with them when Poppy was four. A couple of years later, Gran's arthritis got too bad to cope with a small child, but by then Louise had founded her own company and was making good money. So Elisabetta from El Salvador was drafted in to be Poppy's surrogate mum, which worked out fabulously until the phone bill arrived sending Louise into meltdown and Elisabetta on the first plane back west.

After that au pairs came and went in quick succession. Poppy had lost her heart to each of them. Her earliest memories were of Margarita from Colombia cuddling her when she cut her knee, of Greta from Austria applauding when she rode her bike without stabilizers for the first time, of Adalet from Turkey walking backwards in the swimming pool encouraging Poppy to splash towards her. But Louise had felt differently: the girls were too slapdash, too cheeky, stayed out too late on their nights off. Even the ones who behaved impeccably had to leave as soon as Louise noted her daughter growing too fond of them, because it wouldn't do to get too attached.

With each departure Poppy wept bitterly. The girls all felt wretched and swore they'd keep in touch with the sweet blonde girl with Caribbean-blue eyes, but after a couple of postcards, communication slowed and eventually halted, as they found new families, boyfriends, proper jobs and got on with their lives.

In the end, Louise decided the best thing by far for Poppy was boarding school, which, thanks to her thriving business, she could now afford. She sold the semi in St Albans, bought herself a bijou two-bedroom flat in Clapham and rung round for the prospectuses. Everyone gasped when they heard Poppy had been sent to Watershead when she was only nine, but actually it had been great. Matron was kind, the headmistress was lovely, she'd had lots of little friends and Gran came to visit every other weekend.

It was at Brettenden House that the misery had kicked in. That was a really snobby place – all the other girls seemed to live in huge country piles and own at least four ponies and their mummies had all been to Brettenden too. Poppy was aware that behind her back most of the girls called her 'noov' short for 'nouveau', which in their limited world was one of the cruellest insults. She only had one real friend, Meena, whose dad was an accountant from Wembley by way of the Punjab, who'd slaved to send their daughter to a smart school only to find she was mercilessly dissed for being lower middle class. 'Does your dad do my dad's tax returns?' landowners' daughters would ask, sniggering. To make it worse, Meena had no interest in academia whatsoever and kept begging her parents to arrange a marriage for her to the richest man they could find.

On Saturday nights when most of the other girls had gone home to their country estates, Poppy and Meena would curl up together in the common room and watch a DVD of their favourite film, *Pretty Woman*. The idea of a world where a Richard Gere type hero solved your problems with a flash of his credit card was incredibly appealing.

'That's what we want,' Meena sighed. 'If you were married to a man like that you wouldn't need to worry about exams.'

Poppy agreed. 'Much more fun than being my mum and working all the hours God sends and always being exhausted.'

The Richard fantasy became even more pressing when, just a month before GCSEs, Gran died. Poppy's prospects had been poor anyway but, griefstricken, she only obtained two passes: a C in art and a D in English. Brettenden suggested that perhaps the sixth form was not the right place for her and Poppy wholeheartedly agreed. Happily, Meena was ousted too, so the pair of them found a flat together in Kilburn. Meena got a job in a Starbucks on Oxford Street and Poppy found one selling swimsuits at Harvey Nichols.

In retrospect Poppy realized it was the happiest period of her life. Work was a laugh: there was a nice crowd available for drinks most evenings, and watching rich women squeeze themselves into five-hundred-pound bikinis every day was very entertaining. But a few months later a woman with a face like a hawk had begun quizzing her about Eres versus Missoni, then suddenly diverted into asking if Poppy had ever done any modelling and would she like to come to her office for a chat?

And so, at eighteen, Poppy Price had found herself persuaded to hand in her notice at Harvey Nicks and set off pounding the streets of London with an *A–Z* and a book full of pictures of herself to be studied by hard-faced women in tiny dark offices, who turned to each other and said things like 'Pretty face but needs to lose at least a stone' as if she didn't even exist. Poppy wasn't at all sure about her new career; she was naturally a size eight, but the pressure was on to be a size six or a four. It was generally agreed that she was not edgy-looking enough to appear on the catwalk, but had a more 'commercial look', which meant she appeared in a couple of adverts for bathroom warehouses and detergents. She also did some shoots for teenage magazines that involved standing on a street corner wearing a sweater dress and stripy tights, arms linked with another (prettier) model, pretending to laugh, even though the cold wind was biting her face, while passers-by sniggered at her, and a photographer yelled they were supposed to be going out on the razz not to a funeral. But her friends, Meena especially, were so excited at the idea of knowing a real-life model that she decided to stick with it for a couple of years before going back to swimwear. Then Luke and love entered her life, and their arrival seemed to sprinkle fairy dust into every cranny of her existence. After her rocky start, mod-elling jobs suddenly started to rush in: a shoot for *Elle*, the cover of *Cosmo*, a shoot for *Glamour* (in Cuba), another for *Harper's Bazaar*.

Poppy and Luke's relationship had lasted nearly a year. She adored him with every ounce of her being. She worried increasingly about the fact he still hadn't left Hannah, but she was sure it was just a matter of biding her time. She saw him usually two nights a week and occasionally for a stolen hour or so at weekends. They didn't go out as much as they used to, they mostly stayed in bed, but that was enough.

Then came that terrifying yet amazing day when

Poppy's period was so late and she'd been feeling so weird and off the booze that she decided to buy a pregnancy test. She peed on the stick and saw the line turn blue. It wasn't a massive surprise. Even though Luke had asked her frequently if she was on the pill, and she'd frequently assured him she was, she'd never actually picked up her prescription. After all, Meena said the pill made you bloated, and Poppy kept reading in the papers how it was virtually impossible for any woman to have babies these days, except by expensive and painful IVF. And – although she could hardly admit it even to herself – she wanted a baby to love more than anything else, plus Luke would *have* to leave his wife, so she didn't see how getting pregnant could really be a bad thing.

She toyed with the idea of calling Meena who was surfing in Cornwall for the week in the hope of picking up Prince William or at least one of his friends. Then she decided Luke had to be the first to hear the news. She had to wait forty-eight hours until he came round after the show. She meant to tell him straight away, but he was feeling very frisky and steered her straight to the bed before she could even open her mouth. After a session which hadn't been quite as vigorous as usual because Poppy was terrified of hurting the baby, whom she had already christened Isabelle, she took a deep breath.

'Luke,' she said, stroking his chest, 'I've got something to tell you.'

'Mmm?' Luke's eyes were closed; he was drifting off to sleep.

'I'm . . . we . . . we're having a baby.'

'What?' Luke sat up. He looked horrified. 'You *are* joking?'

'No,' Poppy said, confused.

'Fucking hell, Poppy! How the fuck did this happen? You're on the pill.'

'I . . . Yes, I am, but I guess it didn't work.'

'The pill *always* works. Shit. Well, we'd better get you to the doctor quickly. How far gone are you?'

'I'm not sure. Maybe a couple of months. I didn't want to go to the doctor until I told you. I thought we could go together.'

'Fucking hell,' Luke said again.

Poppy started to cry. This was not the overjoyed reaction she'd expected.

'I thought you'd be pleased.'

'Pleased? How could I be pleased? I don't want you having an abortion, but I don't see what bloody choice we have.'

She gasped. 'An abortion?'

'Well, what else were you going to do?'

'Have the baby of course. Little Isabelle.'

Luke's face turned a shade of plum. 'Isabelle? You know it's a girl?'

'No, I just have a feeling. I—'

'My middle daughter's called Isabelle. Christ, Poppy.'

Poppy cried a lot. She said there was no way she was going to have an abortion. She said, not very convincingly, that she'd be fine as a single mother, that her mum had coped and she would too. Luke had snapped back that, of course, she couldn't go it alone, he'd support her, but he couldn't leave Hannah and the children, she had to understand that.

'But why not? You don't love *her*.'

Suddenly, Luke looked all of his forty-nine years. 'I'd forgotten how young you are, Poppy. Of course I love Hannah. She's my wife. The mother of my children.'

'But you love *me*.'

'I love both of you,' Luke said, looking very agitated, 'but in different ways. I mean, if things had been different, if I'd met you at another time, I would have married you. But I'm married to Hannah; I can't leave her. You must see that.'

'But men leave their wives all the time. What's the problem?'

Luke looked aghast. 'You really can't see what the problem is?'

'You could still see your children.'

He got out of bed and started getting dressed. 'It's not that simple. I'm a public figure, you know. The papers would have a field day if I left my wife for a younger woman.'

'No, they wouldn't,' Poppy said. 'You're not *that* famous.' After all, since Mrs Angry on day one, the only person who'd recognized Luke had been the waiter in the Indian round the corner, and it turned out as the conversation progressed he'd thought Luke was one of the contestants in *The X Factor*.

It was the wrong thing to say. 'Your little friends may not know me but, believe me, I'm a household name.' Luke knotted his tie. 'I have to go now. Don't cry. We'll sort all this out. I'll find you a doctor, the best doctor. But you can't have this baby.'

She cried all night, finally falling asleep as dawn broke. She completely forgot a car was coming at nine to pick her up for a shoot for a new low-calorie chocolate bar and was in such a deep sleep she didn't hear the doorbell. Her phone's battery had died, so when she did rise at eleven, it was to a barrage of irate messages from Elsa at her agency. But no messages from Luke. Nothing.

The car came back for her, she went to the shoot, where the make-up artist tutted over her red eyes and blotchy skin and told her not to be such a naughty girl in future. Between every shot she checked her phone for messages.

Nothing.

She left messages all day for Luke, but his phone was switched off. She texted him continuously. In the end, he rang her shortly after eight when she was howling on the sofa, while spooning her way through a tub of Skinny Cow ice cream.

'Sorry I haven't been in touch,' he said, sounding as distant as if he was calling from the moon. 'It's been frantic at work, but I will find you a doctor.'

A large rock was lodged in Poppy's chest. 'I told you, I'm not getting rid of this baby.'

He sighed. 'Well, just think about it. I have to go now, Poppy. I'll call you tomorrow. Bye.'

Poppy had known unhappiness before, but now she was becoming acquainted with true misery. That night and the following day passed in a blur of sobbing and sleeplessness and fruitless attempts to call Meena, then Luke, then Meena again. Neither returned her calls (later, she discovered that Meena couldn't get a signal at the seaside). But then at nine the following night something miraculous happened. The doorbell rang and when Poppy answered it, expecting the Chinese food delivery man, she heard Luke's voice on the crackly intercom.

'Poppy, it's me. Please let me in.'

She opened the door to see him climbing the stairs, carrying a large suitcase.

'I've left them,' he called up to her, stopping for breath on the first-floor landing. 'I've come to live with you, Poppy. You're going to have the baby. I'm going to make you my wife.'

My Husband, the Bimbo and Me

BY HANNAH CREIGHTON

Hannah Creighton was devastated when her husband, Luke Norton, anchorman of *Seven Thirty News* on Channel 6, fell for a 22-year-old model. With Luke now remarried and a new father, Hannah is rebuilding her life with children Matilda, 15, Isabelle, 13 and Jonty, 8. Here, with heart-searing honesty, she writes about the most painful period of her life.

It was a bright late-summer's afternoon when the news came that would change my life for ever. I was sitting in my study, looking out over the garden of our glorious family home in Hampstead, North London, sipping a cup of Earl Grey, enjoying the sound of the birds singing and watching sunlight play in the leaves of the willow tree. It was a brief lull between putting an organic chicken to slow-cook in the bottom of the Aga for a family dinner and getting in the car to pick up Jonty from school then heading on to meet Isabelle from lacrosse practice.

I jumped as my computer announced I had email. Without much curiosity, I turned to the screen. I expected a message from our dear friend Cheryl, thanking me for picking up her daughter from school the previous day, but I saw Luke's name at the top. Probably him warning me he'd be late home. Annoyed, because getting all five of us round the table was as rare in our house as coconuts in Antarctica, I opened it, read it, then blinked in confusion.

Darling Luke

I'm emailing u becoz ur not returning my calls or texts and I'm desprat. I'm sorry u had such a shock about the baby but we need 2 talk. I'm going to keep it whatever and I understand if u don't want 2 b involved but we just need to talk some more. I love u, I love u so much and I thought u loved me 2. Please, please, please get in touch.

Again, I love u with all my heart
Your, Poppy xxxxxOOOOO

Blood pounded in my head. I thought my eardrums might be about to burst. Forgetting to put the potatoes on, I googled Poppy Price, the name attached to the email. Thanks to modern technology, within seconds I knew my enemy. A picture of a gangly, doe-eyed blonde, barely older than Matilda, smiled out at me. This bimbo, I read, was 22 and a model. Everything took on a surreal tone, as if events around me were happening in slow motion. Surely this could not be true.

When Luke and I met in a bar in Israel, eighteen years ago, it was like a bolt of lightning for both of us. I was a newspaper journalist, he was an up-and-coming foreign correspondent for the BBC. At first I was wary of his advances. I knew all about his womanizing reputation, but gradually his charm wore me down. Back in England, we started seeing each other and within a few months we were inseparable. Eighteen months after we met we were married in a village church with our friends and families weeping as my husband held my hand and pledged his troth, promising to forsake all others. Fool that I am, I believed him.

A year later came the first of our three children. Of course, as with every relationship, life seemed a bit more humdrum now we were being woken by crying babies in the middle of the night. There were times when both of us, no doubt, felt like running for the hills. But, somehow, we continued to love each other and our children. With Luke still jetting all over the world, I soon realized the best way to maintain a happy home for my family was to abandon my beloved career to provide a stable base for everyone. I missed the buzz of the office, of foreign travel and meeting celebrities, but most of the time I was more than content to be nest-building for my 'team'. Yet for the past few years I had had to hold my head high and ignore friends' 'concerned' comments about Luke's 'friend-ships' made on long trips away from home, or his 'closeness' with various girls in his office. Mostly, I'd ignored such hints, desperate to sustain a happy home. Once or twice I'd tackled Luke, but he'd laughed off my suggestions as paranoia, saying his family was his world.

But this was different. A baby – if it was really true – was something else altogether. I felt as if someone had put a knife in my stomach and was twisting it round. I ordered Luke home. Over the next few hours we had a lot of conversations straight out of Mills & Boon along the lines of: 'How could you do this to me?' 'It was a mistake. She means nothing to me.' After an evening of this, I told him to leave. 'Where shall I go?' he asked. 'To that bimbo,' I replied. And so he left.

For the next few days, he called, emailed and texted repeatedly begging me to have him back, but something inside me had snapped. After so many years of tolerance, the wife had turned.

Gradually, over the weeks and months that followed fury gave way to despair. As my anger diminished, I found that –

despite myself – I couldn't help missing Luke. I loathed being a single mother. I wondered if I had been too quick to kick him out and if there was any way back. But the fact remained: the Bimbo was pregnant.

Misery threatened to engulf me. I considered anti-depressants, but I decided the only way to get back on track long term was to start enjoying myself again. At first I didn't feel like seeing anyone, but I forced myself. I organized dinner dates with girlfriends, started swimming at the local baths and even joined a wine-appreciation society. Slowly, I started to have fun, and every time I heard myself laugh, I knew I was one step further towards dealing with my emotions.

Little by little, I began to see light at the end of the tunnel. Having found the courage to kick Luke out, my new confidence affected other areas. Although many of our old 'couple' friends drifted away, others came to the fore. What really changed things for me was resuming my writing career – the one I had abandoned to be a perfect wife and mother. Hands trembling, I lifted the phone and called a few old contacts. To my everlasting gratitude, it transpired many of them had been where I was and were happy to give me a hand restarting my career. Seeing my name in print for the first time in years gave me a buzz similar – I imagine – to the Viagra I discovered about the time Luke moved out that he had been ordering on the internet.

Despite such moments of sunshine, there is still no denying that the break-up with Luke has been unbelievably traumatic, not only for me but – worse – for our children, who worship their father. In those first few months, Jonty got into trouble at school for hitting other children. The girls became sullen and withdrawn. They vowed never to see their father again, something that caused me both intense pain and deep satisfaction.

My jealousy was overwhelming. I knew that Luke had moved his little strumpet into a palatial apartment overlooking the canal in one of the swishiest parts of London. How different to the start of our own married life in a poky one-bedroom flat in Willesden, where Tilly slept in a drawer and the boiler was constantly on the blink. No penury for his new trophy wife; she'd stolen my husband once he was famous and well-off. What would she know of stress and struggle?

But much as I hate him, there are still many times when I miss Luke as I might a limb. I married him because he was a clever, funny, handsome man but I have to remind myself he was also a liar and a cad. I can't bring myself to take down the family photos – some from our early days together before his hair started thinning and his paunch developed. Friends have told me this is unhealthy, that it will keep new lovers away. But I don't feel I can adopt a scorched-earth policy. It is the children's home, too, and why should all traces of their dad suddenly be deleted?

Apparently he and the Bimbo have just had a baby girl. I have to swallow my vicious feelings and hope my children will learn to love their new half-sister. Some people have found themselves permanently excluded from my Christmas-card list for informing me I should count my blessings that Luke has granted me a generous divorce settlement and 'allowed' me to stay in the family home by paying the mortgage. The implication that I should somehow be grateful to stay in the house I have lovingly restored, cared for, brought up our babies in, sends me virtually to boiling point.

Nonetheless, I keep telling myself, I have no choice but to move on. I must find a way of coming to terms with my new situation. Thousands of families endure this same pain every year and – though I find it near impossible to do – we have to be forgiving. If my children, and I, are to be happy, then we all need to believe in a rosy future, just rather different from the one I dreamt of when I pledged my troth.

3

The month after Luke arrived on Poppy's doorstep was a whirl. They spent a week in her flat, before Luke said he couldn't stand any more of this student lifestyle and not being able to get into the bathroom in the morning when Meena was doing her make-up. He rented a large flat in Maida Vale right next to the canal. It was in a handsome white stucco building, based over two floors. It had two bedrooms, a study for Luke, a high-ceilinged living room and a Poggenpohl kitchen/diner.

'It's lovely,' Poppy breathed, unable to believe how quickly she'd moved on from Kilburn. She'd known Luke was rich; he was obviously well paid by the network, plus he'd inherited a lot from his father who had been something in the City. Only now, however, did she begin to realize how rich. 'Do we need such a big place?' she added.

'Well, the kids will be coming to stay,' Luke said.

'Oh,' Poppy said. 'Of course. I can't wait to meet them.'

In a weird sort of way she was quite looking forward to it – after all Luke's daughters weren't that much younger than her. But in the end, they never came. They said they had no desire to meet the woman who had ruined their own and their mother's lives, so Luke was obliged to spend every other weekend taking them to

Pizza Express and – they scornfully dismissed his suggestions of the zoo – on shopping trips, which he complained bankrupted him. Poppy had dreamt of spending weekends strolling hand in hand along the canal, but instead she was left all alone for forty-eight hours with a pile of DVDs and a growing bump.

Even during the weekends he was with her, he was busy working on his book about the Balkans and spent nearly all the time secluded in his study. Poppy would bring him snacks and offer him head massages, which he gratefully accepted but then he'd wave her out again.

No one had reacted to her news in the way she'd hoped.

'You're up the duff!' Meena had screamed. 'Poppy, you idiot!' She paused and then added, 'I mean, congratulations. I suppose it's one way to get a ring on your finger. But, Poppy, you don't want a baby, you'll get all fat and then you'll have an agonizing birth; you'll never sleep again and spend the rest of your life covered in puke and poo.'

'I love babies.' Actually, Poppy loved the idea of babies, crooning softly to them wrapped in pink fluffy blankets. She'd never spent any time with a real one.

'Then go and be a nanny. Don't have one of your own. You're not twenty-two yet. You've got the rest of your life for all that. Plus,' Meena paused for a second, 'plus I know Luke's on telly, but it's boring telly. Couldn't you hold out for someone from *Hollyoaks* or something? I mean I'd never heard of him, and you're so pretty, Poppy, I reckon you could do better for yourself.'

Poppy decided it was sour grapes. After all, Meena

made no secret of the fact that her game plan was to bag a member of the royal family or, failing that, a Bollywood mogul and spend the rest of her life shopping. To help achieve her goal, Meena worked as a receptionist at a ludicrously swanky health club in St John's Wood where she could get discounted manicures, facials and hair cuts, plus meet plenty of potential husbands. So the fact Poppy had managed to net a rich husband first had put her nose seriously out of joint.

Her mother, who was in a bad mood anyway after yet another romance had fallen through, was even less delighted.

'I can't believe you've been so stupid, Poppy. You're making exactly the same mistake I did.'

'No, Luke is standing by me,' Poppy said, then realized too late that as usual she'd said the worst possible thing.

'He may be standing by you, but he's leaving a wife and three children. What kind of man is that? Do you really want him to be the father of your child? Poppy, you're so pretty. I've always thanked God for your looks because heaven knows there isn't much else to recommend you. I always hoped you'd marry a lovely guy, not shack up with some shit.'

'He's not a shit.'

Louise sighed. 'Poppy Price, how did I raise such a clueless child?'

'You didn't raise me, the au pairs and Gran did.'

'I was doing my best,' Louise hissed. 'You have no idea how hard being a mother is. Well, you'll soon find out.' She put her hand to her brow. 'Now I can feel one of my migraines coming on. I feel nauseous. I'd better lie down.'

Poppy didn't bother saying that she felt permanently nauseous herself. After four months her ballooning belly meant she had to stop working. She greeted her new life as a stay-at-home mother-to-be with enthusiasm, but it turned out to be a lot lonelier and a lot more boring than she'd expected. She had found modelling scary, but at least it had given her something to get up for in the morning and there had been people to chat to all day. In contrast, Luke was almost never at home – sometimes she thought she'd seen him more when he was her lover. He went out early and returned often about midnight, tie askew, the smell of Chianti on his breath and his Black-Berry still buzzing.

'Entertaining contacts, darling,' he'd say, crawling into bed. 'That's what my job's all about. That's what enables us to live in this beautiful flat.'

'But I don't care about a beautiful flat. I'd rather just see more of you.'

He shrugged. 'This is my life. I've lost my family because of you. You can hardly expect me to give up my job as well.'

In the dark, tears stung Poppy's eyes. She was learning not to cry in front of him, because it only made him angry.

'I didn't ask you to lose your family. You left them; I didn't make you.'

'Didn't you?' he muttered and rolled on to his back.

There was a brief silence.

'I felt the baby kick today.'

'Did you? Poppy, I'm really tired. I'm going to sleep now.' And within seconds she heard him snoring.

So Poppy spent her days and nights in front of the television, waiting to hear Luke's key in the lock, gently stroking her growing stomach and flicking through her pregnancy book to see what her foetus was doing this week (somersaulting, kicking, possibly sucking its thumb). She did ask Luke if she could attend some of these work dinners with him, but he sighed and said he hardly thought it would be suitable.

'Most of these people know Hannah from way back. I can hardly just wheel up one day with you.'

Hannah rushed through a divorce on grounds of adultery. Poppy didn't know many of the details, but she gathered Luke had made her a huge settlement. When Poppy was eight months pregnant, she and Luke married.

'We don't have to do this, you know,' Poppy said as they sat in the back of the taxi en route to Marylebone Register Office. Of course she wanted to more than anything else, but Luke looked so bleak you'd have thought he was on his way to a funeral, not his own wedding.

'Don't be silly,' he said, trying to smile, 'of course we do.'

And so they plighted their troth in a small room that reeked of Pledge, with Poppy in a blue-and-white maternity dress from Topshop rather than the Princess Diana meringue she'd always envisaged. There were two witnesses: Meena and Gerry, an old war-correspondent friend of Luke's, who had a red nose from too many nights in bars and a scar on his cheek where a melanoma had been cut out. Luke's parents were dead.

Louise said she would have loved to attend but she was chairing a huge conference in Glasgow that week. 'You understand, don't you, cherub?' As usual, she hadn't waited for a reply. 'Got to go, sweets. Hope you have a lovely day.'

Afterwards they had lunch at Orrery in Marylebone High Street. The food was probably delicious but Poppy didn't really notice, so awkward were the vibes between the four of them. The others got very pissed until Meena eventually threw up in the loo and had to be put in a taxi and sent home. Gerry stumbled off into the afternoon. She and Luke got in their own taxi and went back to Maida Vale. To Poppy's relief they made far more passionate love than they had for several weeks, after which Luke fell into a deep sleep. When he woke up they ordered an Indian and ate it on the bed, giggling and feeding each other bites of naan almost like in her early coffee-ad fantasies. So Poppy had gone to sleep on her wedding night reassured that now the fairy tale was about to begin.

The Demise of the Trophy Wife

Golddiggers who take their rich husbands for a ride are on the verge of extinction, says HANNAH CREIGHTON.

Not so long ago it was a truth universally acknowledged that a man with a kick-ass job must be in want of a trophy wife. These divine, docile brood mares were the perfect addition to the mansion, the Maserati and the holidays in Mauritius.

But how times have changed. According to recent research the earnings gap between married couples is narrowing. These days men are bored with stay-at-home parasites and are looking for high-fliers. To paraphrase Jerry Hall, whores in the bedroom, masterchefs in the kitchen – but also queens of the boardroom. Some have interpreted this as a victory for the feminists, along with burning our bras. Sadly, however, the truth says something much less appealing about our sex. Powerful men, I believe, have only just latched on to the downside of the stay-at-home wife. Either marry a woman prepared to pay her own way, or end up spliced to a spoilt, lazy, bloodsucker.

I can feel the finger pointing at me. OK! I put my hands up. I, too, used to be one of those stay-at-home wives I am laying into. My husband, Luke Norton, was a distinguished foreign correspondent who, in the dying days of our marriage, became the anchorman for Channel 6's *SevenThirty News* and consequently a household name.

We lived with our three children in our glorious family home in Hampstead, North London and I didn't go out to work. But there the resemblance between me and the trophy wives ends.

I was of a different generation, you see, the *Cosmo* generation who believed in 'having it all'. We children of the 1970s were brought up to understand this meant running a home, entertaining regularly, raising charming children, keeping our husbands happy and having some sort of career to keep our brains ticking over and our bank accounts seperate.

I confess I failed at the last hurdle. Although I had a high-flying journalism career before I met Luke, I found the challenges of three small children too difficult to combine with the logistics of a job. But, feeling guilty I had not managed to be a ball-busting career girl, I worked doubly hard to make sure I raised happy children, who lived in a beautiful house, played in a glorious garden and who sat down to eat nutritious meals every night. When my husband came home there was an equally nutritious meal waiting for him, plus a large glass of wine. I listened to his tales of office in-fighting and *Boy's Own* derring-do and told him how brave and clever he was. I never shared my own anxieties about arguments with builders or changes to the school run. I thought this was part of the pact: I kept the home fires burning while he earned a wage.

How naive I was. When the last of the children were finally old enough not to need me full-time and I began to explore plans for some kind of part-time work, my husband announced he was leaving me. For a 22-year-old model. Who was pregnant with his fourth child. The years I had put into creating a stable home environment counted for nothing. The story of my anger and my recovery have been documented. Suffice to say, I was devastated but I got over it, and today I am happier than I have ever been.

But what interests me is the trophy wife my husband seemed to think it was his right to acquire, much as a man of his position might crave a chauffeur-driven Bentley or membership of the Garrick Club. Of course I can't speak for the second Mrs Norton, but what I have observed in general, is a fascinating new breed of trophy wives, women who seem to think their whole function is to be provided for, while giving their husbands nothing in return.

If they are rich enough, they employ a chef; if not, the poor husband must make do with TV dinners. Ditto a cleaner. If they can't afford one, then the husband must simply live in squalor. The children are dumped in nurseries or looked after by nannies. This does not stop the new breed from constantly complaining how exhausted they are and demanding the husband spends every moment of the weekend taking the brats to the park, so they can enjoy their 'me time'.

More and more I bump into men my age who are bitter and disappointed at the non-working wives they have acquired. 'I wouldn't mind providing for her and my daughter if she just occasionally did something for me,' whispered a shattered husband to me recently. 'But she doesn't clean, she can't cook and she can't even seem to get our child potty-trained. I thought relationships were meant to be about give and take, but I do all the giving and she does all the receiving. I'd divorce her, but I've already lost one wife and I just can't face doing it again.' 'My wife's so vacant, not only does she never throw dinner parties, she never wants to meet anyone outside her little circle of other pampered wives,' said another. 'She's boring and completely self-obsessed.'

But now, it seems, the tide is turning. I couldn't possibly speak for my own ex-husband, but from other twice-married men I hear rumblings of discontent as they realize the price attached to their decorative little trophies and how well off they were with their first hard-working spouses, who either laboured at home or in the office, or both to provide them with the standard of living they deserved. So take heed you leeches, you parasites! Your time is nearly up. There's no such thing as a free ladies' lunch.

4

It was a grey Tuesday in January. In the offices of the *SevenThirty News* the temperature was at fever pitch. Gossip had been circulating for weeks ever since Jonathan Chambers, the channel's genial head of news and current affairs in charge of hirings, firings and budget had 'retired' sooner than expected to be replaced by Roxanne Fox or 'Foxy Roxy' to give her her office nickname, who was already proving to be about as generous with the company purse strings as a nun with her sexual favours.

Last night the rumours had solidified like cold lava into hard news when it was confirmed that Chris Stevens, the programme's bufferish editor since its launch a decade ago, had suddenly 'resigned'. His replacement, it was announced, in a short press release, was to be Dean Cutler, poached from the BBC.

'So what do we know about this Dean guy?' Lana, the newsdesk secretary, asked, twisting the gold chains round her neck with her claw-like hand. Lana was a forty-something single mother of three and any threat to her livelihood was to be taken very seriously.

'He's young,' said Luke Norton, looking up from the news list for that evening's show. He'd read it about six times but his brain refused to absorb it, such was his anxiety. Not to mention the fact that he found it very hard to read close up these days, but refused to wear glasses. Luckily the autocue was placed near enough so he could still just make it out without squinting.

'Not that young!' chirped senior reporter, Marco Jensen, from his desk, just behind him. 'He's thirty-seven.'

Luke looked at Marco with ill-concealed dislike. With his thick eyelashes, dimpled cheeks and blond curls, a fortuitous blend of his mother's Italian and father's Norwegian genes, he was too pretty ever to be completely trusted by other men. Everyone who met Marco suspected he was gay but in fact he had a gorgeous long-term girlfriend called Stephanie. He was also only thirty-three, which meant he'd been in short trousers when Luke had been out dodging bullets in the Gaza Strip. The most dangerous thing Marco had ever done in his life was accidentally leave the gas on overnight when he came in high on E after a rave.

Recently, Marco had been promoted to the upper echelons of co-presenters, the four chief correspondents who took turns to be Luke's sidekick and who hosted the show in his absence. Whenever it was Marco's turn, the show was inundated with appreciative emails and texts, which was why Luke had been taking less and less time off of late. Even though he worked a four-day week, he frequently volunteered to do five, so paranoid was he becoming about his young rival.

'One day that'll seem young to you, pipsqueak.' Lana smiled at Marco so her crow's feet were etched deeply in her coppery face. 'What else do you know, Luke?'

'He's a dumber-downer. Obsessed with the yoof audience. He was the one who caused all the fuss at the BBC by interviewing Jordan and Peter Andre on *Newsday*.'

'The viewing figures for that were amazing,' said Marco.

'It's not all about viewing figures,' Luke said with as much pomposity as he could muster. 'It's about providing groundbreaking, incisive news.'

'Not according to our shareholders. Our viewing figures keep going down. That's why Chris got the boot.'

'It wasn't Chris's fault we've lost viewers,' said Lana. 'It's the bloody internet's. Everyone gets their news from there now.' She eyed her computer balefully, as if it was that particular PC's fault that Chris Stevens was now on his way home clutching a P45.

'Well, the shareholders think we should be doing more to fight our corner.' Marco smirked as he bent his head over the pile of newspapers on his desk. There was a moment's silence. Lana chewed her nails and applied some lip gloss that smelt of pear. Luke returned to the news list again:

1 Mad cow disease outbreak in Shropshire.
2 Rumours of PM calling early general election.

He was temporarily distracted by the sight of Alexa Marples, recently promoted to producer, wiggling past in a pair of trousers that adhered to her splendid buttocks like clingfilm. Tempting. Stop it, Luke. He turned to his screen. Two new emails. One from a PR, which he deleted without reading. Another from his eldest daughter, Tilly. Oh Christ, no doubt wanting the dosh for the bloody skiing trip Hannah had promised her she could go on. He really should get on with drafting that email to the president of Syria, demanding an exclusive interview, but he just couldn't summon the energy.

'Oh look,' Marco said with cheery malice. 'Nice picture of you here in the *Daily Post*.'

Luke's heart sank. He knew what that meant. 'Oh yes,' he said, trying to sound as bored as possible.

'Mmm. Hannah's written another article: "The Demise of the Trophy Wife". Sounds interesting.'

'I need a slash,' Luke said brusquely. He got up and strode across the newsroom to the gents. He didn't really need to pee, but he needed a moment away from that little shit Marco and the generally febrile atmosphere.

'You all right, Luke?' said Emma Waters, one of the chief correspondents and another co-presenter, looking up from her screen where she was probably doing her Ocado shop. Emma was an old friend of Hannah's and there was no mistaking the malicious glint in her eye.

'Great, Emma, never better. Excited at the prospect of a breath of fresh air in this place.' Luke decided he'd swipe back. 'Love your jacket, by the way. My wife was saying the other night that green really suits you.'

He carried on to the gents, hugely cheered. One of Emma's pet peeves was the way, even after she'd interviewed the prime minister, the only thing viewers seemed to register about her was what she was wearing and whether it suited her or not. 'Luke and Marco don't get emails all day saying their hair's too long,' was her constant complaint, to which no one had an answer.

At least I'm not a woman, thought Luke, as he always did when he really needed to count his blessings. But then, having peed, he stared in the mirror with all the consternation of a former starlet on the eve of middle age. Shit. He'd definitely lost some more hair. Since he'd had to give up on the gym – no time or money thanks to having to divide his time between two families and the alimony – he was fatter too. Worse, however, were the furrows that almost overnight had started to etch themselves into his brow like cross stitch. There was no getting away from it. At fifty-one (fifty-two in a couple of weeks, he thought with a shudder), he was beginning to look his age. Of course the make-up girls could help a lot. But they couldn't do anything about the wrinkles and sagging, the bags under his eyes like the Austrian blinds in his ex-mother-in-law's cottage in Dorset. It was hardly bloody surprising he looked so exhausted, given his set up. Since Clara had been born nearly two years ago, he was lucky to get about four hours sleep straight. He'd accepted that when she was first born, but the months had passed and, still, she screamed in the night.

'Just leave her,' he'd moan to Poppy. 'That's what Hannah did with the children. They soon learn.'

'That's *cruel*,' Poppy would retort tearfully, jiggling and cooing their bawling baby who always ended up in their bed, where she'd snuffle and snort all night long. When there'd been disturbed nights with his other three, Luke had gone into the spare room. But now there *was* no spare room. Sometimes he retreated to the living-room sofa, but it was fiendishly uncomfortable, too hot in summer and arctic in winter thanks to the huge picture windows with their views of the canal.

Even on the rare nights of relative peace, Luke's worries kept him awake: how he'd damaged his three elder children by leaving them; how much cash his two families required, especially now the kids were all at boarding school, since Hannah had insisted it was the best possible babysitting arrangement for a single mother; how Hannah, with her newly invigorated career, kept publicly attacking him. How Poppy, sweet pretty Poppy, looked lovely on his arm but how a pot plant would have made a better wife. How he could hardly be blamed for searching for 'companionship' elsewhere, a search which had included a brief fling with – at this point Luke would kick the sheets – Foxy Roxy, who was now one of the people who held his future in her hands.

Why had he ended it with her? he'd think with the despair that always assailed him around four a.m. Why couldn't he have just let it trickle on? But Luke knew why: he'd been freaked out after that time she'd left her knickers in his pocket. Envisaging a second divorce and the bailiffs coming round, Luke had called it a day with a lot of waffling about 'It's not you it's me'. Foxy had appeared philosophical, but Luke knew better than almost anyone about the dangers of a woman scorned.

But more than his faltering new marriage or his shaky career, what kept Luke awake most was the question of how he could have forwarded that email to Hannah. Had he taken leave of his senses? It just didn't make sense. But here they all were.

The door opened.

'Aha, we thought this was where we'd find you,' cried Marco. 'Dean Cutler wants to see you. Now.'

If Luke's heart had been attached to a monitor, it would have started bleeping frantically.

'This minute?'

'You heard me. Chop, chop!'

Straightening his tie, Luke walked across the newsroom floor towards Chris's old office. Phones rang softly. Emma had headphones on and was recording her voice-over for a story about heroin in prisons into a microphone. 'Jermaine Franks had never touched drugs until he was sentenced . . .' she intoned, while beside her the story's producer clicked his mouse, shuffling the images they planned to use like a pack of cards.

Above his head, a row of clocks showed the time in London, Washington, Brussels, Baghdad, Bangkok. Screens continually broadcast the latest from Sky News. An earthquake in Mexico. Albanian slave ring exposed. Coach crash in France – a handful of Britons hurt: one seriously. Striker Duane Bryonne scoring a glorious goal. Luke loved those screens: loved the idea that all the dramas of the world were contained there for him to pronounce on. He didn't know why he was so nervous. He was the 'face' of the show. Naturally one of the first things Dean would want to do was meet him. But still his heart was running double time. All new editors liked to make sweeping changes to stamp their authority. What could be more sweeping than replacing the old anchorman with a new one?

Lindsay, Chris's old secretary, was still at her desk outside her former master's den. She looked shell-shocked.

'All right, Lin?'

'Fine, Luke,' she said, rolling her eyes to imply she was anything but. 'Go in. Dean's waiting for you.'

Luke pushed open the door of the glass box. Dean Cutler stood up behind Chris's mahogany desk and held out a hand. He was tall, skinny, with cropped blond hair and bulging green eyes that made it look as if he was impersonating a frog. He wore a dark grey polo neck, pinstriped trousers and black Chelsea boots. Anyone more different to the donnish Chris with his rumpled suits was hard to imagine.

'Luke.' They crushed hands, both determined to show the other who was the more manly. 'What a pleasure. A real pleasure.' Dean had a nasal mockney accent that failed to hide his public-schoolboy origins. It took one to know one. 'I've been a fan for so long, it's a dream come true to finally get to work with you.'

'Thank you.' Luke smiled, despite his reservations. 'Err . . . likewise. I loved what you did with *Newsday*.'

'Thanks, man. Sit down, sit down.' Luke sat. Overnight, all traces of Chris had been expunged: the family photos, the assorted awards the show had garnered over the years, the slightly tatty prints of Oxford colleges, the bookcase with its battered copies of *Who's Who* and various dictionaries. Now the walls were bare, the shelves empty. It was as if Chris had never existed.

Luke swallowed.

'So, it's just a preliminary chat. In the next few days we'll get to know each other better. Have lunch. Or dinner. Yeah, dinner. Maybe you and your wife would like to come over and meet me and my wife.' He picked up a dictaphone and spoke into it. 'Tell Farrah: Luke and his wife to dinner.'

Luke's heart sank. Now he'd have to try to persuade

Poppy to leave the house. One of the advantages of having such a beautiful wife ought to have been showing her off, but Poppy was so shy their outings were almost always torture – not to mention the hostile vibes that came off Hannah's many old friends at the sight of them, which made him feel like he was walking through a field of radiation.

'What a great idea,' he said.

'Now, Luke,' Dean leant forward and began rolling a hideous red and green paperweight from one hand to the other, 'in the meantime, just a quiet word. As I say I am a great fan of yours. A *great* fan. But . . .' With a flourish like a magician pulling a rabbit from a hat, Dean produced that day's *Daily Post.* 'It seems not everyone feels the same way.'

Luke shrugged. 'My ex-wife. What can I do?'

'I agree, man. What *can* you do? I can't think why she's got such a downer on you. I mean, you didn't do anything wrong, you just left your devoted wife and three children for a girl young enough to be one of your daughters. Can't think why she's pissed off with you at all.' There was a brief silence, then, 'Aha! Had you! I was only joking, mate. You lucky bastard. We'd all do the same given half a chance. You're just bloody unlucky to have the menopausal old bunny boiler getting a column in a national newspaper.'

'Uh,' Luke managed.

'So! I have every sympathy but . . .' A dramatic pause. Dean rolled his eyes. 'The shareholders do *not.* I've argued that there's been a slight increase in viewing figures since Hannah's columns started. People tuning in to see what 'the cad' actually looks like. But the *shareholders* think it's bad for the show's image. Plus – and I'm telling you this strictly *entre nous* – they're concerned you're getting a bit past it. There's been talk of wanting a new face for *SevenThirty*. Now, *I* have defended you to the hilt. Said there's no way we're getting rid of such a distinguished newsman. You bring the show gravitas. But *they've* said, 'Well, he did bring it gravitas, until his ex made him a laughing stock.' So . . .' Dean winked, 'I am here to warn you, Luke. You need to be squeaky clean. We can't stop your mad ex attacking you, but what we *do not* want is to provide any fuel for her fire. Capeesh?'

'Capeesh,' Luke agreed.

'You are a happily married man, Luke. You've found true love with your pretty, young second wife and your baby girl. End of story. *N'est-ce-pas?*'

'Absolutely.' Luke's heart was off again. Shit. Did he know? How could he?

Dean winked. 'So it won't bother you in the slightest to hear that Thea Mackharven is coming back from New York as a senior producer. She's an excellent journalist and I'm delighted she's agreed to return to be part of my crack team.'

Thea? Luke almost collapsed in relief. Did Dean think she was an old girlfriend? Of course there'd been the odd shag over the years, but that hardly made them Romeo and Juliet.

'That's excellent news,' he said sincerely. 'She'll be a great asset to the show.'

'I'm glad you think so. She was wasted in the States.' Dean grinned, showing a row of pointy teeth, then stood

48

up, indicating the talk was at an end. 'It's great to have finally met you, Luke. I'll arrange dinner for us all to get to know each other asap.' He pronounced it *ay-sap*. 'In the meantime, just remember, not everyone's on your side but *I am*.'

'That's great to hear. And it's great to have you on board. I know the show's going to improve hugely with you at the helm.' Luke cringed at his disloyalty to Chris, but what could he do? Everyone knew the rules. They'd all join Chris in the Bricklayer's tonight for his impromptu leaving do. They'd get plastered, swear they couldn't work without him and in the morning they'd get up, take some Resolve and start sucking up to Dean. The editor was dead, long live the editor.

5

On that same grey Tuesday, oblivious to the upheavals in her husband's life, Poppy Norton was pushing a buggy containing her toddler, Clara, round Tesco's in Maida Vale. She was desperately trying to remember what she'd written on the shopping list she'd so carefully compiled then left lying on her kitchen table. Organic milk for Clara. Orange juice. Glenda, the cleaner whom Luke had hired even though Poppy had protested she was perfectly capable of cleaning the house herself, had wanted some kind of product for getting limescale off the bath, but for the life of her Poppy couldn't remember its name.

And then there'd been all the ingredients for the dinner she was going to cook for Luke on Friday, which was both his day off and their second anniversary. Poppy had decided to treat him to salmon – Luke loved fish – in a creamy herb sauce, but what were the herbs again?

Damn. Poppy had been quite excited about her culinary foray. When she and Luke had got together he'd been shocked at her lack of cooking skills, demanding how anyone could seriously exist on a diet of Pot Noodles and long-life apple juice. 'And what's this?' he'd asked, brandishing her pot of Crème de la Mer she'd pinched from a photo shoot.

'Don't eat that! It costs about two hundred pounds a jar!'

'Christ,' he'd sighed, 'two-hundred-pound face cream and there's not even any decent bread and butter in the house.' He paused, then added, 'Any more,' making it clear Hannah had always paid attention to such details.

When Poppy had dreamt about marriage and children it had been a misty montage involving a lot of scampering and cuddling and certainly no wiping of filthy bottoms and laundering of stained bibs. If the vision was more concrete, she saw herself as Maria in the *Sound of Music* with dozens of children snuggled up in bed round her as a thunderstorm raged outside.

It hadn't occurred to her that having them still snuggled in bed with her at three a.m. when her grumpy husband wanted sex might not be quite such fun. Not that her imaginary husband was ever grumpy – oh no, he was an adoring man gazing at her across a crystal-laden, candle-lit dinner table saying things like 'You have made my life complete'. It hadn't crossed her mind that *she* would have to put that crystal and candles on the table, that *she* would have to make the dinner, satisfying Luke's demands for home-cooked food. That *she* would have to make sure there were always three different types of muesli in the house, plus 'decent' bread, posh French butter, chunky marmalade, Bonne Maman jam, Marmite. *Good* coffee (i.e. Lavazza not Nescafé). Fresh orange juice. And that was just breakfast.

'Usually Luke leaves for the office about ten,' she whispered under her breath. 'And in the evenings, of course, he's presenting the news and usually has dinner either in the work canteen before the show, or goes out afterwards with colleagues. So usually I just microwave a baked potato for myself and then I have a tub of Skinny Cow ice cream while I watch Luke on TV.'

Poppy couldn't remember when she'd started giving interviews. Some time after Clara was born, she'd begun to enjoy little chats in her head explaining to a sympathetic lady from a magazine about how she was rooting for Nisha, the former children's TV presenter, to win this year's *Strictly Come Dancing*. How she'd just been to visit Hogarth's House in Chiswick and couldn't believe such an oasis of tranquillity existed just off one of the busiest roads in London. How Clara's favourite thing at the moment was to feed the ducks in the canal while shouting 'Quack, quack.' All the little things she longed to share with Luke but which he was rarely around to listen to; and even if he was they seemed to bore him.

'Mummeeee!' Clara interrupted her mother's train of thought.

'Yes, darling?'

'Mummeee, Clara get out.'

'In a minute, darling. Just let Mummy finish her shopping.' She looked up and caught the eye of another buggy-pusher. Tall, dark, probably quite pretty once, but old, at least forty, and haggard. Poppy recognized her from the baby clinic. They'd both been regulars in the hellish newborn days when Poppy had been so tired she'd once scattered formula powder over Luke's pasta thinking it was Parmesan and cleaned Clara's filthy bottom with a Flash floor wipe. Poppy smiled at her.

'Hi!'

The woman frowned as she tried to place her. 'Oh, hi, how are you?'

'Fine.' She smiled into the buggy at the woman's little boy, whose name she couldn't remember. 'How are you sweetie? Wow, you're so big now.'

'She's sweet,' the other woman said dutifully, eyeing Clara. 'What's her name again?'

'Clara.'

'Oh? I know two other Claras. And a Clare.'

'Right.' How was Poppy supposed to react to this? Change her child's name? 'I'm trying to find something to get limescale off the bath,' she said with a little laugh. 'Do you know what it might be called?'

'Viakal,' the mother said, jabbing a finger in the direction of cleaning products. Then her expression lit up as she saw another buggy-pusher, this one with grey hair in a bun. 'Marcia! Hey, how are *you*? You weren't at Gymboree yesterday. Do you have time for a coffee?'

'Bye,' said Poppy. 'Thanks.' But she was ignored. It was always the same. Because she was so young, the other mums seemed to think she was beneath their contempt. She'd tried the mother and baby groups, the music sessions, but all the mums were so much older. Occasionally, she'd see someone of her own age and her heart would quicken, but when she spoke to them they always turned out to be the nanny or the au pair, always with their own network of nanny and au pair friends, who regarded mothers in the same way the Palestinians did the Israelis.

That was the main thing that had never featured in Poppy's fantasies: that as a wife and mother she'd be so lonely; that she'd have days when her only adult exchanges would be with the bored-looking Indian men at the supermarket checkout. Days when she actively listened for the postman because, if she timed it right, she could collar him on the doorstep and engage him in a couple of minutes' chat about the weather – despite the fact he was all the while backing away.

Luke was frequently away and he often neglected to call for days, ignoring her anguished messages and texts. Poppy would send them frantic with worry that he'd stepped on a landmine, only to turn on the news at seven thirty and see him right as rain. 'Sorry, darling,' he'd say absently when she tackled him about it. 'Often we have no signal and when I'm on a deadline I don't do personal stuff. I will try harder.' And he did for a while, but then the calls dropped off and Poppy eventually got used to it, just as she got used to him being very terse with her when she did call, and to life alone with a baby. The early, sleepless days had been incredibly hard with a screaming baby, no friends in the same boat and no support from her mother. 'Babies are a nightmare. I went to hell and back with you,' had been Louise's helpful contribution.

Luke did find Clara sweet, but he just wasn't around much, either working late, or away on foreign trips and, despite his three children, could offer no advice. 'Hannah did the baby side of things,' was all he said vaguely whenever Poppy asked him for tips on burping or weaning.

But gradually things had got easier. She'd always loved Clara even at her screechiest worst and now she was walking and talking, she had become Poppy's little buddy. They spent long days together reading stories, watching the ducks drift down the canal and, especially now Clara was older and marginally more civilized, exploring hidden corners of London. Together, they'd discovered the graceful church of St Andrew-by-the-Wardrobe in Blackfriars with its cosy wood interior; the magnificent paintings of the Wallace Collection with its enclosed garden and fountain with a golden snake; the quirky Middle Eastern shops on the Edgware Road with their piles of pomegranates and dill, unripe mangoes and dusty Turkish Delight.

'Mummeee!'

'Yes, darling, Mummy will just pay and then you can walk home.'

Now her basket contained organic milk, orange juice, Cheerios (the health visitor had told Poppy she should be giving her daughter porridge for breakfast but Clara loathed it and threw it at the walls) and Viakal. Sod the fish. She'd buy some tomorrow from the fishmonger in Chapel Street market. That would be the day's project. Poppy had long since realized that one of the skills for making motherhood bearable was time management. She never bought more than a basket of stuff because, firstly, if she put too many bags on the back of the Maclaren buggy it tipped over, and, secondly, because she needed an excuse for leaving the house tomorrow.

Out of the corner of her eye, she saw the new *Tatler* on the magazine rack. Grinning from the cover was Daisy McNeil, Poppy's biggest rival from her modelling days. They were both healthy-looking, blue-eyed blondes with big teeth and had always been sent for the same jobs. Usually Poppy got them, but not any more, obviously. Below it, with the newspapers, was a *Daily Post*. Oh fuck, it was Tuesday. Which meant . . . yes, there above the masthead was a grinning Hannah. THE DEMISE OF THE TROPHY WIFE, the paper screamed and underneath 'Hannah Creighton on the death of the bimbo spouse'.

Oh, no. Oh, no. Not another attack. Hannah had been silent for a few weeks. But just as you knew the axe-wielding serial killer in a horror movie was pretending to be dead, so he could suddenly jump up and terrify the heroine, Poppy knew she could never relax as long as she and Luke's ex-wife shared the same planet.

It had been a nasty shock when just a few weeks after Clara was born Poppy had opened the *Daily Post* to see a huge picture on page eighteen of Luke and a pretty redhead with their arms round each other, next to a headline screaming: MY HUSBAND, THE BIMBO AND ME by Hannah Creighton. The picture caption read 'Luke and Hannah in Happier Times' and there was a smaller picture of Poppy looking particularly stupid in a red, flowery hat, with the caption 'The Other Woman – Poppy Price'.

There then followed the heartbreaking story of Hannah's marriage break up. Since when, there had been a weekly bulletin about Hannah's wonderful new life as a divorcee, overflowing with friends, exotic holidays, interesting work and incredible sex.

At the same time, frequent digs were made at the 'cad' and the 'bimbo' (after the first column she had never again mentioned Poppy by name, which was something, Poppy supposed). Hannah described how she had heard the marriage had run into trouble once the baby had been born, how she couldn't help but feel sorry for

Poppy lumbered with a man who bought Viagra on the internet.

Of course, the columns raised all sorts of questions. Timidly, Poppy tackled Luke about them and he responded furiously. 'Of course I didn't beg her to get back with me; of course there weren't dozens of women before you; of course I didn't order Viagra on the internet.' After the last, he softened. 'Why would I do that? Do I need any help in the bedroom?' Poppy had had to believe him or she would have gone insane, but the doubt still lingered just under the surface, like a splinter the tweezers couldn't quite grasp.

Initially, there'd been a flurry of calls and letters and emails from various newspapers, including the *Post* itself, asking if Poppy would like to give an interview defending herself. She'd been up for the chance to put her side across, but Luke had said absolutely no way in a tone that brooked no argument and after a while the approaches had stopped, even though Hannah's attacks continued.

Glancing round the supermarket, Poppy stuffed the paper in her basket as if it were a porn mag. She paid, and outside, released Clara from the buggy for the torturously slow walk home, with stops to examine every stone, twig and cigarette butt that lay between Clifton Gardens and Blomfield Road. Poppy's phone rang in her pocket. Meena. Bored at work again.

'Hi, gorgeous.' Poppy tried to sound chipper.

'Hiiii, trophy wife. I've just read that bitch in the *Post* slagging you off again. Silly cow. She's just jealous because you're young and beautiful and she's a forty-something has-been.'

57

'Oh right. I haven't seen it,' Poppy lied. Meena always got cross with Poppy for letting Hannah get to her.

'Good. Don't. It'll just upset you. So how are things?'

'Well, Clara's had a bit of diarrhoea but—'

'Too. Much. Information.' Meena was very sweet to Clara when she saw her, pulling faces and tickling her, but like most childless people she had simply no inkling of the gigantic space a child took up in your life. Poppy didn't blame her, not so long ago she'd been equally clueless. 'So what have you been up to?'

'Oh, the usual. Shopping.'

'In Westbourne Grove?' Meena perked up.

'No, Tesco's, you muppet.'

'Poppy! I don't get it. You've married a rich man, why don't you spend more time flexing his plastic?'

'You know I don't like shopping much. It's boring.' Plus, the joy of wandering around boutiques, flicking through racks of clothes and fingering fabrics, was somewhat diminished when your daughter had a habit of lifting up the changing-room curtain just as you'd thrown your bra on the ground, or dashing off into the shop when you were wearing nothing but knickers and tights. But Poppy wasn't going to go into that. In any case, Meena was moving on.

'Listen, you've got to help me. Dan's texted.'

'Oh yeah?' Dan was a banker from Goldman's or Salamon's – Poppy forgot which – who Meena occasionally slept with. 'What did he say?'

'"R U around Saturday nite?" What do you think? Do you think that's good?'

'Of course it's good.' Poppy never quite understood

the arcane rituals surrounding Meena's love life. Because her only proper boyfriend had been Luke, she'd missed out on the rite of passage that was flirting in bars, one-night stands, waiting for texts, studying his page on Bebo, all the things that dominated her friend's existence. Poppy tried to give useful advice, but she felt often as if she were trying to translate that day's *Financial Times* into Mandarin, so limited was her vocabulary in the language of emoticons and poking.

She knew Meena thought she had the perfect life, but often Poppy felt a little jealous of her friend who had nothing more to worry about than whether to wear the red or the green top to Boujis on Friday or alter her Facebook status to 'in a relationship', while Poppy – who'd thought Luke would free her from all cares – found herself hassling the landlord to send someone round to mend the dishwasher. Sometimes when she looked in the mirror, she was surprised at the fresh, unlined face that stared back at her, so staid and careworn did she feel inside.

'I don't know,' Meena was musing, 'I think he thinks I'm easy. He always gets in touch, just like that out of the blue. It's not respectful. I think I'm going to ignore it.'

'But you like him, don't you?'

'Mummmmee. Whassat?'

'Just a minute, darling. I . . .'

'Mummeee!'

Poppy shrieked. Clara was holding out a clear plastic bag containing a fresh dog turd.

'No! No! Put that down. Dirty! Dirty! Dirty!'

Clara burst into tears as her mother threw the offending

object into the road. Help! Poppy was sure dog shit had some bug in it that made you blind.

'Clara, don't touch your eyes, don't touch your eyes.' She picked her up. 'Come on. We have to get home quickly and wash your hands. Meena, I'm sorry, I've got to go.'

'What about the school reunion?'

'Oh . . .' They'd been invited to a reunion at Brettenden in a month's time and were still debating about whether to go or not. Meena was pro, Poppy had been anti. But right this second, she was more concerned with saving her daughter's eyesight. 'Say yes, if you like. I'll talk to you later.'

They marched up the road, Poppy pushing the buggy laden with shopping with one hand, while under her other arm a thrashing Clara screamed at a volume that could have been put to good use in Guantanamo Bay. A passing man in a suit averted his eyes in horror. Not so long ago he'd have scanned Poppy admiringly. But now Poppy was another victim of buggy blindness syndrome, which made all women pushing children completely invisible, except to dotty old ladies and other women pushing children. Poppy sometimes thought she should offer her services to MI6 as an undercover agent. So long as she had the Maclaren with her, she could infiltrate meetings to nuke London without anybody being the wiser.

Her phone rang again. Luke. Probably warning her not to read the *Post*. She'd promise him she wouldn't, then had to remember to hide her copy carefully at the bottom of the recycling.

'Hello, darling?' she said, adding to Clara, 'It's Daddy.'

'Down, Mummeeeee!'

'Is she OK?' Luke asked, then without waiting for a reply, 'Listen, can Glenda babysit on Friday?'

Poppy's heart soared like a lark. He'd remembered their anniversary.

'I don't know. I expect so. I'll ask her right now.'

'I bloody hope so, because there's a work do we have to go to.'

'Oh.' Poppy might once have begged to go to Luke's work gatherings but now she was regretting it. As soon as they arrived he would disappear into the crowd, leaving his shy wife to move from group to group, smiling nervously. But everyone simply carried on talking vociferously and even though, here and there, people moved aside to let her pass, nobody interrupted conversations for her. She looked pretty, but she didn't look important enough to actually talk to. And when she did finally find Luke and attach herself to him, the men would lech at her, while the women greeted her with the same enthusiasm they'd reserve for a dose of chlamydia.

'It's non-negotiable. Chris Stevens has been sacked and his replacement Dean's having a small dinner.' There was a pause. 'You do know who Chris Stevens is, don't you?'

'Of course!' Poppy tried very hard to keep abreast of all Luke's work matters; it was what a good wife should do. 'Your editor. That's terrible.'

'It is. It's the end of an era. But now we've got to schmooze Dean. Mightily. It's very important I show up with my wife.'

Poppy stalled. 'Now I think about it Glenda might be busy on Friday.'

'Glenda seems to be busy a lot these days,' Luke said sharply.

'She babysits for a lot of people,' Poppy lied, feeling guilty because she knew Glenda would love the cash. Maybe she'd just slip her some extra.

'If Glenda can't do it, you'd better find someone else. I've told you, Poppy, it's really important you accompany me to this party. It's the kind of thing good wives do for their husbands.'

'OK,' she said.

'Listen, I've got to go. I'm recording an interview with the head of the TUC. But call Glenda. You need to get over this fear of going out before we become more of a laughing stock than we already are.'

So he'd seen the *Daily Post*. 'I'm not frightened—' Poppy tried, but Luke said, 'Gotta go. See you later,' and the phone went dead.

6

The paper boy, in the village of Dumberley, Surrey, made his way up the crazy-paving path of 'Stumpers' and pushed the Mackharvens' copy of the *Daily Post* through the brass letter box.

'Paper's here, Dad!' cried Jan Mackharven, gasping slightly from the effort of bending over in her floral dressing gown to retrieve it from the doormat.

Sitting at the pine kitchen table, cradling her coffee, Thea Mackharven winced slightly. She loved her mother, but the way she addressed Thea's step-father, Trevor, as 'Dad' still made Thea cringe, just as she shuddered at their extensive collection of Phil Collins and Level 42 CDs, their painting-by-numbers of a little boy with a hand over his mouth because he'd just wet himself, their battered orange MFI sofa and their wall of red-and-gold, leather-bound Reader's Digest 'classic' books.

Thea wished it were not so, but there was no doubt she was a snob. She blamed it on her paternal genes. Trevor Mackharven was a kind, if stodgy, man, who'd always treated her as his own, but Thea had never ever been able to shake off the knowledge that she wasn't; that she came from a better place.

Like Poppy, Thea had never known her father. There, however, the similarities ended. Thea was twelve years older than Poppy for a start and her father hadn't left Jan but had died before Thea was born. Poppy had been a beautiful baby, Thea had not. Brown-toothed ladies who bent over her pram to coo backed away in shock at the sight that greeted them. Just so no one should forget this, Jan had placed a huge photo of her infant daughter in pride of place in the middle of the mantelpiece. It showed a baby with a shock of bright red hair and a face like a pug dog with worms.

Fortunately, the photos surrounding it showed a slow improvement. There was Thea aged four at Jan's wedding to Trevor: still a plain little girl but the red hair replaced by thick black locks that fell down her back like wires. Then there was six-year-old Thea at the christening of her first brother, Paul, her face thinner now though still blighted by NHS glasses with sickly pink frames. Thea at the christening of the twins, Edward and Nicholas, her face ravaged by the fierce acne that had endured throughout her adolescence.

She took another sip of coffee and studied the other pictures in their tacky brass frames. There she was on her graduation day, looking embarrassed in a mortar board and gown, flanked by Trevor in a cheap suit from Burton and Jan, beaming in polyester lilac. Thea's looks had definitely improved by this time: the specs and the spots had gone and John Frieda had invented Frizz-Ease, but her eyes were still too slanted and her mouth too wide, with nothing to be done on either count. There she was in the family line-up at Paul's wedding: eyes closed but wearing a gorgeous green Jasper Conran suit, proof she was now earning good money. And then there was Thea in a divine cream Stella McCartney dress accepting an award for best TV news item of the year at the BAFTAs. Three years ago, the last night she and Luke had spent together.

To her annoyance, Thea felt a pinching at the bridge of her nose as her tear ducts started to fill.

'Are you all right, sweetheart?' her mother asked.

'I'm fine,' she said briskly, getting up and heading to the door. 'I'm going to get dressed.'

As she left the room, Trevor and Jan exchanged concerned looks over their bowls of Shredded Wheat.

'Do you think she's all right?' Jan said, sotto voce.

'Of course,' Trevor reassured her, picking up the teapot, 'fill this up will you, love? She's probably still jet-lagged. Remember how it took you days to get over it after you came back from visiting her?'

Jan liked this answer. 'You're right,' she agreed eagerly, switching on the kettle. 'She's only been back a couple of days. Or maybe she's got a boyfriend? She could be missing him.'

Trevor snorted. 'Thea with a boyfriend? I can't imagine that.'

'Oh, don't say that, Trev,' cried Jan, stricken. 'She's thirty-six. I do worry, you know. I keep reading about these girls leaving it too late to have babies. I don't want Thea to be one of those.'

'Paul has children,' Trevor pointed out, somewhat irrelevantly. 'And Thea's always said she doesn't want babies. After all, sweets, she *has* got a great job.'

'I know,' Jan said. For a moment she was silent, reflecting on how different her daughter was to her, how – having watched Jan's struggles to bring up four children on a limited income – Thea had always sworn she was going to devote herself to her career. And that devotion had paid off, Jan thought proudly. A producer for the *SevenThirty News*, Thea had spent the past couple of years in New York. But now the programme had a new editor, and Thea had been recalled to London, just like that, as a senior producer. It was very impressive. None of Jan's friends could believe Thea was actually on speaking terms with the likes of Luke Norton and Emma Waters and, especially, the gorgeous Marco Jensen.

But still . . . Jan's floppy face sagged.

'Every woman wants to be a mother, Trev.'

'Shh,' Trevor hissed. 'She's coming back.'

They both gazed into their bowls, as the subject of their conversation re-entered the room, dressed in tight jeans and a beige chunky-knit sweater. Trevor stood up.

'I'm off to work now, love. Will you be here when I get back?'

'No, I'm leaving in a minute.'

Trevor gave her a diffident hug. 'Goodbye then, my love. See you again soon, I hope.'

'Mmm,' Thea said. Irrationally, it annoyed her when Trevor called her 'my love', even though he had every right to. Most people didn't even know he wasn't her real father. After all, she had taken his surname when her mother married him. Thea's real father, Leo Fry, had worked in an accounts office by day, but at night was a singer in a rock band. Mum had met and married him when they were both twenty-one. He'd died, only weeks before Thea was born, in a motorbike crash. Throughout her childhood, Thea had obsessed over how different her life would have been if Leo's back wheel hadn't hit that patch of oil. In her parallel life, she would have grown up an adored only child, touring the world with her rock-star father.

But Leo *had* died, so Thea's fate had been to grow up in this run-down semi, on the fringes of an industrial estate, littered with plastic cars, trucks, diggers and aeroplanes that belonged to her three boisterous younger brothers. It was a solitary childhood. Mum loved Thea, but the boys' demands meant she had little time to spare for her. Thea had spent a lot of time locked in her room listening to her father's precious Bob Dylan albums.

The only person who actually had time to really listen to her was Leo's mother, who lived in Guildford, a short bus ride away. Thea visited her every Sunday without fail. Mum just nodded vaguely and said, 'That's nice, angel', when Thea brought home a good report. Gran would put her specs on, read it carefully and note with approval that Thea was 'excellent' at French and frown when she saw she hadn't been paying attention in biology.

'You've got to work as hard as you can, Thea,' she'd say. 'There are so many opportunities for girls these days. Opportunities I'd have killed for. You can get out of Dumberley and do something with your life. Don't let me down, love.'

'I won't, Gran,' Thea promised. And she hadn't.

'I'm going to make you some tuna sandwiches to take back to London with you,' Jan wittered as the front door slammed. 'They're your favourite, aren't they? At least, it used to be. Maybe there's some American sandwich you like now. If you tell me, I could make it for you.'

'I doubt you can buy lox and pastrami in Dumberley,' Thea muttered.

'Sorry?'

'Oh, nothing.' As always, Thea felt guilty. Her mother was only trying to look after her. The problem was Mum was always trying to look after everyone, with the result that she had neglected herself. Even now the boys had grown up and left home, she still seemed to have no time for herself, busy as she was baking for Trevor, washing Trevor's dirty underpants, cleaning Trevor's facial hair out of the basin, while Trevor sat in the pub with the darts team watching Sky Sports and nursing a pint.

'Here, have another slice of toast,' Jan said, shoving the rack under her daughter's nose. As penance for her earlier nastiness, Thea smiled.

'Thanks.' But as she continued flicking through the *Daily Post*, she couldn't help another swipe. 'I can't believe you're still getting this vile newspaper. It's obsessed with Princess Diana and how Britain is being swamped with evil immigrants.'

'Dad likes the football reports,' Jan protested feebly, 'and I like the horoscopes. I suppose we could try another paper . . .'

But Thea wasn't listening. She was opening an email that had just arrived on her BlackBerry from her best friend Rachel. 'You're back' read the subject field.

Yo, girlfriend, so glad you're home. Def on for dinner on Tues. But no boozing, sadly now am up the duff. Can't wait to catch up.

Scowling, Thea pressed delete. She was getting sick of this. Having fulfilled a lifelong ambition to live in Manhattan, Thea had nonetheless been thrilled to get the call from Roxanne Fox asking her to come home.

'*You* are exactly the kind of talent that is missing from the newsroom,' Roxanne had said. 'Dean and I want you at the heart of things, jazzing this programme up.'

Within forty-eight hours Thea had packed her belongings and was on her way to JFK to catch her one-way flight to Heathrow. From the back of her kamikaze taxi, she had sent out a flurry of emails and texts announcing her return. After her lonely childhood, Thea had grown into an extremely gregarious adult who considered a night in to be a night wasted. She could quite easily go for several weeks without cooking a meal in her pristine oven or picking up the TV remote.

Things had slowed down a bit in Manhattan. She'd made a handful of friends — mostly gay — through introductions or work, but she'd found herself having to try much harder to keep things on the boil than she had in her twenties, and she'd found the whole dating culture utterly soul destroying. By the end of two years, she couldn't wait to come home. Three days ago, she'd disembarked at Heathrow, expecting to be deluged by messages from friends, welcoming her return. But the greetings had been discomfortingly lukewarm. There was the odd text or email, saying 'Gr8 C U Soon I Hope', but no one had made any firm plans to meet.

The people she had spoken to all said how pleased they were to have her back, but were all unwilling to commit to anything definite. 'I'd love to, but my in-laws are in town/the new nanny's just started and I don't dare leave her to babysit/I don't live in London any more, didn't you know, we've moved to Scotland' were the kind of answers she received.

Pussies. What the hell had happened to all the old party crowd? Even Rachel, who'd always laughed at women who stroked their bumps and said things like 'we're pregnant', was probably playing Mozart to her foetus now and reading it Tolstoy in original Russian to improve its chances of getting into the best nursery.

'So now you're back in London, how does it work for lunch?' Jan asked.

'How do you mean?'

'Well, what do you do? Take in sandwiches and a flask?'

Inwardly, Thea groaned. What was it with her mother's obsession with food? 'No, Mum. Mostly I'll have lunch in the canteen. Sometimes I'll go out if there's time.'

'Go out?' Jan was scandalized.

'Yes. To a caff.'

'That must be pricey. Wouldn't you be better off taking sandwiches?'

Thea ignored this.

'I could make you some if you like? To take in on Monday.'

'No, thanks, Mum.'

'Are you sure? I could do you — what did you say you had in New York?'

'I'll be fine. *No one* takes in sandwiches.'

'What? You all eat in a caff *every day*?'

'Usually in the canteen. It's subsidized.'

'But it still must cost a bomb.'

'We can afford it,' said Thea, thanking the Lord she had to get back to London for meetings and, of course, for Dean Cutler's dinner party on Friday night. She carried on leafing past articles about how useless the government was, what Victoria Beckham had worn to some party, the latest cure for cellulite when – wham.

'Oh my word,' said Jan, looking over her shoulder. 'It's Luke.'

'Yes,' Thea said. Blood was drumming so hard in her temples, she could hardly hear herself.

'He is a handsome man, isn't he? Mind you,' continued Jan bending over her daughter and peering at a second, smaller photo, 'that Hannah is very attractive as well. Do you know her at all?'

'Mmm. Vaguely.'

'I must say, I do enjoy her column. It makes me laugh. Cry sometimes too. I mean, it was a terrible thing Luke did leaving his family for a younger woman. Pretty as she is. But Hannah seems to have really pulled herself back up again. She's becoming quite a celebrity. She was on *Loose Women* the other day and she did make me laugh with some of her comments.'

'Don't call them Luke and Hannah, Mum. You don't know them.'

'Sorry,' Jan said reproved. 'You're right. I don't. But I feel as if I sort of do. After all, I see Luke on the telly most nights and you worked with him for years, so . . .'

'But you don't know him.'

'You're right. I don't. I'd better get back to the sandwiches . . . Oh. Telephone. Hello? Dumberley *six* nine *oh* two seven. Oh, hello, Faye. Yes, Thea's back. Yes, lovely

. . . Yes, I'll tell her Emma Waters really shouldn't wear those Peter Pan collars. I know, it does nothing for her . . .'

While her mother babbled away, Thea studied the photographs. There was Luke. Of course in New York she'd still seen him on screen virtually every day, so no big shock there, but she couldn't stop herself from studying those high cheekbones, that firm mouth, those wide shoulders.

But what about Hannah? Last time Thea had seen her she'd been a pretty, but worn woman with sensible hair framing a tired, round face. But the woman who smiled out at her here was a vixen with a feathery hair cut that showed off high cheekbones and sparkly eyes. So much for the woman who'd confided in Thea that when Luke left her she thought she'd die of the pain. If Hannah had died, she had quickly resurrected herself as something of a siren.

Greedily, like a dieter left alone with a bowl of M&Ms, Thea devoured the article. Bloody hell, Hannah. It was an out-and-out attack on Poppy and all her kind. For the first time that morning, Thea's mouth widened into a smile.

'Are you going to visit your gran?' Jan asked, as she hung up.

'Very soon.' Leo's mother was senile now and lived in a home that Thea paid for. Guilt about not seeing her enough had been one of the main reasons she had wanted to come home.

'You *are* a good girl.' Jan leant over Thea's shoulder again. 'What are you looking at? Oh, still reading Hannah.

What's she on about this week? The Demise of the Trophy Wife. I'm sure that will be a laugh. She's very funny, though I do think she can be a bit unkind to that new wife, calling her a trollop and a bimbo. I mean, I'm sure she played her part, but Luke's the real villain in the case, isn't he? I mean, in the end it was *him* who left his family. The Bimbo didn't force him to go at gunpoint.'

'You know exactly what happened, do you, Mum?'

Another metaphorical slap in the face. 'Well, no. Of course not. But—'

'So Hannah's been writing a lot of these articles for the *Daily Post*?'

Relieved that her daughter no longer seemed on the attack, Jan smiled. 'Yes. She has a weekly column. It's called "Story of a Split Up", but then she writes other stuff as well. Like I say, she's been making quite a name for herself. I'm surprised you didn't know.'

'I haven't been reading the *Daily Post*. I've been in New York, remember?'

'You could read it online.'

Thea looked up, as astonished as if her mother had revealed she and Trevor were founding members of the Dumberley devil-worship society.

'*Online?* You read newspapers online?'

'Of course. You know I know how to use Dad's computer. How do you think I send you all those emails?' Which none of you ever respond to, Jan thought.

'Yes, but reading newspapers ... Anyway, I guess I could have read Hannah online, but I didn't know she was writing for the *Daily Post*.' Why didn't you tell me, Rachel? With superhuman force of will, Thea collected herself. 'Not that I care, anyway. Why would I? I have no interest at all in Luke Norton's private life.' Having uttered that enormous lie, she stood up. 'OK, Mum. I really must be getting back to London.'

'I wish you could stay longer.'

'Me too,' Thea lied again. 'But it's *work*, you know.' It was the cast-iron excuse that got her out of everything, every time. What would she do without it?

7

It was just after six on Friday. In her bedroom, Poppy was poring over the copy of the *Post* she'd bought earlier that week, re-reading Hannah's trophy-wife article for the twentieth time. She'd vowed to rip it up, but just as she'd loved to pick at her playground scabs until they bled, she couldn't resist returning again and again to Hannah's words.

Leech. Parasite. Every phrase ripped through Poppy like a labour pain. That so wasn't how it was. She'd married Luke for love, not money. That was why he always said he loved her. Used to say, she corrected herself sadly, realizing Luke hadn't made any such declaration for quite a while. OK, so perhaps she neither held down a twenty-hour-a-day job in the City nor was she a brilliant hostess and cook, but she was busy – way too busy, bringing up Clara. In her articles, Hannah never mentioned that her superwoman stance had been made considerably easier thanks to the teams of au pairs she'd employed or, post-divorce, by sending all three children to boarding school, giving her plenty of time to tend the garden and re-establish her brilliant career.

For the millionth time since the columns had begun Poppy turned her attention to Hannah's photos. Meena insisted she'd been airbrushed, but even allowing for that, there was no doubt she was a really attractive woman. Perhaps not as pretty as Poppy, but certainly nothing like the frump she'd imagined on the rare occasions Luke had reluctantly referred to his wife. Much as it pained her, Poppy couldn't help nursing a grudging respect for Hannah. She hated the way she kept attacking her in print and now – more and more – on TV, but at the same time Poppy knew the attacks were justified. Before she'd married Luke and especially before she'd had Clara, she'd had no understanding of how much a wife *needed* her husband, how much a child needed its father. She'd taken Luke from Hannah almost as casually as she might have finished Meena's shampoo and it was beginning to dawn on her what a bad and selfish thing she'd done.

Poppy believed in karma. So even though Hannah's attacks were humiliating, she meekly submitted to them knowing that, if anything, she was getting off lightly for her evil behaviour.

'Oh Clara! Put that down!'

Clara continued rubbing Poppy's favourite Shiseido lipstick all over her face.

'Clara, that's Mummy's, give it to me.'

'No-wagh.'

Poppy struggled to recall the techniques imparted from all the childcare programmes she watched when Luke was out entertaining contacts. 'Then Mummy will have to take it from you,' she threatened.

A sly look came over Clara's pretty face, as she backed towards the wall.

'No-wagh.'

Poppy looked round helplessly as if Supernanny might be hiding in the cupboard ready to jump out and help her subdue this ferocious toddler.

'Please?' she asked meekly.

Clara turned her back and started drawing on the wall.

'Oh, sweetie, don't do that. No!' Luke would go mad. Poppy bounded across the room and snatched the lipstick. Immediately, Clara's face creased and she began to scream a scream that could lead warriors into battle.

'Noooo! Noooo! Noooo! Give me, Mummy. Give meeeee!'

Luke stuck his head around the door. 'For God's sake! What's all the racket for?'

'Nothing,' said Poppy, positioning herself in front of the graffiti. She was sure the marks would come out with a bit of soap and water. 'Clara's just tired. Aren't you, poppet?'

'No, Mummeee. No tired.'

'Did you have a good day?' Poppy asked. It had been Luke's day off and she had hoped he might spend it with them, but he'd lunched in town with a contact.

'Yeah, not bad,' he said absently. 'Will Glenda be here soon? You should be getting ready.'

'Half past seven, I told her.'

'That's now,' Luke said, flopping on the bed. Poppy's heart started to thud. If he discovered the *Post* under the duvet cover she'd be in big trouble. Happily, he was distracted by Clara trying to scramble on to his chest.

'Clah-Clah, I just told Mummy, it's time you got in your pyjamas.'

'I don't think she's ready yet,' Poppy said, rearranging

the bedclothes to hide the paper better. 'She had a really long nap this afternoon.'

'You just said she was tired.' Luke sighed. 'You let her sleep too long in the afternoons. Hannah had some kind of routine for the children, where you only let them sleep a bit in the day at set times and then they always went to bed at seven and were always up at seven. That way you got the evenings to yourself.'

'Mmm,' Poppy said, trying surreptitiously to shift the cheval mirror, so it covered the red marks on the wall. It was what she always said when Luke praised his ex-wife. Bloody control freak. Why on earth would you want your child up at seven every day? She didn't want Clara going to bed at seven sharp either. Well, sometimes it would be nice, but Luke was out so often in the evenings; Poppy relied on her daughter for company.

The doorbell rang. 'Ah, that'll be Glenda. I'll let her in. The cab's coming at quarter to. Think you can be ready by then?'

Poppy knew a dig when she heard one. She always did everything to delay these outings, in the vain hope Luke would suddenly decide he'd rather spend an evening in with her than go out schmoozing. She looked in the mirror on her dressing table. Not bad, she thought, looking at her floaty blue top from Portobello and the grey pinstripe trousers she'd found on a market stall in Dalston when she and Clara were on one of their adventures in the East End. Poppy had never been that into clothes and had quite happily slipped into the new-mum's uniform of stained sweatpants and T-shirts, not worried if she ever wore a pair of heels again. But she knew she had to make some effort when she and Luke went out together. It had taken some time to shift the baby weight after Clara was born and she was still not quite as skinny as when she had been modelling, but she thought a healthy child was more important than getting to size zero.

'Hello, darlin'!'

Glenda came bustling into the room. She was forty-five, with four children of her own in the Philippines whom she visited once a year for a fortnight. Compared to her, Poppy knew her problems were small. But the Alonto family's loss had been Poppy's gain. She hadn't wanted a cleaner, but she hadn't realized Glenda would end up being an unpaid shrink as well. Without her weekly visits, Poppy thought she would have gone a bit doolally for want of another mother to confide in.

'Hey! How are you?' She smiled.

'Fine, my love. How are you?' She swooped on Clara. 'Hello, darling. How are you? Oh, I missed you, sweet angel.'

'Gwenda!'

'Why you no in your pyjamas? Come with Auntie Glenda, I make you all cosy.'

Obediently Clara toddled off with her. Poppy watched, stricken. How come Clara never did that with her? Was there *anything* she wasn't rubbish at? The doorbell rang again.

'Poppy, that's the cab,' Luke yelled from downstairs.

'Just a second.' She ran into Clara's room, where her baby was looking angelic in her flowery pyjamas. She fell to her knees. 'Goodnight, darling. Can Mummy have a cuddle?'

'No-wagh.'

'I'll read you a story.' Poppy always tried this one on the rare occasion Luke had friends over, even though she knew she should be making witty and erudite conversation downstairs. She could spend hours tucked up cosily with Poppy, avoiding the 'grown-ups' as she couldn't help thinking of them by invoking the cast-iron excuse of introducing her daughter to the glory of the written word.

But as usual Clara was wise to her mummy's ruse. 'No wanna story.'

Luke stuck his head round the door. 'Poppy! The taxi's here.'

'But Clara needs a story.'

'No wanna story,' Clara repeated, as Luke said. 'Well, Glenda can read you one.'

Defeated, Poppy knelt down and kissed her. 'I'll see you in the morning, then. Be a good girl for Glenda.'

'She's always a good girl for me,' Glenda purred.

In the back of the taxi, Luke leant back against the burgundy upholstery and sighed.

'At long last we're going out together.'

'I'm looking forward to it,' Poppy lied. 'Tell me more about it. Dean Cutler's your new editor.'

'Yup, so be very, very nice to him because the rumour is that Dean has the knives out for everyone on the show over forty. Which means me.'

'You mean you might lose your job?'

'I might indeed.' Luke stared out at the Marylebone Road. 'How old is Clara now?' he asked suddenly. 'Nearly two?'

'Twenty-three months.' It never failed to amaze her that Luke couldn't remember pieces of information that were tattooed on her heart.

'So she'll start nursery soon.'

'I suppose so,' said Poppy vaguely. Despite nagging from everyone from the man at the dry cleaners to the health visitor, from Louise to Meena, she had steadfastly refused to put Clara's name down for nursery, so much did the prospect of sending her baby out into the big, bad world terrify her.

'So you'll soon be able to go back to work.'

'Mmm.'

Luke reached out and took her hand. 'I've been thinking about it, Poppy. It would be good for you. Get you out of the house. Earn your own money. Be able to talk to people about something more than nappies and *Teletubbies*.'

He'd been reading bloody Hannah. 'Mmm,' she said then, deciding it was worth another try, she squeezed his hand. 'But I was thinking maybe soon we'd have another baby.'

As always when the subject came up, Luke sighed heavily. 'You know what I think about that. I've got four children already. I can't support another one.' He ran his fingers through his hair. 'Look, sweetheart, just think about the work thing. You can't stay at home doing nothing for ever.'

'I don't do *nothing*,' Poppy protested, but the cab was drawing up outside Dean Cutler's terrace house in West Hampstead.

8

About an hour earlier Thea Mackharven was turning this way and that in front of the mirror of her one-bedroom flat in Stockwell to the strains of Bob Dylan singing about Black Diamond Bay on her favourite of all his albums *Desire*. Not bad, she thought of her dark green Joseph trouser suit and her hair piled in an unruly topknot, that she hoped was sexy rather than bag lady.

Thea knew she was not a natural beauty. As with everything in her life, she'd worked damn hard with her raw materials and – as with everything else – she'd succeeded. No one would ever say Thea was gorgeous but they would say she was 'very attractive', a tag which she'd managed, heroically, to retain even after passing the watershed of thirty-five. Only in the past few months had the mirror occasionally revealed a tired woman with a sunburst of lines round her eyes and mouth that thousands of pounds of rhinoceros's innards and penta-peptides had been unable to keep at bay.

Tonight, however, her reflection was on her side. She smiled triumphantly, then glanced round the room. It had a rather corporate feel, she had to admit. Thea had owned it for nearly nine years but beyond a quick paint job when she bought it, she'd done little to make it feel like a real home. She had about as much interest in interior decoration as she did in the sex life of the aardvark. Her flat represented somewhere she slept for a few hours after rolling in after a long night in Soho House rather than any kind of nest. Its highlights were its proximity to the Tube and the twenty-four-hour shop below. All right, it did look a little bleak, but it would be better once she got round to unpacking her New York stuff, not that that amounted to more than a couple of boxes. Thea prided herself on travelling light, on being available to up sticks at a few hours' notice. Possessions just slowed that process down.

It was unsettling to think that just a month ago, this space had been full of the clutter of Parveen; she worked for an accountant in the West End. Luckily, she'd been transferred to the Leeds office before Thea had been called back to London and before she'd found a new tenant, meaning she'd been able to move straight back in. Who had Parveen entertained in this bedroom? Thea wondered, then swallowed hard as she thought back to the last time she had been naked there with a man.

'Come on,' she snapped at herself, triple-locking the door and tapping down the stairs. She strode down her Victorian terraced street and on to the main road, inhaling the South London smell of fast food and petrol. Head in the air she walked even faster past a gaggle of hooded youths sitting on a wall, but they seemed more interested in their mobiles than in her. Thea felt a pang for the days when gangs of men had meant wolf whistles rather than potential stab wounds.

She had been staggered by how much London had changed in the short time she'd been away. Bits of it had got so much richer, with everyone floating round with blow-dried hair and threaded eyebrows (and that was just the men) as if they were on Rodeo Drive. Other bits, however, like Stockwell seemed to have got poorer and nastier, with an unsettling undercurrent of violence. She'd love to move to a smarter area, but with Gran's care-home fees, she couldn't afford it.

Still, she thought with a sudden swing in her heart, it was great to be back. Despite the dirt, the noise, the crowds, the grey, the rain, the incredible expense, Thea adored London, adored it – to everyone's surprise – far more than New York, which she found a little bit too sanitized and populated by wannabe Gwyneth Paltrows with bleached blonde hair and perfect teeth who said 'that's funny' to all Thea's jokes as if she'd just told them they had terminal cancer. No, London was better. She adored the sense of possibility that existed here, the way anything was available: Portuguese custard tarts, dog yoga teachers, Swarovski-studded burkas. She loved how Poles lived next door to Brazilians, who lived next door to Nigerians, Bangladeshis, Canadians; how three hundred languages were spoken within the M25; the way the city was so big and noisy you could lead whatever life you chose without fear of a moment's silence in which to question if that choice was the right one.

She'd yearned to live here ever since she'd come on a school trip to see *Annie* at the London Palladium when she was twelve. As a teenager, she had thought 'sashimi in Soho' was the most glamorous phrase known to man and now she could eat sashimi whenever she liked in whichever parish she chose. Sometimes Thea had to pinch herself when she realized this life was actually hers. All right, television didn't pay like banking or law, but she lived comfortably *and* she got to travel the world and have adventures that someone from Dumberley could never have dreamed of.

Yes, all in all, Thea's life was pretty perfect. Once she'd thought she needed one thing to complete it, but she was over that now.

She strode past the motley collection of drunks, drug-pushers and losers waiting for their dates at the Tube entrance and hurried over to the kiosk selling sweets and cigarettes. As embarrassed as if she was buying an ounce of crack, she picked up a bag of Skittles and handed over 55 pence.

Thea liked to see herself as the kind of woman who, in times of high anxiety, might sip a herbal tea or inhale some Rescue Remedy, but truth be told in times of trouble the thing that calmed her down best was a packet of brightly coloured sweeties stuffed with additives, which she would munch in strict colour order, first the yellows, then oranges, then greens, then reds and finally – having saved the best until last – the tangy purples.

Purchase achieved, she swiped her Oyster card on the barrier and hurried down the escalator. Thea was far too impatient to stand still and let the stairs carry her. As she waited for a Victoria line train – eight bloody minutes according to the electronic sign – she popped on her headphones and, to the strains of Bob telling her not to think twice, contemplated the evening ahead.

She was going to see Luke again. Not that it was that big a deal; she was long over him. But still, she couldn't help being a bit nervous.

Like Poppy, Thea had always had a thing about older men and like Poppy, it wasn't hard to see why. As a spotty, flat-chested teenager, the boys at school had had no interest in her whatsoever. Being proud, she pretended to have no interest in them either. Teenage boys were oafs, she had decided. She preferred older, cleverer men. Men who could drive. Men who read broadsheets and novels by dead Russian authors. Who ate frogs legs and played chess. Who listened to Bob Dylan rather than Wham! With those attributes in mind Thea conceived the first of her crushes on her history teacher, Mr Lyons, spending hours on her essays, sitting attentively at the front of the class, only to be rewarded by a 'Thea is a very good student' in her reports, before she discovered he was having an affair with Miss Jones, the French teacher.

The same pattern was repeated at college. Although by now her fellow students gave her plenty of attention, she couldn't reciprocate it. She lost her virginity to one of the grey-bearded lecturers, who then told her his wife was pregnant with twins and it couldn't go any further. Following that she had an affair with another lecturer; it lasted two years until he and his family moved to Bath.

She'd fallen in love with Luke before she'd even met him, watching his reports on the BBC. There couldn't be much doubt that he was the perfect man: brave, clever and astonishingly good-looking with his dark, thick hair, Easter Island head and Roman nose. He was one of the reasons she applied for a job as a researcher at the organization, although she never met him in her time there. But when the *SevenThirty News* was founded she jumped ship to become a junior producer. The first time she had to brief him on a story, she stuttered and her hands, clutching a sheaf of papers, shook uncontrollably.

At first, he took virtually no notice of her, just grabbing the briefing from her with a snappy, 'Thanks'. But in the months and years to come, they travelled all over the world together. She produced his coverage of the Oscars, presidential inaugurations, elections in South America, disaster zones in the Far East. Inevitably, spending so much time together they'd become friends. At the end of the day, in far-flung places, they'd talk about books and films and world affairs and how annoying everyone else in the office was. Once, in the Sudan, they'd even shared a scuzzy hotel room, where cockroaches crawled across the floor. Thea had suffered agonies of constipation rather than poo within Luke's hearing and had slept in full make-up, so he'd always see her at her loveliest.

Inevitably they had sex. The first time was in Pakistan, when their car had been in an accident on a narrow mountain road and they had luckily escaped with only bumps and bruises. That night they got drunk on illegally imported alcohol and ended up in bed. The next morning, Thea's heart was singing like a karaoke freak, but the expression on Luke's face told her plainly he didn't want to go there. So she left it, said nothing, acted as if the night had never happened and, because she played it cool, four months later they had a repeat in Malawi. So it went on for the next four years, the occasional night of carnal knowledge, followed by eye avoidance the next day, before they settled back into their familiar colleagues' routines.

Thea was in love with Luke, wholeheartedly, passionately. They were intellectual equals and soulmates. In every conversation, Thea looked for points of contact. He loved Marmite – well, so did she! He loathed jazz. Ditto. His idol was the Polish war reporter Ryszard Kapuscinski. Same here! He hated sushi – oh well, it would be boring if they had everything in common. She was sure if they'd met at another time, they'd have been together. But she never let her love show. She'd seen his other girlfriends getting obsessed, texting him constantly, leaving lipsticks in his pocket in the hope Hannah would find them. They never lasted long. Luke loathed any form of pressure. To win him, Thea knew she needed to play the long game, to make no demands, simply to be there when the time was right.

In the meantime, she wasn't a nun. There were no serious boyfriends. All the travelling her job entailed made relationships hard to maintain, as the divorce statistics for journalists showed. Besides, whenever Thea was free she wanted to catch up with friends, not wander hand in hand round a farmers' market discussing what to cook for the next dinner party. When she had an itch, it was never hard to find a guy to scratch it.

She never discussed her private life with Luke and if one of her men rang when they were together she'd snap: 'I'll call you back, I'm busy.' As for Luke, he rarely mentioned his family except to complain: about how much they cost him, how infuriated he was that even now the kids were all at school Hannah said she was 'too busy' to return to work. When he was speaking to

Hannah, it was invariably to argue: about the fact he was going to miss Jonty's sports day or Tilly's end of term concert or the church bazaar. Thea listened in astonishment. Hannah obviously didn't understand him at all, saddling him with this mundane, domestic nonsense. Thea genuinely didn't understand how people got bogged down with such boring stuff. If she was with Luke, he would be her number one and nothing would get in the way.

She stepped off the train at Green Park. With Bob crooning his ode to Corrina in her ears she followed the arrows pointing to the Jubilee line, harrumphing loudly as she found herself stuck in the narrow corridor behind an elderly couple holding hands and walking at the speed of a disabled tortoise. Obviously tourists. Londoners didn't amble on the Underground, or anywhere for that matter, they strode and shoved and overtook on the inside. Sighing loudly, Thea squeezed past them. As she hurried down the stairs to the platform she heard the sound of a train departing. Two minutes later the country bumpkins sat on the bench beside her. Thea glared at them. It was all their fault she was having to wait. Though, she reminded herself, she didn't want to get to the dinner too nerdily early. But not too late either, or Dean's wife would get in a strop about her soup going cold.

Slowly rolling a red Skittle round her mouth, savouring its artificial redness, before crunching into it, she thought back to the last proper night she'd seen Luke. BAFTA night. The *SevenThirty News* had been nominated for an award in the current-affairs category (which no longer existed now, so dumbed-down had this country become) for their reporting of an Al-Qaeda bombing of a train in Italy.

Thea hadn't had particularly high hopes for the evening, knowing Luke would be accompanied by Hannah, in some safe but boring Phase Eight dress. But Hannah, it turned out, had caught the flu from Isabelle, so Luke arrived alone. Thea sat next to him at the dinner, and they won the award and both went up on stage and made a witty and gracious acceptance speech and after that everyone at the table had got very drunk and they'd all ended up in Soho House with Luke and Thea squeezed up next to each other on a leather sofa, legs brushing against each other. She sensed there was something different about Luke that night. He seemed nervier than usual, strangely unrelaxed for someone who'd just received an award. Still, they'd ended up back at her place and she'd given what she considered the best sexual performance of her life. Afterwards they lay in dazed silence.

'Shit.'

Thea decided to take that as praise. 'Yeah. That was good,' she mumbled.

'Fuck,' he said.

He'd been more eloquent. She waited.

'Christ, Thea, I don't know what to do,' he said. 'Maybe Hannah and I . . . I don't know . . . Maybe I'll have to leave her. Leave them . . .'

He was asleep. Thea, however, felt as buzzy as her electric toothbrush after a day's charging. She lay beside him, heart hammering, absorbing this unexpected triumph. He was going to dump Hannah. He'd realized.

She'd won. No wonder he'd been so edgy all night, he'd been coming to this momentous realization.

'You've done the right thing, Luke,' she whispered. 'We'll be so happy together.'

By the time he woke up, she had very quietly slipped into a Janet Reger silk robe, retouched her make-up and perfume and fetchingly mussed her hair. As he opened his eyes, she smiled at him sexily and breathed, 'Good morning.'

He sat bolt upright. 'Shit! What time is it?'

'Nearly nine,' she purred.

'Oh Christ!' he yelped. 'What's Hannah going to think? I've got to go.'

Before Thea could open her mouth, he was out of bed and pulling on his clothes. 'Oh my God,' he said, 'she's going to kill me.' He pulled his phone out of his jacket pocket and stared at it despairingly. 'Battery dead. Help! I'm going to have to get Gerry to give me an alibi.'

Thea still couldn't speak.

'What's the best taxi number? Oh no, don't bother. How do I get to the Tube? It'll be quicker.'

'Turn right out of the front door, then left and straight up the road. It's about ten minutes.'

'OK.' He stopped for a second and looked down at her, so prettily arranged in her white satin. A wry smile crossed his features.

'That was great,' he said. 'Thank you.' He bent and kissed her briskly on the lips. 'Take care, Thea.'

She stared at him in confusion. A few hours earlier he'd been about to leave Hannah. What the hell had changed? There was no way she was going to ask.

'You too.' She smiled bravely.

'You're very sweet,' he said and hurried out of the door.

Standing on the Tube, surrounded by the raucous Saturday-evening crowd so different from the weary commuters in the week, her cheeks still burnt at the memory of what happened next. Thea had Monday off work. Luke was off on Tuesday and Wednesday. She waited for a call, a text, an email, but nothing. When she finally saw him on Thursday morning in conference, he studiously avoided eye contact. When she later contrived to bump into him by the water cooler, he smiled in the nervous way you do when a wild-eyed stranger starts making conversation with you in the street.

'Hi,' she said.

'Oh, hello.'

'Was everything OK with Hannah?'

'Yeah, yeah, it was fine. Look. I've got a meeting with Chris now.' And he hurried off.

Thea felt as if she'd been slapped. It wasn't as if she and Luke had never been to bed before, so why was he treating her like a stalker? Back at her desk, her head buzzed and she found it impossible to concentrate on pulling together an interview with the Minister of Agriculture. On the other side of the room, she could see Luke sitting at his desk. He looked pale, drawn, stressed. Had Hannah found out? Thea sort of hoped she had and sort of hoped she hadn't. She watched him frown at his screen, sit back in his chair, then get up and head toward the gents.

She knew she shouldn't do it, but something seized her.

Glancing round to make sure no one was looking, she tapped out of her email account and then tapped in luke.norton@sevenoclock.com. Years of working with him meant she knew his password – Matilda – and Thea was always reading his emails to check who he was fooling around with, although annoyingly Luke tended to double-delete everything as soon as he read it, so she rarely got much joy there.

She was in his email account. She searched for some angry missive from Hannah, but there was nothing. A load of guff from PRs wanting to meet him. Something from Gerry entitled, *Let's have a beer.* And then one from *PoppyPrice.* Nothing in the subject field.

Heart staccato, Thea opened it.

Darling Luke
I'm emailing u becoz ur not returning my calls or texts and I'm desprat. I'm sorry u had such a shock about the baby but we need 2 talk. I'm going to keep it whatever and I understand if u don't want 2 b involved but we just need to talk some more. I love u, I love u so much and I thought u loved me 2. Please, please, please get in touch.

Again, I love u with all my heart
Your, Poppy xxxxxOOOOO

The Tube pulled in to West Hampstead. Stepping out through the doors, Thea recalled the murderous, white-hot rage that had enveloped her as she read it. And she remembered how she, Thea Mackharven, who prided herself on her cool and collected approach to life had clicked on the forward button, then rapidly tapped *Ha* into the address field. *HannahNorton@Norton.com* flashed up. An icy calm descended on Thea as she clicked on send. 'Ding! Your email has been sent.'

Rapidly, she logged out of Luke's account. Seconds later he returned to his desk.

Thea wasn't sure now what she'd intended by sending the email. She wondered about this, as she turned right out of the station. There were other, simpler ways of taking revenge, like organizing a secret online account to deliver monthly packets of Viagra to his home address. That was what Thea did when she heard Luke had left Hannah and was living with the illiterate Poppy Price. But it was poor compensation for the havoc she'd wreaked.

When she discovered Luke was going to marry Poppy, Thea had gone to Chris Stevens and asked if she could spend a couple of months in the New York office, filling in for the producer David Bright, who had just announced his wife was pregnant with twins and wanted them all to come back to Britain for the birth.

'Really?' Chris had said incredulously. 'But you're doing great work here, Thea.'

'I need to be challenged,' she'd said.

Chris's eyebrows wiggled in an uncomfortably knowing way. 'Well, for you I'm sure we can arrange anything. Because one thing's sure, we don't want to lose you.'

Within a fortnight Thea had packed up her life and was on a plane to New York. The Brights decided not to return to the US and Thea acquitted herself so well that she was a shoe-in to take the job permanently. Beyond the odd word with Luke in a work context, she had not spoken to him again. To her pain, he had not spoken to her.

Now she was tapping up the tiled pathway that led to Dean Cutler's redbrick terraced house and within minutes she was going to see him again.

She took a purple Skittle out of the bag, crunched on it fast, took a deep breath and rang Dean's doorbell.

9

A skinny man in jeans and a lumberjack shirt opened the door.

'Oh-ho,' he said, 'you must be Thea! We meet at last. Great to put a face to a voice.'

'Dean.' She smiled her most winning smile and held out her hand but he was already kissing her on both cheeks, in a way that would have given Chris Stevens a heart attack.

'It's great to meet you.' He examined the bottle she offered him. 'Hey, Cloudy Bay. My kind of woman. Come in, come in.'

Thea followed him into a living room which had a beech floor, grey Farrow & Ball walls decorated with huge black-and-white pictures of unattractive babies. Bebel Gilberto crooned from hidden speakers. A group that included that irritating twerp Marco Jensen and Roxanne Fox in one of her trademark dull little skirt suits, was standing by the window, another by the fireplace. No sign of Luke. A blonde woman in black leather jeans and a diaphanous grey top approached.

'Thea, meet my wife, Farrah. Farrah, remember I told you about Thea? She's one of our best producers and I've just lured her back from New York to be part of my crack team.'

'Oh yes, I remember.' Farrah smiled. 'Dean's so chuffed to have got you back.'

'That's nice,' purred Thea, as the doorbell chimed.

'I'll get that,' Dean exclaimed and hurried out into the hall, leaving the two women together. Thea's heart sank. She hated wives. But one of the many things that made her brilliant at her job was knowing they were the people you absolutely had to get on side. So she smiled in her friendliest fashion.

'And what do you do, Farrah?'

'What an interesting question. I'm mainly a mother, of course, but now the kids are both at school I'm retraining as a colour therapist. It's just amazing. When you get a person's colour right you can totally change their lives.'

'Oh.' Thea nodded.

'You would not believe how many people's energy is being sapped by *disastrous* colour choices. Some people are cool and some are warm and they should never mix it up. But you'd be *amazed* how often they do. It's shocking.'

'Oh yes, it must be.' Thea tutted, listening to male voices laughing in the hall. Luke's. She didn't care, she told herself. It was ancient history. She was long over him.

'I saw one client recently, who was head to toe in browns and oranges and I said, "Sweetheart, I'm telling you this for your sake, you should be in spring-colours with that pale skin" and she said, "But surely I should wear the opposite of my colouring." I mean, I was speechless. Speech. Less.'

'I can imagine.'

'Now you, Freya, you would look stunning in orange. That green does not do a thing for your colouring.'

'Oh. Right.' Thea smiled, wondering if she should set Farrah straight about her name.

'I'd be very happy to give you a consultation, Freya. Mates' rates, of course. I'll make sure to give you one of my cards.' She looked Thea up and down. 'You're a Gemini, am I right?' Before Thea could reply, 'No, but *you* are an idiot', she continued, 'Now *there* is a lady who knows what colours are right for her.'

Turning round, Thea felt as if she'd been punched in the stomach. Standing in the doorway was Luke, looking even more charismatic than she remembered him. Like a double espresso he sent a jolt through you.

And holding tightly to his arm was a girl, no one could reasonably call her a woman, looking absolutely petrified. Fuck, though, she was pretty with her fine blonde hair and tiny feet in gold ballet slippers. Jealousy crackled off Thea's body in green lightning forks as all the insecurities she nursed about her appearance: that she was too dark, too shapeless, needed to trowel on make-up to look even halfway presentable, danced for attention in her head. Her vision narrowed as if she was about to faint. With superhuman effort she smiled.

'Luke.'

'Thea.'

Kiss. Kiss. Soft, newly shaved cheek. Smell of Imperial Leather. Once Thea had discovered it was his soap (he didn't believe in aftershaves) she'd gone out and bought a bumper pack and slept with it under her pillow.

'It's great to have you back,' he said warmly. 'Now, I don't believe you've met Poppy. My wife.'

'So, Poppy, what have you done with your incredibly short life? How have you filled it in the ten seconds since you were a child? Do you want to see the tattoo on my spine I had done when I was backpacking in Laos? Do you want to hear about the awards I've won? Do you want to know how often I've fucked your husband? Or that you're only married to him because of an email I was stupid enough to send?' That was what she wanted to say. What came out of Thea's mouth was: 'Pleased to meet you. I'm Thea. I used to work a lot with Luke as a producer. But I've been in America for the past couple of years. Just got back.'

She waited to see if her name would bring a flicker of recognition, but Poppy just smiled politely.

'Where were you in America?' Her voice was so soft Thea had to strain to hear her.

'Thea, hi! How are you?' It was Emma Waters, one of the chief reporters and Luke's regular female co-presenter. Emma was in her forties, pretty, if a bit haggard. She had three kids she never spoke about and was a very good friend of Hannah Norton's.

'Emma, hi! How are you? You look *great*.'

'Thanks,' Emma said somewhat less gushingly. Too late, Thea remembered how huffy Emma got about compliments on her appearance rather than her journalistic skills. She nodded brusquely at Poppy. 'Hello, you must be Poppy.'

'Yes,' Poppy said. 'Hi.'

Emma ignored the hand that was offered. There was an ugly silence, then Poppy hastily turned back towards Thea. 'Have you been anywhere especially interesting recently, Thea?'

'I was in Cuba not that long ago.'

'Oh? I did a modelling job there once. In Varadero.

99

The beach was beautiful. Did you go swimming with dolphins?'

Thea knew she was trying to be friendly, but she couldn't help the bitchiness that rushed over her. 'Hardly,' she said, catching Emma's eye in a we-are-women-of-the-world way. 'I was researching an item about the effect the revolution has had on the Cuban health system, so I spent most of my time in one-horse towns deep inland not *tourist* resorts.'

'Oh,' said Poppy.

'You're not modelling now, though, are you, Poppy?' Emma asked. There was no mistaking the hint of mischief in her voice.

'I . . . Well, no. My daughter's very young still, so—'

Luke interrupted. 'We've agreed to look for an au pair or a nanny or something so Poppy can get out and about a bit more.'

'Oh, that'll be nice.' Emma smirked. 'Give you more time for the health club and shopping.'

Poppy flinched as if she'd been hit. To her astonishment, Thea felt a moment's pity for Luke's very young wife. But only a moment's.

'It's very fashionable to be a stay-at-home mum these days,' Emma continued. 'You should see my local branch of Fresh and Wild. You can hardly get into it with all the yummy mummies sitting around decoratively with their designer prams. It wasn't like that when my kids were born; then it was just assumed you'd be going back to work otherwise you'd be letting the side down.'

'So you're looking for a nanny, are you, Poppy?' said Farrah, who'd been hovering on the sidelines.

'Well, I hadn't really thought . . .'

'Because mine is up for grabs,' she said. 'Now my youngest is at prep school, we don't need her any more. She really is fabulous. You should snatch her while you can. Shall I give you her number?'

'That sounds good,' Luke said. 'You should take Farrah up on that, Poppy. Word of mouth is always the best way to find a nanny.' He gave Farrah his most dazzling smile. Watching him, Thea's heart felt as if it had been ripped in two. She'd thought she'd got over Luke, but she'd just been in remission. And now, just like that, she had relapsed.

'Do you have children, Thea?' Farrah was enquiring.

'No.' A tiny pause and then, 'I don't want any.'

Silence fell like a safety curtain in front of a stage set. People always reacted like this when Thea told them she didn't want children. Anyone would have thought she'd confessed to a fondness for fried puppies in a burger bun. It infuriated her the way everyone assumed she must either be a heartless witch or, worse, that she was actually desperate to breed and putting a brave face on things. But the truth was as predictable as $E = mc^2$, rivers running downhill or your boyfriend wanting all the details about how you French-kissed your best friend at a party when you were fifteen. Thea wanted a family as much as she wanted to ski down Mount Everest dressed in a chicken suit.

Farrah laughed.

'Very sensible, I must say. If you should be stupid enough to change your mind you can always adopt mine.'

'That's our Thea,' said Luke, who had somehow joined

the group. 'She's the ultimate career girl. Too busy burning the candle at both ends to fit in a family.'

'Well, I've managed,' Emma said sharply. She turned to Roxanne Fox, who was hovering on the sidelines. 'And so have you, haven't you, Roxanne?'

'Managed what?' For a woman who liked to sack six people before breakfast, Roxanne had a bizarrely babyish voice to match her china-doll face. There was something about her Thea found creepy.

'Manage to have kids and a career.'

'Oh, yes.' Roxanne didn't sound pleased by this conversation. Thea grinned. There was a famous story in the office of Roxanne calling home and declaring, 'Hello, darling, it's me!!' There was a pause before she snarled: 'Your mummy, darling.'

She hid her smile as Roxanne said, 'And how are you, Thea? Good to have you back.'

'Good to be back,' Thea said for the umpteenth time, just as Farrah put her arm on hers.

'Sorry to interrupt, ladies, but it's time to go in for dinner.' She turned to Emma. 'Hi, Emma, we haven't been introduced. I'm Farrah, Dean's wife. Just wanted to say that necklace you were wearing last night on the programme was *beautiful*. Where did you get it?'

Poppy was seated between Marco Jensen and a middle-aged man called Bill.

'Do you work for the *Seven Thirty*?' she asked as they sat down.

'Christ, no! I've got a real job.'

'Oh.' Poppy nodded and smiled at Dean, who was hovering behind her with two bottles of wine. 'Red, please.' Another glass, she hoped, would make this evening, which had started so horribly, pass a little quicker.

'I'm a writer,' Bill continued, 'do a little bit more for my money than her indoors.' He nodded at Emma Waters. The penny dropped.

'You're Mr Waters!'

'Mr Pearce actually,' he corrected snippily. 'Emma kept her maiden name. Unlike you.'

'How do you know that?'

He laughed. 'Everyone knows who you are. You're the bimbo.' Luke, who was deep in ingratiating conversation with Farrah Cutler, looked up, annoyed. 'I don't know how you put up with it.' Bill continued, 'It must be so humiliating.'

'Oh, I don't mind,' Poppy said with all the sincerity of Prince Philip asking a factory worker if he enjoyed his job. 'It's just fish and chip paper. What kind of writing do you do?'

'Bill's a civil servant,' Emma cut in icily.

'That's not true, darling. What about my play?'

'Oh yes, the play.' Emma sounded as if she was referring to a particularly large dog turd on her front path. She turned back to Dean and started chattering vivaciously.

'What's the play about?' Poppy felt bound to ask.

'Just something I've been working on for a while. It's influenced by Anouilh. Do you go to the theatre much?'

'Well, no, I've got a baby so . . .'

But Bill had suddenly turned his back on her and was making animated conversation with Marco's girlfriend, Stephanie, who – Poppy knew from Luke's bitching – worked in the City and earned about five million pounds a second.

'Of course I love Jean Genet,' she was saying earnestly. Bill nodded and smiled. Poppy winced, took a large gulp of wine and a mouthful of her pomegranate and feta salad. She wondered how on earth she was going to get through the night. She felt so intimidated by all those other confident, eloquent, older women. Look at Thea, laughing vivaciously at something Dean had just said. Why had she shot her down so vilely about Cuba? She'd only been being polite.

Poppy looked at her again. Something about Thea made something in the depths of Poppy's mind stir, like a long-sleeping beast. She realized with a jolt that she was the perfect woman she'd seen talking to Luke that first morning at Sal's. That was the kind of woman her husband ought to be with, she thought sadly. A woman who talked about what was on the Booker Prize shortlist and what to do about global warming rather than the fact their toddler hadn't yet started potty training, but they were going to get round to it soon. A woman who had been friends with Hannah and showed admirable loyalty by her disdain for her successor.

'Did you have a good Christmas?' she said to Marco, on her other side.

'Sorry?'

'How was your Christmas? Did you go away?'

'Uh. Yeah. Steph and I hired a chalet in Verbier.' Marco wasn't making eye contact, his expression was fixed on Dean, a few tantalizing places away, who right now was in intense conversation with Emma. Poppy glanced again at her husband, who was gallantly laughing at Farrah's every word. She was saying, 'And I looked at Highgate, but it's really very academic and − I don't know − I've got a feeling maybe the boys are more creative. It's a tricky one, schools. Where do your kids go?'

'Are you good at skiing?' Poppy tried.

'Sorry?' Marco zoned in on her. 'Um. Yeah. I'm pretty good. Do you ski?' He sounded as if he'd just come round from a general anaesthetic.

'No, no. I've always wanted to. My mum would never let me go on the school trips. Said she couldn't afford them. But I'm not very coordinated anyway, so—'

'Sorry, sorry, Dean!' Marco shouted. 'Did I just hear correctly? Did you say the show's being cut down?'

A murmur went round the dinner table.

'That's right,' Dean said. 'As of next month, the channel's cutting fifteen minutes from the show, so it will end at eight fifteen instead of eight thirty.'

Fantastic. Luke will be home fifteen minutes earlier.

But Poppy's delighted thought was drowned out by the cries of protest.

'But this is outrageous!'

'How could this be allowed to happen?'

'What are you saying?'

'Guys, guys! Don't shoot the bloody messenger, all right?' Dean threw up his hands. 'I'm just telling you what the channel has decided. I can't say I'm exactly thrilled about it, but what can you do? Having a news programme that finishes at eight thirty is no good for the schedule. Sadly, we're taking up too much of the all-important eight p.m. slot. When people turn on the telly after their Vesta curry they want to watch a movie with George Clooney or, failing that, Peter and Jordan going shopping for a new cot for Princess. They don't want to see Luke interviewing the prime minister of Japan.'

'Oh come now, you're not saying Luke isn't every bit as delectable as the Cloonester?' There was a sarcastic note to Emma's question.

'Of course he is. And you, darling, are Britain's answer to Nicole Kidman – we all know that. And Marco is . . .'

'I think he looks a bit like a young Val Kilmer,' Farrah said dreamily.

'Oh, for Christ's sake.' Luke had got where he was partly because his voice could cut across a room and hold everyone's attention. 'Listen to how this conversation is degenerating already. Look, this is a disgrace. The *Seven Thirty* is one of the last bastions of decent TV journalism still standing and you're telling us that our paymasters are cutting fifteen minutes of it in order to feed the masses more Hollywood pap.'

Dean and Roxanne looked at each other.

'That's the long and short of it, yes,' Dean said.

Roxanne hastily interrupted. 'Look, guys, I know this must seem like a dramatic step, but then dramatic measures are needed. You know how badly viewing figures – not just for the *Seven Thirty* but for the channel as a whole – have been falling. We had to do something about it urgently.'

'Look on the bright side,' Dean continued. 'Fifteen minutes less work a day for you all.'

'And of course no one is taking a cut in salary,' Roxanne added.

'I think it could be a good thing,' Marco said quickly. 'It could make the whole show sharper. Snappier.'

'Thanks, Marco.' Dean beamed.

Luke's look couldn't just have killed Marco, it could have disembowelled, diced, sautéd and braised him overnight.

'And what about the content?' he snarled. 'Are we dumbing that down in accordance with our shorter running time?'

'I wouldn't say dumbing down—' Roxanne said.

'But we will want more of an emphasis on showbiz,' cut in Dean.

'And human interest.'

'Fewer foreign stories.'

'Focus groups are telling us they just aren't interested in what happens abroad.'

'Unless the sun's shining and they can buy cheap lager and fags there.' Dean guffawed. Roxanne rolled her eyes. Farrah got up and started collecting plates. Poppy jumped to her feet.

'Can I help?'

'Oh, thank you, Poppy.' No one glanced at her as she collected the crockery, they were all too busy being aghast.

'The budget is going to be cut overall by fifteen per cent, so that will leave far less funding available for foreign travel,' Roxanne was saying.

Poppy followed Farrah into the gleaming kitchen, where a sour-faced woman was garnishing a vast tray of roast lamb.

'Is it nearly ready, Elisa?'

'Very nearly, Mrs Farrah.'

'Hello, I'm Poppy.'

Elisa looked startled. So did Farrah. 'Oh yes, this is Elisa, our housekeeper. Elisa, Poppy's looking for a nanny. I told her she should call Brigita.'

'Yeah, good idea,' Elisa said glumly. Raised voices filtered in through the half-open door.

'Oh shit, Dean's put the cat among the pigeons, hasn't he?'

'It's not his fault,' Poppy said. 'I mean, he's just obeying orders, isn't he?'

'Like the SS.' Farrah giggled. 'You're very sweet, Poppy. Sounds like you've had a bad rap. Got any pictures of your little one you'd like to show me?'

Poppy got out her phone and she and Farrah spent a happy ten minutes cooing over photos of each others' children.

'We'd better go back in now,' Farrah whispered to her, as if they were naughty school girls, who'd been sneaking fags behind the bike shed. 'I don't know about you, but I find these corporate-wife evenings a right pain in the backside. I don't understand half the shop talk and no one wants to know about me because I'm just a mother.'

Poppy smiled nervously. She longed for another glass of wine.

'They don't seem to understand that we do the hardest job in the world. I mean, you can't imagine Dean or Luke putting up with more than a morning of wiping bottoms or making Lego towers. Mind you,' she continued before Poppy could say that she could quite understand why no one wanted to hear about Farrah building a Lego tower, 'you need a break or you'd go bonkers. If I didn't get my me-time at the gym I don't know what I'd do. That's why you should call Brigita, Poppy. You'll be amazed how much better you'll feel with an extra pair of hands.'

'Mmm,' Poppy said evasively. She hated the idea of a nanny; it brought back too many memories of her own miserable childhood. Even if things weren't quite right between her and Luke, at least Clara was happy at home with her mummy.

'Just gives you time to get dressed properly,' Farrah continued with a kind wink. 'Know what I mean?'

'Sorry?'

'I should have told you earlier, but I didn't want to embarrass you in public – your top's on inside-out. Now, I think the meat's rested long enough, Elisa. Let's take it in. Poppy, if you could bring the gravy that would be a real help.'

A week had passed. Luke Norton's heart was beating fast: faster than when he had found himself under fire from the Taliban in Afghanistan, or even when Hannah had confronted him about Poppy. He'd finished presenting the show half an hour ago and now he was sitting in the back of a cab negotiating its way through London's doctorland, the streets that lie between Regent's Park and Oxford Street. Behind the anonymous Georgian facades, smooth doctors wrote stressed businessmen prescriptions for Valium and legendary beauties got out their credit cards in return for losing their stretch marks. Every problem could be solved here, as long as you had the cash to pay for it and knew the right address. Or so Luke hoped.

'What number Harley Street did you want?' the driver asked.

'Ninety-five.'

'Here we are then.' They pulled up outside a discreet grey door.

Luke got out and paid. 'A receipt, please.' He'd put the taxi fare down on expenses, everyone did.

'Do I know you from somewhere?' the driver asked.

Normally Luke loved that question. But not tonight.

'I don't think so.'

'You look very familiar.'

'Can't help you, mate.' As the cab drove off, Luke

inspected the names attached to the various doorbells. Complementary health clinic. Oculoplast. Foetal medicine. He put his finger on the bell for Dr Mazza.

'Hello?' squawked the intercom.

Luke glanced over his shoulder. 'Um, hello, I've got an appointment.' He lowered his voice and whispered into the grille. 'Luke Norton.'

'Sorry?'

'Luke Norton,' he repeated just as an enormous lorry trundled past.

'I can't hear you above the traffic noise. You'll have to speak up.'

'LUKE NORTON TO SEE DR MAZZA.'

'Oh, Mr Norton. I'm sorry. Do come in. You know where we are. Second floor.'

The door buzzed open. After months of surreptitious research and phone calls, on the eve of his fifty-second birthday Luke found himself climbing a thickly carpeted stair, pushing open a heavy door and entering a gleaming reception area filled with orchids. The platinum blonde behind the desk smiled at him.

'Mr Norton. Welcome. I'm Dahlia, Dr Mazza's assistant.'

Luke felt a faint flicker of alarm. Dr Mazza had obviously used her for practice and the results weren't quite as impressive as one might have hoped. Her face was frozen in a semi-smile and it looked as if there were ping-pong balls under her cheekbones. But before Luke could bolt down the stairs, Dahlia continued, 'Oh hello, Mrs Lyons. How are you feeling?'

Luke swung round. Kelly Lyons stood behind him,

proffering her credit card. Shit, shit and double doo-doo. Of all the people in the world: one of Hannah's closest friends from the school-run crowd. Their eyes met. To his relief, even though Kelly's face was paralysed, her eyes were full of panic.

'Shh,' she said, raising a manicured finger to her plump lips. 'I won't tell if you don't.'

'OK.' Luke gulped. Well, well. Kelly. Whose fresh features Hannah had always envied. 'Why do *her* kids sleep through the night?' he remembered Hannah wailing after their annual Christmas drinks when Kelly had looked peculiarly energized for someone who had just bought and wrapped thirty-seven presents and sent two hundred and three Christmas cards. Well, it turned out they probably didn't, but Dr Mazza had helped hide the evidence. For a mad second, Luke itched to get out his mobile to text his ex-wife the news.

Kelly smiled at the receptionist. 'Thank you, Dahlia. I'll see you in three months then.'

'Lovely, Mrs Lyons. Take care.'

'You too.' She turned again to Luke. '*Not a word*. All right?'

'Never,' Luke said, as earnestly as if they were two members of the French Resistance agreeing on a plan to smuggle British soldiers to the coast.

As she departed, Dahlia turned to him smiling apologetically. 'Sorry about that, Mr Norton. It's very unusual for our clients to recognize each other. As you know, this is Dr Mazza's late night for his very favourite clients – he only fitted Mrs Lyons in because she's got her sister's third wedding next week and she's *such* a regular. But don't worry, I'm going to put you in the celebrity waiting room now, so no one else will spot you.'

'Excellent,' Luke said, chuffed his status had been acknowledged.

'Gianluca's running a bit late,' she said as she ushered him to a small room decorated with prints of Scottish lochs. 'Would you like a glass of champagne while you're waiting?'

'Why not?' Luke said, picking up an *Economist* from the pile of magazines in front of him. But he couldn't concentrate. He couldn't believe it had come to this, that he, Luke, the brave war correspondent, was reduced to secret appointments with a Botox doctor. His thoughts turned to Kelly Lyons. Christ. He'd always fancied her, and they'd once had a slightly too-long kiss under the mistletoe at another Christmas party, but now Luke was glad he hadn't fucked her. The knowledge she was having Botox diminished her in his eyes, though he didn't pause to wonder what she might think of him.

Luke's attitude towards women was schizophrenic, to put it mildly. An only child, his mother had been a rather cold and distant figure who made it plain to him from a very early age that he ranked far, far below her husband in her affections. Luke couldn't help suspecting she would have loved him more if he hadn't been three stone overweight. Unsurprisingly, as a fatty, he found it hard to get a girlfriend. His teenage years were filled with girls laughing at him when he asked them to dance and lonely Saturday nights masturbating in his bedroom.

But while backpacking round India after his A levels,

Luke got a terrible case of food poisoning and the weight melted off. By the time he got to university, the ugly duckling was most definitely a swan. At first he'd been amazed when girls started to pay attention to him; quickly he became blasé about it.

Luke entered a phase of serial monogamy. He always had a steady girlfriend and another waiting in the wings to replace her. He liked the security that came from being in a couple, but he also loved the buzz of the chase, so as soon as one challenge had been conquered he would look round for the next. Between the ages of eighteen and twenty-eight, Luke got through women faster than some of his friends changed their bedsheets.

He adored this new Casanova version of himself. Knowing he was such a hit with the ladies infused the rest of his life with confidence. He'd always wanted to be a journalist and, on graduating, he won a prized news traineeship with the BBC. Thanks partly to his handsome face, but mostly to talent, within a few years he was a foreign correspondent, working all over the world. He quickly discovered that – even more than the kick he got from sexual conquests – he loved the adrenalin jolt of working in a danger zone. He first made his name reporting from Chernobyl, then did some fine work in Israel and the Occupied Territories. It was during this stint that he first set eyes on Hannah Creighton, dancing on a table in the bar of a Jerusalem hotel where the world's press had been despatched to cover a new peace treaty.

Luke was instantly attracted to the lively redhead from the *Daily Post*, not least because she didn't seem in the least bit interested in him. In the hotel bar, she flirted with the Japanese, German, French and Italian reporters but paid not the blindest bit of notice to her compatriot. When he bought her a drink, she said 'Thanks', downed it in one, then turned her back on him and carried on talking to Ulrich from Swedish TV.

Naturally, Luke's blood was up. Omitting to call Annie, his girlfriend at home, he spent the next few days love-bombing Hannah, buying her more drinks, taking her on trips to obscure corners of Jerusalem that only insiders knew about, telling her she was the most beautiful girl he'd ever seen, until finally, after five days, they went to bed.

But in the morning she slipped out of his room before he was awake and avoided him next day then returned to London without telling him. Back home, he'd bombarded her with calls, but she stonewalled, saying she was busy. When he finally bumped into her at a party she ignored him all evening. It took another six months to get her back into bed and then during the following six months she only occasionally returned his phone calls and often cancelled dates at the last minute. Intrigued, in lust, Luke asked her to marry him. She said no, then three months later said yes. The wedding was planned to take place a year from that day, and Hannah moved in to Luke's flat in Willesden.

And suddenly everything started to change. Hannah began cooking for him. She began taking his suits to the dry cleaners. She started to get cross when he got home late from a night out with the boys. She no longer wanted to go out on Saturday night and paint the town red, but to stay in snuggled together in front of the TV. She kept wanting to talk about marquees and invitation fonts. In short, the woman Luke walked down the aisle with was no longer the devil-may-care woman he'd proposed to.

Soon Tilly was born and the mews house was swamped with dirty nappies and drying babygros. Luke adored his baby daughter and was impressed by how brilliantly his wife adapted to motherhood, so brilliantly in fact that she decided not to go back to work. But coming home from work to find Hannah making purées and talking about what happened at playgroup was about as sexy as a bottle of formula. Luke loved his wife but he was no longer in love with her.

It didn't really prove a problem. He was constantly away on assignments where temptations were plentiful and indulging them was seen as par for the course for the war crowd. After twelve hours dodging bullets, a warm body in your bed at night was incredibly affirming, proof you had made it through another day. Usually the flings only lasted a couple of nights. Sometimes longer. When he'd been in Sarajevo he'd enjoyed a four-month affair with Anne-Marie Gleen from Irish TV. But the same rules applied: as soon as he returned to their Hampstead house Hannah had made so beautiful he slipped easily into the role of devoted family man, even if occasionally he'd meet Anne-Marie for a quick 'drink' when she was passing through town.

Tilly was followed only a year later by Isabelle and then, when she went to primary school, Hannah confessed she was getting broody again and so they conceived Jonty. It was around this time that Channel 6, which was launching in the spring, contacted him to ask if he'd be interested in the job of chief foreign correspondent for its flagship evening news programme; he accepted and after seven years was promoted to anchorman.

Luke was in two minds about the change of job. He didn't know if he could let go of the endorphin rush when his phone rang with orders to get on the next plane to Bosnia or Somalia or East Timor. On the other hand, Hannah was getting increasingly shirty about his lengthy absences, especially now the children were old enough to question why their father was risking his life. Mainly, however, the idea of being the face of the programme was very appealing to his vanity.

On the whole, it had been the right decision. He missed those war-zone thrills, but he still got sent on just enough foreign trips to satisfy his wanderlust. To compensate for the lack of excitement in his work life, the affair quotient increased. Nothing heavy, naturally. Luke always made the ground rules very clear: he wasn't going to leave his wife; he had no time for girlfriends who tried tricks like calling him at home.

No one serious. Especially not Poppy. Poppy's role in Luke's life was, quite simply, to make him feel better about the way he was slowly shedding hair and his belly burgeoning. It was embarrassing to admit it, even to himself, but Luke liked the fact she was a model. It was an affirmation of his alpha maleness that he could attract the very cream of the crop. Still, she was nothing but a delightful diversion.

Until she became pregnant.

Even then, disaster could have been averted. The baby could have been got rid of (though in retrospect Luke found it very hard to imagine life without Clara). While he worked out how to deal with the problem, he went into slight meltdown. He got wasted after the BAFTAs and ended up in bed, with Thea, as he occasionally did. But, happily, Hannah swallowed his excuse about crashing on Gerry's sofa. He was just congratulating himself on having got away with that when, two nights later, he arrived home to find four suitcases packed and sitting in the hall. And a very angry wife telling him to leave. For ever.

He'd done everything he could to try to change her mind. Begged. Pleaded. Promised. But Hannah was adamant. She'd known about the other women all along, it transpired, and this time she'd had enough.

Luke went to their friends Grahame and Fenella's for a night, but Hannah got on the phone demanding they kicked him out, so kick him out they had. In retrospect, he should have gone to a hotel but, wounded and needy, he'd decided to spite Hannah and headed to Poppy's horrible studenty flat. Luke was a proud man. He couldn't bring himself to admit he was there because he had no choice, so he told Poppy he had left Hannah, that he wanted to marry her. Of course, even after Poppy's overjoyed acceptance, he'd carried on frantically negotiating with his wife, but Hannah had been deaf to all pleas for forgiveness. After Luke received the decree absolute in a shockingly short space of time (and this after he'd agreed to give Hannah pretty much everything, in the hope she'd be touched by his generosity and forgive him), he decided the best way to spite his ex was to marry Poppy as quickly as possible.

But even as he sat at that miserable wedding lunch at Orrery, slowly getting plastered and trying to laugh at silly Meena's jokes, Luke knew he'd made a terrible mistake. Poppy was divinely beautiful, he kept reminding himself, and sweet, and young. Other men would envy him, marvel at his virility to be with this peach while their wives were turning into prunes.

Two years from that day, Luke was still telling himself the same thing. But it sounded increasingly hollow. Having a woman only slightly older than his daughter on his arm didn't make him feel like a stud but like a dirty old man.

He cringed, thinking about the dinner at Dean's. Hannah would have lit up the whole room with her raucous laugh and spirited gossip. Poppy, on the other hand, had contributed about as much to the evening as one of the silly scented candles on the mantelpiece, spending half the evening hiding in the kitchen. All right, she was the most beautiful woman there by a mile. But – just as with Hannah – Luke found it increasingly difficult to be sexually attracted to his child's mother. He didn't know why, it just didn't seem right.

So, even though he'd sworn he'd turn over a new leaf, since Clara was born there'd been a steady stream of women. Nothing serious: a waitress he met in a coffee shop in Denmark where he was covering race riots; a quick fling with an American political researcher he'd met when he was covering the US primaries. No one on home turf, apart from that insane dalliance with Foxy, which had only hammered home the fact that you should never piss on your own doorstep.

He had to admit, Thea was looking especially hot right now. She'd always been a good lay, but Luke had never been that bothered about her: she was too dark, her tits were too small and, although her professionalism made her a joy to work with, it was also distinctly unfeminine. He knew she was besotted with him, that if he said 'limbo dance', she would immediately reply 'how low?', and he found that devotion rather a turn-off. But then again, she had always known how to make Luke laugh, and laughs were in rather short supply at the moment. He wondered if she was seeing anyone. They should have a drink soon. Catch up.

Dahlia stuck her head round the door.

'Mr Norton, Dr Mazza is ready to see you now.'

Dr Mazza was a perma-tanned Italian, who pulled off the challenging trick of looking both baby-faced as proof his needle worked and swarthy so as not to put off the macho men like Luke. He came over to London from Milan twice a week working a fourteen-hour day to satisfy demand. He examined Luke's face like a forger might the work of a great master.

'Mmm. Not bad. I 'ave seen worse. But *terrible* sun damage. I think you don't use the SPFs, Mr Norton. And you smoke!' He said this last in the same tone reserved for accusing someone of having sex with their pet hamster.

'Not any more. I gave up twenty years ago.'

'Still, the damage is done now.' Dr Mazza sighed. 'Yes. What a shame you didn't come to me twenty years ago. Then I could 'ave really helped you. Now, it is not so easy. Of course you are already a long way behind most of your rivals. They all have regular work.'

'Who? Jon Snow? Huw Edwards?'

'Naughty! Naughty!' Dr Mazza wagged a finger. 'You know I can't breach patient confidentiality. All I'm saying is you won't be the first newsman to come to me. Or the last.'

He pulled a black marker pen from a drawer and started dabbing it all over Luke's forehead. He looked as though he was about to undergo a weird tribal initiation rite in Papua New Guinea.

'This won't hurt. I promise.'

He was right, it didn't hurt too much. At the end, Dr Mazza stood Luke in front of the same mirror. His face was covered in dozens of tiny red blotches as if he'd been stung by a wasp.

'Don't worry,' Dr Mazza reassured him. 'They will fade in a few hours. Couple of days at the most. You're not planning to go anywhere this weekend are you?'

'No, I'm having a family weekend.' He sighed as he thought how he was going out for lunch with the children tomorrow. In the old days his birthdays had been riotous affairs, involving one of Hannah's most delicious cakes and a drinks party for all their friends, including the Lyonses. But now they meant forking out a fortune in Royal China in St John's Wood while the kids texted their friends from boarding school and made snide jokes about 'Snotty' as they called their stepmother, before he drove them back to their boarding schools just outside the M25. Then he'd return home, depressed, to what would no doubt be another badly-cooked dinner by Poppy. She tried so hard to feed him well, but the cooking gene just wasn't there.

He shouldn't be so hard on her, he told himself as he settled up with Dahlia. It wasn't Poppy's fault he'd married her out of a twisted mixture of guilt and revenge. He should stop brooding on her lack of cordon bleu skills and focus instead on her loving heart and how she laughed at his jokes, the way she devotedly watched the programme and plied him with questions about it that he was usually too tired or preoccupied to answer. She was trying; he had to cut her some slack.

The roads were empty and he was home in just fifteen minutes. The light was on in the living room. As he inserted his key in his front door, he could hear the television blaring in the living room. Face tingling, he opened the door to be greeted by the sight of his wife, fast asleep on the sofa with Clara beside her. He looked down at her, his exasperation melting at the sight of their two angelic faces. Luke could never admit it publicly, but Clara was the most gorgeous of all his children, a wonderful blend of his and Poppy's beauty, and for her presence he could be nothing but grateful.

Sensing him there, Poppy stirred.

'What time is it?'

'Eleven. Sorry I'm so late.'

'Are you OK? What's happened to your face?'

'I've been to the dentist. He gave me a filling.'

Poppy sat up, concern etched on her brow in a way that no patient of Dr Mazza's could ever emulate. 'Oh, poor you. I didn't know you had toothache. Why didn't you tell me?'

'I thought I did,' Luke said, as usual feeling irritated by her concern. He picked up Clara. 'Come on, missy, let's get you to bed.'

'It's nearly midnight,' Poppy said, 'almost your birthday. I've got a lovely surprise planned for tomorrow.'

Bugger. Luke hadn't told her he was having lunch with the children. But he wasn't going to lose a valuable chunk of their limited sleeping time by breaking that news now. He'd disappoint her in the morning when he'd have regained just enough energy to deal with her tears.

How I Lost a Husband but Rediscovered My Sex Life

HANNAH CREIGHTON, 48, is the ex-wife of the *Seven Thirty News*'s anchorman Luke Norton. A mother of three, she was devastated when Luke left her for a 22-year-old model. Here, in a hilarious and moving piece every woman will relate to, she reflects on the pros and cons of her new life as a divorcee.

It was dawn on Sunday morning. I opened my eyes. Something didn't feel right. Had I left the gas on? I wondered dreamily. And then it clicked: no children. They were with their father for the weekend. Silence. Tranquillity. No screaming. No demands to help with homework. No stamping feet demanding we get in the car and drive to a mall to buy the latest brand of trainers. No announcements that they had all gone vegan and would I please throw out all the cheese in the house and replace it with Quorn.

Heaven. I decided to get up and make breakfast. But, delightfully, as I pulled back the duvet, my new boyfriend grabbed me and we stayed in bed until lunchtime. Ah, ha! Now I remembered how I used to fill my time BC (before children). Yowza! As with everything, there are upsides and downsides to being a divorcee. The pros are more plentiful than I anticipated, the cons surprisingly few. And one of the biggest pros is sex. Like every couple I know, after eighteen years together and three children Luke and I didn't see much bedroom action. Twice a month was about average. Sleep was far more important and – to be honest – I often granted my husband his conjugal rights while mentally composing the next day's shopping list. But now I am with my new boyfriend I think nothing of staying up half the night, contorting myself into positions from the Karma Sutra. In comparison, just last week, the postman rang the doorbell with a package to sign for. I'd 'accidentally' opened it before I realized that – whoops – it was meant for my ex-husband. He has a nubile young wife, so why does he feel it necessary to order Viagra on the internet? One of life's great mysteries like the *Marie Celeste* and why there's always one odd sock in the wash.

If I sound cruel, I have to confess there are still many, many downsides to my new life. I wanted to be with Luke until death did us part. That's something every girl aspires to along with a music box with a revolving ballerina and Jennifer Aniston hair. It's only recently I have forced myself to remove my beautiful wedding and engagement rings, putting them in a drawer – for what? I can hardly give them to my daughters; they're so ill-fated. It was the end of a long-held dream and made me weep bitter tears.

Even more humiliating, although Luke and I are long divorced and despite his many, many failings, I still can't help missing the old fool, just as I might miss some moth-eaten cardi even though it's shapeless and long, long out of fashion.

The children and I took a summer holiday this year in Norfolk – a far cry from the jollies we used to enjoy in Florida or Tuscany, but of course Luke has another family to take to exotic places now. We had a wonderful time, but they missed their old dad. At the end of the summer Luke called and said he'd missed me too. I suppose any couple who's shared so much is going to remember occasionally that life together wasn't totally terrible. Call me vindictive, but I can't help being just a little chuffed that now nappies and sleepless nights have entered the picture Luke isn't finding life with the Bimbo quite as glamorous as he expected.

12

Ever since dinner at the Cutlers', Luke had been grumpier and grumpier. He said he was stressed about all the changes at work.

'But you won't lose your job, you're far too important,' Poppy had said trying to reassure him

'Want to bet?' he'd growled. 'Marco's regularly hosting the Saturday night show now, Emma's doing more as well. I'm going out of fashion, like flares in the eighties.'

'Sorry?'

'Christ, I keep forgetting you were Clara's age then.' He sighed and pushed his half-eaten plate of pasta away (OK, it was a bit *too* chewy, Poppy had been aiming for al dente, but perhaps she'd got carried away). 'Anyway, even assuming I *do* hold on to my job, the question is do I want it any more now it's all pop stars and old ladies in Torquay getting locked in the lavatory for a week?'

'No! Did that happen? Poor woman, how awful.'

'I was being facetious,' Luke growled, standing up. 'I'm going to have a bath. Unwind.'

'There are other ways to unwind,' Poppy said, in what she hoped was her sexy voice, though she suspected it just made her sound like she had a bad cold.

Luke paused for a second and then said, 'No, I really fancy a bath.'

As she cleared away the half-finished dinner, Poppy

wondered what she could do to make Luke proud of her. Perhaps she should start an Open University degree? Something to do with architecture or history of art, so she could find out more about those hidden corners of London she was so passionate about. But a degree would cost money and Poppy was tired of being another expense on Luke's long list. Maybe she should find a job? But then what would she do with Clara? Farrah Cutler had texted her Brigita's details, but the idea of handing her daughter over to another woman still made Poppy deeply uneasy.

'I don't know,' she confided to Glenda the following morning, as she followed her and her can of Mr Sheen round the flat. 'I mean, I don't think things are quite as good as they could be between me and Luke. Sometimes I wonder if he's having an affair, he's out late so often, but I don't think so.'

'I'm sure he isn't.' Glenda, who was privately convinced he was, reassured her. 'Not when he's married to such a pretty woman as you, Poppy.'

'We hardly ever see each other. We need to spend more time together. It's his birthday on Saturday, so I thought I'd take him out to lunch. A bit of time alone together, getting to know each other.' The thought crossed her mind that perhaps this was something they should have done before they married, but she hastily put a lid on it. 'You're not free to babysit on Saturday, are you?'

'Oh darling, I wish you ask me earlier. I'm looking after the Bristow children that day.'

'Oh.'

'You could ask your mother. That is what I would do.'

'I don't think your mother is the same as my mother,' Poppy said gloomily, comparing Anna-Maria who was currently bringing up Glenda's brood with Louise, who complained regularly that she'd hoped for a few years respite from childcare.

'This is the real problem, I think, Poppy. You have no one to help you with Clara. Maybe it would be good to have a break from her some time. You haven't had a night away from her in two years. It's a long, long time for any woman to do alone.'

Not you too! The problem was that on one level Poppy agreed with Glenda, she just hated to admit it for fear of sounding like her mother. 'You know I love being at home with Clara,' she said defensively.

'You need time off every now and then. You've been a hero, Poppy. No Clara, don't pick that up, darling. No, it has bad, dirty things in it. No, listen to Auntie Glenda. No, is not for drinking!'

'I'm hardly a hero,' Poppy argued above Clara's anguished shrieks as Glenda removed the bottle of Flash to the highest bathroom shelf. 'What about you? You've got all those kids at home and here you are . . .' Cleaning my toilet, Poppy thought, but instead she let the sentence trail off.

'Yeah, but when they were babies it was much easier for me than you. I had my mum, my aunties, my cousins around to help. You have nobody.'

'I'd be happy leaving Clara with you for a couple of days a week,' Poppy hinted, but Glenda sighed regretfully.

'You know we've been here already, Poppy. I got no work permit. Luke's already worried I'll be caught cleaning your house and he'll be in trouble for employing an illegal.' Seeing Poppy's disappointed face, she continued, 'You should look for someone else. You can't just think about Clara's happiness, you know. You've got to be happy too. I know you, Poppy, you're not happy right now because things aren't going too good with Luke.'

'But I've told you, I'm working on that. If Mum will look after Clara, I'm taking him out to lunch.'

And to Poppy's amazement, Louise had agreed to babysit.

Poppy woke up some time around six on Saturday, brimming with excitement.

'I'm taking Luke out for a surprise lunch at Orrery, which is where we went after our wedding,' she told her invisible interviewer. 'I think it's really important to spoil each other, don't you?'

No time to start like the present. She rolled over and gently kissed Luke on the cheek.

'Good morning,' she breathed.

'Uh? Wuh?'

'Happy birthday.' She slipped her hand under the duvet and into his pyjama trousers. Still floppy. Never mind. Poppy set to work.

'Mmmm,' said Luke.

'An early birthday present.' She grinned.

'Mummeeee!' came floating through the door.

'Oh, no,' they both groaned.

'Ignore her,' Luke implored.

'Mummeeee!'

'Come on.'

'No! I can't.'

Luke groaned again. 'You've got to stop running to that child,' he said, but Poppy had already crossed the hall to her daughter's room. 'Hey, gorgeous,' she said to Clara, who was standing up in her cot, grinning at the sight of her. 'Come into bed with us. It's Daddy's birthday. Will you say happy birthday, Daddy?'

'Ha'ee birthday,' said Clara, as Poppy plonked her down beside her groaning father.

'Aah. That's so cute.' Poppy kissed her. 'Now I'm going to tell Daddy what I've got planned for today. Granny Louise is coming over and so Mummy is going to take Daddy out for lunch.' She realized uneasily that more and more she communicated with Luke through the medium of their daughter.

'Oh?' said Luke. He sounded less than delighted.

'Yes, I've booked Orrery.' She looked at him. 'Is that OK?'

'It's just . . .' Luke sighed. 'Sorry, darling, I should have told you. But I've got to go somewhere.'

Poppy felt as if she'd been hit. 'What?'

'I'm really sorry. I meant to tell you. It slipped my mind. The children are taking me out for lunch. So . . .' He flailed around like a drowning wasp. 'It's great that Louise is going to babysit, though. Why don't you take advantage of it? Go out. Meet your friends. Or something.'

'I was all excited about our lunch,' Poppy said in a small voice.

'We could go out for dinner.' Luke's heart sank at the

131

thought of two big meals. His hand drifted down to his waist. He could definitely pinch more than a couple of inches. He was haunted by the ghost of his chubby younger self. He glanced in the mirror. His face was still a little red, he just hoped Dr Mazza was right about it fading over the weekend.

'I don't think we can get a babysitter,' Poppy said. 'Glenda can't do it this weekend. That's why I asked Mum. Ow, Clara. Stop pulling Mummy's hair!'

'Well, we'll go out at some point in the week.' Luke rolled out of bed and padded into the en suite. Poppy lay trying to cuddle Clara, who was completely uninterested, preferring to rip pages out of a toy catalogue. Tears pricked Poppy's eyes. She'd been so keyed up about taking Luke out for a romantic lunch, coming back to a – hopefully – empty house and making love and then, perhaps, having that discussion again about another baby. But as ever, Luke's other family took priority. And as ever, Poppy could hardly complain, given how she'd stolen him from them.

Luke emerged from the shower. 'I tell you what: why don't I take Clara down for breakfast and you can get some more sleep.'

'But it's your birthday!'

Luke smiled ruefully. Poppy was still at an age where birthdays were something to celebrate rather than to make you groan in horror. 'That's why I'd like some quality time with my daughter. Come on, Clah-Clah. Shall we have breakfast together?'

'Croissant!'

'I got croissants for a special birthday breakfast,' Poppy

explained. 'And your present's on top of the fridge.' She peered at him. 'Ow! Your face does look sore. Are you sure it was a dentist and not a butcher you saw?'

'It looks worse than it feels,' Luke said abruptly, kissing her on the forehead. 'Now go back to sleep.'

Poppy didn't think she'd be able to. She lay listening to Clara clashing pan lids and Luke opening and shutting cupboard doors, still brooding on her disappointment. Still, she thought, Luke was right, she could do something with this unexpected time off. But what? She thought of activities where Clara was distinctly unwelcome. The cinema, maybe? But only losers went to see films alone. A museum? Usually Clara came with her, but it might be an idea to go somewhere like the John Soane Museum in Holborn, which was so densely packed with trinkets it had been a bit of a nightmare to negotiate with a buggy. On her own Poppy could take a really good look at things.

Cheered at the idea, she drifted off to be woken a couple of hours later by the doorbell ringing and then voices in the hall. Of course, Mum had said she'd come about eleven. Rolling out of bed, she went to the landing. Sure enough, she could hear her mother talking to her husband

'Happy birthday, Luke. Fifty-two, eh? God, how does that feel? It's bad enough being forty-five. You are looking very well on it, I must say. Is that a shaving rash? Your skin is a little bit blotchy.'

'Granny!'

'Now you know I don't like to be called that, Clara. I'm Louise. Louise who has brought the most *gorgeous* party dress for you. It was in the Moschino sale. I just do hope you won't put your sticky fingers all over it.' She knelt down and clapped her hands so her discreet silver jewellery rattled. Clara giggled and Poppy felt a little surge of hope. All right, so Louise hadn't been the best mother, but maybe it wasn't too late for her to redeem herself.

'Hi, Mum,' she said, coming down the stairs and inhaling the familiar aroma of Obsession. As usual, her mother was dressed more for a day trawling Bond Street than rolling on the floor with her granddaughter. Louise's tiny figure, maintained through a diet endorsed by Gillian McKeith and a weekly regime of two step classes, one power-yoga session and daily sit-ups, was encased in a knee-length denim skirt, a black leather jacket and a cream silk blouse that radiated dry-clean-only vibes. Her black hair gleamed, her make-up was subtle but immaculate. As ever, Poppy wondered if two such different physical types could truly be related. She presumed she got her Viking looks from her father, but she'd never know for sure.

'Hello, darling,' Louise said, eyeing her stained dressing gown warily as if it might be contagious. 'How are you?'

'Fine. I—'

'I have the most *appalling* headache again,' Louise continued. 'And my hay fever's started already.'

'Oh, poor you.'

'Yes. Well. That's the price you pay for working every hour God sends to build up a business.'

'It was really kind of you to take time out to babysit,' Poppy said humbly. She knew the script backwards.

Louise looked down at her tan, knee-length boots. 'Um. Actually. There's a bit of a problem about that, darling.'

Familiar disappointment thudded in Poppy's breast-bone. 'Right,' she said cautiously.

'You see my chiropractor just called and she can fit me in at half past one, which is just as well as my neck is killing me. So I'm afraid I'm not going to be able to babysit over lunchtime after all.'

'Mum!'

'I can stay for an hour now, if you like. I don't see why it's a problem. You can take Clara with you, can't you?'

'I—' Poppy began, as Luke interrupted, 'Well, that's a shame, Louise. But don't worry, I understand. And luckily your services aren't needed because as it happens I'm going out to lunch with my other children. So all's well that ends well.'

Louise turned to Poppy, outraged. 'What? You mean you got me to babysit for nothing?'

'You weren't going to do it anyway. You could have said!'

'No, *you* could have said.'

'Luke only told me this morning.' Poppy pushed her hair away from her eyes and grabbed Luke's arm. 'Did you open your present?' she said softly

'Oh yeah. Thanks.' He kissed her on the cheek. 'It's great. I'm going to get dressed.'

Poppy felt steamrollered. She'd spent a purgatorial morning pushing a very vocal Clara round the shops find-ing the perfect cashmere T-shirt to match the colour of Luke's eyes. She'd paid a vast price for it – well, Luke had paid really, but still . . . and this was all the thanks she got. She felt like an old pair of socks that no one could be bothered to retrieve from the bottom of the laundry bin.

Louise cleared her throat. 'I don't suppose a cup of tea would be too much to ask for?'

The kitchen was its usual clutter of dirty cereal bowls, the floor was covered in plastic toys. Sometimes it made Poppy despair that she spent all day tidying up only for Clara to displace it all again. Louise navigated her way through the mess, wrinkling her nose.

'This place is a tip, Poppy. I can't believe you have a cleaner.'

'She only comes once a week.'

'And what do you do on the other six days? Honestly! You should be so lucky. When you were Clara's age I certainly didn't have the luxury of someone to help me out.'

'You had an au pair,' Poppy said softly.

'Sorry?' But Louise was never that interested in what anyone else had to say. 'Have you got any herbal? Tea and coffee is incredibly bad for the skin, you know, sweetheart. All that caffeine. Makes you old before your time. Like kids.'

'So what's the news, Mum?' Poppy said, determined not to rise to the bait. 'How's Gary?'

Gary was Louise's on-off walker, a bald widower with a heart of gold. Louise wouldn't dignify him with the term boyfriend. When asked why, she'd reply: 'He works in insurance and he's got a hearing aid.' Gary was a very useful escort to the cinema and to tennis-club functions, who was shelved whenever someone more appealing came on the scene.

As usual, at the mention of Gary, Louise wrinkled her nose as she might at one of Clara's used nappies. 'He's fine. He's booked a little holiday for us in the Lake District.'

'Oh, how lovely.' Poppy yearned for a holiday, but even though Luke got a very generous six weeks off a year, three of them had to be spent with his children and the other three had to be spent finishing his book. 'We'll fit in something,' he said, whenever she asked him about it, but they never did.

'Hmmm. The hotel's only four stars, but it does have a spa. Of course, we're sharing a room, but that shouldn't be a problem, thanks to these new sleeping pills I've got.'

'Mum!'

'One in his glass at dinner and one in mine and there'll be no hanky panky,' Louise continued.

'Why didn't you just ask him to book separate rooms?'

'He'd have been upset, and I can't stand it when Gary gets upset. This puppy-dog look comes into his eyes and . . . Oh, Clara! Off Louise please! I don't want you laddering my tights.'

Poppy opened her arms. 'Come to Mummy.' She hugged her daughter tight, inhaling her sweetness, marvelling at the softness of her skin and hair.

'Oh, darling, I *was* hoping for fresh.' Louise plucked the teabag out of her mug and gazed at it balefully. 'Did I tell you Christine and I are off next weekend to a spa in Malaga? Should be lovely. I've booked a facial, a full body scrub and a Thai head massage so far.' She looked her daughter up and down. 'Anyway, enough about me. What about you? Any more thoughts about going back to work?'

Not you too! Poppy felt a sudden flash of resolve.

'Actually, yes,' she said. 'I'm about to hire a nanny.'

Louise put down her cup in surprise. 'Really?'

'Yes. She's just finished working for a colleague of Luke's. They say she's great.'

'Polish is she? I hope so. They're the best girls at the moment, so loving and excellent at housework, which wouldn't go amiss. And cheap. I wish there'd been more of them around when you were growing up.'

'I don't know where she's from. Her name's Brigita.'

'Almost definitely Polish. Don't hire an Australian whatever you do, they're always picking up venereal diseases and getting drunk on duty. Still, that's the best news I've heard in ages, Poppy. Get you out of the house at last. Maybe you're a chip off the old block after all.' Louise looked dubious at this pronouncement. She took a sip of her tea. 'Ugh. This tastes like mud.'

'The teabags are quite old,' Poppy admitted. She vaguely remembered buying them when she was pregnant with Clara and being good about what she put in her body.

Luke reappeared, in chinos and a stripy shirt looking very Ralph Lauren. 'Well, I'm off now,' he said sheepishly.

'And I'd better be going too.' Louise pushed her mug aside. 'Can't finish that anyway.' She bent down and kissed Clara on the nose. 'Now you be a good girl for your mummy,' she said, then she pecked Poppy on the cheek. 'And *you* think about what I've been saying.' She pulled a copy of the *Daily Prophet* out of her bag and dumped it on the table. 'I'll leave you this.'

Luke kissed Clara and then his wife.

'Look, I'm sorry about this. You should have told me

you had something planned. Let's get Glenda to babysit and we'll have a special birthday celebration in the week. Wednesday's my day off.'

Watching her husband and mother walk down the front path together, Poppy felt more desolate than ever. Everyone else was going out, having lives and here she was stranded at home with a child she adored but, she could only whisper it to herself, was beginning to resent. She hated to admit it, but much as Louise infuriated her, she was slowly beginning to understand why she'd made some of her choices.

'Where Daddy?' Clara asked.

'He's gone out,' said Poppy, going back into the kitchen. She picked up the *Prophet* and began flicking through it, enjoying the paparazzi shots of Minnie Maltravers, her model icon, scowling into the camera as she left a restaurant, a feature about Robbie's readmission to rehab. She turned another couple of pages and . . .

HOW I SAID GOODBYE TO MY HUSBAND AND HELLO TO GREAT SEX

With a howl of fury, Poppy threw the paper across the room. Bitch. Bitch. Bitch. Now Hannah was attacking her in the bloody *Prophet*. Was nowhere safe any more? She retrieved it and read on, infuriated. All this guff about the children being away with their father when the truth was the children were locked in their boarding schools. It was all so unfair.

Suddenly she had had enough. The flicker of resolve she'd felt earlier, hardened into something steely, like Sarah Connor in *Terminator* squaring up to save the planet. She picked up her phone, scrolled rapidly through her texts and retrieved a number.

'Hello, is that Brigita? Yeah, hi, my name's Poppy. I gather you're looking for a nanny job . . .'

13

If Poppy's Saturday wasn't much fun, Thea's was proving to be as about enjoyable as a colonoscopy. After her first couple of gruelling weeks back in the London office, it was time to visit her gran, a visit which, since she'd sold her car when she moved to the States and hadn't yet got a new one, involved a train ride to Guildford and a taxi to the small village where the nursing home was.

Thea felt as if a toad was lodged in her throat. She hated these visits although she never dodged them. When she'd lived in London, she'd tried to go twice a month but her time in New York had put paid to that. Gran doesn't know if I come or not, she would tell herself, all she does is sit in her armchair talking to herself, watching old films on her enormous television. But it didn't make Thea feel any better. Even if that was true, she knew her grandmother's family should be with her, at least some of the time, not some random nurse ignoring her ramblings.

It was so hard to accept how Toni Fry's life had altered in just a couple of years. Thea had always loved her grandmother's perkiness, the way she took such an interest in everything. Once Thea left home, she returned to see her mother and Trevor perhaps four times a year, but whatever else was going on in her life she visited Toni at least once a month to tell her about her achievements and where she was going next. Gran loved hearing stories about trips to Iraq and Afghanistan. 'Girls these days are so lucky to have such adventures,' she'd say longingly. 'Make the most of it for your gran. I'm living through you.'

But one Sunday four years ago, Thea arrived at the bungalow to find the front door wide open. She hurried inside calling: 'Gran, Gran?' No answer. She searched the house. Toni was nowhere to be found; there were no signs of an intruder. She was about to call the police, when the front door opened and her grandmother walked in wearing her dressing gown and slippers.

'What have you been doing?'

Gran looked taken aback. 'Me? I just went for a walk.'

After that, this sort of incident became more frequent. Thea remembered bumping into Rosa, one of her grandmother's oldest friends, in the street. The three of them had a good chat. When Rosa finally said goodbye, Toni had turned to Thea and said, 'Darling, who was that?'

Toni was an avid reader. She'd loved books all her life, treasured them and looked after them. To help her get her brain back, Thea started sending her regular packages from Amazon. She returned from a trip to the Sudan to find Toni sitting in an armchair methodically tearing the pages into strips.

Thea could no longer avoid the truth. Something dreadful was happening. It was very, very frightening. She loved Toni so much, knew her so well, but it was as though she was becoming another person. Thea was tortured by what she might find on her next visit. Each time there were a few subtle changes. After a lifetime as a demon Scrabble player, Toni announced one night when

Thea had yet again beaten her (she could have thrashed her but had deliberately held back) that she was giving up playing. She got in a muddle over her bills and red letters started arriving threatening to cut off the gas.

Thea tried to reassure her with jokes, inventing stories about how forgetful she was too, saying it must be in the genes. She wished she'd taken the situation more seriously and sent her to her GP. That might have bought them at least a few more months. Or it might not have. At the nursing home Thea had talked to a woman, whose mother's GP had laughed when he heard she was becoming forgetful and said she was just suffering from 'old age'.

How cosy that phrase sounded as opposed to the grim reality which Toni was facing. Things were becoming dangerous. She would mix up the gas cooker and the fridge. On one visit, Thea found she had singed her eyebrows. She cooked a joint in the oven but forgot to take off the plastic wrapping. She fell down a step she'd forgotten was there and was lucky to escape with only grazes and bruises.

The game was up. Thea couldn't bear it any more, but equally, she couldn't bear the thought of giving up her job to be a full-time carer. Rachel and her other friends assured her she wasn't being selfish, only realistic, but it didn't make the guilt any easier to bear. Thea had tried various combinations of carers but in the end she'd realized the only way to provide Gran with the level of help she deserved was to put her in the best home she could find, although even on her good salary, she could only just afford the fees.

Today was the first time she'd have seen her grandmother in four months. To stop herself from brooding during the train journey, Thea bought an extra-large bag of Skittles and all the papers. Aggressively, she spread them out over two seats, so no one could invade her space. As London's jagged edges ebbed, she trawled through them, searching for nuggets that might appeal to Dean. Thea wasn't at all happy about the new, shorter, more airheady *SevenThirty News*, not least the fact that foreign travel, which was what she lived for, was going to be severely curtailed. Since that announcement Thea had had severe doubts about staying with the programme. But where else could she go? The other networks were just as bad and she could hardly jack the whole thing in and go travelling – not with Gran's care fees to pay for.

She'd worry about that later, she thought, as she spotted an item in the *Mail* about a Russian woman who'd just given birth to quintuplets. Thea reached in her bag for her red biro and ringed it as worthy of a follow up. 'How M&S went from dowdy to dazzling'. Another ring. Hey, they could interview Hannah Creighton, Thea thought, popping an orange Skittle in her mouth, she'd always bored Thea rigid at parties by going on about how superb the Autograph range was.

Thea picked up the *Press* and lead about the *American Idol* scandal. God, she thought she'd left all that behind in New York. She flicked on.

HOW I LOST A HUSBAND BUT REDISCOVERED MY SEX LIFE

Thea was seized by a mixture of outrage that Hannah could be so nasty, and amusement. A tiny bit of her felt guilty about ordering the Viagra. Since Dean's dinner party, Thea hadn't spoken to Luke; he seemed pretty studio-bound at the moment, and most days she was out on a story. She couldn't quite work out her feelings for him. Every time she saw him in the distance, her insides felt as if they'd been given a good going-over by the tumble dryer. Then she remembered his child-bride wife and she felt nothing but cold scorn and fury that she'd wasted so much time on such a feeble excuse for a man.

The train pulled into Godalming station. It was a twenty-minute taxi ride to Greenways. As it bowled up the gravel drive, Thea thought, as she always did, that at least she couldn't have chosen a prettier place for her grandmother to spend her final years. It was a white-washed, rambling Edwardian villa. Toni had a room on the ground floor with French doors leading straight out into the pretty gardens.

Not that she knew where she was.

Gritting her teeth, Thea paid the driver and rang the doorbell. A smiling nurse – twenty-something, Polish, like they mostly were – opened it, releasing a smell of overcooked vegetables and bleach, a smell that concealed something much more unpleasant that only hit you occasionally.

'Good morning.'

'Good morning. My grandmother, Mrs Fry, is in room twenty-seven.'

'Of course. Mrs Fry. I bring her breakfast this morning.'

'Oh yes.' That thought gladdened Thea. 'Did she like it?'

The nurse wrinkled her nose. 'She's not a breakfast person, I think.'

Alarm bells rang in Thea's head. Gran had always loved her breakfast. 'Not today? Or not always?'

'Not always, I think. Mrs Fry, she not eat much.' The girl smiled and moved off. 'Have a nice visit.'

Perturbed, Thea hurried along the corridor with its plastic handrails. It was so peaceful: thick green carpets, prints of flowers on the walls. She pushed open one fire door, then another. Then she heard the screaming.

'Oh my God, please, no! He's going to kill me.'

A tiny woman in a pink, sprigged nightie was standing in a doorway, weeping hysterically in the arms of a young man with dark hair and bushy eyebrows.

'Take him away, take him away, he's come to kill me.'

'Mum, it's OK. Mum, it's me. Jake. Your son.'

Thea quickened her pace as she walked past, trying not to look. But she couldn't help noticing the woman seemed to have some sort of food matted in her hair. She averted her eyes. Funny how she'd coped with meeting victims of bomb blasts, famine and war but the inmates of Greenways freaked her out far more, even the ones who still had their marbles but were just frail. This was partly because her own grandmother was one of them, partly because every visit brought with it the unpalatable reminder that this was likely to be her destiny too.

She was not going to feel sorry for herself, she told herself furiously as she knocked on the door of room twenty-seven with its little nameplate: Mrs Fry. There was no reply, but then there wasn't usually, so Thea pushed it open, heart in her mouth as to what she might find.

What a relief. Gran was sitting in her armchair by the French doors, staring into space. She was wearing a green polyester skirt and a white blouse, quite unlike the jeans and fleeces she used to favour – Greenways had asked Thea to buy clothes for her that washed easily and were simple for a carer to put on. She appeared much the same as last time, but thinner, definitely thinner. Wasn't she eating?

She didn't look round.

'Hello, Gran. It's me, Thea.'

Silence.

Thea kissed her. 'Hi, Gran. It's Thea. I've brought you some flowers.'

Gran's eyes flickered. 'Flowers. Oh, how nice.' She buried her nose in them. 'Lovely. Lilies: my favourite.'

Even though they were roses, Thea's heart expanded. It was going to be OK. They were going to have a good visit, where they looked at old photos and perhaps had a gentle stroll round the lawns. 'They're nice, aren't they, Gran?'

'Beautiful. Thank you.' She smiled at Thea. 'How have you been, my darling?'

'I've been really well. Got back from America a couple of weeks ago. I'm sorry I didn't come and see you before, but I've been very busy.'

Gran nodded sagely. 'Always busy. Working?'

'Yes, working. I've had another promotion to senior producer.' She turned to look at the black-and-white photo of a young, skinny laughing man. 'I wish my dad was here so I could tell him. I bet you do too.'

'How's that Luke?'

Thea's heart lurched. Apart from Rachel, her grandmother was the only person she ever confided in because she was fairly sure she wouldn't remember a thing. But obviously she'd been wrong.

'Luke's all right. He's married that young model I told you about. They've got a baby. It's a bit weird. I thought I was over him, but then I saw him at a party and . . . I'm not,' she admitted finally. 'I still love him. I can't help it. I know it's pathetic to be obsessed with a married man, I know I'm on a hiding to nothing, but he's just so handsome and clever and brave and—'

Suddenly Toni's face changed. 'I asked my mother to come. Who are you?'

Oh shit. 'I'm Thea. Your granddaughter. You know me.' She kept her voice soft and low.

'No. No. You're not my granddaughter. I don't have a granddaughter.'

'Yes, you do. Sometimes you forget about me, but I *am* your granddaughter.'

Gran shook her head violently. 'Where's mother? And Maria? I want to see them. Are they coming?'

Maria was Thea's great aunt. 'Your mother's been dead for thirty years, and Maria lives in Spain. She'll come and see you next time she's over, though.'

Toni started to cry, not loud hysterical tears like you sometimes got, but soft sobs. They were just as bad.

'Go away. I don't know you. Go away.'

'But Gran . . .'

There was a knock on the door. 'Is everything all right?' It was Corinne, the home's manager.

'We're fine,' Thea trilled.

'Tell her to leave. I want my mother. *I want my mother.*'

Corinne opened the door, her usual faintly disapproving expression in place. 'All right, Toni,' she said gently. 'Don't worry, sweetheart, it's your granddaughter.'

'I don't have a granddaughter! Tell this woman to go.'

Corinne winked at Thea. 'Playing up a bit today,' she whispered. 'If I were you, I'd skedaddle. She'll have appreciated your coming.'

'Do you think so?' Thea asked, eager for reassurance, standing up.

'Oh yes. I'm sure the dears know on some level you're there.' She went over and patted Toni on the shoulder. 'Now, don't worry, love, your granddaughter's off now. But she'll be back soon, won't you?'

'Of course,' Thea said with a forced jollity she didn't feel in the slightest. Gran continued to weep softly. 'I can't just leave her like this,' she said, panicked.

'Don't worry, I'll get one of the girls to check on her,' Corinne said. 'Now, I'm glad I caught you, Thea. I'd just like you to come into my office for a moment, because I need to talk to you about fees. I'm afraid we've had no choice but to put them up again and I wanted to give you plenty of warning.'

14

It had been a depressing conversation. Another hundred pounds a month was going to be needed. At the end of it, Thea called a taxi. As light drizzle fell, she stood shivering in the drive, doing calculations in her head. She could afford it, but it was getting tighter and tighter. She pulled her jacket more closely round her and fumbled in her bag for her iPod. Some Dylan would cheer her up.

'Excuse me,' said a voice behind her.

She turned round. It was the dark man she'd seen comforting his mum in the hall. He was short, only coming up to Thea's shoulder. Twenty-seven? Twenty-eight? He had pointy ears and sideburns. All in all, he looked like a character out of *Lord of the Rings*, albeit dressed in a Stone Roses T-shirt and denim jacket.

'Are you waiting for a cab to the station?' he asked. Home Counties accent. 'Only I was wondering if you'd mind sharing?'

Thea did mind. She wanted to be alone with her thoughts and her bag of Skittles. She didn't want to share any purple ones, particularly with a stranger. But she couldn't think of a way to refuse him.

'Sure,' she said ungraciously, as a black Mondeo pulled up in front of them. They climbed in.

'Going back to London?' he said after travelling the first few minutes in silence.

'Mmm. You?'

'Yes. Visiting family?'

'Yes,' she said brusquely, then softened slightly. 'My grandmother. What about you?'

'My mum.'

Thea wasn't sure what to say. 'She must have been very young when she . . . fell ill.'

'Sixty,' he said. He shrugged. 'It's hard, isn't it? I feel guilty that I don't go to see her often enough, but my job takes me away a lot and . . .'

'Most of the time she doesn't know you're there anyway.'

'Exactly.'

Thea eyed him. He didn't look like an international jetsetter with his beaten-up leather satchel over his shoulder. Curiosity got the better of her. 'What do you do?'

'I work for a charity based in Guatemala. I'm here most of the time, but I go there a lot.'

'Oh right.' She was mildly interested now. It took her mind off her gran in any case. 'What kind of charity?'

'We work with street kids. I'm the press officer.'

'I work for the *Seven Thirty News*. Senior producer.'

She was showing off and she was punished immediately. 'Really? That's my favourite news programme. Only one with a serious agenda any more. I'd love to get something about our work on your show.'

'Mmm,' she said, as the cab pulled in to the station forecourt. Damn. He'd be forever bombarding her now with dull press releases. 'Oh look, the twelve eighteen's there. Quick!'

They jumped out of the car, fumbled for their tickets

to get through the barrier and dashed on to the platform. He held the door open, allowing her to scramble on to the train.

'Thanks.' She smiled politely.

'You're welcome.' There was an empty block of four seats beckoning them. Shit. Thea wanted to read and listen to music in peace, not talk to someone barely out of their teens about his page on MySpace and what his favourite ringtone was. But she could hardly move off to the other end of the train. So they sat down together.

'Would you like a paper?' She offered him one. That should shut him up.

'Love one.' He took the *Guardian* from the pile. Typical charity worker, Thea thought, amused.

'Um. Do you mind if I listen to some music? I just need to clear my head a bit.'

'Of course not.'

Relieved, she slipped on her earphones and for once not being in a Bob mood decided to go for some Joni Mitchell. For a while she lost herself in the music. She was snatched from her reverie by a hand waving in front of her face. Thea looked up. A man in uniform. She pulled off her headphones.

'I was saying tickets, please, love.'

'Oh sorry!' She fumbled in her bag while the inspector mumbled, 'Bloody iPods.' She looked up. The press officer grinned at her. There was a cockiness about him Thea found a bit unnerving. After the inspector had stamped her ticket, he handed the *Guardian* back to her.

'There you go. Thanks for that.'

'Keep it if you like. I've finished it.'

'Oh, OK. I will.' A pause. 'Nice, Greenways, isn't it?'

'It's beautiful,' Thea said. 'But you can't help wondering whether it makes any difference.'

'I console myself that Mum's in a lovely place, but then I wonder if she'd be better off at home with me.'

'That would be a hell of a burden,' Thea said.

'I know. But I still think I should be up to it.'

'I feel the same way.' Their eyes locked. Embarrassing tears welled in Thea's eyes. She rarely talked about her grandmother. Mum hated any references to her dead husband's mother because – ridiculously after thirty-three years – she thought it upset Trevor, and Thea's friends didn't want to know about an old woman for whom there was no future. No hope.

'I'm Jake, by the way,' he said.

'Thea.'

The train was passing the grey, rain-streaked streets of South London, about to pull in to Waterloo. Thea was surprised at how quickly the journey had passed.

'Well, here we are,' he said, standing up. He smiled at her. 'It's been nice talking to you, Thea. You don't have a card, do you? You never know, there might be a story we could work on together.'

'I've forgotten them,' she lied.

'Oh well, never mind. Here's one of mine. Perhaps we could have a drink some time? Or – I don't know – maybe lunch now, if you're not doing anything?'

Thea looked up startled. He fancies me, she thought. Half of her was flattered, half taken aback that someone so much younger than her, shorter than her, in such a lowly job might think he stood a chance.

'Um . . . I'm busy now. Meeting some friends. Sorry.'

He shrugged. 'Shame. Maybe some other time.'

'Yes, maybe.'

He stood, obviously waiting to see if she'd follow him off the train, but she sat motionless.

'OK, then,' he said, 'see you around.'

'Absolutely.' Through the window, she watched him walk briskly up the platform towards the Tube. She glanced at his card: 'Jake Kaplan, Guatemala Children', followed by an address and phone numbers. She stuffed it in her bag, where she knew it would nestle among Tampax, keys, lipsticks and her Oyster card for several years until some time towards the end of the next decade she had a clear out. Thea's bag was full of identical tatty cards from press officers all trying to get a profile for their cause. Brutal as it was, most of them were ignored. Thea was sure Jake's charity did a lot of good work, but it was just one of thousands trying to make a difference. She saw no reason to give it special treatment.

15

The following evening Thea stood on the doorstep of Rachel's maisonette in Islington, a huge tray of sushi in one hand, a bottle of sake in the other. Her heart was beating with excitement as she waited for her best friend to open the door. Ridiculously, it had taken them nearly three weeks to get together. Two dinners had been cancelled because Rachel's pregnancy was tiring her out and another because Thea had been called away overnight to Newcastle where a child, feared drowned, had been reunited with her family. But tonight they were finally meeting, having agreed that the best venue was Rachel's house, so she could loll dribbling on the sofa when exhaustion got the better of her.

To further conserve energies Thea had promised to bring the food. She was chuffed with her choice: sushi had always been their favourite and this was from Ikkyu, the battered dive next to the Scientology Centre in Tottenham Court Road, where the pair of them had spent probably one fifth of their twenties gorging themselves from the hand-roll sushi set and analysing every two-word text Luke had ever sent.

'Ta dah!' she cried as the door opened, waving the goodies above her head like a cheerleader.

'Oh,' Rachel said.

'I know, I know. You can't drink the sake,' Thea said.

'That's for me. But you can have as much sushi as you can stuff in.' She tried not to stare at the small, yet still obvious, swelling below Rachel's green cashmere sweater. Last time she'd seen Rachel was five months ago in Manhattan when she'd spent the entire weekend telling Thea how her boyfriend, Dunc, didn't want babies until he'd got together the finance to direct his first movie and how that was fine by her. A couple of weeks after returning home her coil had 'accidentally' failed.

'But I can't eat sushi any more,' Rachel wailed, 'raw fish.'

Thea had seen it a dozen times before: former Amazons metamorphosed into wusses who panicked at the sight of peanut butter and spent hours debating whether to get their hair coloured. But she was determined to take Rachel's pregnancy in her stride, so she smiled patiently.

'What do Japanese women eat when they're pregnant?'

'I don't know. I think they make sushi differently there or something.' Rachel looked pained. 'I'm really sorry, Thee. It was a brilliant idea of yours. Don't worry. I'll have something from the freezer. Dunc will be happy to finish what you don't eat.'

'Dunc's here?' Thea tried and failed to keep disappointment out of her voice as she followed her friend into the gleaming kitchen. Despite her job as a high-earning lawyer, Rachel had always been brilliant at homely stuff. It mattered to her that her fridge was full and her surfaces like mirrors, whereas Thea could not have given the tiniest hoot.

'No, he's gone to the pub with his mate Stan. There's some football match on.' Rachel riffled through the freezer drawers. 'Look, there's a lasagne here, so I'll eat that and you can have the sushi, you lucky thing.' She sighed melodramatically. 'Still, only five months to go, then as soon as the baby's out I'm going to buy the most enormous Stilton I can find and devour it in one sitting.'

'So how are you feeling?' Thea was determined to empathize.

Rachel smiled as she jabbed the ready meal's plastic film with a fork. 'Very tired. Very sick. Not throwing up, but constantly nauseous. And my boobs hurt all the time. It's supposed to get better from the third month but I think that's just one of the many lies they peddle, like childbirth doesn't hurt much, to ensure the human race keeps going.' She opened the microwave and shoved in the lasagne. 'Anyway. Boring. How's work? How's *Luke*? God, I saw the article on trophy wives.'

Thea giggled. 'And they say journalists make things up. Every word accurate.'

'Have you met her yet? I mean the Bimbo?'

Thea found she couldn't make eye contact. She picked up the sake and studied the label. 'Yup. At a dinner party.'

'And?'

'Hannah's let her off too lightly. She's virtually an imbecile.'

Actually, in her heart Thea knew that was unfair. She couldn't really judge Poppy's intelligence, because she'd hardly had a chance to open her mouth all evening with the amount of chatter going on around her. And so much of that chatter was shop talk about the various news networks and their staff; no one outside the business could have been expected to understand it. Thea had heard her making an effort to engage Marco in conversation but he was so busy arselicking to Dean that he had cut her off at the pass.

Deep down, Thea also recognized that the women had been less than kind to Poppy because she was a) so pretty, b) so young and c) was a stay-at-home mother which would have unleashed a tornado of self-doubt in Emma and Roxanne. The fact that she had stolen Emma's closest friend's husband hadn't helped either. Thea shuddered to think how Emma would react if she ever found out about her and Luke. But how could she?

'Tell me more,' Rachel was saying eagerly. 'Is she like this client I had to deal with the other day who didn't know that birds laid eggs? When I told her, she said: "Well, you learn a new thing every day!"'

'On that sort of level,' Thea said shortly.

'Bloody hell – Luke! What an arse. Why are men always so obvious? Have you seen him yet? Properly I mean.'

'Hardly spoken to him. It's all over. You know that.'

'Yes.' Rachel nodded. 'You know I always thought you were far too good for him. Any man who cheats on his wife is only going to do it again.'

'You never said that at the time.' Rachel had always been encouraging about her and Luke, saying it wasn't Thea's fault if he'd so obviously married the wrong woman and assuring her one day he'd see the light and they'd come together.

'Didn't I? I'm sure I did.' The microwave pinged. 'Oh, what sweet music. Let's eat. I'm always starving; I'm going to get so fat.'

'You're not, you're growing a baby,' Thea said dutifully.

She picked up some toro and dipped it in the wasabi. 'How's Dunc about it all? Is he excited?'

'Much more than I expected him to be.' Rachel sipped some pear juice. 'I've been very lucky, Thea. When my coil failed, he could have left me, or put pressure on me to have an abortion but, instead, he's taken it in his stride.'

'Mmm,' Thea said. She believed the story about the coil failing as much as she did in the tooth fairy. Before she could come up with a more eloquent reply the door slammed.

'Oh, that'll be him.' Rachel looked at the microwave clock. 'Back earlier than I thought.'

'All right?' Dunc grinned, ambling into the room. 'Good to see you, Thea.'

'You too.' Thea smiled, although she felt like a bicycle wheel that had just run over a broken bottle. However happy Rachel seemed, Thea couldn't help being depressed that her beautiful, bright, funny friend, who could tie a knot in a cherry stone with her teeth, would now always be linked to a man who – while undeniably handsome – could boast that he knew every word of *The Office* DVD boxed set off by heart. A man, what was worse, who seemed content to live off Rachel's vast salary while he tried to get various projects off the ground; not to mention a man who absolutely refused to marry her because, as he charmingly put it, he found the thought 'too depressing'.

'Yum, look at that sushi,' Dunc exclaimed, grabbing the only piece of yellowtail sashimi, which Thea had been looking forward to.

'So how are things, Dunc? What are you up to at the moment?'

'It's really exciting actually. Me and my mate Stan are setting up this new internet venture so you can order takeaways online.'

'Like Hungryhouse?' Thea ventured politely.

'Who?'

'Hungryhouse. I use them all the time. You type in your postcode and they list everyone near you who delivers.'

'Oh. Right.' Dunc scratched his curly head uneasily. 'I'll have to check them out.'

'Might be an idea,' Thea said. She didn't meet Rachel's eye. The doorbell rang.

'That'll be Stan. We're having a meeting.'

'On a Sunday evening?' Rachel sounded calm, but Thea knew she was annoyed.

'We won't bother you, babe; you can still have your early night.' Dunc headed to the door and returned with a plumpish man with an unnervingly low hairline. 'Hey, Stan, meet Thea. Thea, Stan.'

'Nice to meet you.'

'Likewise. Shit, look at all that sushi.'

'Help yourself,' Dunc said generously.

And so an hour passed, during which Dunc and Stan ate all the best bits of the sushi and showed no sign whatsoever of convening a business meeting, preferring instead to engage in heated debate about the merits of Facebook versus MySpace with many detailed anecdotes from friends. Thea yawned discreetly and drank as much sake as she could get away with. Rachel caressed her stomach as though it was a lazy Siamese cat.

'What is it you do, Thea?' Stan said turning to her, after a long discussion on the evil that was TalkTalk broadband, which had ended with Dunc hurrying to his office to check some fact.

'I'm a journalist.'

Stan made the sign of the cross. 'Oooh, better be careful what I say. Don't want you misquoting me.'

Why did the dullest people always say this? Thea smiled stiffly.

'Thea's not that kind of journalist,' Rachel said loyally. 'She's a senior producer on the *SevenThirty News*.'

'Oh yeah? Never watch the news. Get it off the internet. Hey, have you ever met Ricky Gervais?'

'No. But I hear he's a complete arsehole.' This wasn't actually true, but it was worth it because Stan looked like a three-year-old who'd just been told there was no Santa Claus.

'I can't believe that.'

'Well, that's up to you.' Thea grinned as the lie began to take shape. 'But he was the only star who refused to contribute to our summer charity appeal. He said charity began at home.'

'Stan,' Dunc yelled from the other room, 'come and look at this. It proves my point one hundred per cent.'

'Excuse me, ladies.' Stan got up. As soon as he'd left the room, Rachel smiled.

'He's nice, isn't he?'

Thea looked at her friend in astonishment. She might as well have asked her to affirm that Pol Pot was a cutie.

'Quite good-looking?' Rachel pressed on.

'He's OK. I mean he hasn't got a harelip or a disfiguring skin condition.'

'He split up from his girlfriend recently.'

'Did he?' Thea yawned.

'So what do you think?'

Trying to hide her irritation, Thea filled her glass with sake. 'Rach, stop this at once!'

'Stop what?' Rachel said with mock innocence.

'Trying to matchmake. I don't want to be part of the smug marrieds club.'

'Nor do Dunc and I,' Rachel said rather sharply.

'True,' Thea agreed hastily. Just as Rachel knew without asking how she felt about Luke, Thea didn't need to be told that Rachel's 'I don't care about marriage, it's just a piece of paper' line was an out and out fib. She added, 'But Rachel, I don't fancy Stan. Sorry. I don't fancy anybody at the moment. I'm sure I will again in time, but I don't want babies so where's the rush?'

Rachel's hands moved protectively to her bump, as if such words might harm her unborn child.

Hastily Thea carried on, 'Look, I'm thrilled you're having a baby. I'm going to be its big bad godmother, and stuff it with sweeties and buy it make-up if it's a girl and violent computer games if it's a boy and generally love it to pieces. But I don't want one of my own. You know that.'

'But *why*?'

Because babies didn't drink, didn't have interesting conversations, went to bed at an absurdly early hour. They curbed your freedom, meant an end to all passion and spontaneity and turned you into a drudge like Thea's mother. They made you settle for an oaf like Dunc, because at thirty-six, time had run out before you'd found someone better. But naturally Thea was going to say none of this, just inwardly thank the good whoever was up there that she had somehow miraculously been born without the urge to breed and was therefore spared such hideous compromises. 'Why not?' She shrugged.

'I don't know,' Rachel said tentatively. 'I just somehow thought maybe you had this anti-marriage and babies line because of Luke. You know, because he already had kids and you thought he didn't want any more. But now it's all over . . . Or maybe it isn't competely finished yet?'

'It *is* finished. I told you. It took me long enough, but I really have seen the light about Luke. Being his lover was such a cliché. It's up there with peasants in movies always having filthy hair but perfect white teeth.'

Rachel chuckled. 'Or women wearing bras but no knickers when they have sex.'

'Or returning from the shops with a baguette sticking out of their string bag.'

'Or the villain leaving at least an hour for your bomb to explode, so the hero has plenty of time to defuse it and rescue the girl.'

They were giggling when the men came back into the room. Suddenly Thea felt cold. She looked at her watch. 'Listen, I've got an early start. I'd better get going.'

'Maybe you could give Stan a lift,' Dunc said hopefully.

'I was going to get the Tube,' Thea lied. She'd had every intention of leaping in a black cab. Taxis were her great indulgence, you could put them all against expenses, though rumour had it that Foxy Roxy was planning to put a halt to this practice. Well, all the more reason to enjoy it while it lasted.

'I could walk you there,' Stan said eagerly.

Thea looked at her watch again. 'Gosh, actually, it's later than I thought. Maybe I will get a cab.' She looked unwillingly at Stan. 'Where do you live?'

'Acton.'

'You're nowhere near me. I'm in Stockwell. I could drop you at the Tube if you like.' She made her offer sound like a doctor asking the patient to choose between amputating a leg or an arm. Stan got the hint.

'No, don't worry, I'll walk. Fresh air would do me good.'

Rachel stood up and hugged her friend. 'It's been great to see you. We'll do it again soon.' She lowered her voice. 'Just the two of us next time.'

Thea felt a lump in her throat. For a second, she'd been worried she'd lost Rachel. But maybe there was still a chink of hope. All the same, as her taxi accelerated down a virtually deserted, Sunday night Upper Street, Thea felt a bleakness inside, a realization that in her absence her London life had changed unalterably. She'd better find a hot foreign story quickly to take her away for a bit. The joy of life on the road was that you lived in a bubble where you didn't have to worry about the mundanities of everyday life. Tomorrow she'd start scouring the foreign sections for something that could take her away from this new, earthbound existence.

16

Having decided at least to give Brigita, Farrah's nanny, a try, Poppy was surprised how easy it was to organize. After her call, Brigita came over the very next morning with a big smile and a cuddly elephant for Clara.

'Now then!' she cried from the doorstep. 'Good morning, Mummy. Pleased ta meet you.' She had a very peculiar accent, half Slavic, half Yorkshire. She bent down and chucked Clara's cheek. 'And you too, my beautiful princess.'

'G'waaay!' shrieked Clara, burying her face in Poppy's crotch.

Poppy smiled. She'd been hoping for a matronly type in a brown uniform and cap. But Brigita seemed a good second best. She was in her late twenties with cropped brown hair tidily framing a round face. She wore a long patchwork skirt, a baggy brown jumper, sturdy lace-ups and blue woolly tights. She looked like the kind of nanny whose days would be spent making toys out of old egg cartons and romping round the playground, while at night she would be tucked up in her bed at ten with a mug of cocoa and a copy of the Bible.

'Where are you from?' Poppy asked, leading her into the house.

'From Latvia!' Brigita cried, as if she'd said from Jupiter. 'But my boyfriend he is Englishman. From 'artlepool.

I come here to study astronomy but I need to earn money and I discover a real love for children, so I get a job with Farrah and I am . . . oh . . . I am as 'appy as a pig in muck with her. But now she don't need me any more, because the boys are both at school so she say to me, "Go and work for Poppy and Luke. They are good 'uns. They will treat you right."' She looked Poppy up and down. 'Farrah say you are model, but this is no true, I think?'

'I used to be. Before Clara.'

'Well, the bairns they make the women fat. This is the life.'

'Er . . .' Nonplussed, Poppy gestured at the sofa. 'Sit down. Would you like a glass of water?'

'No, Mummy! Don't be like this. I get *you* a glass of water. Tell me, where is the kitchen?'

'No, it's OK.'

'No, really! I find it.' Before Poppy could stop her, Brigita had disappeared into the kitchen. It was a while before she returned.

'Here you go, Mummy. I'm sorry, kitchen is dirty so I need to clean up first. And I can find no ice. Would you like? I can go and search in freezer again.'

'I'm fine,' Poppy said faintly.

She tried to conduct a bit of an interview, though that was a total misnomer since, unless Brigita had confessed to a penchant for freebasing, the job was hers. But in any case, Brigita surpassed herself by pulling a print-out from her bag with a list of toddler activities in the area and asking which ones Clara attended.

'None of them,' Poppy said, embarrassed. She'd tried, of course, but she found it so difficult sitting alone on a hard chair, watching Clara fighting with other children for a battered doll's buggy, while all the other mothers sat in tight, cliquey circles she hadn't a clue how to infiltrate.

'Oh right. So what do you do all day together?' She chucked Clara under the chin. 'Pretty girl. You don't look nothing like your mummy.'

Potter about. 'You know,' Poppy shrugged, 'go to the playground. Read stories.'

'Of course, Mummy. But it's time Clara was mixing a bit with other children, I think.'

Then she asked a lot of questions about allergies and what Clara liked to eat and potty training, and then Clara did a poo right on cue, so Brigita rolled up her sleeves and changed her nappy without visibly holding her breath, then blew a big raspberry on her tummy to make her giggle. Poppy said the job was hers, four days a week, if she wanted it and Brigita said she did, very much indeed. Could she start a week on Monday? Poppy asked.

'I can start tomorrow if you like!'

'Oh no, no, no,' Poppy said. The thought of being catapulted so abruptly from her old life into her new one was more than she could take. She needed a week to prepare herself and Clara mentally for the new regime.

'As you wish.' Brigita shrugged. 'I'll come at eight, Mummy.'

'Eight? That's a bit early, isn't it?'

'I start for Farrah at eight.' Brigita looked taken aback.

'Maybe nine?' Poppy bargained.

'Well, if you are really sure. I mean, Farrah she is fair throng.'

'Sorry?'

'Very busy,' Brigita said a little impatiently. 'She always goes to gym every morning for one hour before work.' She looked Poppy up and down again and shrugged. 'But every woman has the different priorities, I guess.'

Poppy had meant to say they'd have a trial period of a month, she meant to discuss pay and holidays and the things Luke had told her to ask, but in the flurry of it all, she totally forgot. Never mind. They'd talk about it later.

And so, a week on Monday, the doorbell rang at nine sharp. Brigita bustled in and before Poppy knew it, Clara was sitting in her high chair eating a large bowl of porridge.

'That's amazing,' said Luke, entering the room in his suit. 'Clara usually chucks the healthy stuff on the floor.'

'I make a smiley face out of these blueberries,' Brigita said with false modesty. 'That makes her hungry.'

'She's great,' Luke mouthed at Poppy, as he switched the kettle on. Poppy nodded, dumbstruck with jealousy and nerves.

Brigita lowered her voice. 'Now, don't take this the wrong way, Mummy, but I think is best if you stay out me way today. If you're around Clara, she will get confused and be a little monkey. The more time we are alone together the quicker she will get to know and love Brigita.'

'OK,' Poppy agreed meekly.

Not quite knowing what to do with herself she had a shower and dressed. Poppy couldn't deny it: it was a joy to perform these two seemingly simple tasks without Clara exploiting her mother's brief unavailability by either throwing soap and toothpaste in the loo or deciding to climb in with her fully dressed. But Poppy was too anxious to enjoy her new freedom. She dried and dressed as hastily as she could then dashed downstairs to find Brigita buttoning Clara's coat without any of the screaming (Clara) or yelling (Poppy) that usually accompanied this deceptively simple-looking manoeuvre.

'We're going to the playgroup at the church,' Brigita said. 'Come on, Clara, let's go!'

'Oh, right,' Poppy said, as her daughter skipped out of the door without even a backward glance. As the door slammed, she stood slightly dazed. She'd anticipated tears and resistance and clinging to Mummy. Instead, it was as if she'd never existed.

A sudden vision of the future presented itself to her: a vision of Clara getting older, going to school, making friends, not needing her any more. It had started already. So what was she going to do? Both short and long term, Poppy hadn't a clue. She glanced out of the window. The sun was shining in a watery blue sky. She felt as redundant as Jake the Peg's extra leg. She could go for a walk on her own, she supposed, it might be more relaxing, but she didn't think that was why Luke had wanted a nanny.

'I keep myself very busy, you know, running the house. Doing a bit of charity work. Working out . . .'

Her phone rang. Mum.

'Hello?' For once Poppy was quite glad to hear from her.

'Just calling to see how the new girl's settling in.' Louise was clearly behind the wheel of her Porsche Boxster. She only ever called when she was bored and stuck in traffic.

'She only started an hour ago, but I'd say really well.'

Louise snorted. 'Typical you, Poppy, ever the optimist. Well, you won't listen to my advice because you never do, but I'll tell you anyway: lock up your booze and put a code or something on the phone. God, when I remember the trouble I had with your girls—'

'OK, Mum.' Poppy decided to needle her. 'How's Gary?'

'Gary?' Louise sounded like Scary Spice learning she wasn't allowed to fly business class. 'I haven't a clue.'

'Weren't you going on holiday with him?'

'Was I? I don't think so. No, no.' Louise lowered her voice. 'Actually, there's someone new on the horizon. Jean-Claude.'

'Oh yes.' Poppy's heart sank. She'd heard this hushed, excited tone so many times and it always spelt disaster. 'Where did you meet him?'

'When Christine and I went on our girls' spa trip to Malaga. He was in the same hotel as us for a conference. He's a professor of linguistics at the University of Marseilles. So good-looking, Poppy. I can send you a link with his photo.'

'So he's French?'

'Mmm. Isn't that exciting? But he speaks excellent English.'

'How much time did you spend with him over the weekend?'

'He joined me and Chris for dinner on our second night and then the next morning I had a lovely chat with him at the breakfast buffet which was *very* lavish, I must say, though I forced myself to steer clear of the croissants. I gave him my card and he said he'd be in touch.'

'And has he?'

'No. So yesterday I googled him and found his email address and sent him a nice email with my number on it, because he probably lost it, you know what men are like, and now I'm waiting for him to get back to me. He's wonderful, Poppy, I know you'll like him, he's really clever and—'

Poppy couldn't bear it. She resorted to her usual standby. 'Mum, Mum! I'm really sorry but there's someone at the door. I've got to go.'

'Oh. All right.' Louise was miffed. It was *her* role to end calls. 'Call me later and let me know how the *girl's* settling in. And I'll email you Jean-Claude's details.'

'OK. Thanks for calling.'

'Oh, and just one more thing.'

'Yes?'

'Now you have this girl, what are you going to do with yourself all day?'

'I've just called my agency,' Poppy lied. 'They've got loads of work lined up for me and I'm going in to see them about it this afternoon.'

'Oh yes? Well, that's very good.' A noise of honking. 'Oh, thank heavens, finally we're moving. All right, Poppy, speak soon. Bye!'

Exhausted from the conversation, Poppy flopped back on the bed. Talking to her mother always left her drained. Perhaps she'd go back to sleep for a bit. But then she thought about the lie she'd just told and the same new icy resolve that had made her call Brigita tingled in her veins. Wanting to feel businesslike, she went into Luke's study, shut the door and, heart doing a samba in her ribcage, dialled her agency.

'Hello, Prime Models. Jenny speaking.'

A new receptionist since her day. 'Hi. Could I speak to Barbara please?'

'Who may I say is calling?' Jenny yawned.

'It's Poppy.'

'Poppy who?'

'Poppy Norton. I mean, Price.' It had been a while since she'd used her old, unmarried name. It took her back.

'Will she know what it's in connection with?'

'I'm a client of hers,' Poppy said stiffly. She was starting to remember why exactly she'd hated modelling so much; how soul-destroying it was to be constantly treated as if you were something to be scraped off a shoe.

'Hold, please.'

As she waited to the strains of Amy Winehouse, Poppy looked round the room. The walls were covered with pictures of the highlights of her husband's career: Luke in a flak jacket in the desert in Iraq; Luke shaking hands with the Queen; Luke with President Bush. As so often, Poppy had the sense of being a visitor rather than the mistress of this flat, where the furniture had been chosen by David, their landlord, and delivered in a John Lewis van and virtually everything that made a house a home – pictures, ornaments, books, CDs, DVDs – belonged to Luke, Poppy having had virtually no time in her short life to acquire mementoes. She'd thought about redecorating, because she had a vague idea that was what stay-at-home mothers were supposed to do, but when she'd suggested it to Luke he'd pointed out that David wouldn't be too pleased.

'Poppy!' cried a voice that sounded as if it had been gargling bleach. 'Long time, no hear. We were wondering what the hell had happened to you. How's it all going?'

'Really well, thanks, Barbara. Still alive, despite the baby, ha ha.'

'Oh, yes, the baby. How *is* he?' Poppy could hear Barbara tapping rapidly on a computer.

'It's a she, actually.'

'Sorry, *she*.' Now she sounded as if she was opening a giant-sized packet of crisps. 'Do you think you're about ready to return to the real world, Poppy? After all, it's been – what – more than two years?'

'Something like that. And yes, I do think I'm ready. I've got a nanny now you see, so—'

'Great, great. Well, come in and see us. Soon. Bring some baby piccies.'

'Oh yes, I will. I've got some lovely ones of her on the slide. She looks—'

'Ah. Bless. Sweet.' Barbara sounded as interested as if Poppy had tried to tell her about last night's dream.

'I could come in on Friday,' Poppy gasped, desperately trying to keep Barbara's attention like a bad comedian with a drunken audience. She wanted to say 'today' but she knew it would sound too eager.

'Friday? Well, I suppose so,' Barbara said reluctantly.

'About eleven?'

'All right, then. Oh, sorry, gotta go. See you Thursday.'

'Friday!' Poppy shouted at the handset. She remembered how Barbara had once chased her round the swimwear section at Harvey Nicks desperate to get her signature on the contract. Now she was lower on her priority list than a packet of Japanese rice crackers. But she wasn't going to dwell on such thoughts. Poppy wasn't going to be a leech and a parasite. She would go and wow Barbara on Friday and she would make Luke proud.

17

Thea had spent that Monday in a hospital in North London putting together a story about a doctor who'd given a child a near fatal dose of medicine. Now, at five, two hours before the show began, she was in one of the editing suites checking the astons – the names that appeared under each talking head. Astons were very important: the times when Hillary Clinton had been billed as the Duke of Westminster or Nelson Mandela as Johnny Rotten were legion. But it had never happened on Thea's beat. And it never would.

Satisfied that all was in order, she opened the sound-proofed door and was back in the buzz of the newsroom. As the deadline approached you could almost touch the adrenalin. Reporters gesticulated as they gabbled into their phones. Producers barked as they tried to lure inter-viewees on to the show. Monica Thomson, that day's programme editor, was trying to persuade Emma Waters to go to Heathrow where a man had breached the perimeter fence and run naked across the runway.

'Don't be ridiculous, Monica. I'm not going to Heathrow! It's bloody raining out there.'

'Please,' Monica tried timidly. She was newly promoted to the job and, like dogs, the reporters could smell her fear.

'No.' Emma gestured at Bryn Darwin, one of the oldest and laziest reporters, who was bent over his sudoku. 'Send Bryn. Go on.'

'Oh, OK,' Monica said and scuttled off nervously to try him.

Dean strode through the room like Napoleon overseeing his troops.

'Have we got a fat teenager yet?' he shouted at the room in general. 'Well, why the fuck not? I want a roly-poly. Hoisted into the studio with a crane preferably. Come on, everyone. Find me a lardbutt. Fifty quid for the winner.'

'Got one!' shouted creepy Rhys, one of the GAs – general assistants – much mocked for his over-eager manner. 'Sixteen. Twenty-three stone. Lives on Coke, crisps and KFC. Claims she's got a hormonal problem.'

'Bingo, my boy. Well done! Details to Amanda.' Dean nodded at the guest booker, who was responsible for interviewees arriving at the studio.

'She says she'll need a people carrier,' Rhys told Amanda, 'and even then they may have to move the seats to fit her in.'

Thea grinned. She loved the way that at work there was scarcely time to breathe, let alone think. Thinking too much wasn't healthy; she'd had a near sleepless night brooding about whether her friendship with Rachel could ever be the same.

'How's your day been?' asked Alexa Marples, who was sitting at the desk behind her. Smart and ambitious, Alexa reminded Thea a lot of herself ten years ago, except Thea would never have had the confidence to wear such low-slung jeans. Before Thea could answer, she continued. 'God, I'll be glad when today's over. Woke up with a mouth like a dog's bum. Too many Bacardi Breezers last night.'

Thea smiled. 'I know that feeling.'

'Do you?' Alexa looked as if the Queen had just told her she was feeling a bit bunged up but hoped a vindaloo would clear it. Since she'd got back, Thea had had a few exchanges like this. She'd only been gone two years but in that time the office appeared to have been repopulated by babies who spent all day updating their profiles online and rushing off as soon as work was over to get bladdered in Shoreditch. Thea was no longer part of that gang, but on the other hand she wasn't part of the late-thirties office crowd who rushed home immediately after the debrief to read their kids a bedtime story. Just as she had at Rachel's, Thea felt a flicker of unease, a sense of not belonging anywhere.

At the newsdesk, Luke was practising tonight's headlines. 'Six out of ten teenagers are obese,' he intoned in his crisp, clear voice as Dean and Georgina, the lawyer, listened intently. 'The Mexican earthquake: two hundred feared dead. The doctor who accidentally poisoned a toddler—'

'You know you can't say that, Luke,' Georgina interrupted. 'It hasn't been proven yet. The doctor will sue.'

'Oh bloody hell.' Luke was never patient with lawyer's stipulations. 'The toddler who received a fatal dose? How about that.'

'Is it just me?' Alexa said softly. 'Or is something a bit weird about Luke's face?'

Thea looked. Now Alexa mentioned it, the skin did seem to be stretched even more tightly than ever across his cheekbones and, although his eyes were full of expression, his brow stayed strangely smooth. Thea glanced sideways at Alexa, but her attention was now fixed firmly on the monitors. Thea hated the idea of everyone knowing there had been something between her and Luke.

'He looks the same as ever to me,' she said shortly.

'Don't you think he's been a bit off form recently? Apparently Dean's compiling a dossier of bad performances and Luke's in the lead.'

'Really?' Thea sounded bored. She wanted to kill this conversation dead.

But she knew Alexa was right. Luke's performances had been a bit lacklustre recently. He'd omitted a really obvious question when he was talking to the head of the Prison Service on Thursday. Dean hadn't been amused.

'Don't think much of Emma's jacket,' Alexa continued, nodding at the senior reporter – who having successfully evaded the journey to Heathrow – was dictating her eldest son's history homework to him over the phone. 'No Magna Carta, darling . . . not C-A-R-T-E-R, C-A-R-T-A.'

'Does nothing for her complexion,' Thea agreed. She clicked on her screen to bring up the 'viewer base', the file of viewers' emails that Dean was insisting everyone studied daily for feedback. 'Yup and the general public agree. There were three emails criticizing it after the lunchtime news. Red does nothing for her.'

They both giggled and suddenly Thea felt a spark of kinship. Even if Alexa was half her age, perhaps they could be friends. Her mobile rang. 'Hello?' she said, still smiling.

'Is that Thea?' said a male voice she didn't recognize.

'Yes?' she answered frostily. Nutters rang the newsroom all day long telling her they were Princess Anastasia and for ten thousand pounds they would grant her an exclusive interview. You didn't want to do anything to encourage them.

'This is Jake Kaplan. We met at Greenways.'

Even worse. That charity guy wanting to tell her that – newsflash – tragically children were living on the streets.

'Hello,' she said haughtily.

'Hi. I'm just back from Guatemala and I was wondering if you'd like to meet?'

His directness took her aback. 'Sorry?'

He laughed. 'I didn't phrase that very well. I just got back from Guatemala yesterday and there's a story brewing there I think the *Seven Thirty News* might be very interested in, so I was wondering if you'd like to have a drink and talk about it.'

'I'm pretty busy right now. Can't you just tell me on the phone?'

'No,' he said. 'It's quite an important story. We really need to discuss it face to face.'

Presumptuous sod. Thea was annoyed. 'I'm really sorry, Jake, but I'm totally booked up this week. You could send me an email giving me some idea of the story and then maybe we could pencil something in for next week.' And then I'll cancel you.

'I won't be here. I'll be back in Guatemala. So the sooner we meet the better.'

Thea rolled her eyes. The boy had a nerve. 'Look, I can't promise anything. And I really have to go now, Jake, it's mid programme and—'

He cut her off cheerily. 'OK. It's the *Seven Thirty News*'s loss. I'll have to take the story to the BBC. They'll want it for sure.'

Oh no, they won't; you pushy short man. 'Well, I'm afraid I'll just have to live with that,' Thea said and hung up. He wouldn't call back. They never did.

18

Poppy was in two minds about meeting Barbara. All week she kept remembering more and more things she'd loathed about modelling: the competitive undereating, the bitchiness, the obligatory fag-haggery involving cooing over pictures of Kylie Minogue, necessary if the guys who did hair and make-up were not to make you look like Bet Lynch on a bad-hair day.

But after three days with Brigita in the house, Poppy knew she would expire from a combination of boredom and sadness if she didn't find some work. Now the novelty of being able to have a bowel movement in private had worn off, she missed Clara's company desperately. Hearing her laughing in another room caused her physical pain. Poppy was forever rushing in to pick her daughter up and smother her in kisses but, whenever she did, Brigita's lips would curl into a sulky snarl

'I tell you is best Mummy keeps out of the way. You go enjoy.'

Poppy decided she had nothing to lose by at least dropping in to see Barbara. So having doublechecked she was in the diary for Friday, she spent fifteen times longer than usual getting dressed in jeans that held in her post-Clara muffin-top and a turquoise T-shirt the same colour as her eyes. She never normally used her hairdryer because Clara was petrified of the noise, but with Brigita in charge she styled her blonde locks with her round brush, then applied her make-up. When she looked in the mirror she scarcely recognized herself. She hadn't looked so polished since – well, probably since her wedding day.

'Poppy!' cried Glenda, sticking her head round the door, Pledge in one hand, duster in the other. 'Good morning to you!'

'Hi, Glenda, how are you? How are the children?'

'They are well. I spoke to them on Sunday after church. Fernando he is playing good football, I am so proud. Maribel is worried because she has a fight with a friend. I miss them.'

'It must break your heart.' As always, Poppy felt overwhelmed at how pathetic her problems were in comparison with Glenda's. But her cleaner just shrugged.

'At least I make a good living. Do my best for them.' She looked at Poppy. 'But you look so pretty today, darling. Where are you going?'

'I've got a sort of job interview.'

'Looking so beautiful, you will get any job you want. Good luck, my sweetheart. Let me know what happens.'

'I will. I'll text you.'

It was one of those dishonest spring days when the sun shone down so boldly people began to think of putting their winter coats away. A day when the evening papers would be full of pictures of two pretty girls sunbathing in Hyde Park next to some early daffodils and everyone would feel guilty about enjoying what was such a sure sign of global warming, only to wake the next day to find the mercury had dropped again and start investigating foreign holidays on the internet. As Poppy headed towards the Tube, she realized men were looking at her in a way they hadn't looked for a long time. It felt surprisingly good.

'You sad woman. You're married,' she chided herself.

At Oxford Circus she emerged into the light and headed off through the maze of sleazy but exciting Soho back streets towards her agency with its tatty black door. The waiting room was just as she remembered it: the walls lined with framed magazine covers featuring the agency's top girls. Once Poppy had been among them, but she'd been quietly removed. A girl who looked about twelve with legs that stretched on forever was lounging on the sofa, reading *Harper's Bazaar*. She glanced at Poppy pityingly as if she'd wandered in from the Help the Aged offices four doors down. The receptionist, who appeared all of thirteen, cleared her throat.

'Can I help you?'

'I'm here to see Barbara.'

'Do you have an appointment?'

'*Yes*. I'm Poppy Price.'

'Oh, yeah. Go on through.'

Poppy pushed open the plate-glass door and walked into the main booking room with its intoxicating aroma of Jo Malone candles. Tiny speakers boomed out cool tunes that competed with the noise of nine skinny women sitting round a huge rectangular table yelling into mouthpieces as if they were trading copper in the City rather than finding the ideal candidate for a new anti-dandruff shampoo. 'Has anyone checked the photographer for Alix?' 'Have you found a hotel for Kate?' No one even looked at Poppy as she headed towards Barbara's office in the back right corner.

She tapped at the glass door and was motioned to come in. Surprise, surprise, her old mentor was on the phone. 'Yeah, OK, well, maybe she should go to the Priory? Or that other clinic in Jersey? Hi, Poppy, sit down, angel, be with you in a second . . . Yeah, I know last time the staff sold stories on her, but the woman in question's been sacked . . . Look, if she wants to do rehab in Arizona that's fine by me – whatever. Just get her there soon . . . because clients are starting to ask questions . . . They noticed the needle marks between her toes.'

Poppy looked at a huge signed photo of Daisy McNeil on the desk in front of her. 'To Babs, Love, love, love yoooou! D xx'

'Look, I gotta go. An old friend's here.' She smiled at Poppy. 'OK, keep me posted, bye. Poppy!' She got up and kissed her. 'Poppy! Back from the dead! It's a miracle.'

'Well, not *dead*. I just had a baby.'

'I'm sure you used to have a sense of humour,' Barbara said and then, seeing Poppy's hurt expression, 'Joke! Ha! Proving my point rather,' she added under her breath. 'So let's have a look at you.' A long silence followed as she scanned her. 'Yes. Pretty good. Probably could do with shifting another seven pounds, but you're almost there. I'm sure there's some catalogue work I could put you up for. In fact, I think the Mothercare catalogue just called.'

'Oh,' Poppy said. Catalogue work was the Bernard Matthews turkey twizzlers of the modelling world. 'Not editorial?'

'Well, possibly. I think Sharon mentioned a cookery magazine looking for girls. I'll have to have a chat with her. Sweetheart, don't pull that sulky face. The wind might change. We might get you back doing editorial, but like I say, you need to shift the last few pounds. They're on your face you see, sweetie, that's the problem. Also, you're how old now . . . twenty-six?'

'Twenty-four.'

'So obviously your shelf life is coming to an end. In high fashion at any rate. There's always plenty of work for the mature lady, obviously. Plus, don't take it the wrong way, but while you've been away, fashion's changed completely. The wholesome look's out. Edgy is in again. It'll swing back in a year or so, it always does, but what the magazines are all asking for now is grungy. Which I am very happy to say, you are not.'

'But I could be!' Poppy cried, full of regrets at having washed her hair and scrubbed her nails that morning.

Barbara laughed and shook her head. 'Poppy, you're a California girl who got lost in London by mistake. You should be jogging along the beach in Malibu not trudging round the West End.' She glanced at her Tag Heuer. 'Look, sorry to cut things short but I've got a lunch and I need to speak to Tokyo first. Off you run. But don't worry. I'm sure something will come up. I'll be in touch soon.' She pressed her buzzer. 'Sweetheart, send Jasmine in please and tell her I'm sorry to have kept her waiting.'

And before she knew it, Poppy was back on the street, blinking slightly in the daylight. She couldn't believe how briskly she'd been dealt with. The rest of the day still stretched ahead of her as empty as Westbourne Grove on Christmas morning. She could go to an exhibition, she supposed, but even her normally voracious appetite for art was dulled as if she'd eaten a packet of cotton wool, that popular modelling trick. She'd go for a walk, she decided, clear her head.

She wandered through Soho Square with its tiny patch of grass that in an hour or so would be obliterated by picnicking office workers, funny, half-timbered gardener's hut in the middle and statue of King Charles II and the bench commemorating Kirsty MacColl. Down the narrow, urine-soaked alleyway that ran behind the Astoria where Poppy had once been with her still-in-the-closet boyfriend Alex to see Geri Halliwell, then across the road past the vast, ugly Centrepoint and down shabby New Oxford Street and into the Georgian streets of Blooms-bury. The dejection she'd felt just a few minutes ago disappeared, replaced by the exhilaration of being out alone, without a buggy to slow her down containing a passenger demanding juice and rice cakes.

Finding herself outside the British Museum she decided to go in. She'd taken Clara here to see the mummies several times; she'd go back now and enjoy some other pieces. She crossed the great domed lobby where Clara loved to charge about. A woman, coming out of the door that led to Egyptian antiquities, stood back to hold it open for her.

'Thank you,' Poppy said and then as her brain switched into gear, she exclaimed, 'Oh! Hello.'

'Hello,' said Thea Mackharven.

'What are *you* doing here?' Poppy immediately realized

this sounded rather rude. 'Sorry. I mean not that there's any reason why you shouldn't be here but . . .'

'It's not that far from work. I often come here in my lunch hour.'

'Of course,' Poppy said, then desperate to please, 'Which bit do you like best?'

That scornful look from Dean's dinner party that had scorched itself on Poppy's soul was out again in force. 'I quite like the Sumerians,' Thea said loftily.

'Oh, me too. I find it amazing that Sumeria is now Iraq. I always used to love reading about the hanging gardens of Babylon. It sounded so idyllic and now it's this dusty, messed-up country.' Poppy knew she was gushing but nerves had got the better of her. 'At least, Luke says it's dusty and messed up.'

'Mmm. Luke and I have worked in Iraq a lot.'

The way Thea said it made Poppy's insides shrivel. 'Well, nice bumping into you,' she gabbled, looking at her watch. 'Is that the time? Oh, dearie me! I'd better be off now.'

'Bye,' said Thea, as Poppy hurried out of the museum into the sunlight, wondering why that horrible woman hated her so much.

19

A week had passed. All day it had been raining torrentially. Parts of Britain were suffering from the worst flooding in centuries. But not, to Poppy's bitter disappointment, the village of Brettenden in Oxfordshire, where their school reunion was being held that night. At six sharp Meena was sitting outside Poppy's front gate in her shiny Audi, a present from her doting dad, ready to ferry her friend back to their alma mater.

'God, what took you?' she yelled when, fifteen minutes later, Poppy, sodden from running just three yards from the front door down the garden path, jumped into the car beside her. 'I've smoked at least ten fags while I've been waiting for you.'

'Sorry, sorry. Clara threw her supper all over the dress I was going to wear, so I had to get changed at the last minute.'

'Christ, I've been cacking myself,' said Meena, with her usual poetic charm. 'I'm so bloody nervous I think I'm going to have to drop a Valium.'

'I don't think that's a very good idea if you're driving,' Poppy admonished her gently, but Meena was too busy checking out Poppy's outfit to notice.

'Oh God, Poppy. I mean, you look pretty and everything like you always do, but couldn't you have worn something a bit funkier?'

'Oh.' Poppy had thought she'd looked all right in her floaty black chiffon skirt and blue cardigan. She glanced at Meena in skinny jeans and a green T-shirt. Somehow she'd got it exactly right – looking as if she hadn't made any effort while still being dazzling. Poppy, on the other hand, looked like the boring dependable mum she had become.

'Christ, I'm dreading this,' Meena squawked, scrutinizing her eye make-up in the mirror as they sped up the outside lane of the A40, rain tom-tomming on the bonnet. 'Why did you make me go, Poppy?'

'I didn't make you! You made me. I told you it would be terrifying.'

'What's the problem for you? You're married to a rich and sort-of famous man. You've got a beautiful baby. What about me? Single. Receptionist. I was meant to have it made by twenty-one.'

'Being married doesn't mean you've got it made,' Poppy said softly.

Meena glanced at her, hitting the motorway and roaring into fifth. 'Is Luke giving you grief again?'

'Well . . . he's a bit cross because I told the nanny we'd pay her twelve pounds an hour. But it was him who wanted a nanny, not me.'

'Mean git.' Meena cut in front of a white van. Poppy grasped the edges of her seat. 'He's loaded, isn't he?'

'I don't know. He keeps complaining about how broke he is with all the other children's school fees.'

'Shouldn't be sending them to posh schools then. I always told Dad he'd be better off putting the cash in the bank to buy me boob job. Or pay my dowry.'

'So what's the latest man news?' Poppy asked.

'Boring. Quiet. No City boys around at the moment; they're all trying to get their bonuses. I keep begging Mum and Dad to fix me up with this cousin of ours who's a software mogul in Bangalore, but they say arranged marriages are old-fashioned. Like I care.'

Despite the weather, it seemed no time at all before they were passing through the high gates that marked the beginning of Brettenden's long, gravel drive.

'Oh, help. I'm seriously spooked out. Turn the car round, Meena. Let's go and have a curry in Henley. I can't face this.'

'Shall I?' They were pulling up in the car park now, tyres fizzing on the wet tarmac. 'I could, couldn't I?'

'Go on.' Poppy nodded. Meena placed her hand on the gear stick but just as she was about to reverse, there was a tap on the window.

'Meena! Poppy! Hey!'

Gurning through the rain-streaked glass was a round face set off by black-rimmed spectacles. Strawberry-blonde hair in bunches. Green spotty raincoat.

'Oh, fuck me,' Meena said. 'It's Lolly Frickman. Shit, last time I saw her she was crying because she'd lost out on being Yum Yum in Mrs Grinder's production of the *Mikado*.' Lolly tapped again. Meena sighed and wound down the window. 'Lolly! God, look at you! You look *great*.'

'Thanks,' beamed Lolly, 'you too. Nice to see you, Poppy.'

'And you,' Poppy said, realizing the game was up. She

got out of the car, looked up at Brettenden's Gothic facade, shiny in the rain. 'Yuk. Return to Colditz.'

'Didn't you like BH?' Lolly was astounded.

'No, I hated it,' Poppy said, as they hurried up the wet stone steps and pushed open the vast green doors that led into the entrance hall. It still smelt of polish and pubescent sweat and its walls were still covered with green boards where the achievements of OBHs, as they were known, were set out in gold leaf. Meena and Poppy always used to giggle about them 'Greatest number of doughnuts ever consumed without licking the lips: Meena Badghabi.' 'Largest number of excuses concocted to get out of netball: Poppy Price.' Poppy turned her attention to Lolly, who, after exchanging animated boasts with Meena, was now tugging at her sleeve.

'So, Meena's an executive for the Holmes Place group. And what about you, Poppy?'

'I'm married.' A touch defensively, she added, 'Happily married.'

Lolly laughed. 'No way! You are joking aren't you?'

'No,' Poppy said as they walked in to the old assembly hall, full of screeching women. God, was that Amelia Crinch? She *must* have had a nose job. 'I've got a baby.'

'Really?' said Lolly taking a glass of white wine from a trestle table and downing it in one. 'How grown-up. I don't think I could be coping with a baby just yet. Nappies, eeeuch! And sleepless nights. No thank you.'

'It's not that bad,' Poppy said, a bit hurt she hadn't congratulated her or asked to see photos. 'What are you up to, Lolly?'

'I'm an accountant.' Lolly fiddled with one of her hair slides. 'Got a traineeship when I graduated. It's pretty amazing. I meet all sorts of interesting people and the money's great too. I've just put a deposit down on a new-build flat in Paddington.'

'I live near there! In Maida Vale.'

She didn't know why, really, because she'd never even liked Lolly who had the dubious distinction of being Brettenden House's most boring girl despite stiff competition, but it was still a bit of a blow when instead of saying, 'Oh how great, we must meet up some time', she responded, 'Oh. Right.'

'Yes,' Poppy said. She felt oddly humiliated. Her life was meant to be every woman's Holy Grail: married to a handsome, successful older man, with a beautiful daughter, a lovely home in a desirable part of London and childcare to boot. Why did people with their nine to five office jobs look at her so condescendingly? 'Must find the loo,' she mumbled, 'see if they're still as stinky as they used to be.' But as she turned on her heel, a voice cried.

'Poppy? Is that Poppy Price?'

A glamorous woman with short brown hair in a green minidress, long black boots and sporting what Poppy recognized as the latest Balenciaga bag came towards her. Poppy thought of pretending she had no idea who she was, but what would have been the point?

'Migsy Remblethorpe!' She'd been one of the coolest girls in the year, always surrounded by other cool girls who giggled at her catty put-downs and copied her outfits. Apart from asking Poppy to pass the salt a couple of times at dinner, they'd never exchanged a word. 'How are you?'

'Really well. *Really* well. It's funny to be called Migsy, I've been Michelle for years now. So what are you up to?'

'I'm a model,' Poppy said. No way was she peddling the 'mother' line again.

'Really? I thought they had to be, like, anorexic. How refreshing to see a real woman doing it.'

Perhaps she shouldn't have lied. 'Well, I *was* a model, but I've got a small child now, so . . . How about you, Migsy?'

Migsy smiled smugly. 'I work for *Wicked* magazine. Do you know it? I'm the features editor. It's so much fun. I get to travel all over the place and meet so many celebrities.'

'Oh, yes. Like who?'

'Well, tomorrow I'm going to interview Marco Jensen. You know? The gorgeous guy who reads the *SevenThirty News.*'

'He doesn't read the *SevenThirty News*! My husband does.'

'Your husband?' Migsy shouted, so loudly that the huddle next to them, including Fleur Mappleton-Wise, whose father apparently owned the whole of Northamptonshire, stopped talking and stared at them.

'Yes.' Poppy could almost feel her chest puffing up. 'His name's Luke Norton.'

'*Luke Norton?*' Migsy shrieked, so the sleek blonde heads turned again. 'What? You mean the cad?'

'I . . .'

'*You're* the Bimbo?' From the expression on her face,

you'd have thought Migsy had unearthed Lord Lucan disguised in a gymslip.

'Well . . .'

'God, Poppy, I love those columns. They're *hilarious*. And they're all about *you*. Oh my God.' A slow smile crossed her face. 'We should keep in touch. Are you on Facebook?'

'Um. No. It's not easy for me to do stuff on computers, my daughter keeps pulling the wires out.'

'Not on *Facebook*?' Migsy looked as if Poppy had admitted to a fondness for pulling down her knickers in public. 'Right. Well. Do you have a card?'

'I'm afraid not. Sorry.'

Migsy fumbled hastily in her huge green tote bag and pulled out her phone. 'Quick, what's your number?'

Poppy told her and Migsy jabbed it in.

'Great,' she said, kissing Poppy on both cheeks. 'I'll give you a call really soon. Let's go for a drink. Catch up on old times.'

'I'd like that,' Poppy said, and wondered what her life had come to that she actually meant it.

20

Shortly before Poppy and Meena set out to dazzle Brettenden, Thea was standing knee-deep in water on the village green of Fordingley, somewhere on the border of Wales and Gloucestershire. She was wearing an unflattering cagoule and mascara was streaked down her face. One hand held an umbrella over her head, the other held a mobile phone.

'Yeah, I've just sent you the package,' she was saying smugly over the noise of the drumming water to Johnny, that day's programme editor. 'Village devastated by worst floods in thirty years; people canoeing down the High Street; mother with newborn baby homeless; everyone complaining that the government knew this would happen but did nothing to intervene.'

'Excellent, Thea. And well done for getting it over to us so early. I'm well impressed.' Thea beamed. Getting a package in a whole hour before the show kicked off was quite a feat, but then she *was* superbly efficient. 'So is Marco ready to do his live?' Johnny continued. 'It's scheduled for seven oh eight.'

'Of course.'

'Is he there now? I'd like a quick word.'

'Um. He's not actually, he's just popped into the pub to use the loo.'

Actually, this wasn't quite true. Marco was in his

bedroom at the Pig and Whistle, the local pub where they were staying, probably reapplying his foundation. Thea was delighted to have a break from him. He had been a pain in the arse ever since nine that morning when he had climbed into the company Ford Galaxy, driven by George the cameraman, which was carrying the three of them to the worst-flooded village in Britain. From the minute Marco emerged from his Chiswick cottage, Thea knew the day was going to be a long one.

'Christ,' he groaned, getting into the front seat (as 'the talent' he automatically got to sit there). 'I can't believe Johnny's assigned me this story. I've got a fucking awful hangover. I was out with Jonathan and Jane last night . . .' He paused slightly. Like all namedroppers Marco never attached surnames to his famous friends because that would imply he didn't know them quite as well as he claimed. But at the same time, he had to be totally sure everyone knew who he was talking about. It was a thorny dilemma.

'Out with Jonathan and Jane,' he continued when Thea and George refused to rise to the bait. 'Bloody great laugh. Jonathan's very naughty given he has to record his talk show today, but he's such a pro—'

'Do you mean Jonathan O'Connor? Oh no, it's Des O'Connor, isn't it?' Thea grinned at George's sarcastic tone. There was no point trying to impress a cameraman, the breed were so jaded that if Kate Moss had climbed in the back naked and asked to be driven straight to the nearest five-star hotel and ravished, they would barely blink.

'Jonathan Ross, actually.' Marco could resist no longer. 'Great, great mate. Got to know him doing Sports Relief last year. Anyway, I've got this freakin' hangover, plus it's Stephanie's birthday tonight and she's bloody furious. I should be making reservations for the Ivy, not heading off to the wild west to talk to a bunch of sheep shaggers.'

'You should have made a reservation for the Ivy months ago,' said Thea. 'If you haven't done it by now, you're better off leaving town.'

'Daring, don't you know who I am?' Marco said it in a silly voice, so Thea would think he was joking. But she wasn't fooled. 'I am a celebrity, my sweetness. Able to get a table at the Ivy at the drop of a hat. I'll have to take you there some time.' There was silence. George drove steadily. Thea continued researching the story on her BlackBerry. Marco loathed the thought of nobody listening to him. 'Why couldn't someone else have covered this and I could have stayed in the nice, dry studio?'

'Because it's a really important story, Marco, and as one of our best reporters you were the natural choice to cover it,' Thea said patiently above the whine of the windscreen wipers. George was a demon driver but in these conditions even he could only manage 40mph and she was terrified the competition would get there first.

'Whatever.' Marco shrugged. 'It's bandit country where we're going. You know Fred West is from round there. Best thing that could happen to those yokels is to have them all swept away.'

Determined not to rise to the bait, Thea was relieved to hear her phone ring. 'Hello, Thea Mackharven. Oh, hello, Mrs Emory. Yes. A *SevenThirty News* team is on its way to Fordingley now and as chairwoman of the village association we'd love to interview you . . . it'll be Marco Jensen. Yes, I know! . . . Well, he can't wait to meet you either . . . Did you like Emma's necklace on yesterday's show? . . . Of course, I'll pass the compliment on.' She hung up, happy, having persuaded Mrs Emory to find her a homeless mother of a newborn baby to speak exclusively to Marco.

'I still can't believe this is getting such attention,' Marco whined on like a particularly persistent mosquito. 'Do we *have* to stay the night?'

'Yup. Until the rains abate Dean says he wants us there.'

'Christ. It'll probably be like Noah's flood, forty days of it, to punish the peasants for sheep rustling and incest.'

'So where are we staying, Thea?' George interrupted. He was a man of few words but his question was vital. 'Does it have a bar?'

'I would imagine so. It's rooms in the pub.'

'Rooms in a pub!' Marco exclaimed in horror as George cried, 'Nice one.' It was the same with all cameramen. No matter how important the story or exotic the location they were in their priority was always the bar. Nine Eleven: great, New York hotels have fantastic bars. Diana's funeral: will we be able to slip away and get to the bar? Saddam Hussein's execution: Iraq better than many Muslim countries for availability of alcohol. First daytrip to the moon, news teams invited. Fine, but will the bar be open?

Of course once they'd arrived in Fordingley it had been an entirely different story. George had been efficiency itself, while Marco had charmed Mrs Emory with auto-graphs and exclamations that she didn't look a day over forty-five. He'd blown raspberries at the homeless mother's baby. Thea watched in grudging admiration. Just like Luke, he'd got whatever it took to charm serpents down from trees. It was a source of much irritation among all producers that the 'talent', aka the presenters, got paid so much more than them. But wielding their charm, they could wheedle the devil into unlocking the gates of hell.

Now Marco was shaking his head sympathetically as Mr Willis of the village council complained how they'd lobbied for years for effective flood barriers but nobody in power cared.

'Though it's a bit different this time what with the election coming up,' he added. 'I would have thought some of the bigwigs might have wanted to suck up to us, but it seems even the thought of winning our votes isn't enough to swing it.'

'Politicians. What do they know?' Marco said, shaking his head.

'I think he was confusing me with someone who actu-ally gave a fuck,' he sniggered an hour later as they sat on the lumpy double bed in Thea's room at the Pig and Whistle. They'd spent the past two hours putting the package together, a process that involved editing the footage and Marco doing a voiceover. All that was needed now was the 'live', which would take place once the show was on air, when Luke – via satellite link – would ask Marco, standing in the wettest possible corner of the village, for an update on the situation.

'All done,' he said briskly, after viewing the package

for the second time. 'Nice work. I'm going to phone Stephanie and then I'll have a quick kip. See you later.'

'Be back at the village green at six fifteen,' Thea warned him as he headed to the door.

'Six fifteen? Don't be silly, that's miles too early. I'll be there for six thirty.'

'Six fifteen, Marco.'

'To stand around in the rain for an hour? What for?'

Thea smiled sweetly. 'Marco, in these conditions all sorts of technical things could go wrong. Six fifteen.'

'Whatever.' He shut the door just a little too loudly behind him. Thea stared at it with dislike. When she'd left for the States, Marco had been an eager beaver, volunteering to work weekends, Christmas day, bank holidays and his mother's funeral in order to get a leg-up the ladder. Now he did the occasional presenting he'd transmuted into a prima donna who'd give Mariah Carey a run for her money. Once again, Thea was struck by a wave of weariness. Not so long ago she'd adored this life: the never knowing where she might end up that night, the challenge of getting the right interviewees, even the arguments with the reporters. Yet increasingly, she was thinking she'd seen and done it all before. She was turning into George – minus the beer belly and the rather dubious Clark Gable 'tache. But where did you go from the best job in the world? Anything else would be a come down.

Perhaps she should book a holiday. Have something to look forward to. Egypt could be good this time of year; she could do some diving. Only a year ago, she'd have called Rachel and asked if she fancied a break, but now of course that was impossible. Thea was going to be one of those women people pitied who ate dinner alone with a book and had to wear a wedding ring to fend off the attentions of amorous waiters wanting a British passport. Still, too bad. She'd always wanted to see the sphinx and pyramids. The thought of ancient Egypt took her mind back to the bimbo and bumping into her in the British Museum the other day. Thea often went there when she wanted a break from the office, but finding Poppy Norton there had seemed about as likely as stumbling across Paris Hilton at a brain surgeon's convention.

Thea wondered how on earth she filled her days. Dean had mentioned in passing that she'd hired his nanny, so she didn't even have to look after her child any more. How could any woman stand not to have a career? It was a concept as far removed from Thea's understanding as women who had little pictures of ponies painted on their nails or wore jeans endorsed by Victoria Beckham. Mind you, the bimbo probably did both of those things. How could she have wasted so much time on a man who liked that kind of thing? Thea berated herself, slamming shut her laptop. Thank God, she had finally seen the light.

No point sitting brooding in this dingy room. She pulled on her rainwear and went down to the bar, where, sure enough, George was nursing a pint and chatting up the barmaid.

'Sorry to break this up, but it's time to get down to the village green and set up for the live.'

'Okey-dokey.' George downed his pint in one. 'Truth be told I was getting a bit paranoid in here, Thea. Everyone else is still working. It's making me nervous, as if we're missing something.'

'We're not missing anything, we're just super-efficient,' she replied. 'But that's why we want to set up now, in plenty of time.'

It was just a five-minute wet walk from the hotel to the village green, hidden under three feet of water. All the other networks were already in place: the BBC, Sky, ITN, Channel 4. Thea waved at them, as she and George splashed towards the corner they had designated as theirs.

'It's twenty past six,' George warned her once everything was in place. 'Shouldn't Marco be here by now?'

'Yes, he bloody should,' Thea said. 'I told him six fifteen, but I'm sure he's on his way. He's just got a few sweet nothings to whisper down the phone to his girlfriend.'

'Maybe you should raise him.'

'I will, I'll call him.'

But Marco's phone went straight to voicemail. Thea left a message telling him to hurry up, then continued checking everything was in place. Five minutes later, she called again. Five minutes later, a third time.

'Fucking hell, he's cutting it fine.'

'He's only a five-minute walk away,' Thea said, determined not to reveal how much she was inwardly fuming. 'If he doesn't turn up by six forty-five I'll just run to the pub and physically drag him here.'

As she spoke, there was a shout from behind them. Thea whipped her head round and her jaw dropped like a cartoon character's. Just a few yards behind them stood the prime minister wearing waders. A small team of minders stood round him as he held both Mr Willis's hands in his and listened to his concerns.

'Fuck! What the hell is he doing here?'

'Making a frigging flying visit,' George said, picking up his camera and starting to wade towards him. 'Shit, look. Everyone's descending on him.'

Sure enough, all the other teams were splashing across the green, brandishing cameras and waving microphones in a race to be first to talk to the main man.

'Buggeroony!' Thea yelped. All right, her home hadn't disappeared under five feet of water, but in her eyes this was still a disaster. When the prime minister appeared it was a chance for the reporter to tackle him fiercely about how and why the government had managed so spectacularly to cock up. It was the kind of thing that gave a programme its reputation – the knowledge that its reporters weren't afraid to ask frank and fearless questions. But if Marco wasn't there, then there was nothing she could do. She jabbed at his number, but the phone was still switching to voicemail. 'Shit, shit, shit. This is a nightmare,' she hissed. Francesca Broome from Sky had her bloody microphone under the Prime Minister's nose and was nodding energetically.

'. . . appalled at the situation here. Promising a full aid package and an enquiry . . .'

Thea's phone started ringing. 'Marco!' she yelled.

'No, this is not fucking Marco, it's Dean. Where *is* Marco? We can't see him anywhere.'

Shit. That was the problem with bloody Sky. It ran 24/7 in the office, so whenever you were out on a job with the pack, which was more than 90 per cent of the time, your bosses could easily keep an eye on you.

'Marco's gone AWOL,' Thea snapped at Dean. 'We're trying to raise him.'

'A professional like Marco? Not like him not to be on the spot.'

'He'll be here any second.' Thea hung up and grabbed the arm of a skinny young man she took to be a press officer. 'What the hell is going on? Why didn't anyone warn us the PM was coming?'

'It was meant to be a surprise visit. We knew you'd all be here anyway.'

'Shit!' This was hideously embarrassing. They couldn't have all the other news networks tackling the PM and nothing on Channel 6. It would look ridiculous. Heads would roll.

'Will he be having a word with all of us?' she asked the press officer, as Lola Brindleman from the BBC stood forward to take her turn.

'Of course. But he's only going to be here for the next ten minutes. The helicopter's waiting to take him to Brize Norton, then he's flying straight to Germany for a banquet with the heads of the EU.'

'Marco,' Thea hissed into his voicemail for the fourth time, 'where the hell are you? Bloody hurry up.'

'I'm sorry,' the press officer said, 'he's really got to go now.'

'OK, OK! I'll do the interview!' Fumbling with the microphone, Thea stepped forward. 'Prime Minister, Thea Mackharven, *SevenThirty News*.'

Seeing her sodden hair and streaked mascara, the prime minister took a nervous step backwards.

'Just wondering how the government can possibly justify introducing this aid package so late. After all, this is the third time in three years this area has flooded.'

George was a pro. He kept the camera steadily focused on the prime minister's face, as – despite his alarm at being accosted by a mad gypsy woman who might try to pin some lucky heather to his lapel – he still smoothly spun out the usual array of platitudes.

'Thea!' shouted a voice behind them. Thea glanced over her shoulder. Marco was galumphing towards them, the collar of his raincoat turned up so he looked like a glamorous private eye.

'It's OK, Marco's here,' she said to the press officer. 'Quick, can we do it just one more time with him asking the questions?'

'No, no, sorry. Got to go now.' And the prime minister was ushered away to dry land in a flurry of crackling radios.

'Where the fuck have you been?' Thea yelled.

'You know where I've been. In the hotel. Why the fuck didn't you raise me?'

'I *did* raise you. I've been calling and calling.'

'No you haven't.' But Marco's face made it clear he was lying. He'd bloody been on the phone to Stephanie and had been ignoring the bleep of his call waiting. Thea knew better than actually to tell him he was a liar.

'Whatever. You should have been here already.'

'You told me I didn't have to get here until six forty-five.'

Thea stared at him coldly. 'No, I didn't,' she said with slow deliberation. 'I said six fifteen.'

'You said six forty-five.' They eyed each other like two dogs about to go for each other's throats. Marco was going to lie, Thea realized with a pang. The shit was going to hit the fan and Marco was going to make out it was all her fault.

Already her phone was ringing. Recriminations had begun.

'Thea!' said Dean's voice menacingly. 'What the fuck has been going on?'

Dean wasn't just angry. He was livid, furious, choleric, enraged, incensed, riled, splenetic or – as he put it – 'Fucking pissed off!'

'I am about as happy as a rhinoceros on a date with a big-game hunter. Last night's cock-up was inexcusable. We looked like total tits in front of all the other networks.'

Jammed into his office for morning conference, the staff of the *SevenThirty News* looked at their feet, their fingernails, anywhere but at Thea.

Dean lifted his finger and pointed like a Roman emperor ordering the lions to be let loose on the Christians. 'Thea! You were responsible for this lumpen turd. I'd sack you if I could, but Roxanne says I've got to give you an official warning first. So here you go, Thea, you are officially warned. Fuck up again and you swim with the fishes.'

There was an uncomfortable silence.

'OK,' Thea said eventually. She looked meaningfully at Marco, still hoping despite herself he might shoulder just a milligram of the blame, but he was staring into space. Only his left foot twitching in his Prada loafers hinted that he might be experiencing even a smidgeon of guilt.

'Good.' Dean turned to that day's programme editor. 'Sunil! I want tonight's show improved fifteen trillion per cent. And I want the Cancer Dad.'

'Excuse me?' Sunil Syal pushed his glasses up his sweaty nose.

'Get with the programme! The fucking Cancer Dad. It's page five in today's *Express*. He's a single father of three, because his wife died in childbirth with twins and he's just been diagnosed with terminal lung cancer. Having never smoked. Isn't that great? We need to get an interview with him.'

'Oh the *Cancer Dad*. Of course. Rhys is on the case already. *Aren't you*, Rhys?'

'No. I —' A look from Sunil silenced him. Fortunately, Dean didn't notice so carried away was he with his vision.

'We want him weeping; all the kids round him, their little faces distorted with grief. It'll be great.'

'No worries,' Rhys gabbled.

'It's still not enough,' Dean warned them all. 'I'm looking for something extra special. Thea, I can't have you horsewhipped, unfortunately, but I'm going to look into buying a rack to spreadeagle you on. I brought you back from the States because I thought you were talented. So after last night's cock-up I am going to be looking for a super-duper scoop from you and I don't mean of dog poop. A revelation that brings the government down. Or better . . . a showbiz exclusive. An interview with Tom Cruise where he confesses he's really a woman. Elvis revealed to be working as a lift operator in Harrod's. Prince Philip admitting he murdered Princess Diana. In other words, something really fucking special. Capeesh?'

'No problem,' Thea said, as smooth as a duck pond on a windless day.

Inside, however, she was a raft on the Atlantic tossed

by a force-ten gale. Thea had never had such a public dressing-down. The injustice of it all made her want to throw something hard against a wall. All the way back to London the previous night (Dean had ordered them home for the inquest) they'd argued about who'd been at fault. Marco had simply denied she'd asked him to be in place for six fifteen. It was his word against hers and she was merely the producer, while Marco was the talent. And, as all behind-the-scenes players knew, the talent always got the benefit of the doubt. Channel 6 might miss Thea if she left, but the outside world would know nothing about it. If Marco departed Women's Institutes across the land would commit mass suicide. She could do nothing, just repeatedly tell herself she'd been in the right.

What made things worse was that no one outside the news industry would ever understand what all the fuss was about. After all, the package had run smoothly. Marco had still been in place for the 'live' to the studio, in fact the only element that had been dodgy had been the interview with the PM. They'd still managed to drop it in as an extra half minute of 'breaking news since we came on air' but while the other networks all had a slot where their reporters ferociously grilled him for his government's lack of foresight and not caring about the country-side, *SevenThirty News* viewers had just got thirty seconds of footage of bland remarks about how this was a terrible disaster and the government would do its utmost to help. Either way, Thea knew, it wasn't going to change the history of journalism, but in offices where they prided themselves on perfection, it was an almighty cock-up.

Having been dismissed, she returned to her desk, head

held high, back straight. Everyone was avoiding her gaze. She stared at her screen, unable to focus because of the tears swimming in her eyes. Find a scoop. Yes, fine, Dean, she'd just order one on the internet. She needed a sympathetic ear. Picking up her phone she dialled Rachel.

'Hi, I'm busy right now. If you—'

Thea hung up and dialled Dumberley.

'Dumberley, *six* nine *oh* two seven.'

'Hi, Mum, it's me.'

'Thea?' Jan sounded thrilled, but then an anxious note crept in. 'Won't you get in trouble calling from work?'

'No, it's fine.' She paused, wanting to tell her mother how bruised she felt, but – as always – wanting to protect her feelings. 'How are you?'

'Really well. Are you watching that Andrew Lloyd Webber show? All competing for parts in his musical. Oh, Thea, it's marvellous. They're all so good, I don't know who to single out, though if I was forced to choose . . .'

Thea was overwhelmed with an unexpected rush of affection. 'Would you like me to book you tickets for the show? We could go together. You could come up to London and stay the night.'

'Oh, thank you, darling, but no thanks. Who would cook Trevor's tea?'

'Can't he microwave it for once?' Thea felt very alone. Gran would have understood. She sensed a presence behind her. She glanced round to see Luke.

'Hi,' he said.

Her face turned terracotta. 'Hi,' she mouthed, then, 'Just a minute.' She turned back to the phone, cutting her mother off mid-sentence. 'Mum, Mum, I'm really sorry, but I've got to go. Work problem. I just wanted to check you were OK. I'll call you soon . . . Yes . . . Great . . . all right, see you then. *Bye!*' She hung up and tried to smile.

'So,' he said, 'how are you doing?'

'Fine, thanks. You?'

'Great.' Luke smiled, then lowered his voice. 'That was out of order. Dean's an arsehole. He completely overreacted.'

Thea smiled faintly. 'Thanks, Luke.'

'Well, it's true.' Luke looked at her. Direct eye contact. Thea felt like butter being spread on hot toast. 'Look,' he said under his breath, 'everyone knows that that little prat Jensen landed you in it. George is putting the word about. Don't worry; it'll get back to Dean quickly enough. In any case, how about a drink tonight?'

Thea's stomach swooped, like when she skied a black run. She'd often fantasized about this moment, how she would turn Luke down flat, tell him she was too busy eloping with Sir Trevor McDonald. But now the moment had arrived all she could come out with was. 'I . . . ah . . .'

Luke started to move away. 'If you're busy don't worry.'

'No! I'm not busy!' she said, just as Rhys appeared behind him. 'That would be great.'

'Don't let the bastards grind you down. See you later, then. And sod the idea of a drink, let's make it dinner.' He walked off. For a second, Thea stared after him, then said, 'Hi, Rhys. What can I do for you?'

'Um, sorry about what happened to you.'

'That's OK.' Thea couldn't stand it. A GA who'd been learning his five times table when she was jetting round the world getting exclusives on the Taliban was feeling sorry for her.

'I had an idea. For a possible big interview.'

'Oh, yeah?'

'Yeah. I was wondering about Minnie Maltravers.'

Thea smiled politely, deeply unimpressed at the unoriginality of the suggestion. Minnie Maltravers was a forty-something supermodel turned all-round phenomenon. She was famous mainly for three things: being gorgeous, being angry and being very, very late for everything. She was American, from humble origins, who'd risen to fame in the eighties, spent most of the nineties having a drug problem and most of the noughties in rehab. Now she was sober, married to a British film director called Max Williams and lived in a castle in Scotland and little was heard of her, apart from the occasional court case when a maid or whoever would sue her for wrongful dismissal among tearful tales of how Minnie had thrown a fax machine at her. Everyone was fascinated by Minnie, everyone would love to watch an interview with her, there was just one problem . . .

'Rhys, you know Minnie never gives interviews. That's the whole point of her. Her mystique.'

'Yes, but' – Rhys proffered a print-out – 'I saw this tiny piece on the news wires. Apparently, she's about to go to Guatemala on a charity visit. I thought maybe we could tie something in with that. Even if she only talks about her charity work it would be getting Minnie Maltravers to *talk* and that would be something.'

Slowly, Thea took the piece of paper. 'Guatemala, you say?'

'That's right.' Thea read the brief print-out from Reuters.

Guatemala City

There was excitement this morning as rumours spread that supermodel Minnie Maltravers is planning a visit in association with the charity Guatemala Children to open a new health clinic and visit some orphanages and children's centres . . .

'You have email,' her computer trilled. She glanced at the screen. 'Luke Norton'. He'd written in the header field:

Booked Wolseley for 8.30. Looking forward to catching up x.

Glancing anxiously at Rhys as if she were browsing nude pictures of Justin Timberlake, Thea pressed delete.

'So what do you think?' Rhys asked.

'I think there could be something in this,' Thea said calmly. 'I've got a contact at Guatemala Children. I'll give him a call.'

'You don't want me to do it?' Rhys was disappointed.

'No thanks. It's *my* contact. In fact he'd already hinted to me this could be a way to Minnie.' Thea ignored the look of disbelief on Rhys's face. She felt a bit ashamed, after all, he'd made a good spot and was entitled to want to run with it, but after how Marco had stabbed her in the back she wasn't feeling charitable towards anyone. 'It probably won't lead to anything, but it's worth a shot.' A beat and then, 'Good work, Rhys.'

'Thanks.' As Rhys moved off dispiritedly, Thea – knowing it would take too long to sift through her bag – googled Guatemala Children. It was a number beginning 7485, which meant Camden Town. Rapidly, she dialled.

'Hello? Yes. Jake Kaplan please.'

As she waited to be put through, she typed an email.

Afraid can't make tonight. Urgent work thing. Sorry. Another time.

As she pressed send, regret crashed over her. Quickly, she pressed a mental button and her emotional portcullis came down. Luke had got to her in a moment of vulnerability. She should never have said yes to him. She wouldn't do it again. It was all long over between them and Thea was not going to look back.

22

Jake didn't sound surprised to hear from Thea, but he did sound quite pleased.

'Sorry I was so brusque when you called the other day,' she said. 'We were coming up to deadline and it was a bit tense. I'd love to meet soon if you're free.'

He laughed. 'So you've heard about Minnie?'

'Minnie who?' Thea tried to sound innocent.

'Minnie Maltravers. There was some tiny mention on her website about her going out to Guatemala with us. Popped up five minutes ago and since then the phones haven't stopped ringing.'

'Is that what you wanted to talk to me about?' Thea asked.

'I told you I had a hot story.'

'I believed you,' she lied. 'I was just so busy I didn't see how we could meet. But, like I say, if you're still up for it . . .'

Jake sighed teasingly. 'How do you know I didn't give the story to the BBC? Or ITN? Or Sky?'

There were all the people gossiping about Channel 6's failure to knobble the PM. 'Did the BBC or ITN or Sky ask if you'd like to have dinner at a restaurant of your choice to discuss the story?' Thea tried.

There was a brief pause, then Jake said, 'You're lucky, Thea, for some reason I decided to hold on to the story until things were a bit firmer, so it's still up for grabs. But I may be too busy for dinner now. Things are crazy here today and they're not going to get any quieter. And I'm back off to Guatemala bright and early tomorrow morning.'

'You have to eat!' Thea yelped. 'Just a quick bite tonight while you fill me in.'

'Oh well, if I must,' Jake said cheerily.

'Good,' Thea said after just the tiniest pause. She was right, Jake definitely fancied her. Which was odd, given he was so much younger than her. And too short. Still, if it led her to Minnie Maltravers she wasn't complaining. 'Where would you like to go?' she asked. 'Gordon Ramsay at Claridge's? Locanda Locatelli?'

He laughed. 'Both if possible. And maybe the Savoy Grill as well? We could have a course in each.'

'Um . . .' That wouldn't go down too well with Foxy Roxy.

'I'm joking. Don't worry about the fancy meal. I'm going to be working late. I wouldn't have time to do it justice. There's a good gastropub round the corner from my office. Why don't we go there? Save me the schlep into town.'

'No problem,' said Thea, a thought formulating in her mind that she could treat someone else – say her mother if she could persuade her to come up to town – to a meal at Gordon Ramsay and then expense it as wooing Guatemala Children. Everybody did it.

At half past eight, Thea pushed open the door of the Sceptre and Pony in Camden Town. She'd been a bit miffed at how easily Luke had responded to her cancelling their dinner, with a brief, emailed: 'No worries, another time'. But it was for the best, she reprimanded herself. She was not to go running after Luke again just because she'd had a bad day at work. He was as over as cheques, as telephone boxes, as puffball skirts – oh, not puffball skirts, they'd made a comeback recently. Well, anyway, he was over.

Jake was sitting at a corner table, a pint of Guinness in front of him, poring over an orange file. As he saw her approach, he stood up. She'd forgotten how short he was.

'Hey!' he said. There was an awkward moment when they both wondered if they should kiss, then both decided they shouldn't. 'How are you? Can I get you a drink?'

'I'll get them,' she said and was vaguely annoyed when he said, 'Oh, OK, thanks.' Weren't men supposed to say, 'No, no, let me.' But this wasn't a date, she reminded herself. She was here to woo him and, infuriating as it was, he held all the cards.

'Thanks,' he said again when she returned from the bar with a large glass of Barolo for her and another Guinness for him. 'It's been a bit of a day as you can imagine. One tiny item about Minnie going to Guatemala and it all goes beserk. The phones have rung more in one afternoon than they have in the past year.'

'So *is* she going?' Thea asked, trying and totally failing to make it sound like a casual comment about the weather.

Jake smiled. 'I couldn't possibly comment.'

'You mean she is?' Thea leant forward.

'Maybe,' Jake said. They both eyed each other, working out who was going to crack first and fill the silence. Time for another tactic.

'How's your mum?'

Jake grimaced. 'Not making a miracle recovery, shall we say. How about your gran?'

'The same.'

'It's crap, isn't it?'

'To echo your eloquence: it's a sack of shit.'

They grinned at each other.

Jake gestured at the blackboard.

'Maybe we should order some food?'

It took half a bottle of red wine and most of two rare ribeye steaks and chips before Thea could bring herself to acknowledge that Jake might be young and small, but he was still quite good value.

'I checked your website,' she said. 'It said you're an artist liaison officer, whatever the hell that means.'

He dipped one of his chips in a pool of ketchup. 'Every charity worth its salt these days has a celebrity division. I'm head of ours. It's our job to massage the egos of stars who want to do a little *charidee* work.'

'To enhance their profiles?'

'How cynical!' Jake waggled a Roger-Moore-type eyebrow at her. 'Maybe they're genuinely motivated by a desire to help the poor and needy.'

'Yes, I'm sure.'

'You journalists. Why can't you ever believe anything good about anyone?' He grinned as he popped a cherry tomato in his mouth. 'It's a tricky one. They need us to boost their images; we need them even more, but so often it backfires. When I worked for World Hunger we took a film star out to Malawi who insisted on staying in a five-star hotel and flying first class. She drank the mini bar dry, then freaked out at all the flies and squalor and refused to do a photoshoot with a starving child in case she caught something. It cost us thousands of pounds and we got bugger-all back in return.'

'Who was that?'

He shrugged and made a zipping motion over his mouth. Fair enough. Anyway, Thea knew it was Justina Maguire: everyone had had a laugh about it at the time. PRs were so naive, thinking they could keep a lid on gossip like that. 'What were you doing before all the charity stuff?' she asked.

'I started off at ParaShoot,' he said, naming one of the biggest celebrity PRs in town. 'But the work was so vacuous I moved to World Hunger and then to Guatemala Children.'

'Are you religious?' Thea was genuinely curious.

When he laughed you could see Jake's tonsils. 'No. Do you need to be religious to want to help people?'

'Not many people do something for nothing.'

'Cynical, again! I get paid. Just not as much as in my old job. And I'm happier now.' He looked at Thea. He had nice eyes, humorous ones, but there was a directness to them she found oddly unsettling. 'Are *you* happy?'

It was as if he'd asked her if she used vaginal deodorant. Thea felt prickles zigzag along her hairline. 'What an incredibly personal question.' She paused for a second, then snapped, 'Of course I am. As happy as anyone is.'

'Good,' Jake said. 'Just wondering. Do you have a boyfriend?'

An image of Luke flashed up in Thea's head, like an annoying pop-up on a website. Mentally, she pressed the 'close' button. 'Are boyfriends the key to happiness?' she asked. 'Do you have a girlfriend?'

He looked her straight in the eye. 'No, I'm single. For now.'

'And so am I,' she said, irritated by the 'for now'. Presumptuous little so and so! 'I'm getting sick of being treated as if I've got some terminal disease. I like the way I am. I love my job. I love travelling. I love knowing I can get on a plane in the next hour and wake up the following morning anywhere in the world. If you have a boyfriend you can't do that kind of thing.' Unless your boyfriend does it too, she thought, then gulped some more wine.

'What happens when you get old though?' Usually people sounded critical of Thea's footloose approach to life. But Jake's tone was merely curious.

'You can't spend your life worrying about getting old.' Thea realized she was drunk. God, in the old days half a bottle of red would have just been the warm-up act before getting seriously stuck in. What was happening to her? 'Sorry, what was I saying? Oh yeah. You can't worry about getting old. Well, not much anyway. You have to live in the moment.'

'I agree,' Jake said.

'Really?'

'Yeah.' He took a gulp of wine. 'After what happened to Mum, you have to think that way. She was so active, so busy, enjoying life when – wham! – her brain starts to wither and within months she's the living dead. That's why I packed in ParaShoot. Life was just too short to waste promoting the winner of *I'm a Celebrity*'s auto-biography. I had to seize the day.'

'To seizing the day,' Thea cried, raising her glass.

'Seizing the day!' They clinked.

'Ahem,' said the waitress, plonking the bill in front of Jake.

Thea looked at her watch. 'Jesus, it's nearly midnight.'

Jake laughed. 'And I've got to be at the airport at six.'

'And you still haven't told me what's going on with Minnie,' Thea slurred.

'Are you drunk?'

'Cheeky! I'm . . . relaxed.'

'If you say so.' He smiled. 'OK, I'll put you out of your misery. Minnie *is* going to Guatemala to do some work for us. I think you should send out a team to cover her visit.'

'Will she give us an interview?' Thea said.

'I very much doubt it,' he said, 'but you never know. And if you're not there you won't get it.'

'We can't spend a huge chunk of budget sending a team off to Guatemala on the off-chance Minnie talks to us. I need a guarantee.' Crossly Thea jabbed her pin number into the waitress's machine. She felt as if she'd just indulged in a long foreplay session only to be denied the climax.

'I can't give you a guarantee, Thea. I'd be lying.' Jake held out his hands. 'Wasn't that what we were just talking about? Was it Abraham Lincoln who said there are no certainties in life, just death and taxes?'

'I think it was actually Cliff Richard. No, it was Benjamin Franklin.'

'Know it all.' He scratched his head. 'Look, I can't say

too much at this point but a big news story may come out of this and Minnie may decide to talk to someone. If the *SevenThirty News* has a team in place then I will do my best to make sure that someone is you. I can't say more at this stage, I'm sorry.'

'All right,' Thea said sulkily. She stood up. 'I'm going to get a cab. What about you?'

'Bus for me. Charity worker, you know.' Jake pushed open the door, dousing them with a sobering blast of fresh air.

'Look, there's a cab with its light on.' Thea waved frantically. As it stopped she turned to face him.

'Well, good to see you,' she said. 'I'll talk to the powers that be about sending a team out, though if you can't promise me anything, I can't promise you.'

'I'm not trying to con you. Minnie is going to go to Guatemala City very soon and you'll be grateful to me if you have your boys in place.'

'I'll see what I can do.'

'And I will too.'

They both looked at each other for a second, then he leant forward and standing slightly on tiptoe kissed her on the cheek.

'Safe journey,' she said. 'I've got your numbers; I'll keep you posted.'

'Ditto,' he said, then paused. 'Maybe I'll see you when I get back.'

'Maybe,' she said, climbing into the taxi. 'If you get us an interview.'

He laughed and shut the door for her. As the cab pulled away, she turned round to see him waving. Tentatively she waved back. And smiled. Something felt weird. It took her a second or two to realize it was the unfamiliar sensation of having enjoyed herself.

An Open Letter to Carla Bryonne from Hannah Creighton who knows just how it feels to have a straying husband

When HANNAH CREIGHTON read about the marital difficulties of WAG Carla Bryonne this week after her former PA Gloria Wilkins alleged that her husband, England and Arsenal striker Duane Bryonne, had had a string of affairs, she felt a tug of sympathy. Here, as one neglected wife to another, she offers Carla some moral support.

Dear Carla

When I read about the pain Duane has allegedly put you through these past few weeks, I felt touched to the soul. Your travails brought back the agony of my own marriage breakdown.

If what I read is the truth, then your husband is an unpleasant, vain philanderer with utter control over you. You feel weak, ugly: used goods. Duane, I would guess, knows how desperately you want him to stay and I suspect he's loving this power.

The sordid tales of your former PA Gloria Wilkins must have shattered your confidence. Your husband's behaviour is said to have left you a physical and emotional ruin. I feel for you because I've been there. My husband, *SevenThirty News* anchorman Luke Norton, cheated on me God knows how many times during our eighteen-year marriage before eventually leaving me and his three children for his 22-year-old pregnant girlfriend, known to my nearest and dearest as 'the Bimbo'.

The first time I discovered my husband was playing away, I
– like you – had just had my third baby. My self-worth was at
an all-time low as I struggled to lose the baby weight and to
leave the house without pieces of mashed banana clinging to
my hair. No wonder my husband didn't want me, I thought.
My heart palpitated, my breathing was out of control. I felt as
if I was losing my mind.

It is the toughest thing imaginable to discover that the man
who is supposed to be your lover and protector has betrayed
you. It's even tougher when you think about all those times
you confronted him only to be told that you were ridiculous,
paranoid, that you'd imagined it all. Did Duane call you neur-
otic? Did he tell you you were so delusional he was inclined
to dump you anyway? In public you've continued to assert that
you believe in Duane, but in private you must at least suspect
he has been unfaithful.

Yet, if you're anything like me a piece of you will still
stubbornly cling to the belief that he is telling the truth. I
tackled Luke so many times over his affairs, only to be met
with angry denials. Like you, I found myself humiliated into
looking for hard evidence just so I could know I wasn't going
mad. Having to sneakily read your husband's text messages
makes you feel like the lowest of the low.

For years I too stood by my husband. Unlike you, I didn't
even have a job. I had given up work to concentrate on raising
my family and I didn't know how I would be able to make a
go of things financially without him. But finally the discovery
of an email made it impossible to avoid the truth any more.
When I learned he'd knocked up the little floozy, I had no
choice but to kick him out. And do you know what? I survived
– though admittedly at times it was touch and go – by focusing

on my own well-being and by starting to work again. Today, I am more confident and happier than I ever have been. I have a great new boyfriend and relations with my ex are cordial, if cool.

Carla, I know what hell you are going through. As one woman to another, I urge you to distance yourself from Duane and find strength from friends and family members. Concentrate on *your* career as a tracksuit designer. Have some nights out with the girls.

However hard you may find it, you *must* find out if Duane has strayed. Call those involved yourself. What you hear may be unbearably painful but it may also set you free, because the ball will be in your court as to whether to continue with your marriage or not.

You have a long life to look forward to overflowing with adventures and promise. You have your beautiful children. But if you carry on behaving like an ostrich, it may mean the end of not only your marriage but also your sanity. And, believe me, no man is worth that.

Thinking of you
Hannah Creighton

23

Time was dragging for Poppy. With Brigita coming four days a week, she quite simply had nothing to do. It was a catch-22 situation: until she had childcare she couldn't work, but until some work materialized she had to pay someone to look after her daughter (well, OK, technically Luke had to pay, but what was his was hers) when she would have preferred to be doing it herself.

She knew Luke had hoped by employing a nanny they'd eventually be earning more money, but in the short term their expenditure went up. To get back in shape for modelling Poppy joined the Harbour Club just up the road where she managed to eke out her days doing slow lengths of the pool, drinking smoothies in the bar and leafing through old copies of *OK!* magazine. The place, after all, was full of other bored mothers who sat in huddles bitching about their lazy housekeepers and swapping tips on holiday destinations with kids' clubs. But, as usual, they were all at least ten years older than Poppy and she knew she'd have nothing to say to them, so she watched them timidly out of the corner of her eye, while reading about Lindsay Lohan's new boyfriend.

She spent a lot of time cooking elaborate meals for Luke, but she always burnt them or put in too much sugar or too little salt. When she apologized, he'd shrug and say it was OK, he wasn't very hungry anyway and the rest of the meal would be eaten in silence.

Luke grunted. Poppy cleared up the plates in silence, watched a bit of television and went to bed early.

'Are you all right?' Poppy asked after a couple of nights of this.

'I'm fine,' he replied unconvincingly. 'Work is stressful. The shareholders are putting on pressure to bump up the viewing figures. Give the channel a more youthful image.'

'What does that mean?'

'It means,' Luke snapped, 'that my job is on the line. I'm over fifty and the channel wants viewers who don't know who Adolf Hitler was. They want to watch baby faces like that hairdresser Marco Jensen.'

'Oh, yes,' Poppy said unthinkingly. 'Someone I saw at the school reunion works for *Wicked* magazine. She was off to interview Marco.'

Even as she finished the sentence, she saw Luke's face turn purple. 'See, that is typical of the way things are going at the moment. It's all about who looks like they belong in a boyband, not about who's got experience.'

'Clara sat on the potty today.' Poppy tried to change the subject. 'Brigita says she's doing really well.'

She wanted to make a cake for Clara's second birthday, but when Brigita caught her digging around for scales and a mixing bowl in the kitchen, she was outraged.

'That's my job, Mummy. You sit back. Relax.'

The cake Brigita made in the form of a chocolate hedgehog with flakes for prickles and cherries for eyes was much nicer than anything Poppy could have created.

Brigita invited some of her nanny friends and their charges over for a birthday tea and, as usual, Poppy hovered on the edges of the group not knowing quite who to talk to and feeling vaguely resentful at having to share her daughter's special day with strangers.

She was so bored she even resorted to looking at the link her mother had sent her for Jean-Claude. She found a video clip of a tall, white-haired, self-consciously groovy man in his late thirties giving a lecture on 'Roland Barthes: from Phenomenology to Deconstruction'. Poppy wasn't exactly sure what he'd have in common with a woman whose favourite read of all time was *Flowers in the Attic*, but Poppy's was not to reason why.

Louise had called her when she was stuck in traffic on the M27 to tell her the latest news.

'He didn't get back to me, so I called him. He was ever so surprised to hear from me, but he said he'd take me out for dinner next time he's in London.'

'And when will that be?' Poppy said teasingly.

'He didn't say. But it's not a problem because I've decided to go on a spa weekend to Marseilles at the end of the month and surprise him, so we can have dinner there.'

It was a relief when, on Thursday morning, Michelle née Migsy Remblethorpe rang.

'Hi!' said Poppy, as obsequiously as Jonathan Ross greeting Madonna. 'How *are* you?'

'Fine. How are you? I thought of you because I've just been reading Hannah Creighton's article about Carla Bryonne. It's savage, isn't it? I felt for you. Everyone at work's talking about it, saying how awful it must be to be publicly known as "The Bimbo".'

'I haven't read it,' Poppy said, feeling slightly sick.

'Haven't you? Oh well, don't, that's my advice. It's so gratuitously nasty. But it made me think. It was so much fun us bumping into each other at the reunion and I was hoping we could meet for lunch.'

'Today?'

'Today? I don't know. It's press day; we're quite up against it. But I could sneak out for an hour if you met me near our offices. We're in Farringdon, so how about Smith's of Smithfield?'

'That would be lovely,' Poppy said.

Excited that Migsy Remblethorpe wanted to know her, she carefully applied some make-up, put on her cleanest pair of jeans and headed to the Tube. At the little newsagent's in the concourse she bought the *Post* and read the article. The usual cocktail of emotions jiggled inside her: one part anger at Hannah's viciousness mixed with two parts meek acceptance because she deserved no less.

'I'm sorry, Hannah,' she breathed, 'I didn't know what I was doing.'

But it was too late now, she thought as she walked up the steps at Farringdon Tube. This had been her regular stop when she'd worked at Sal's. But then Luke took me away from all that, she'd always tell her interviewer.

But what had he actually taken her away from? Poppy wondered now. She'd been happy at Sal's, earning a pittance but spending hours gossiping in the kitchen with him and his wife, Maria, then strap-hanging home to Kilburn where she'd sulk a bit about the appalling state her flatmate had left the kitchen in, but then cheer up when Meena got home. They'd spend hours getting dressed up to go into town while swigging from a bottle of wine and dancing to Kiss FM.

But I didn't have Clara, she reminded herself as she tapped along the cobbled streets. But I'm not happy. But you *have* to be happy, you have a beautiful, healthy daughter. But I'm not. Maybe I'm too greedy. What else do I want from life?

Even though she was five minutes late, she still had to wait twenty minutes for Migsy. A happy twenty minutes, though, at a sunny table on the roof terrace with a magnificent view over the dome of St Paul's. She relished being in a restaurant without free crayons, high chairs and children's portions, browsing a menu without being in a perpetual state of alertness in case Clara stabbed herself in the eye with a fork or ate all the sugar cubes.

'Poppy, hi! Sorry I'm late.'

Yet again Migsy looked immaculate.

'It's so great to catch up,' she twittered as she sat down. 'Wasn't the reunion fun?'

'Mmm,' said Poppy, who'd left about five minutes after her conversation with Migsy when it became apparent Meena was so drunk she was going to have to drive her home.

'Did you talk to Laura Lightman? She's a sex therapist now and she changed her name to Laura Lightwoman.' Migsy tittered. 'Who would have thought it? But who would have guessed *you* were the Bimbo. A bottle of sparkling please,' she said to the waiter. 'By the way, I had *such* fun interviewing Marco Jensen. Isn't he cute?

He was telling me all about the *Seven Thirty News*; what an honour it is to work with a veteran like your hubbie. Said he really respects him, like he does all the old-timers.'

'Oh that's nice,' Poppy said.

A waiter hovered. 'Hi.' Migsy smiled. 'Right, I'll have the pear and fennel salad. Poppy?'

'Um, I'll have the pheasant,' said Poppy, naming the first thing she spotted on the menu.

The waiter disappeared. Migsy leant forward.

'I'm going to cut to the chase because I can't stay long. Busy, busy, busy. You know how it is, I'm sure.'

'Oh, yes, indeed.' *Indeed?* Poppy sounded like the host of a religious-affairs programme. She really did need to get out more.

Migsy continued, 'We're looking to launch a new column. A sort of It-girl about town diary. You know, the parties you've been to, the shops you've shopped in, the celebrities you've hobnobbed with. I think you'd be perfect for it because you're a model, which is what all our readers aspire to be, but you're also a mum, which they are too – poor cows – so you can give us a few cute little anecdotes about your baby which other mums seem to like for some reason. Oh, and don't take this the wrong way, but you're also "The Bimbo". I mean, obviously you're not really, but that's how people know you because of Hannah's columns.' She waved away the proffered bread basket before Poppy could help herself to a delicious-looking crusty roll. 'So what do you think?'

Poppy felt like Dorothy after the hurricane struck Kansas.

'Um . . .'

'Don't worry, I know you can't write,' Migsy continued. 'That will be my job. You'll chat to me once a week about what you've done. The pay'll be three hundred pounds a column to start with, and then if it goes well we can talk about a rise.'

'I . . .'

The food was placed in front of them. Migsy skewered a fennel leaf and placed it between her lips. Poppy lifted her knife and fork. Why the hell had she ordered pheasant? As soon as she attacked it, the bird started skidding round her plate like a drunk on an ice rink. She tried to saw off a corner and ended up with enough to sustain a very thin flea.

'What do you think? I'd like an answer now, because we've got a new editor and I need plenty of ideas to impress her.'

'I never go to parties,' Poppy confessed. 'I haven't really had a social life since my daughter was born.' Or much of one before, she could have added.

'That's fine,' Migsy said airily. 'We can sort out all that for you.'

'What, you can get me invited to parties?'

'Course we can.' Migsy fumbled in her bag. 'Here's a few to get you started. Look. The *Murder Police* première. It's tomorrow night. Meant to be amazing. Brad Pitt's in it. And an after-show party at the Natural History Museum.'

'Really?' Poppy looked at the colourful piece of cardboard. 'And all I have to do is tell you what it was like?'

'And who you saw. It's the easiest job in the world. Up there with being an usherette.' Migsy snorted. 'I'll call you once a week on Thursday morning, say at eleven, if that's not too early, and we'll have a chat about what you've done that week. Basically, two parties, a couple of comments about someone in the news – Kerry Katona, for example – and something cute your baby's done. Then I'll email you a version of what I'm going to write, and that's that.'

Poppy leafed through the pile of stiff-backed cards, not knowing where to begin. She bit her lip.

'I think I'd better just run this past my husband.'

Migsy shrugged. 'If you want to, but I don't see why he'd mind.'

'Maybe not. I'm sure not. He says he wants me working again. But all the same . . .'

'Sure, sure, well run it by him,' Migsy said a tad more impatiently, as her mobile rang. 'Oh, excuse me. Yes? Shit! OK. Well, don't worry, I'll be straight back.'

She hung up. 'Crisis. There's a rumour Minnie Maltravers is going to adopt a baby. We've got to alter the whole front cover. I need to get back. You know how it is, Poppy, but don't worry. You take your time here. Linger. Have a dessert.' She stood up. 'Really nice to see you again. So thrilled you'll be working for us.'

With a jaunty wave, she was gone. Poppy stared after her retreating form in bemusement.

She stared out of the window at the higgledy-piggledy rooftops. A proper job. Just like Hannah had. The chance to go to parties, leave the house again. And a column in a magazine. The thoughts that raced round her head would finally get some kind of outlet. I'm so busy with my column, but I still manage to make as much time as I can for my daughter. Motherhood is the most important thing in the world to me . . .

Back home, Clara was sitting on the floor, scribbling on a large piece of paper. Brigita was washing up at the sink, her phone tucked under her chin.

'Mmm. Hmmm? Well, I love you . . . No, I love you more.' She giggled girlishly, then sensing Poppy's eyes on her, whirled round. 'Oh! Got to go, me duck. Bye, then. Yes. Ta, ta.' She put the phone down on the kitchen counter. 'Hi, Mummy. I didn't hear you come in. How is your day been? Is a little parky outside, no?'

'Good,' Poppy said, wondering if she dared ask Brigita to stop calling her Mummy. She squatted down to her daughter's level. 'Hey, chickabiddy. How are you?'

Clara grunted, not even looking up.

'She's been really good,' Brigita said fondly. 'Did another weewee in the potty. Soon she will be using the big bog. We made star chart. Show Mummy.'

'No. Wanna draw!'

'OK, you show me later.'

Clara continued scribbling. Brigita returned to the sink. More than ever, Poppy felt like a stranger in her own home.

'Was that your boyfriend you were talking to?' she asked.

Brigita turned round, flicking a damp strand of hair out of her eyes. 'Sorry, Mummy. Usually I don't make personal calls during work time but it was an emergency, he . . .'

Poppy waved her excuses away. 'What's his name?'

Brigita smiled and her usually puddingy face was suddenly transformed. 'Phil,' she said lovingly.

'What does he do?'

'He's a roofer.'

'How long have you been together?'

'Two years. Our dream is to make enough money to go back to Yorkshire, buy a house, then I can continue to study for my PhD.'

Don't go home too soon, thought Poppy, appalled at the idea of Brigita abandoning her now she had this new opportunity. But she said, 'Oh, how lovely.'

'Dinner's is ready, Clah-Clah. Wash your hands, please, angel.'

Obediently, Clara jumped up and padded over to the sink. Poppy watched in astonishment. How come it took her hours to persuade her daughter to do something as simple as sit in her high chair? An unexpected wave of inadequacy crashed over her. On paper, she was so much more fortunate than Brigita: far prettier and with a handsome, rich husband, gorgeous daughter and lovely flat. But she and Luke never spoke on the phone in the way Brigita had to Phil. And it had been a long, long time since mentioning Luke's name had made her light up like a firework display.

But she wasn't going to think like that any more. She'd been offered a job. An exciting job. She would be going to parties and earning money again. As soon as Luke got home from work, she'd run it past him, but she didn't see how he could say no. She'd prepare him a lovely

236

dinner and open a bottle of wine and they'd make love, which they hadn't done for quite a while.

Just then her phone beeped.

Having dinner with a minister. Back midnight-ish. Big kiss to C, L x

Oh. Well, never mind. She'd talk to him when he got back. Or no, she had a better idea.

'Brigita, I know it's a long shot but you're not free to babysit tomorrow night, are you?'

'No worries!' Brigita said instantly.

'Great. I'm going to book Orrery. It's where Luke and I had our wedding lunch. I'll take him out for a romantic dinner and tell him some news I have.'

'You are up t'duff again?' Brigita's hand flew up to her mouth. ''Appen as I think your tummy is getting a little porky, but I don't like to say.'

'No, no. Nothing like that.' Quite the opposite, Poppy thought, as she picked up her phone and scrolled down contacts for Orrery's number. But her phone bleeped again.

Change of plan. Off to Paris now to cover riots. Hope to be back Sunday depends how story develops. Will call from Eurostar if I get chance. x

Poppy stared at the phone in disbelief. Another lonely weekend with just her and Clara. She turned to Brigita to tell her babysitting was off. But then she thought again.

Tomorrow was the *Murder Police* party. To which she had two invitations. She might as well go. What did she have to lose? All she needed was a date, and Poppy knew someone who'd be delighted to come.

She scrolled down her address book and pressed Meena's number.

24

Naturally, Meena was thrilled.

'A film première? Yay, Poppy! I'll take the day off work.'

'You don't need to do that. It starts at seven thirty.'

'But we've got to get ready. That's gonna take hours. I'll be round yours at three.'

True to her word, Meena was on the doorstep the following afternoon as punctual as a Japanese bullet train.

'Ta-dah!' she cried, flicking her long black hair over her shoulders and gesturing to the vast Samsonite suitcase she was wheeling behind her. 'I've bought outfits! Where's Clara? I have a fairy number for her.'

'She's with her nanny.'

'Oh yeah, I forgot. You're a proper trophy wife now. Staff and everything. Well . . .' She produced a bottle of cava from a plastic bag. 'With no child to keep up appearances for, let's get ourselves in the mood.'

They turned the radio dial from Luke's Radio 4 to Kiss FM and Meena set to work with her tools. It was just like old times.

'Though really we should have got in a make-up artist and hair stylist,' Meena declared, mouth gaping as she applied her fourth layer of mascara.

Poppy laughed. 'Don't be silly. That would cost a fortune.'

'Yeah, but you're a professional It-girl or whatever now. You need to dress up properly for these things. Paparazzi will be taking your photo.' Meena hugged herself in excitement. 'Oh my God, do you think Prince William will be there tonight?'

'I doubt it.'

'Brad Pitt? He's the star, isn't he?'

'He's married.'

'No, he isn't. He and Ange won't tie the knot until American law changes so gays can get married too.' Meena's knowledge of such things was encyclopedic.

'I'm still not sure I fancy getting into a fight with Angelina. You can imagine her getting nasty down a dark alleyway.'

'Whatever. There'll be plenty of chances now to meet famous guys. Because if you do this column, you'll get invites like this all the time.'

'*If* I do the column,' Poppy said cautiously.

Meena placed both hands on her hips and glared ferociously at her.

'What do you mean *if* ? It's a no-brainer. You're getting paid to attend parties every night. And you'll be *famous*. I mean properly, glamorously famous, not like your boring husband sitting behind a desk reading an autocue. God, if you weren't my best friend I'd want to kill you I'd be so jealous.'

'I need to check with Luke first.'

Meena snorted just like one of the ponies all the other Brettenden girls had been brought up with. 'Luke wanted you to get a job and you have one. So what's the deal? He's off swanning round Paris. Why can't you have fun?'

'I'm sure he'll be fine about it. I just think I should check with him first. As soon as he gets back I'll ask him.'

Meena sat down on the bed. 'Poppy, you've never said it in so many words but you've had it hard the past couple of years: you've basically been a single mum; you've hardly gone out, you've missed out on so many laughs and you've never once complained. I'm proud of how you've dealt with things, but I bloody think you deserve to have some fun now.'

Poppy felt a lump in her throat. Happily, she was spared from some kind of wind-beneath-my-wings moment by Meena, who'd been teasing her hair into a ponytail, saying, 'What outfit is it going to be then?'

'I'm not sure, I thought maybe my blue dress.'

'No, no, it needs to be much funkier for a première.' Meena started briskly leafing through Poppy's wardrobe. 'God, I can't stand it. Don't you own anything except fleeces and tracksuit bottoms?'

'They wash easily.'

'Oh, listen to you.' She flicked on. 'Right. These jeans. With this jacket.'

The jeans were an old pair of Radcliffes that were too smart for Poppy ever to wear now; the jacket a sequinned silver number she'd been given after a shoot and packed away at the back of the wardrobe because she suspected it made her look like a crooner on a cruise ship.

'I don't know.'

'Well, I do. Put the jeans on.' Poppy obeyed dumbly. 'And now the jacket.'

'But I need a T-shirt or something underneath.'

'No you don't; it'll be far sexier without.'

Dubiously, Poppy followed her orders.

'Perfect. Now ... how about this necklace.' Meena fastened a black jet number round her friend's neck. 'And those shoes.' She pointed at a pair of snakeskin stilettos.

'I can't walk in those. I'll break my ankle.'

'Girlfriend, looking like you do, you ain't gonna need to walk anywhere.' She pushed Poppy in front of the cheval mirror. 'Look.'

Poppy looked. As always, she was amazed at what a difference several litres of make-up and a decent hairdo could make.

'Wow! Either I look like a complete tit or I look fantastic.'

'The latter,' Meena said smugly.

'Are you sure? How do you know?' Poppy twisted and turned.

'Mummy pretty,' Clara cooed, toddling in, Brigita behind her.

'Hey! Brigita, this is my friend Meena. What do you think of our outfits?'

Brigita sucked her teeth, like a surgeon about to embark on a coronary bypass. 'Yes, this jacket is good for you Poppy. It covers the top of your arms.' She turned to Meena. 'With that bum, I think this no skirt. Wear a trousers instead?'

'I can't believe Migsy Remblethorpe is responsible for this,' Meena gasped, as the Bakerloo Line whisked them to the West End. 'She always hated us. Used to call us the chav sisters.'

'That was a long time ago,' Poppy said.

'Still, seems a bit weird to me, her suddenly being so nice to you. But I'm not complaining if it means loads of party invitations.'

'I don't know about loads. We'll have to see how it goes.'

They emerged from the Tube at Piccadilly Circus. Three searchlights were combing the sky. Above Leicester Square floated a huge airship bearing the words *Murder Police* over the pouting features of Brad Pitt.

'Oh my God!' Meena screamed, linking her arm through Poppy's. They crossed the square, passing nutters praising the Lord from soapboxes, cartoonists on fold-out stools doing bad drawings of grinning tourists, Peruvian Pan-pipers and a man selling roast chestnuts, hen-night parties, legs blue from the unseasonably chilly night, to the far corner of the square where a crowd was gathered round a metal gate, guarded by two bouncers. A white limo drew up and disgorged a tall, black girl in a purple taffeta balldress.

'That's Vonzella from *Celebrity Love Island*,' Meena said. 'That must be the way into the cinema. Quick, get out the invitations.'

Diffidently, Poppy showed them to the bouncers, convinced they'd be rejected as forgeries. They brusquely nodded them through.

'We're on a red carpet!' Meena had always been fond of stating the obvious. It wasn't quite like Poppy had imagined it would be. She'd had the impression you floated up it alone while adoring fans scrutinized your every sartorial decision. But in fact it was as busy as

Selfridge's on the first day of the sales with gaggles of sequin-clad women posing for the camera phones on the other side of the barrier. At the northern end a gang of photographers stood like cattle behind a pen, shouting at a small woman who expertly twisted and turned before them.

'Amanda, here! Amanda, this way! Amanda, smile a bit more. Show us some leg, love.'

'That's Amanda Holden,' Meena whispered. 'Do you think *we* should pose for them?'

'Don't be silly,' Poppy said, 'they don't know who we are.'

'They soon will. Oh my God – there's Trinny and Susannah!' She fumbled for her phone. 'Do you think it would be really uncool if I took their photo?'

'Yes,' Poppy said firmly, as a voice said, 'Meena!'

'Hey, Toby!' Meena flung herself on the most handsome man Poppy had seen in a long time. Tall, with bushy brown hair, big eyes and a slightly hooked nose like a Red Indian chief. He was dressed in black jeans and a grey shirt.

'Poppy, this is Toby. He used to work out at the club. What's happened to you? I missed you.'

'I moved to Shoreditch.' He turned to Poppy and his eyes widened like a five-year-old in front of a cake-shop window. 'Hi, Toby Hastings.'

'Poppy Norton.'

A beaky-faced woman in a black suit wearing a headset hurried over to them.

'Guys, you've got to take your seats *now*. The film's beginning in five.'

'Coming to the party afterwards?' Toby said in a low voice to Poppy.

'Oh, yes.'

'Come *on*, guys!'

25

Poppy found it hard to concentrate on the film. So, it seemed, did everyone else in the audience who, despite dire warnings on the tickets banning mobile phones, seemed to spend the entire two hours texting their friends, talking to each other, munching loudly on the free ('Free!' Meena cooed) bags of M&Ms or getting up to go to the loo. None the less, at the end everyone clapped wildly. Then they all trooped outside and across the square to Panton Street where a line of coaches waited to carry them like children on a school trip, to the Natural History Museum.

'How lovely,' Poppy breathed, entering the cathedral-like room with its dinosaur skeleton in the middle. She'd been here a dozen times with Clara but the place had been transformed with huge stands of exotic flowers and the vaulted ceilings with sparkling fairy lights. Two clowns in illuminated body suits were hopping round on stilts. A smoke machine tucked in a corner breathed out puffs of pseudo mist that whirled across the room and round the ankles of a group of toned men wearing dinner jackets and bearing wide, silver trays.

'Canapé?' said one.

'Yes please! What are they?'

'Deep-fried halloumi with a lemon dressing.'

Poppy took two, then had to cram them both in her

mouth as another man with a tray of champagne approached. 'Thank you,' she managed to mumble, seizing a flute.

'This is the life,' said Meena, as they clinked glasses. 'To many more of these.'

'Assuming I can get a babysitter,' Poppy said.

'What's that Brigita for? Or why can't Luke do his share? I told you, you've sat in nearly every night for two years while he's been out on the town. It's your turn.'

'I was hoping I'd see you again,' said a deep voice behind them.

They turned round. It was Toby Hastings. Poppy felt suddenly nervous.

'Did you enjoy the film?' she twittered.

He shrugged. 'Not really. A bit derivative, I thought. What about you?'

'Oh, I thought the same,' Poppy said, as Meena chimed in. 'Oh my God, I see cocktails. I'm going to get one.' She dashed off into the crowd.

'How do you know Meena?' Toby asked. Poppy's dull reply was interrupted by a skinny girl with blonde dreadlocks. '*Tobes!* How are you, sweets?'

'Trina!' He turned his back on Poppy. She stood, nursing her glass looking nervously from side to side. It was just like being at a party with Luke. No one wanted to talk to her. She'd been a fool to think the column could ever work. She downed her glass and looked about for somewhere to put it, just as Meena rushed back to her, bearing two wide frosted glasses.

'Look! Vodka gimlets.'

With her friend by her side and a cocktail in her hand,

things quickly improved. They wandered from room to room, gawping at the number of famous faces they recognized. Occasionally, Poppy would stop to study the glass cases full of stuffed exotic birds, but Meena dragged her away.

'Don't be boring, Poppy. Look, there's Jude Law! Oh my God, he's so much shorter than I thought he'd be. Is that Nicole Richie over there?'

'No, I think it's someone from *Emmerdale*. But *that* is definitely Gwyneth. Or at least someone who looks like her. Still no sign of Brad Pitt though.'

Time flew by. They helped themselves to a buffet as lavish as something from the last days of the Roman Empire, then found themselves in a room made out entirely like a sweet shop where they stuffed their faces with dolly mixtures. A DJ had set up beside a gently dripping ice sculpture. Meena started dancing. Poppy watched from the sidelines, wishing she could join in, but dancing always made her feel as though she was wearing concrete moon boots. She yawned slightly. Toby reappeared at her side.

'Need something to help you stay awake?'

'Sorry?' Poppy blushed, unsure what he meant, but before she could ask there was another 'Toby!' This time it was a man. Old, perhaps not as old as Luke, about her mother's age. He wasn't exactly handsome but had a long, lean body, flaxen hair and a ruddy face that spoke of a lack of care with sunscreen. His eyes were crinkly and smiling in a way that suggested an absence of troublesome wives and children.

'Charlie!' The two men pumped hands. Poppy started

to back away, but Toby said, 'Charlie, have you met Poppy?'

'Hello,' she said shyly, holding out a hand.

'I'm Charlie Grimes. What a pleasure.' He grinned and winked at Toby. 'Are you one of my friend's harem?'

'Piss off, Charlie,' Toby said cheerfully. 'We've only just met.' He smiled at Poppy. 'Though I'm hoping we're going to see a lot more of each other.'

From the dance floor, Meena came bounding towards them like an over-excited puppy.

'This is *great*!' she yelled. 'I'm having *such* a good time. Oh my God, look, there are the Dastardly Fiends.' She pointed to the bar, where two members of the indie band of the moment were standing. Girls flocked round them like seagulls to a fish and chip van. 'I'm going over to say hello.' She pulled Toby's arm. 'Do you know them?'

Toby shrugged. 'A bit.'

'Can you introduce me?'

He laughed. 'I don't see why not.'

Meena dragged him off. Poppy watched them. Of course she already had a husband and Toby seemed ideal for Meena. But she couldn't help feeling a little . . .

'Jealous?' said Charlie softly beside her.

Poppy started slightly. How had he read her mind? 'Of Meena and Toby? No. Why should I be? I'm married.'

'*Are* you? Surely, you're a bit young. How old are you?'

'Twenty-four.'

Charlie grinned ruefully. 'That's the age I still feel inside. You lucky thing. I envy you. All that time ahead of you; make the most of it.'

'I'll try,' Poppy said, eyeing Meena and Toby. Meena

was laughing hysterically, then went on tiptoes and whispered something in his ear. He grinned and nodded. Together they started pushing through the crowd. With an effort, Poppy turned back to Charlie.

'Um, if you don't mind me asking, what are *you* doing here?'

'Too old for all this?' he asked, grinning.

'Oh no, no,' she said, then, 'Well, yes, a bit maybe.'

He laughed. 'I appreciate the honesty. It's true. I shouldn't really be here. I should be at home watching *Rebus* in my incontinence pants, but I'm a gossip columnist for the *Daily Post*. Going to parties is what I do for a living.'

'For the *Daily Post*?' Poppy eyed him, suddenly wary, as if Hannah might be about to jump out of his pocket.

'Yes.' He looked at her curiously. 'Do you read it? Most people your age don't buy newspapers any more. They're vanishing more quickly than the Amazonian rain forest.'

'I do sometimes,' she said cautiously. Actually, now she put the pieces together, Charlie's cheery face was vaguely familiar from the top of his page, full of inane tittle-tattle about how Sophie Anderton was launching a new bikini range and Girls Aloud had had a great time filming their new video in Germany. Poppy usually read it straight after Hannah's column, like a sweetie after vile medicine.

'What a glamorous job,' she breathed.

Charlie smiled. 'Don't be fooled. There are only so many halloumi and lemon skewers a man can devour and only so many times he can ask Jade Goody about her new career plans before he starts to go a bit doolally and yearn for a job reporting on advances in uranium trading.' He shrugged cheerily. 'But what can I do? My editor likes my column. Says I have an easy way with people.'

'But all those parties . . .' After all this could be Poppy's new career too.

'Oh, they can be fun. But I've got a terrible case of SID – that's status-income disequilibrium before you rush off to wash your hands. My job gives me high status but it's not reflected in my pay packet. I waltz round hotel ballrooms and make small talk with billionaires and then I catch the night bus back to Crouch End in the pouring rain. I have lunch with a movie star at the Ivy and dinner is a Pot Noodle on the sofa.'

'Just like me! I love Pot Noodles.'

'Good girl. Which is your favourite? Personally I'm a chicken and mushroom man, though I do have a sneaky fondness for beef and tomato.'

But before Poppy could exclaim on their extraordinary shared tastes, Meena and Toby returned, even livelier than before. They'd probably crept off for a passionate snog, Poppy thought. Then she registered the tiny white moustache on Meena's upper lip. Oh.

'I wanna dance. C'mon Poppy, I love this song!' To the strains of Jay-Z, Meena pulled her on to the dance floor and began moving manically. Poppy shuffled awkwardly beside her.

'You're such a cow,' Meena bellowed above the music. 'Toby's been telling me how gorgeous he thinks you are.'

Poppy's heart fluttered, but she asked, 'Were you doing drugs with him?'

'Yeah! Do you want some?'

Poppy shook her head. One go and you're hooked. She knew that wasn't strictly true. After all Meena wasn't suddenly robbing old ladies for her next fix, but the only time she'd toked on a spliff she'd felt nauseous all evening and hadn't enjoyed herself at all.

'Go on! It's really good stuff.'

Poppy could see Toby dancing with another girl, this one impossibly pretty with Cherokee cheekbones in a sort of leather shift dress. He was throwing back his head, laughing, showing very white teeth. She wished he was laughing with her.

'I can go and ask Toby to give you some.'

Toby put his arm round the girl's shoulder and said something in her ear. She smiled, nodded and they disappeared into the crowd.

'Pops?'

Poppy shook her head. 'No thanks.' She nodded at the space where Toby had been standing. 'What does he do?'

'Toby? He's a sort of fixer. He works for one of those concierge services that does rich people's boring little jobs, like get them tables at restaurants, their names on the guest list at clubs, you know.'

'Right,' said Poppy, who didn't know really.

By two o'clock, Poppy, feeling guilty about Brigita, kind of wanted to go. But, fuelled by three more glasses of champagne, she was having fun even though she didn't see Toby again. Eventually, she and Meena piled into a cab at three, with Meena chatting away like an aviary bird.

'I've had *so* much fun. Poppy, I can't believe this is your new job. You've got to go for it!'

'I just need to check with Luke,' Poppy said, firmly.

'Oh sod, Luke. Miserable git. I'm so happy you're finally escaping from his clutches. You were always too good for him.'

26

It wasn't the most pleasant awakening, to have Clara snatch her from a heavy slumber just three hours after Poppy had gone to sleep with cries of: 'Mummy, I done a poo!' Still, Poppy reflected as she blearily changed her daughter's revolting nappy, she was permanently tired anyway. At least this way she was tired and happy.

Fuelled by three cups of black coffee, she and Clara managed to pass a quite enjoyable Saturday together snuggled up in pyjamas watching CBeebies and eating toast. Poppy vaguely wondered if they should do something improving, like go to the park, but then she remembered Brigita. She pushed swings all week long, so Poppy could have a clear conscience.

The highlight of the day came at around six, when Poppy was sitting on the loo seat, watching Clara splashing in the bath with nine multicoloured plastic ducks. A text arrived from a number she didn't recognize. Excitedly, she opened it.

Good 2 c u last night. Hope 2 c u again soon. Toby xxx

It wasn't exactly a Shakespearean love sonnet, but Poppy's heart began to beat faster. Smiling, she texted back.

How did u get my numbr? x

'Mummy. No phone! Sing to me, Mummy.'

Poppy began a spirited if tuneless rendition of 'Five Little Ducks' as her phone beeped.

Aha. That wd b telling. U going out tonight? x

Sadly not. Tonight I'm going to bed at nine because I'm knackered and, anyway, I have to babysit my two-year-old. But that wasn't the most alluring of replies, so she texted:

No, chilling tonight. x

Smiling in anticipation, she waited for an answer.

'Mummeee!'

'Yes, darling? Mummy duck said "Quack, quack, quack, quack."' She was frantically texting Meena.

Did u give Toby my number?

'Want my boat.'

'Say please,' Poppy said automatically, staring at her phone willing it to break into life. Nothing happened. She gave Clara her boat, then endured a long and noisy wrangle when she tried to take it away and get Clara out of the bath. She dried her, put on her nappy and pyjamas and then they watched a double bill of the *Seven Thirty News* – last night's on Sky Plus, followed by this evening's. Clara waved energetically to Daddy standing in front of the Eiffel Tower, while Poppy listened extra attentively to his report. Afterwards she read Clara *Maisie's Birthday* six times. Still nothing from either Meena or Toby. Perhaps he hadn't got her last text? Or perhaps she'd sounded too brusque. She sent him another one.

Will b out next week though. 4 work. Let me kno what parties u will be at. x

The phone stayed silent. Poppy read *Maisie* again, put her daughter in her cot, kissed her, turned off the light and then returned six times to retrieve Clara's mousie, which she had taken to chucking on the floor as a way of getting attention. Downstairs, she stuck a Pot Noodle in the microwave and while she was waiting for it to ping, dialled her mobile from her landline. Oh. Right. It *was* working. Her fingers itched to text Toby again, but she told herself not to. He was probably on the Tube. Or in the cinema. Or asleep. He'd get back to her.

Exhausted, she crawled into bed just after nine with the phone under her pillow just in case. At 21.11, it rang.

'Hello,' she gasped, snatching it like a drowning woman would a lifebelt.

'Hi, it's me,' said Luke.

Usually Luke calling filled her with joy. But now she just felt disappointment. 'Oh, hi. How's Paris? We watched you; you were great.'

'Was I? The idiot producer almost cocked everything up, but we got there in the end. Anyway, I'm calling to say I won't be back until the middle of the week now, because they want me to stay on to cover this scandal about vote rigging.'

Normally Poppy protested vehemently at such news,

but this time she merely said, 'Oh, OK,' because her other line had started to beep. Meena. 'Well, good luck,' she added rapidly to Luke. 'Let me know how it goes.'

'OK.' Luke sounded bemused at her unusually abrupt tone, but Poppy had already gone.

'Meena?'

A giggle. 'Yeah, Toby called to ask for your number. Says he's intrigued by you.'

'Oh.' Poppy could feel her neck flushing.

'I did tell him you were married and had a little girl and he said, "So?"'

'Did he indeed? What a cheek!' Poppy was thrilled.

'That's what I told him. Oh, Poppy, that was such a laugh. When's the next party?'

'I'm not sure,' Poppy said. 'But soon. I'll let you know.'

Even though her limbs ached with tiredness, it was a long time before Poppy went back to sleep. She wondered why she was getting so excited about Toby. She was a married woman, other men shouldn't make her pulse flutter. But Luke was away so much and she was so bored, so often. What was the harm in a little flirtation? It didn't mean anything, it wasn't going to lead anywhere. It was just a welcome reminder that Poppy was still young, that she hadn't been buried alive.

The Other Woman

As the Home Secretary introduces his new lady friend to the world before the ink is dry on his divorce papers, columnist Hannah Creighton asks: What exactly do we call women who steal husbands?

A couple of years ago I had what I now see to be the great fortune of losing my husband, the *SevenThirty News*'s anchorman, Luke Norton, 52, to a 22-year-old model. Initially, of course, I was somewhat put out by this unbelievable manifestation of a midlife crisis.

I didn't understand why Luke couldn't have just got an earring and a Harley, instead of impregnating a girl young enough to be his daughter. However, I got over it, not least by writing a weekly newspaper column (soon to be turned into a book) in which I charted the disintegration of my rotten marriage and the beginning of a new and happy life.

One thing, however, is asked of me constantly – why do I never name the woman who stole my husband? The answer is, why should I? In an era when children want to be famous in the same way they used to want to be train drivers or nurses why should *she* get her name in print? So the question, initially, was what to call her? I racked my brains for a suitable epithet. My solicitor called her the correspondent, but that was far too bland for me. 'Mistress' suggests a lady in a negligée and fluffy mules being kept in a tiny, chintzy flat in Earl's Court, which bestowed an air of glamour on the little girl, as did another brief nickname – Cruella.

I considered the Black Hole because any woman who could so flippantly catapult a family's future into cyberspace with the ping of a bra strap must have been brought up in a vacuum devoid of morality and decency, but there was something faintly gynaecological about the phrase.

So I turned to my trusty *Roget's Thesaurus*, where I took my choice from the following: debauchee, doxy, easy lay, floozy, harlot, hussy, Jezebel, loose woman, slattern, slut, strumpet, tart, tramp, trollop, wench, whore. All of which had a beautiful Dickensian ring to them. But my favourite epithet was the one that came first in this alphabetical list: bimbo! When I looked up its exact definition I found: a young woman indulged by a rich and powerful older man. What better way to describe Luke's brainless piece of fluff?

Rechristening the woman who broke up your marriage is very healing, not least because it irritates the hell out of your ex-husband. 'How's the bimbo getting along?' I say when I am obliged to discuss the children on the phone with him. As he replies in pained tones, some of the agony I have gone through is briefly numbed. I've also been known to share the odd blonde joke with him. For example: 'What do you call a blonde with two brain cells?' 'Pregnant.'

There's something very therapeutic about pronouncing the word bimbo. Who needs Prozac when you can juggle those two syllables on the tip of your tongue before spitting them out? It can be said in rage, which somehow helps douse the fury that at times still threatens to overwhelm me. Or it can be trilled out in a way that makes your long-suffering friends snort with laughter. And laughter, I learnt, was one of the keys to leading me out of this sorry situation and into happier times.

27

Time, which had passed so slowly for so long for Poppy, suddenly started flashing by, like a landscape seen from the window of an accelerating train. On Monday, she went to the launch of a new Janis Lyons perfume where she didn't see Toby, but she and Meena got tiddly on bellinis and left with several goodie bags (Meena grabbed an armful when the cloakroom attendant momentarily turned her back) containing a scented candle, a silver paperweight, a bottle of Janis Lyons perfume and a bar of organic dark chocolate.

The next night she was dead to the world by ten. The night after she went to a party at an art gallery in Mayfair, where she didn't see Toby again, but she did spot Tracey Emin, Brian who'd won *Big Brother* aeons ago, Prince Harry's new girlfriend ('Bitch,' Meena said. 'What's she got that I haven't?') and Marco Jensen and his girlfriend, Stephanie, having a spat at check-in because he refused to put her lipstick in his trouser pocket in case it 'ruined the line'. Luckily they didn't see her; Poppy would have not quite known what to say to them. Instead, she had a conversation with a man called Gus, who told her he was 'the calligrapher'.

'*The* calligrapher? You mean *a* calligrapher?'

'No.' Gus giggled. '*The* calligrapher. For this party. There's an exclusive dinner after this for the most important guests and my job's to be at hand in case there are any last-minute *placement* changes.'

'Is this for real?'

Gus looked a bit put out. 'Of course it is,' he snapped. 'You wouldn't believe how many people are no-shows or turn up with their lover instead of their wife.' Unamused by Poppy's incredulous expression, he sniped, 'Excuse me, darling, but I must go and talk to Freddie Windsor.'

Briefly marooned, wondering how she'd managed to cause so much offence, Poppy picked up a glass from a passing tray. She was relieved to see Charlie, the gossip columnist.

'Oh hello. You again.' He smiled as she hurried up to him.

'Hi!' Poppy didn't know why she was so pleased to see him, but she was. There was something reassuring about Charlie. He was cosy and unintimidating like a tatty old dressing gown, though she thought better of telling him that.

'It never rains but it pours,' he continued. 'I've never seen you in my life and suddenly twice in one week.'

Poppy debated whether to tell him about the column, but decided against it. 'I've got a nanny,' she said. 'I'm able to go out more.'

Charlie smote his forehead in mock shock. 'Hell's bells, I knew you were married but I didn't know you had a child as well. Now I really do feel like Methuselah. When were you born? Don't tell me it was in the nineties.'

'No, the eighties.' Poppy giggled. 'Mid eighties.'

'The mid eighties. God, in the mid eighties I was . . .' Charlie trailed off. 'Well, I won't bore you. Nor will I tell you the decade I was born in. All you need know is electric light had only just been invented and the crinoline was considered the height of fashion. Would you like a drink by the way, sweetheart? Assuming it's legal for you to consume alcoholic beverages.'

'I'd love another glass of champagne.'

'One glass of champagne for the lady and one tonic water,' he said to the barman.

'Tonic water? Without gin or vodka?'

'I never drink,' Charlie said, accepting the glasses. 'Thank you so much.'

'Why not?'

Charlie smiled. 'Now that shows what an innocent you are, my dear. I don't drink because I'm an alcoholic.'

'But alcoholics are always pissed, aren't they?'

'If I had half the chance I would be. But about the time you were born I almost killed myself from too much booze. And pills. And other nasty substances. I was living in the South of France and I ended up getting in some very nasty situations. Hurt a lot of people.' He grimaced faintly. 'Had to spend a year on and off in a drying-out clinic. It kind of put me off the booze.'

'But it must be so strange going to parties and not drinking.'

'It's interesting.' Charlie's eyes twinkled. 'You see the world in a completely different way from everyone else when you're sober. I feel a little bit out of things, but then it's my job to report on what's going on not to take part.'

'Are you married?' It was a rather nosy question but there was something so inviting about him, Poppy didn't think he'd mind if you asked him if he had terrible problems with flatulence.

'Sadly not. Too wild for too long, then once I'd got my act together all the good girls had been taken, and the younger models aren't interested because I'm not a banker or a lawyer.'

'But you're a lovely man. Women aren't all gold-diggers you know.' Poppy knew what she was talking about here.

'You'd be surprised. As soon as they've checked out my payslip, most of them are making their excuses and . . .' Charlie gulped down his tonic. 'On which note, sweetheart, sorry, but I've got to dash. Need to grab Gianluca Mazza. Cosmetic surgeon to the stars. He's always got some good gossip for me, though he keeps trying to laser my spider veins.'

Luke got back on Thursday morning, tired and grumpy. Apparently the hotel in Paris had been dreadful. 'Roxanne's insisting we can't stay anywhere that costs more than a hundred a night. It's ridiculous,' he moaned as he unpacked. 'We were practically in a bed and breakfast.'

'Oh poor you. But your reports were really good.'

'Yeah?' He brightened up. 'Do you think we did better than Sky?'

'Definitely.'

She thought about telling him about the column, but couldn't quite face it. Perhaps she'd just surprise him by showing him the finished object. After all, she'd been to the parties so there needed to be some kind of payback. Her phone rang.

'Hello?'

'Oh hi, Poppy. It's Michelle Rembelthorpe. Calling as promised.'

Poppy glanced at Luke, flinging his dirty underwear into the laundry bin.

'Um, just a minute,' she said. 'I'll take this in the study.' She went into the little room with its view over the canal and closed the door. 'Right, I can talk better now.'

'So how's your week been?'

'Great,' Poppy said. 'I've been to three parties. I got you a Janis Lyons goodie bag.'

'Oh, you're a sweetheart,' Migsy purred. 'So tell me. Who did you see?'

'See?'

'What celebs did you spot?' Migsy sounded a trifle more impatient.

'Um. Well, the first party was the film première. I saw Jude Law and Gwyneth and the Dastardly Fiends.'

Migsy squealed. 'Oh how exciting, Poppy! What was Jude Law like? Was he as gorgeous in the flesh?'

'No, he was actually much smaller than I expected and kind of grumpy-looking. He was sitting in a corner all evening with some girl and I thought "Why did you bother coming out, if you're going to make no effort to enjoy yourself?"'

Migsy laughed. 'Oh yeah? I've heard he can be a bit moody. And what about Gwyneth? How did she look? I've always thought she has awful taste. Do you remember that revolting meringue she wore to the Oscars?'

'I do! But actually that looked stylish in comparison to what she had on on Friday – it was a disgusting orange number. I didn't know she was colour blind. And Denise van Outen! God, it's amazing what you can do with a pair of curtains and a sewing machine.'

Migsy giggled. Poppy felt as if her internal central heating had been turned on. Finally, she was in with the in-crowd.

'And what about Nick from the Dastardly Fiends?'

'He looked really pleased with himself. I don't know why because his music's awful, I think. He sounds like a castrated gerbil. His teeth were so yellow, traffic probably slows down when he smiles.'

'Well, he's a big junkie.' Migsy chortled. 'Anyone else?'

'I saw Brian from *Big Brother* at the Janis Lyons party.'

'Oh yeah, the walking satsuma.'

'That's the one.' Poppy laughed. 'I didn't talk to him either but he looked like he was having fun. And Tamara Mellon was at the art gallery party.'

'With some guy who looked like he'd had his face ironed?'

'Got it in one.' They both laughed again. 'And there was this ridiculous calligrapher man there to do last-minute changes to the place names. I mean, can you *imagine*? They say you can never be too rich or too thin, but I say you can definitely be too rich and too stupid.'

Migsy honked with laughter. 'As a BH old girl, I *so* agree. And what has little Clara been up to this week?'

Just then Luke stuck his head round the door. 'What are you doing?' he snapped.

Poppy put her hand over the mouthpiece. 'I'm on the phone. I won't be long.'

'Do you *have* to chat to your friends in here? I need to get online.'

'I told you: I won't be long.'

At her insubordinate tone Luke stared. But then – to both their surprise – he said, 'OK.'

'Could you shut the door, please?' Poppy asked. It closed quietly. 'Sorry, Migsy, I mean Michelle. You were asking about Clara. Well, she's being toilet trained, but frankly I can't see the point. It's so much easier to keep them in nappies than having to shove them on the potty every fifteen minutes. If I had my way I'd keep her in them until she leaves home.'

'Lovely.' Migsy laughed. 'And finally. What do you think about Hannah's article today?'

Poppy's blood froze. 'I haven't read it,' she said calmly.

'Haven't you? Oh well, don't worry, I'll read it to you.'

Poppy listened, biting her lip.

'What do you think, Poppy?'

Poppy paused. 'Poor Hannah. Going through the menopause must be awful.'

'Oh, touché!' Migsy giggled. 'And do you mind being called a bimbo?'

'Of course not,' Poppy blustered. 'I've heard it all. Bimbo. Dumb blonde. Dolly Parton would say I don't mind dumb blonde jokes because I know I'm not dumb. I'm also not blonde.' Actually, she was but she'd been waiting for years to come out with that gag.

'Excellent,' Migsy purred. 'Well, that's it, darling. We're all done now.'

'All done? That was quick.'

'I told you it wouldn't take long. Good stuff, Poppy.

I'll write it up and it'll come out a fortnight tomorrow. The only other thing we have to do is organize a photographer to take a headshot of you to go over the column. Would tomorrow morning suit? And we're biking over some more invitations later today. We've got our work experience girl calling all the PRs to get your name on the guest lists.'

'Of course.'

'Great, I'll have a snapper with you about eleven, if that's OK. Oh, and you must give me your bank details so you can be paid.'

Having done all that (it took a few minutes to dig out details of her long-dormant personal bank account) Poppy hung up. She couldn't believe how easy it had been. She'd tell Luke about it tonight; she didn't see how he could possibly object.

In the *SevenThirty News* office, Luke was sitting despondently at his desk, going through three months' backlog of expenses. Luke wasn't enjoying life much at the moment. Marco was being allotted more and more of his airtime. School fees had gone up again. The attacks from Hannah continued relentlessly.

At home too, things weren't right. Well, they were never right if he was honest, but they were *different*. Normally, Poppy made him feel stressed and guilty with her tears when he went away on assignment, but she'd been fine about the extended Paris trip. He should feel relieved, but instead he felt uneasy. Since he'd returned two out of three nights he'd get back from work to find Brigita babysitting and his wife out. Luke knew he'd said Poppy should enjoy life more, but it was disconcerting coming home and finding the nanny, rather than his wife, sitting in front of the TV and being woken at some late hour by Poppy stumbling in, smelling of alcohol. Not to mention he'd thought the idea of getting a nanny was so Poppy could find a job, not go out on the town every night. He'd have to tackle her about it – gently, so as not to upset her. Though maybe this new, somehow tougher Poppy would take it in her stride?

He stared at the pile of receipts in front of him. Nine taxis, a hotel bill for Prague, a hotel bill for Paris. Another bill for £175.80 from the Frontline Club for a couple of weeks back. What the hell had he been doing that evening? Oh yeah, he'd got pissed with Gerry and then some other people had joined them and Luke had ended up treating everyone to champagne. When Luke had started out boozy nights like that had been as compulsory a part of his job as shorthand and typing. You *had* to be able to hold your drink; how else were you going to get stories from your contact, unless it was by plying them with liquor? And how else were you going to come down after a long day's war reporting?

But in the past few years, all that had changed. Marco's poncy generation seemed to prefer a Pret sandwich at their desks to a bottle of claret at El Vino's. Increasingly, Luke found himself marooned, like a polar bear on a melting ice cap, searching for someone to share a quick post-work snifter with. So that raucous evening had been a rare treat – a treat which the Channel 6 shareholders could damn well subsidize given the number of times Luke had risked his life for them. The question was, what to attribute it to? He glanced up at the newscreens for inspiration. Aha. Footage of Bellchester Cathedral after the town had been named as having most burglaries per head in Britain.

'Dinner with the bishop of Bellchester', he wrote in the 'Entertaining' column. After all, he'd met the old bugger once or twice. His phone bleeped. A message from Poppy. Luke read it with more interest than he might have done a week ago.

Out late tonight. Don't wait up. x

For Christ's sake. What was going on? Luke looked round the newsroom. Marco was standing by the doors laughing with Dean. Emma was pulling on her cashmere coat, obviously about to go out on a story. At the sight of them, Luke's heart curdled with anxiety. He suddenly, urgently felt the need of a friend. His eye fell on Thea, talking on the phone in her usual bossy way that Luke found such a turn off.

But her hair looked nice today, twisted in a knot on her head and those black trousers she was wearing displayed her legs to best advantage. Luke felt a stirring in his trousers. She had no kids or husband to rush home to, she'd surely go for a post-work drink with him?

Straightening his tie, he headed across the newsroom. She was still talking. At the sight of him, she put her hand over the mouthpiece.

'Hi Luke, can I help?' she said briskly, then back into the phone, 'Just a minute.'

'Just wondering if you fancied a drink after work.'

There was a long pause then she said, 'I'd love to. But I'm busy.'

'Oh. OK.' Huffily Luke turned his back.

Too out of sorts to try anyone else, he went straight home after work to find Brigita occupying Poppy's normal spot on the sofa in front of *Property Ladder.*

'Everything OK with Clara?' he asked her, more for something to say than because he really cared about the answer. Which wasn't to say he didn't adore his youngest child; he just couldn't get too excited about the minutiae of raising her.

'Oh yes, Daddy. Since I come she is so much better behaved. I think before she is a little mardy, no? But I teach her some manners.'

Luke studied Brigita. No one could remotely call her pretty with that sallow skin and slightly stringy hair, but she did have rather magnificent breasts. He slapped himself down. Fancying the nanny was too much of a cliché even for him.

'You don't mind doing all this babysitting?' he asked.

'No. I need t'earn as much as I can so me and me boyfriend can buy a house in 'artlepool. So the more work I do the better. And it's nice to see Mummy enjoying herself. When I started, she always seem to 'ave a monk on, but now it is all much better.'

'Good, good,' said Luke, not having a clue what she was talking about.

After Brigita had gone, he poured himself a whisky, watched his rival Paxman on *Newsnight*, noting with envy his still thick head of hair. Maybe he'd had a weave. He wondered if he'd ever bump into him at Dr Mazza's. Talking of which, he must make another appointment.

He went to bed, but sleep wouldn't come, so he went down to the kitchen and was pouring himself another drink when Poppy burst through the door. She was pink-cheeked and smiling, wearing a purple silk slip dress with a fake fur waistcoat over it and thigh-high green suede boots. Luke's heart stopped at the loveliness of her. He realized he'd forgotten how beautiful his wife was.

'Oh, you're still up,' she said.

'Insomnia.'

'Poor you.' She kissed him on the cheek. 'Shall I make you a camomile tea?'

'Where have you been?' he asked, surprised at the sudden neediness in his voice.

'At a party,' she said, grabbing a Ryvita from the breadbin and taking a bite. 'Launch of some deodorant.' She pointed to a bag she'd deposited on the counter. 'Look, a free one for both of us. Don't say I don't spoil you.'

Luke walked up behind her and wrapped his arms round her waist. 'How come you've been going to so many parties recently?' he muttered into her hair. To his surprise, he felt her stiffen.

'I've been meaning to talk to you about that,' she said.

But Luke didn't really care what the answer was, just as he no longer cared that Poppy wasn't looking for a job. He was distracted by the feel of her breasts in his hands. Cupping them, he kissed her on the back of her neck and was rewarded by her twisting round and kissing him full on the mouth. Twenty minutes later, they were naked on their bed, both breathing heavily.

'That was lovely,' Poppy said.

'It was great,' Luke agreed. Certainly, Poppy had been far more passionate than usual. Maybe it was because she was drunk. Still, Luke wasn't complaining. At last, he felt his eyelids grow heavy, his breathing start to slow.

'Luke,' she said, wrapping herself around him, 'you know you asked about why I was going to so many parties?'

'Uh,' he said. 'I'm half asleep now, darling. Let's talk in the morning.'

28

That same evening, Thea and Rachel were sitting in a vegetarian restaurant in Islington, sharing a thali. Rachel seemed to have doubled in size since Thea last saw her, she'd also had a scan and knew she was expecting a boy.

'Isn't it amazing?' she breathed.

'Incredible.' Thea tried to sound as enthusiastic as possible about the black-and-white picture of a piece of ectoplasm. 'Who do you think he looks like?'

'Dunc, I hope.' Rachel eyed the paper lovingly. 'Bastard.'

'Sorry?' That's what Thea had always thought of Dunc but she was surprised to hear her friend say it.

'That's what I'm calling the baby until Dunc deigns to marry me.'

So much for Rachel being cool about marriage. 'So he's still holding out on that?' Thea said emotionlessly.

'Mmm. Says he can cope with being a father but being a husband is just too grown-up. Doesn't seem to care it's upsetting my mum and upsetting his mum that their first grandchild will be born out of wedlock.'

'For Christ's sake! What would have happened if Dunc had been born in 1920? Would he have refused to go to war because it was "too grown-up". He's what ... thirty-three?'

'He's spoilt.' Rachel's face fell. 'He's had a cushy life

with his mum doing his washing and cooking for him, then various girlfriends doing it, and now me. I've spoilt him, Thea. And he bloody knows he calls all the shots.'

'No, he doesn't.'

'He does. I didn't tell you this before because I was worried you'd judge me, but it wasn't all quite as rosy as I made out when I told Dunc I was pregnant. He hit the roof. Told me I'd trapped him. And . . . I guess I had. So I made him all sorts of promises. Told him he wouldn't have to change a nappy ever, that I'd do all the night feeds, that he'd never have to push a pram if he found it too embarrassing, that if it was all too much for him he could just leave.'

'Oh,' Thea said. It wasn't that Rachel's confession was a surprise – in the shocker stakes it was up there with finding out Elton John was gay or the Queen was rather posh. But hearing her confess so bluntly that she'd trapped her man gave Thea pause for thought. Wasn't that what the bimbo had done to Luke? 'But I'm sure he won't be like that when the baby arrives,' she said in rallying tones.

'Well, I hope not, but he's always going to have the option to duck out when times get tough. It's not that I mind so much for me, it's the bastard I care about. Being born into a world where his dad was more interested in alphabetizing his LPs than singing him lullabies would be sad.' As usual, she did an abrupt Rachel U-turn. 'Anyway, forget it. Boring. How's your gran?'

'Same as ever. I went to see her last weekend and she just stared into space and rocked. It was grim.'

'Mmm. Must be.' Like most people, Rachel wasn't

much good on doling out sympathy about an old, ill person she'd never met. Boyfriend troubles were so much easier to relate to. 'And work?'

'Still in disgrace.'

'That swine Marco.'

'Yeah, that shithead . . . but, you know, his behaviour apart, I think I'm just a bit bored.'

'But you have the most exciting job in the world.' Rachel always pointed this out, when Thea gently compared their salaries.

'*Used* to have. But now all I get given are the most rubbish stories about councils cutting back on recycling and Jordan launching a new range of lingerie. I'm desperate to get back on the road again, but until I crawl my way out of the doghouse, that's as unlikely as . . .'

'As me and Dunc getting married. Why don't you leave?'

'Because there's nowhere else to go. All the networks are cutting back. And because . . .'

'Because Luke doesn't work at another network?' Rachel asked gently.

'Rach! I told you, Luke and I are as dead as the dodo. I never even see him any more. In fact, he asked me for a drink this evening and I turned him down flat. You'd have been proud of me.'

'Yay! Well done.' Rachel grinned as Thea's phone rang.

'Oh sorry. Better answer this in case it's the Prime Minister wanting to confess exclusively how he's been having a ten-year affair with a donkey called Mabel. Hello?'

'Thea? Hi there! It's Jake Kaplan.'

'Oh, hello. Are you back?' She'd been keeping a very close eye on the Minnie website but there had been no more mention of a trip to Guatemala and she had dismissed all thoughts of sending out a team.

'No, still in Guatemala City,' Jake said, although he sounded as if he was out in the back yard having a sneaky fag. 'Looks like I'll be here for a while.'

'Oh yeah?' Thea felt a tingle of interest.

'Want to know why?'

'Of course.'

He lowered his voice. 'Strictly between us, Minnie's visit is booked for next week.'

'Will she give us an interview?'

Jake sighed. 'Probably not. But you might want to cover the visit anyway. Give us some much needed publicity.'

A knot of embarrassment formed in Thea's stomach. 'I don't know, Jake. I mean, the work you guys do is amazing, but without Minnie talking to us it's not really a big enough story.' She paused, surprised at how much she disliked disappointing him. 'Sorry.'

'Look,' Jake said, 'I told you already. Minnie may not give you an interview but there's still going to be a big story. The quicker you can get a team in placer the better.'

'What's the story?'

'I can't tell you in so many words. Just remember what I said about adoption.'

'Minnie Maltravers is going to adopt a Guatemalan baby?'

'Really?' Rachel exclaimed, from behind Thea.

'You didn't hear it from me,' Jake said. 'But as I said you might want a team in place. Just in case.' He paused and then added, 'And if she *were* going to give an interview, it would probably be to the network that offered the most coverage to Guatemala Children's work.'

Thea thought. Minnie adopting a baby would be massive, whether she gave them an interview or not. OK, not such a big story that they'd send the anchorman to cover it, but if there was just the teensiest promise she'd talk to them then they had to have Luke in place. And her. Thea's pulse throbbed. A foreign trip. A hotel. Sun on her back. And Luke.

Just like old times.

Oh stop it, Thea.

'I'll talk to my boss first thing tomorrow, then I'll call you.'

'Good. By the way, how are you, Thea?'

'I'm fine,' she said, 'and you?'

'Looking forward to seeing you again.'

Thea felt a jolt of outrage mixed with amusement. He was flirting with her again. She supposed it would be flattering if he didn't resemble a denim-clad pixie.

'Er, right,' she said. 'Good. I'll be back to you as soon as I can.'

Dean wasn't convinced.

'So you're saying if we don't send a team then we stand no chance of getting an interview but you can't promise the interview will happen.'

'That's right.' Thea nodded, as her mobile started ringing. Without even looking at it, she switched it off.

'But why the hell not?' Dean was asking.

'Dean, you know why. We're dealing with a diva who

never speaks to the press. But giving Guatemala Children as much coverage as possible will give us the best possible chance.'

'I'm not sure Roxanne's going to buy this. We've already gone over budget for this year. What are the shareholders going to say if we fork out all this money on footage of a bunch of kids on a rubbish heap and we don't get Minnie?'

'It's the only way, Dean.' Thea tried another tack. 'They'll be really cute kids, Dean. Cute and starving. The viewers will all have their hankies out.'

'Talking of starving.' Dean reached for the biscuit tin in front of him. 'Shit, who's eaten all the Jammie Dodgers? All right. We'll do it. I'll tell Marco to pack his bags.'

Thea felt as if her ears had been boxed.

'Marco? Not Luke?'

'You heard me. This is more of a Marco story. He's the future face of the network. Luke's got – what? – another year at most before it's time he goes for early retirement. Focus groups show he has no appeal to our younger viewers.'

Thea knew Luke's star was on the wane, but this was the first time she'd heard it stated so bluntly. Part of her crowed, Serve him right. Luke had thrown his wife over for a younger model, now the network was going to play the same trick on him. But still, he was a talent who didn't deserve to be chucked aside. More importantly, she wasn't travelling to the nearest bus stop with a shit like Marco. She hated that man more than she'd hated cabbage as a child, or JR in *Dallas*, or Lucy Randall at school because she'd laughed at the way Thea danced to her

Bugsy Malone record. Doing Minnie with Marco would be about as much fun as a frontal lobotomy without anaesthetic.

'Dean, I've agreed with Guatemala Children that Luke does the interview. Minnie's a huge fan of his.'

'You're telling me Minnie Maltravers watches the *SevenThirty News*?' Dean raised a sardonic eyebrow.

'Maybe her husband does,' Thea said. 'Anyway, that's beside the point. Guatemala Children have told me it's Luke or nobody.'

'Oh bloody hell, Thea Mackharven, why did I ever let you come back from New York? All right, all right. We'll send a team to Guatemala City. Including Luke. Plus a troupe of violin players to help with the sob factor. But if it doesn't work, you are in big trouble. And you wouldn't like me when I'm angry.'

'I don't like you when you're not angry,' Thea said deadpan.

It wasn't a joke, but happily Dean didn't see that. He slapped his thigh appreciatively. 'Nice one! Now fuck off and get me the megastar.'

As she shut his door, her mind was whirling like a fairground ride. So much to do. They should really get going in the morning. She'd have to tell Luke, organize a technical team, get the travel people on to the flights, call Jake . . . She remembered her phone – switched off in her pocket. Absently she pulled it out and turned it on. It started ringing.

You have one new voice message.

Probably Mum, she thought, yawning as she stuck the phone to her ear. She'd better not say she was about to slip out to Pret à Manger. She'd tell her she'd made a salad and brought it in in a Tupperware box.

'Hello, Miss Mackharven. This is Corinne Stiller at Greenways home.'

Thea's mouth went dry. Her legs turned to water. Instantly she called back.

'Thea,' Corinne was trotting out a well-reheared speech, 'I'm so sorry to have to tell you, but your grandmother died peacefully this morning.'

29

Luke was not the only one to board a plane and head off to Guatemala City. Every five-star hotel in the capital was booked solid with news teams from all over the world. As the *SevenThirty* crew landed, headed by Alexa now that Thea had to organize and attend a funeral, rumours were beginning to spread like nits in a nursery that Minnie's visit was not entirely altruistic, that perhaps her trips to see the cute little children in the orphanage might be likened to one of her infamous after-hour sprees in Bergdorf's.

Minnie's people, however, denied everything, insisting that the model was there on a private charity visit to open a health clinic and give the work of Guatemala Children a higher profile. No further statement would be made.

'Are you absolutely sure she's not going to talk to anyone else?' Thea demanded of Jake. Four days had passed and she was talking on her hands-free kit, foot hard on the accelerator of her Peugeot 205. The speedometer was creeping steadily past 90mph as she made her way down the motorway to Greenways and Gran's funeral.

'I'm as sure as I can be,' Jake said sounding remarkably perky, given it was six in the morning his time. 'The *SevenThirty* crew are the only ones who've been allowed full access to our projects. If Minnie does choose to speak, she'll be honour bound to pick you.'

'Thank you, Jake,' Thea said, sticking up two fingers at a lorry overtaking on the inside. The driver made an obscene gesture. Thea gestured back.

'You're welcome. We're doing each other a favour.' A pause and then he said, 'Shame you can't be here.'

'I know,' Thea said, though she didn't mean it in the way Jake did.

'I'm really sorry about your gran.' He'd said it before, when she'd first told him why she couldn't come out, but it was nice to hear it again.

'Thank you.' Thea paused. 'Everyone thinks I should be relieved she's not suffering any more, but I just feel so sad.'

'Of course. You've been in semi-mourning for years and now you can go no-holds-barred. All those emotions you've had a stopper on can come flooding out.'

Terrified they might start flooding out right that second, Thea changed the subject. 'So the adoption is definitely going ahead?'

'Off the record, yes. All the papers were signed last night. There'll be an announcement some time this week.'

Thea sighed with relief. If Minnie had suddenly decided she'd prefer a Chinese baby, she would have almost certainly found herself jobless. 'We were right to send a team, then.'

'Totally right. You'll be on the spot when it all kicks off. Are you sure there's no chance you can join us?'

'I'd love to,' she said truthfully, 'but Alexa's out there already. They don't need me.'

'Shit, I've got to go. Minnie's PA's waiting to see

me.' Jake lowered his voice. 'Could be they'll make the announcement today. I'll talk to you later. Oh, and Thea, good luck.'

'Thanks.' But he was gone. Thea turned her radio back up.

'It's outrageous that some woman with a cheque book should just be allowed to wander in to an orphange as though it's Selfridges and pick the cutest baby she can find,' said a female voice.

'More outrageous than leaving the baby in the orphanage to its fate as a child prostitute and a drug addict?' said another that was vaguely familiar.

'Minnie Maltravers *is* a drug addict. She's done ninety days community service and an anger management course for hitting her maid with a handbag. But it looks as though she's going to get a green light to adopt a baby when so many decent couples are turned down.'

'It's irrelevant if other couples are turned down,' said the woman's voice. Who the hell *was* she? 'The point is one child will be rescued from a life of no hope into a life of opportunities.'

'A life as the spoilt only child of an egomaniac.'

'Look, you don't actually think Minnie's going to bring this child up do you? That'll be done by teams of nannies. She'll see it once in the evening for five minutes before bedtime and occasional photo ops, if they're both lucky.'

'Exactly,' Thea said, as she turned off the motorway. The presenter's voice cut in.

'Thank you, Dilly Wells and Hannah Creighton for adding your voices to the debate. Listeners what do you think? Call us on . . .'

Fuck. Hannah Creighton again. The woman was everywhere, like mercury in the water. For the thousandth time Thea wondered what would have happened if she hadn't sent that email. Would Luke and Hannah still be together? Would Clara never have been born? Would Thea and Luke have ended up together? Would Hannah never have entered the limelight and gone to her grave known primarily for the excellent lentil salad she produced annually for the school fête?

'We'll never know,' Thea said swinging into the Greenways car park.

As she expected the funeral in the home's chapel was a sparsely attended affair. Thea, Corinne from Greenways, a couple of the Polish nurses, Aunt Maria and her husband George, who had flown in from Malaga for the occasion even though they had never bothered to visit Toni Mackharven when she was still alive. Thea managed to get through the service conducted by a bored vicar, who had never met her grandmother, without crying. She saved her tears for the crematorium where another few words were said and the coffin wobbled behind the curtains and the person she loved most in the world was really gone. Then back to Corinne's office for tea and boring plain biscuits. Thea resolved to stop at the first garage she saw on the way home and clean them out of Skittles.

'We always watch the programme on satellite,' Aunt Maria said as soon as she'd got through the usual stock of platitudes about Gran finding herself in a better place. 'It's very good, but I have to ask you one thing – why does Emma Waters always seem to go for those pussy-bow blouses? They make her look like Mrs Thatcher. I mean, I know she was a wonderful woman and all that and she made Britain great again but I still don't want to see her lookalike reading the news. It's a bit scary. Do you think she realizes?'

'I'm not sure she does.'

'There's nothing you could do is there?'

'I could have a word.' For the first time that day Thea smiled as she thought of how Emma would react. She put down her cup, ready to start extracting herself, when an idea struck her.

'Do you think I could go and see Mrs Kaplan?' she said to Corinne.

Corinne looked surprised. 'Do you know her?'

'I met her son here last time I visited. He's in Guatemala at the moment, but she might appreciate a visit from me.'

'I'm sure she would.' Corinne smiled. 'She's in room forty-nine. Just go and knock on the door.'

Thea knocked with some trepidation. She remembered once finding her grandmother sitting in a pool of urine, her room smashed to pieces as if she were some rock star. But Mrs Kaplan was sitting peaceably in an armchair staring out at the beautifully tended gardens.

'Hello, Mrs Kaplan. I'm Thea; I'm a friend of Jake's. My grandmother used to live here: Mrs Mackharven. I've just been to her funeral.'

'On the bonny, bonny banks of Loch Lomond,' Mrs Kaplan sang under her breath.

'Jake's in Guatemala. He's working with some of my colleagues.' Thea noticed a large black-and-white photo of Jake on the mantelpiece, his arm round a very pretty blonde girl. Absurdly she felt a tinge of jealousy. Then she wondered if the girl was standing in a trench, like Tom Cruise's leading ladies, to make him look taller, and she grinned.

'Hot cross buns, hot cross buns, one a penny, two a penny.'

'We went out for dinner. He's a nice man. A credit to you. Though don't be getting any ideas about us. He's way younger than me and he's not my type. And I'm probably not his, though I do wonder . . .'

'If you were the only girl in the world,' she trilled.

Thea squeezed her hand. 'OK, that's all for now. I just wanted to check you were all right and let you know where Jake is. He'll come and see you soon.'

She walked back down the sage-green corridor for what she knew would be the last time. Everyone she'd told had gone on about how at least now there was some kind of closure, knowing she no longer had to come here, that her grandmother had some kind of peace, that her financial burden was lifted. But all Thea could feel was total bleakness: the person who'd loved her most in the world had gone.

'Now I've got no one,' she said to herself, as she got into her car. She rested her head on the wheel for a moment, taking deep breaths.

'Come on, Thea. You'll survive. We all do.'

Her phone started ringing. For a moment, she stared at it, debating whether to pick up. Then she took a deep breath.

'Hello?'

'Thea, it's Luke.'

'Oh, hi, Luke. How's it going?'

'Badly.' No *'How are you, Thea?'* she noticed. 'Do you know what's happened?'

'No. I've been at my grandmother's funeral.'

'Of course. Anyway, it's bloody mayhem out here. They've made the official announcement: Minnie's adopted a little boy.'

'Great,' Thea said, noting the lack of sympathy. Luke had never been good at the touchy-feely stuff. Tosser. What had she ever seen in him? 'So we didn't send you out there in vain?'

'Well, yes, you did. Because Minnie's fucking left the country with the baby.'

'She's left?'

'Yup. Slipped out last night, apparently, in her private jet. No one even snatched a photo of them. We don't know where they are. And we're stuck out here with bugger-all to do.'

30

Just a month ago, Poppy would have felt her heart crumble when Luke called from the office to say he was off to Guatemala City that night. But this time she took it on the chin. Of course she'd miss him but now she had Brigita to share the load in the day. She was happy to chat about Clara's little foibles to the point where even Poppy got a bit bored. And every evening she had a party to go to, flanked by the ever faithful Meena.

'How long will you be gone for?' she asked, buffing her nails, her phone on speaker. She still couldn't bring herself to do the Meena hairdresser and make-up artist thing, but she had had a spray tan at the Bliss spa in South Kensington the other day and she was starting to use more make-up.

'A week maybe.' A pause and then Luke said, 'Sorry.'

'It's fine,' she said cheerfully. 'It's your job.'

'I'll pop home to collect a few things. Say goodbye to you and Clara.'

'Good,' she said, 'but you'd better be quick because I'm going out as soon as she's in bed.'

'Going out? Again?'

Another chance to tell him about the column, but Poppy didn't want to do it on the phone. So she simply said, 'Yes. I'll see you later then.'

But in fact she didn't see him because Luke got stuck

in traffic, by which time Meena had arrived in a minicab and whisked Poppy off.

'Where you going tonight, girls?' said Abdul, the Somali driver, whom they'd had on a couple of occasions, and who appeared to live vicariously through them.

'It's a book launch.' Poppy squinted at the invitation. 'A history of hats.'

'Shit, that sounds a bit boring!' Meena was alarmed.

'No, it's by Lady Emmeline de la Vere, so I think it'll be full of *Tatler* type people.'

'Thank Christ for that.' Meena fanned herself in mock relief.

With each outing, Poppy's shyness was diminishing. It made her feel important to be ushered through the door when she produced her invitation, and a glass or two or three or four of champagne always helped her feel more self-confident and got her in the mood. As soon as she entered the huge, echoing former brewhouse in Brick Lane, she saw Charlie at the bar. She headed straight for him.

'You again.' He kissed her on both cheeks. 'You're becoming one of the fixtures at these events, like the Geldof sisters, or Sienna Miller – she'd turn up to the opening of an envelope. You're going to have to start behaving outrageously so I can write about you.'

'I'll do my best.' She was glad Charlie didn't know she was the bimbo. Long might it last.

Tonight, as every night, she scanned the room for Toby, but once again without success. He hadn't replied to her last text and with almost superhuman force of will she had not sent another one. She told herself not to be so silly. She was behaving like her mother with a new, silly crush. She had to concentrate on the fact she had a very glamorous new job and not mess it up.

So she and Meena drank three pink cocktails ('laced with guarana', the barman told them, whatever that meant), then joined a very small Chinese man in a corset and a very large black girl in gold leggings on the dance floor.

'This past couple of weeks have been so much fun!' Meena screamed over 'Billie Jean'. 'When does the first column come out?'

'Tomorrow!'

'Ooh. I can't wait. After that we'll be getting even more invites, won't we?'

I will, Poppy thought, but she was too kind to correct her friend. Though in any case, she wouldn't dream of going anywhere without Meena. A warm hand fell on her shoulder. Poppy looked round.

'Hello!' she gasped, hoping her moves hadn't been too stupid.

'Hi.' Toby kissed Meena then Poppy on both cheeks. 'How are you, gorgeous? Looking fantastic.'

Poppy's throat suddenly felt as narrow as a spider's wrist. 'I'm well,' she shouted above the music. 'How are you?'

'Very good.' Toby had that look in his eyes that reminded her of Clara the first time she tried ice cream, a look that said 'Why did you keep this from me for so long?'

'Come and have a drink.'

She looked at Meena, but she winked and waved and

carried on dancing. So Poppy followed Toby through the crowd to the bar.

'Champagne?'

'Actually I was on the cocktails.' She smiled, hoping she sounded Holly Golightly-esque.

'Really?' He looked dubiously at the pink concoction. 'Bit girlie for me. I think I'll stick to champagne.' They clinked glasses and their eyes locked. Poppy's heart thudded.

'Have you been busy?' she asked.

He raised an eyebrow. 'Yeah. You know how it is. It's hot in here, isn't it? Shall we go outside?'

'OK.' Feeling almost hypnotized, she followed him through a door on to a roof terrace. Below them, Brick Lane was a kaleidoscopic shambles of neon curry signs, overflowing bins, mini-cabs and girls in high heels. Poppy realized she was more drunk than she'd thought.

'So, pretty married woman,' Toby said, as they leant against the iron balustrade, 'I've been thinking about you.'

'Then why didn't you get in touch?' she blurted out.

He laughed. 'I'm here now, aren't I? Anyway. I didn't know if you wanted to see me. I mean, you *are* married.'

'To a husband I never see.' She was surprised how venomous her words sounded.

Toby shook his head in mock indignation. 'That's outrageous. If you were my wife I'd lock you in a cage. Never let you out of my sight.'

Her stomach flipped, as he turned round and looked into her eyes. It's going to happen. But I'm married. But he's so handsome. And he's my age. But I'm married, she thought.

'Hi guys!' yelled Meena. 'I've been looking for you!'

'Are you OK?' Poppy asked.

'I'm fine, I'm . . . Bleeurgh—'

Poppy and Toby's shoes were drenched in fuchsia-coloured vomit.

'Oh, shit.' Meena giggled, flopping about. 'Sorry.'

Poppy glanced anxiously at Toby, but he was laughing. 'Are you all right, sweetheart?'

'I'm so embarrassed.' She didn't look anything of the sort, far too gone for that.

'Ah, come on. It happens to us all.'

Poppy looked at him, more smitten than ever. Most guys would have been furious to have their shoes puked on. *Luke* would have been furious.

'Awurrgh!' cried Meena, as the pizza she'd eaten for lunch mingling with some Thai mini-bites flew into a conveniently situated plant pot.

'Jesus.' Toby turned to Poppy. 'I think you'd better get her home.'

'I'll be OK,' Meena managed to say. 'I can get home by myself.'

'Well, if you're sure,' Poppy said immediately. She didn't want to leave right now.

'Don't be silly,' Toby said, 'you're in a terrible state. *I'll* take you home.' He looked at her. 'Poppy, are you going to come?'

Poppy knew she'd been judged and found wanting. 'Of course,' she said.

Toby found them a taxi. The traffic was light and it only took forty minutes to get back to Kilburn. Toby sat in the front making calls on his mobile to people called Sergei and Vladimir, Poppy sat in the back with Meena beside her fast asleep. They had to shake her awake to get her out on to the street and through the flimsy front door and up the stairs with its fraying brown carpet.

It was weird being back in the flat, like visiting some Tracey Emin style museum of Poppy's life. Meena had never got round to finding a new flatmate, so the place was virtually identical to when Poppy had lived there: there were the same gaudy Indian prints on the wall, the same tatty throw over the orange sofa, the same pile of magazines on the coffee table, the same curtains that looked like evidence from the Texas chainsaw massacre, probably the same dirty mugs in the sink untouched since the day of Poppy's departure. She'd thought that old carefree side of her had died, but perhaps now it was being reborn.

'I think you should stay the night,' Toby said, once Meena was tucked up in bed in bra and knickers, a bucket beside her. 'She might throw up in her sleep.'

'I can't!' Poppy exclaimed. 'I've got a little girl to get back to.'

'Oh, so you do. I keep forgetting.' He frowned. 'I guess I'd better stay then. It's not safe to leave her on her own.'

A trail of jealousy slithered down Poppy's spine like a fat slug. 'Well, I could call my nanny,' she said. 'See if she can stay over.'

Brigita was as obliging as ever.

'Of course, Mummy. Go out on t'piss. Enjoy yourself.'

'I'm not enjoying myself,' Poppy said loftily. 'I'm looking after my sick friend.'

'Whatever. Clara and I'll be reight.'

'Er, OK,' said Poppy hoping, as so often, she'd understood Brigita's gist. She hung up and turned to Toby who was buttoning his coat.

'Do you know a minicab number?' he asked.

'There's a firm next door.'

'Is there? Great. That'll save me having to wait for hours.' Seeing Poppy's woebegone face, he pecked her on the lips, then more tenderly stroked her hair.

'I'd like to stay but people need me.' He bent down and kissed Poppy on the cheek. 'You're a nice person, Poppy, looking after your friend.'

'Thank you,' she said, guilty that it wasn't quite so simple.

There was a tiny pause. They looked at each other, then Toby leant forward and took her face in his hands and suddenly they were kissing hungrily.

'I can't do this,' she said, just as he gasped, 'You're so lovely.' They looked at each other passionately, then the moment was broken by the strains of OutKast's 'Hey Ya' blaring from Toby's jeans' pocket.

'Shit,' he said, pulling out his phone. Poppy expected him to turn it off, but instead he said, 'Hello, Constantine? Yeah. Fine. Well, look, I'm a bit busy right now but I can be with you in, what, an hour? Is that OK?' He turned back to Poppy. 'Sorry about that, darling.' He kissed her on the lips, but this time perfunctorily. 'I wish I could stay,' he said again, 'but I've got people to see. I'm just going to use the bathroom.'

Poppy sat on the sofa. Suddenly she was cold. She pulled Meena's slightly grimy fake fur throw round her.

Toby was gone quite a while. When he returned he seemed a bit different, brisker somehow, more detached.

'Shit, I've really got to get a move on.'

She'd heard it all before from Luke. But instead of arguing, she smiled like a plucky landgirl.

'I'll see you soon,' Toby said, his hand on the door-knob. 'Call you tomorrow. Now you take care. Look after Meena.'

And he was gone, leaving Poppy with nothing to do but splash her face with water in the old bathroom. The tap Luke had mended was dripping again, while the squeaking windmill vent in the corner was clogged with cobwebs now that Poppy was no longer around to dust.

Poppy went into her old room, which appeared to have become Meena's walk-in wardrobe, removed a pile of clothes from her old bed and climbed under the musty duvet, another fossil from her past. It was late, but sleep took a long time to arrive. Her head was pounding as the alcohol wore off and she pondered on what she'd done.

She was married. She couldn't kiss other men. But she was also – it was the first time she'd bluntly acknowledged it to herself – so miserable. The man she'd thought was her handsome prince had neglected her for so long, she felt like Sleeping Beauty shut up in a tower. But now a new prince was in town and his kiss had made Poppy wake up to a world she'd missed out on, to the prospect that someone else might love her.

31

Two drunks trading insults beneath her window woke Poppy about seven. She groaned and tried to open her eyes, which the fairies appeared to have superglued shut in the night. She rolled out of bed and padded across the hall to Meena's room. Meena was curled up under a blanket, mascara streaked down her face, hair a bird's nest, snoring slightly. She didn't look pretty but she had survived the night.

Poppy showered, taking in the bathroom's greying grout, the lukewarm, dribbly water, the damp patch creeping up the wall. Suddenly she felt desperate to be back with Clara in smart, clean Maida Vale. Home.

She dressed hastily in last night's clothes and, having scribbled a note for Meena, hurried as fast as her heels could carry her down the shabby stairs and out into Kilburn High Road, lined with pound shops selling cut-price shampoos and baby wipes, obscure fruits and vegetables and tight-fitting, synthetic clothes.

As she headed towards the bus stop, guilt about her behaviour the previous night alternated with a fantasy about a possible different life that had opened up to her. What she'd done was wrong, but at the same time it had been so wonderful. Wonderful kisses with a wonderful man, a man who couldn't remember the heyday of the

Beatles, who wasn't a few years away from collecting his Freedom Pass.

Poppy stopped dead, turned round and walked a few steps back down the road to a newsagent's she'd just passed. There, on the stand, nestled between *Closer* and *Now* was this week's copy of *Wicked*. A huge picture of Jordan on the cover. MY BABY AGONY, the headline screamed. Then a smaller picture of two contestants from *The X Factor* – KELLI AND NARGESS: OUR FEUD – and then in the bottom left-hand corner a tiny head shot of Poppy, winking just as the photographer from *Wicked* had asked her to. 'Introducing Our New Columnist: the Bimbo Bites Back.'

Poppy stared mesmerized. She wasn't sure about this. Had there been talk of calling her the Bimbo? But still . . . 'our new columnist'. Hands shaking, she picked up a copy.

'Oi!' yelled the Indian man behind the counter, 'no browsing.'

'Sorry!' She paid him one pound twenty, flashing the magazine in front of him, hoping he'd notice the resemblance between the glossy siren on the cover and the raddled hooker going home after a busy night's trade who stood in front of him. Unsurprisingly, he didn't. She thought about exclaiming: 'That's me! That's me!' but there were many mad people roaming Kilburn and she knew she'd be dismissed as one of them.

On the top deck of the bus, Poppy read the column, then re-read it. She was rather shaken. All the comments she'd made to Migsy about people's hideous outfits and appearances were there in black and white. Poppy hadn't realized Migsy was going to print what she said, she thought it had just been giggly girls-only gossip. And those vile things she'd said about Hannah were now staring at her from the page. God only knew how she'd retaliate. Poppy shivered nervously, but at the same time couldn't stop grinning at her photograph, at her words in print. All right, they were a little unkind but she was a published writer. She wondered what Luke would think. And Mum. And Meena. And Toby.

'You look badly, Mummy. Do you catch sickness from yer mate?' Brigita turned to Clara, who was sitting in her high chair, spooning Weetabix and banana all round her mouth. 'Come on, Clara, eat your breakfast then we go to the museum.'

'Ug,' said Clara.

'The museum?'

'The Science Museum. It's our favourite place, isn't it Clara? I teach her all about the solar system: Mercury, Venus, Earth, Mars, Jupiter, Saturn, Uranus, Neptune, Pluto.' She filled Clara's beaker from the tap. 'And how is Luke? I just hear on the news that Minnie Maltravers has adopted a little Guatemalan baby. Do you think he will meet her? She is my idol that woman. Bloody gorgeous, in'it?'

'I don't know,' Poppy said. 'I haven't heard from him.' And I hadn't even noticed, she thought, surprised. Normally Luke's silence when he was away drove her to distraction. She reached in her bag. 'Have a look at this.'

Silently, Brigita read the column. Then she looked up smiling at her boss.

'Did you really write this? I don't think you're so cleverclogs. Look, Clara, look. And they take nice photo too! Is amazing what they can do with lights and on the computer.'

'More banana.'

'More banana, *please*,' Brigita corrected, as Poppy said, 'I think I'll have a little lie down if that's OK.'

'Of course, Mummy. You definitely need to sleep. Look at those black circles under the eyes. I'm going to call my friends and tell them to buy *Wicked*. And I must send copy to my parents. They will be so chuffed. I am working for not one but two famous persons now. I feel honoured.'

'Don't be silly.' Poppy laughed, secretly delighted that she was suddenly seen on a par with Luke. 'I'll see you later, Clara sweets.'

'Ug.'

She slept and woke an hour later. Turning her phone on, she found she had two messages. One was an over-excited rant from Meena, who'd seen the column.

'I loved it, loved it, loved it. It's hilarious, Poppy, much funnier than the normal celebrity bollocks you read. And thanks for getting me home last night. I owe you my life.'

The next was from her mum.

'Hello, Poppy. Seen the column.' A pause. 'It's not quite what I had in mind for you when I sent you to Brettenden House, but it's still a job of sorts, and some of it I actually found quite funny. Talk soon. Bye. Oh by the way, I'm off to Marseilles for my spa weekend. Fingers crossed. You never know, I could be returning with a new father for you.'

Normally, Poppy would have been infuriated by such a message but now, her mind on Toby, Louise's words drifted over her head. Poppy wondered why he hadn't called. She remembered what she always told Meena in these situations – he was probably just playing it cool. Or he'd be at work. This concierge stuff was obviously very demanding with rich clients wanting you 24/7. Poppy dozed off again. When she woke up it was four o'clock and the phone was ringing with a voice message from her agent, Barbara.

'Darling, brilliant column.' A chuckle. 'I didn't know you had it in you, you always looked so sweet and innocent. Phone's been going crazy all day with various offers. Call me.'

She called. Barbara was on the other line, but this time Jenny on reception knew exactly who she was and organized a lunch date for the following week.

Then Poppy called Migsy.

'*Wicked* magazine, Michelle speaking!'

'Migsy, I mean, Michelle, it's Poppy.'

There was just the tiniest of pauses, then Migsy exclaimed. 'Poppy! We have been talking about nothing but you today and how great you are. The column's been a huge hit. Readers have been emailing us all day saying how much they like it.'

'You said you were going to let me see it before it went to print.'

'Oh? Didn't you get my email? I wondered why you didn't get back to me.'

'You didn't send an email.'

'I did! Oh don't tell me it didn't get through? We've been having a nightmare with our server recently. But there wasn't a problem, was there?'

'Well . . .' Poppy was torn. She wanted to carry on doing the column, but she had to let Migsy know she knew she'd duped her. 'I just didn't realize all those nasty comments were going to be printed.'

'What did you think was going to happen?' Migsy sounded defensive.

'I don't know . . . I thought our conversation was private. I thought you were just going to . . . you know, list the people I'd seen.'

Migsy tutted. 'I have no idea what gave you that impression. Of course we're interested in your opinions. You're a fascinating woman.'

'But I didn't say all those things. I mean . . . you put words into my mouth.'

'But you agreed with them!'

Poppy was feeling too hungover to argue. 'You won't do that again, will you?' she tried feebly.

'Of course not. God, I'm so sorry if there was a misunderstanding but like I say, it really is all's well that ends well, because you're a star now. And I tell you what, how about I negotiate a rise for you? Say five hundred pounds a column in future.'

'Oh.'

'Or six hundred.' Migsy had mistaken her surprise for stalling.

'All right,' Poppy said.

'Great. Now, I have to go, but I'm going to bike round a pile of invitations tomorrow morning for next week's parties. I'll call you on Thursday at eleven again for the lowdown. But honestly, Poppy, well done. You've done terrifically well.'

Poppy stared at the handset. She didn't know quite what to think. Six hundred pounds a week was very tempting, and the feedback she'd had so far had been so positive. So she'd come across as a bit bitchy, but she'd been mauled plenty in the papers before and survived, hadn't she? Why shouldn't someone else take a turn in the ring?

She turned on the television and watched a bit of an afternoon film, then switched to Sky News. A reporter somewhere hot was standing in front of a beaten-up-looking shack.

'So yes, Elsa, I can tell you it has now been confirmed that Minnie Maltravers has adopted a nine-month-old Guatemalan baby called Cristiano Morales. From what we've been able to discover, his mother died in child-birth and his father is unknown. His grandparents raised him for a while, but then, finding themselves unable to cope, had put him in an orphanage. Minnie Maltravers is believed to have left Guatemala. Sources report she has returned to Scotland, where she and her husband Max . . .'

So *that* was what Luke was doing. She should try and remember to watch the *SevenThirty News*, she supposed. Poppy was shaken by the indifference she suddenly felt towards her husband. For nearly three years thoughts of him and how to win him had consumed her, but now she felt a creeping anger at how he'd ignored her.

She reached for the pile of invitations at the side of the bed and as she leafed through them, she picked up the phone.

'Meena, it's me. Take a couple of Berocca and some Red Bull because we're going out again tonight.'

32

Even though Minnie had slipped away in the dead of night, the story of the adoption had gathered pace like a runaway sledge. The world's media descended upon the tiny village in the middle of the jungle where Cristiano Morales had been born, with the result that on Monday Cristiano's aunt was telling everyone who dangled a hundred-dollar bill under her nose how happy she was that her nephew would grow up in the bosom of one of the wealthiest women in the world. By Tuesday she'd changed her mind and was saying how tragic it was that Cristiano had been 'stolen' from his family by gringos.

Meanwhile dozens of aggrieved women who had been refused permission to adopt a Guatemalan baby came forward to complain. Every psychologist in the land was under siege from journalists wanting opinions on Minnie's character and whether such a hard-core hedonist could ever make a good mother. Everyone was discussing the rights and wrongs surrounding the issue. Everyone except the *SevenThirty News* which had a different agenda.

On Thursday evening, Thea was sitting in the gallery – the programme's main operations room – watching the bank of screens in front of her. Bernie, the day's usual programme editor, had impetigo so Dean had decided Thea should take over.

'You've programme edited before, haven't you?'

'Of course,' Thea lied, eager to impress him.

It had been an adrenalin ride, but everything was going to plan. They'd just finished the first third of the show, covering the Russian presidency battle, the new targets for carbon emissions, the German serial killer jailed for life for the murder of fourteen prostitutes and now the adverts were running.

Some of the screens showed Marco and Emma being touched-up by the make-up girls. One showed a still of a giant rubbish dump, the opening shot of Luke's report from Guatemala, which was coming up next.

'OK, Marco, Emma,' said Jayne, the PA, whose job it was to time each second of the programme. 'Going live in three, two, one, on air.' Emma swivelled her chair towards the camera.

'Good evening, and welcome back to the *SevenThirty News*, and now over to Luke Norton in Guatemala City for the third in this week's special reports on the lost children of Guatemala.'

Hilary, the director, pressed the button and the gigantic rubbish tip filled the screen. The camera moved in to highlight two beautiful children dressed in rags sifting through the garbage. Luke's voiceover kicked in:

'On this rubbish dump, just outside Guatemala City, Pablo aged six and his sister Juanita, eight, are trying to make a living. They haven't seen their parents for two years since the end of the bitter civil war that tore this country apart . . .'

Thea sat back with a smile. Tick. Another report under way. Two more to go and they'd have fulfilled their side of the bargain and then Jake Kaplan had better deliver the goods. After Minnie's disappearance, Thea had been more or less constantly on the phone to him. He'd reassured her that even though Minnie was no longer in Guatemala, she'd been seriously shaken by the vicious media coverage and was seriously considering giving an interview to defend herself. Meanwhile, the best thing the *SevenThirty News* could do was keep its team in place.

'Minnie's people are delighted with your guys' work,' he'd told her that afternoon, 'and they love the fact you're the only network not questioning her decision, just showing what a wonderful job she's doing helping these poor people.' Thea smiled at the undercurrent of sarcasm. Jake continued, 'They all met Luke while they were out there and they thought he was just charming and they've assured me that if she speaks to anyone it'll be to him.' A slight pause. 'And Martin Bashir.'

'Martin Bashir?' Thea's voice was so loud, the phone was redundant. She could easily have been heard on the moon, let alone Guatemala City.

Jake sounded sheepish, 'Yeah, Martin Bashir on ABC. Minnie likes him because he's the guy who interviewed Princess Diana. But that's an American network. You're the front runners to get the only British interview.'

'You never said anything about a British *and* an American interview.'

'I didn't know until about twenty minutes ago.'

A vision of chopping off Jake's head and dipping it in boiling oil floated through Thea's mind. 'You bloody owe it to me to let us have this first,' she'd hissed.

Minnie's people had to be pleased with this report, anyway, she thought, concentrating again on the screen.

Luke was on vintage form: succinct, moving, with just the slightest hint of anger about a world that only took an interest in the plight of the poorest when someone like Minnie became involved. As he listened to Maria, aged ten, who lived under a piece of tarpaulin and whose only pleasure in life was sniffing glue, Thea noticed a stillness in the room, her colleagues sobered by what they were seeing. Only one was immune to Luke's spell.

'Fucking hell,' Dean barked from behind her, making her jump. Unlike Chris Stevens who always watched the programme in his office accompanied by a large Scotch, Dean had an unnerving habit of entering the gallery unannounced and making running, critical commentary. 'I'm still worried about this, Thea. We're the only people not debating the Minnie issue and doing worthy reports instead. If we don't get the interview off the back of this we're going to be a laughing stock.'

'I know, Dean,' Thea said, keeping her voice low so the others could concentrate. 'But this is the game plan. We can't abandon it now or we'll have wasted everyone's time.'

'What's your Guatemala Children contact saying?'

Thea took a deep breath and told him about her and Jake's last conversation. Unsurprisingly, Dean was unamused.

'You're telling me the silly cow's going to talk to Bashir first?'

'I don't know. Hopefully not. It depends which country she's in.'

'She – mustn't – talk – to – Bashir – first.' Between each word Dean jabbed his finger in the air. 'I want the world exclusive on this, Thea.' Noisily, he left the narrow, dark room.

'Well, I think it's a brilliant report,' Jayne said, never taking her eyes off her stopwatch. 'We should be running this kind of thing regardless of what Minnie says or does.'

'Thanks Jayne.' Thea's phone started ringing. She picked it up.

'Hi.'

'Thea!' yelled Greg Andrews, the Westminster producer. 'I've got a hot one for you. The Home Secretary's going to resign in the next twenty minutes.'

'Really?' Thea sat up, heart thundering. In the past couple of days there'd been a handful of prison breakouts. Everyone had been demanding a resignation, but the government kept saying it wasn't going to happen. 'Are you sure it's not just a rumour?'

'Yes, but we're getting confirmation anyway. Be back to you in five.'

'Shit! Have you got a package prepared?'

'Amazingly, we do.'

'You darlings!' In theory, the political team were meant to spend quiet afternoons preparing packages summing up the careers of senior politicians to have them ready to run in exactly these circumstances. In practice, they almost never bothered, preferring to use their rare spare time in Annie's Bar or doing their expenses, but for once someone had been diligent. Thea thanked the God she didn't believe in.

Mouth dry, she called down to the newsroom and ordered a photo of the Home Secretary to display in the background when Marco announced the news. As she instructed Bill, the news editor, she checked the rivals' websites. Nothing there, but that didn't mean they weren't on the case. In the studio, Marco was in the middle of a two-way with the arts correspondent about the shortlist for a literary prize. The plan was to finish with an item about a dog who'd fallen over a cliff and been found alive three months later. But Thea didn't want that. Thea wanted a good old-fashioned scoop. She looked at the clock. Why hadn't Greg called back? She dialled his mobile. Busy. Good.

'Five minutes to go, Thea . . .' Jayne warned.

Thea called Greg again. 'It's tight, but . . . he's just outside . . . we're going to get it . . . Hey, Gordon, put your earpiece in.' There were muffled sounds, then Gordon the political editor came on the line.

'Confirmed. He's going.'

'For sure?'

'One hundred per cent. But Sky are on to it too. Get me on air now.'

'Live in forty seconds. Live to Westminster in forty,' Jayne calmly told the studio. 'Marco, newsflash in ten.'

A few miles away Greg was hammering an intro into the system. Before he'd even finished typing, Marco was reading it from the autocue.

'And now over to Westminster for some breaking news. The *SevenThirty News* understands that the Home Secretary is to resign today.' A red strap line flashed up on the screen beneath him, echoing his words. Gordon, Gordon, please let this be true, Thea thought. If they got this wrong her job would be right on the line.

'Our political editor Gordon Cray is with us now.

Gordon, I understand that you're the first journalist to confirm—'

'That's right, Marco,' gasped lanky Gordon, grinning as if all his numbers had come up on the lottery.

Thea imagined the fury at the BBC, the hissy fits at ITN, the tantrums at Sky. There was nothing better than knowing you'd scooped your rivals. She imagined the bollockings in their newsrooms, the 'Why didn't we have this?' and blew her onscreen colleague a kiss.

'I love you, Gordon Cray,' she whispered. 'I want to have your babies.' She looked at the red studio clock. Four minutes left. Thea hugged herself.

'I think I've just redeemed myself,' she whispered, her face lighting up like the Blackpool illuminations.

'Brilliant work,' Dean said, clapping her on the shoulder. 'Maybe you should be programme editing full time?'

'Mmm.' Thea smiled. She didn't want to be a programme editor, even though technically it was a promotion. Editors sat at a desk all day, getting bedsores and grief. She changed the subject. 'What can I get you, Dean?'

'Don't be silly, this one's on me.'

'Thank you, I'll have a red wine,' she said.

They were leaning against the polished bar of the Bricklayers, the *Seven Thirty*'s local. Before Thea had gone to New York, nearly every evening had started here with a few drinks before a crowd of them moved on to the Groucho or Soho House. Since her return Thea had only been in a couple of times for a quick snifter. Tonight, however, Dean had announced he was buying everyone a round and the place was bursting at the seams. Emma

Waters had announced for once she'd skip her children's bedtime. Marco had called Stephanie and said not to wait up. Even Roxanne Fox had deigned to come and was sipping Perrier in the corner, talking to Rhys, who was virtually salivating at this chance to curry favour.

Glass in hand, she turned back to her colleagues who were laughing, gossiping, congratulating each other on their triumph. There was nothing like that sense of team spirit when they'd all worked together to pull off a big story. Shame it happened so rarely. Thea was suffused with well-being, in the way she used to be after a night with Luke.

'We made all the others look like nincompoops,' Dean crowed for the umpteenth time.

'I can't believe we were so prepared,' said lazy Bryn Darwin. 'Totally unlike us.'

'Remember the Queen Mother?' Emma Waters chimed in.

'Oh Christ.' There was general laughter. The death of the Queen Mother had been the most over-anticipated incident in the history of journalism. Packages had been prepared decades in advance; there was an annual rehearsal of how the inevitable event would be covered.

'Happened on a bloody Easter Saturday when there were only three people in the office.' Jayne giggled. 'We'd got a black suit in the cupboard for a male presenter to wear . . .'

'But the only bloke in was me and I had a broken arm from that story I did about army recruitment.' Bryn smiled happily.

'So the buck passed to me and I was wearing a bright

pink dress.' Emma chortled, her collarbone crimson from her third gin and tonic. 'Couldn't have been less suitable.'

'And then we paged everyone to try to get them to come in and Greg Andrews called and I thought he was offering to do a live but it turned out he was at Thorpe Park with his family,' Sunil recalled. 'He ended up having to do a two-way from the monkey house.'

'Disaster,' everyone agreed happily.

'Talking of disasters,' said Marco, looking put out. 'Has anyone seen this?'

He reached for his briefcase and brought out a tacky-looking woman's magazine, emblazoned with Day-Glo pictures of C-list celebrities.

'*Wicked*!' Thea said with disdain. 'Funnily enough, it wasn't on my reading pile this week.'

'Then it should have been.' Like a magician producing a rabbit from a hat, Marco revealed Poppy's page.

'Ta-dah! "The Bimbo Bites Back". It's hilarious. Mrs Norton's views on Gwyneth's appalling dress sense, the waste of time that is potty training and – best of all – the haggard witchery that is Hannah Creighton.'

'Let me see.' Dean grabbed it and scanned the page hastily. Then he slammed it down on the bar. 'Oh fucking hell, this is all we need. Luke's wife starting a catfight with Hannah. She'll never let this one go quietly.'

'It's got nothing to do with us,' Thea pointed out, compelled – though she didn't quite know why – to defend Luke. 'Poppy has no connection with the show.'

'Oh no, Thea, none at all. She's only married to its anchorman.' He put on a silly girly voice. '"Until I saw Denise's orange dress I'd no idea how much you could do with a sewing machine and a pair of curtains." Christ on a bike, I hope she's been commissioned to write the introduction to Luke's book on – what is it again? – the history of the Balkans.'

'Poor girl's got to do something with her time,' Marco pointed out. 'After all, Luke *is* away a lot.'

They all tittered. Thea felt another one of her unaccountable flashes of sympathy for Poppy, as Roxanne tapped her on the shoulder.

'Thea, do you mind? Just had a question. You haven't been working on any religious stories lately?'

'Religious? No, I don't think so.'

'Nothing involving the Bishop of Bellchester?'

'Not that I recall.' Before Thea could ask why, her phone began vibrating in her pocket. 'Oh excuse me.' A number beginning +502. Guatemala calling.

'Hello?' she shouted above the din of the jukebox and her colleagues' chatter.

'Is that Thea Mackharven?' An American woman's voice. Nasal. Sounded as if she'd last laughed circa the sinking of the *Titanic*.

'Yes.'

'Please hold, I have Leanne Martines for you.'

Leanne Martines? But now it was a different voice. Equally nasal, rather weary.

'Thea? Hello. This is Leanne, Minnie Maltravers's personal assistant. Just to congratulate your show on its fantastic work and to let you know Minnie would like to give you an interview on Saturday to discuss the motivation behind her adoption of Cristiano.'

Thea's heart almost stopped with excitement.

'That's fantastic news!' she shouted. Dean banged his pint down on the bar.

'You've got it?' he mouthed. Thea nodded and held up a hand to silence him as the most salient point came into focus.

'Uh. Saturday? You mean the day after tomorrow?'

'Yes, Saturday. Short notice I know, but that's the best time for Minnie. She's keen to put a stop to all this malicious talk once and for all before little Cristiano is irreparably damaged. Five p.m. The Balmoral Hotel.'

'The Balmoral Hotel? Is that in Scotland?'

Leanne gave a dry little laugh. 'Full marks for deduction, Miss Mackharven. That's where Minnie is right now. You'd better get that Luke Norton of yours out of Guatemala and on the first plane to Edinburgh.'

33

It was seven on Saturday morning and Thea was standing tapping her foot by the British Airways check-in at Terminal One. Beside her, yawned creepy Rhys and George, the cameraman.

'Where the hell's Luke?' she snapped, looking at her watch for the fourteenth time in five minutes. 'We're going to miss the plane.'

'His flight from Miami's only just landed,' soothed Rhys. 'He's probably still stuck on the plane with the door jammed.'

Thea took a gulp of her latte and wondered if she had time to run and buy another one. Since that Thursday night call she'd slept a total of three hours, so busy had she been finessing details of the Minnie interview with Leanne. The list of stipulations made sorting out peace in the Middle East look a doddle.

'Why the Balmoral Hotel?' Thea had asked. 'Isn't Minnie's castle somewhere near Inverness? Why don't we do it there?'

'She's going to be in Edinburgh on Friday night,' Leanne explained. 'It's Hope Scott's birthday party at the Balmoral and she's spending the night there, which means she'll actually be in the building on Saturday morning and you'll have no worries about her turning up.'

There was a sinking feeling in Thea's stomach. '*Should* I have worries?'

'No, no, of course not,' Leanne said hurriedly. 'But, you know – cars can break down, or get stuck in traffic. Knowing Minnie is actually on site will mean peace of mind for everyone.' She cleared her throat like a policeman about to give evidence in a black-and-white film. 'Now, some other points. Minnie will only do the interview if she is lit by candlelight.'

'Yes, that's all in hand.'

'She will be wearing an outfit by Bing Parsons and she'd like Luke to be wearing one too.'

'Absolutely,' Thea said cheerily, her mind cartwheeling as she worked out how they could persuade the hottest designer of the moment to lend them a suit.

'Hair and make-up?'

'Yes, it's all sorted,' Thea said sweetly. Minnie was very precise about who was allowed to touch her famous face and mane. 'We've got Carlo flying in from New York just like she requested to do her hair.' First class, she thought. Another budget nightmare. 'And we've persuaded Belinda, the make-up artist, to travel to Edinburgh on the sleeper. She's too pregnant to fly, apparently.' And as a result she's demanding four times her already extortionate rates.

'This interview is going to cost us our entire monthly budget,' Thea warned Dean, when she called him for the sixteenth time shortly after two a.m. on Saturday morning.

'Yeah, but it's going to give us viewing figures to make a donkey cack himself and win us a load of awards.' Thea could hear Farrah mumbling crossly in the background. 'It's all right, babe, go back to sleep. Spend whatever it takes.' There was a tiny pause, then he added, 'You'll have to cut back on flights and accommodation for the crew obviously. Cheapest you can find.'

'I'll book a campsite.'

'That's a good idea.' There was a tiny pause, then Dean said, 'I'm not joking, Thea.'

'Nor am I.'

Rhys said, 'I think we should check in.'

'We can't leave without Luke.'

'We may have no choice. He'll have to catch us up.'

'He's taking a leaf out of Minnie's book.' George yawned. 'I remember one of my photographer mates telling me about a shoot she did for *Vogue* in Cape Town. They waited four days for her to show up.'

'*Four* days?'

'In which case, what's the rush?' Rhys grinned. 'Luke could cycle to Edinburgh. Cut down on his carbon footprint.'

'I'll ring some estate agents. Ask them to show us round some houses, since we're going to end up spending the rest of our lives there.'

George and Rhys chortled. Thea didn't. This wasn't funny. They *had* to catch the plane and Luke had to be with them. But just then, she saw him hurrying across the concourse pulling a wheelie suitcase like a little dog. Alexa was just behind. Thea was pleased to note how rough she looked after a night on the red-eye.

'Jesus, I hope you've got an intravenous coffee drip

on you,' he hailed them. 'I've been travelling for nearly twenty-four hours now. Guatemala–Miami, Miami–here. What a fucking nightmare.'

'It'll be worth it,' Thea said. 'Come on. Let's check in.'

'Economy?' asked Luke suspiciously.

Thea smiled brightly. 'I'm afraid so. Business was fully booked.'

'Christ, I've already gone all the way across the Atlantic in economy. I bet you Jeremy Paxman doesn't travel cattle.'

'It's only an hour's flight.' Thea tried to placate him, but Luke ignored her, striding ahead to the check-in desk.

It *was* only an hour's flight, but unfortunately Thea hadn't reckoned with an hour and a half on the Heathrow tarmac due to engine trouble. Because they had checked in so late, they weren't even sitting together. Luke was at the back of the plane studying the enormous Minnie dossier Rhys had compiled, while the others were fast asleep near the front. Wedged between three burly IT consultants on their way to a rugby match and already downing lagers, Thea tried to breathe deeply but her pulse was racing. They were supposed to be at the hotel at ten, to allow plenty of time to set up before the interview at one. What would happen if they were late? Surreptitiously, she pulled out her phone and texted Leanne for the third time.

Still not moving. Should be there by noon latest.

The reply flashed back.

We understand. Minnie happy to wait for you.

318

By the time they'd landed at Edinburgh at half past eleven, Thea was feeling distinctly edgy, a situation not improved by the twenty-minute queue for a taxi.

'Couldn't you have ordered a limo?' Luke complained.

'They were all booked,' lied Thea. She'd completely forgotten. God, was she losing it already, like Gran? 'Oh, look, we're next. The Balmoral,' she said to the driver, as they climbed in.

'At least we're staying somewhere decent,' Luke mumbled.

'Um,' Thea said as the cab sped off, 'we're not actually *staying* at the Balmoral. It's just where we're doing the interview.'

'So where are we? I stayed at the Scotsman last time I seem to recall. That was nice, and the Sheraton isn't bad.'

Thea shut her eyes and leant back against the sticky vinyl seat. 'We're staying in the Hootsmon.'

'Sorry?'

'It's a hotel called the Hootsmon. It's in a lovely quiet suburb. On the website it looked really cool.'

George and Alexa exchanged glances as Luke exploded, '*The Hootsmon*. Fucking hell, Thea!'

'I'm sorry, Luke. I know it's not ideal. But everywhere's booked. It's this rugby match. And we're not allowed to spend more than seventy-five pounds a head.'

'And people think our job is glamorous,' he said huffily.

'Think of all the awards ceremonies we'll go to as a result of this. They'll be glamorous.'

'I hate awards ceremonies.'

Thea felt wounded. Was he saying he'd hated BAFTA

night? She pushed the thought to the back of her mind as they drew up outside the hotel. The Stone and Crombie suite where the interview was taking place was in complete chaos. A man was standing on a step ladder at the far corner of the room, rigging up a billowing satin sheet, while a young Japanese woman in hotpants with pigtails stood below him shouting: 'Left, left, a bit to the right. No, a bit to the left.' Two young women were setting out a dozen ivory candelabras.

'What's this? Snow White's boudoir?' Luke demanded.

'It's the deal we've done. Minnie has no veto over the questions we ask but she gets to choose the set.'

'Fucking hell,' Luke muttered under his breath. 'From the siege of Sarajevo to this.'

In a bedroom that led off the sitting room, the heavily pregnant make-up artist was gabbling on her phone. A black man with a buzz cut whom Thea took to be the hairdresser – they always had the worst hair – was laying out an array of wigs and hairpieces. The stylists, two women so skinny they looked as if they'd need to run round the shower to get wet, were leafing through a long rack of clothes, consulting urgently. A woman in jeans and a Barbie T-shirt with a haunted look that Thea would soon discover was the trademark of anyone who came in contact with the legend that was Minnie Maltravers hurried towards her, proffering a bony hand.

'Thea? I'm Leanne,' she said. She spoke as if it was a race against the clock. 'So good to meet you finally.'

'Is everything OK? I'm so sorry we're late.'

'It's fine. As it happens Minnie has a bit of a cold, so she's still in bed. But she'll be down in about half an hour. Everything is more or less set up here, so as soon as she arrives you'll be good to go.'

Two hours passed. The make-up was lined up, the outfits selected, the lights were in place. Luke and Thea had been over the questions time and time again. It was three o'clock when Leanne returned. Thea felt like a wilting weed.

'Now, we'll be starting very soon. Minnie's just asked me to go out and buy her a flannel nightgown and *The Lord of the Rings* trilogy.'

'*The Lord of the Rings*?' Thea couldn't help her incredulous tone.

Leanne's eyes filled with panic. 'Forget I said that,' she pleaded. 'Minnie'll kill me.'

'Sure,' Thea said neutrally, filing it away as an anecdote to dine out on for years.

'Minnie's exhausted,' Leanne explained. 'She's finding motherhood a real challenge. All those sleepless nights . . .'

George snorted sarcastically.

'All those sleepless nights, feeding little Cristiano,' Leanne continued.

'She doesn't have a nanny for that?' George asked.

Leanne inhaled.

'No, she doesn't. Minnie is completely hands-on. That's why she went to Hope's party last night. She just needed to let her hair down. A sentiment all moms can relate to. And now she's having a bit of a lie-in.'

'Poor thing,' Thea crooned and then, 'But she *will* be down soon?'

'W-e-l-l. As I said before. She's a little sick. The hotel's called a doctor. But don't worry!' Leanne cried seeing Thea's face. 'Once he's checked her out she'll be along. It's nothing serious. Just a precaution.'

So they waited and waited. They ordered in sandwiches, sushi and pizza. They watched the rugby match on one of the flatscreen TVs. The pregnant make-up artist went to lie down in the bedroom complaining of Braxton Hicks contractions.

'You do realize if I go into labour Channel 6 is going to have to foot the bill for the best hospital in Edinburgh.'

'Of course,' Thea cooed.

'Time to read our horoscopes?' Alexa said, picking up the *Daily Mail*. 'Luke, what are you?'

'Aquarius,' Thea said before she could stop herself. Perfect match with her Libra. Everyone turned to look at her.

'How did you know that?' George teased.

'Years of being bored on the road together,' Luke said lazily. 'Oh, hello, Leanne. Any new developments?'

'Yes, I'm afraid Minnie's still got a bit of a stomach ache, but when the Nurofen kicks in she'll be down.'

Half an hour later, Minnie had terrible period pains. Thirty minutes later it was potential food poisoning. 'But don't worry,' Leanne cried again, as a grinning George made a motion to pack up. 'She really wants to do this interview. She *will* be down in a minute.'

'Models,' Luke said miserably. He was dressed in a slightly too-tight Bing Parsons suit in a rather nasty shade of green that matched the bags under his eyes. 'All flakes. I should know, I'm bloody married to one.'

Thea looked at him. She wondered if he'd read Poppy's

column in *Wicked*. But now was not the time to find out.

The next time Leanne appeared it was half past six.

'She's on her way,' she announced in the tones you might reserve to announce a battalion of enemy tanks moving in to your village.

'Here I am,' bleated a cartoon helium whine. Everyone's head turned to the threshold where one of the most legendary beauties of all time stood dressed in a purple Juicy tracksuit, head bowed and a hand over her Cupid-bow mouth. Minnie Maltravers sniffed loudly into a purple spotted handkerchief, then looked up, dazzling them with her moist violet eyes. 'I don't feel good,' she said heading, arms outstretched, towards Carlo the hairdresser.

'Oh, Minnie, poor baby.' They exchanged kisses. 'Would you like one of my head massages?'

'Yes, pweeze.'

'What's wrong with her?' Thea said softly to Leanne, as Minnie slumped in an armchair and Carlo began running his hands through her thick blonde locks.

'Oh, you know what hotel air-con systems are like. They make the air dryer than the Sahara desert. And they just pump bugs round the system like there's no tomorrow. Poor Minnie.'

Thea looked at the object of all their attention in fascination. She'd always imagined Minnie Maltravers as Amazonian, but like most famous people she was, in fact, unnervingly petite. Her ego, on the other hand, was colossal. Head massage over, she leafed dismissively through the stylists' rack of clothes, refusing to wear any of the outfits they'd selected.

'I hate red,' she muttered. 'Bing knows that. Why the fuck are there so many red dresses? I'm not sure I want to be wearing one of Bing's outfits. Maybe we should call Marc and see if he has anything for me.'

After much flattery, she was finally persuaded to put on a velvet violet dress that matched her eyes. Then she turned her attention to the jewellery.

'But this is all Tiffany! I never wear Tiffany!' She turned to Leanne. 'Go up to my room and fetch my Bulgari necklace,' she snapped.

It was nearly seven. Thea had been awake for what felt like a week by the time Minnie in full make-up allowed Alexa to usher her into the interview chair.

Luke sat in his, straightened his tie and flashed her the legendary Norton smile. Minnie looked right through him. Luke cleared his throat.

'OK,' said Thea, 'lights, camera—'

Dring, dring. Dring, dring.

'Oh my God I have to get this!' Minnie bolted across the room and snatched her phone out of Leanne's hand. 'Hellooo? Oh hi, bunny rabbit. Yeah, I'm *really* well. The baby is adorable, thank you, yes! I know, he *does* look a bit like me. Weird, isn't it? Though God, changing diapers is the pits. I mean, of course, Rosalita does most of them but . . . uh, huh, uh, huh . . . So did you hear about Lily? Uh huh. Uh huh.'

Everyone looked at their watches, but Minnie was oblivious. Ten minutes passed, then fifteen. The chatter continued until suddenly: 'Nicole? She's coming? But you know how I feel about her. No, forget it.'

She flung her phone on to the floor. 'Bloody Nicole,'

she said to the room at large. No one dared answer. Minnie stood up and headed towards the bedroom. 'I've got a headache, I need to lie down.'

'Don't worry,' a panicked Leanne said to Thea. 'I'll go and talk to her.'

She was gone for half an hour. Raised voices could be heard. Finally, a battle-weary Leanne emerged.

'She'd like a word with you,' she said to Thea and Luke.

In the bedroom, Minnie was curled up in an armchair, her twenty-thousand-dollar gown replaced by a towelling dressing gown. At the sight of them, she groaned.

'Do I have to talk to them now? I feel really sick.'

'No, no, Minnie, of course not.' Leanne sounded like a doctor about to perform a smear test with a freezing speculum. She turned to Thea and Luke. 'Perhaps you should go outside again?'

They backed out of the room, like minions at the court of the Sun King.

'This is getting beyond a joke,' Luke growled.

Leanne reappeared.

'Thea, Luke, I am *so sorry*. Minnie really doesn't want to do the interview now. You've been kept waiting so long, she thinks you'll give her a hard time.'

'Sorry?' Luke said, as George stuffed his hands in his mouth to contain his mirth.

'Yeah, she was really angry that you'd been kept waiting so long. But she *will* give you an interview. Soon.'

'Like how soon?' Thea asked. 'Tomorrow?'

Leanne twisted uncomfortably. 'Actually, tomorrow she and Max and little Cristiano are going to Barbados.'

'So the interview's not going to happen?'

'No, no, it will! We'll just have to reschedule.'

Suddenly, Minnie's head popped out from behind the door. 'Sowwy,' she whispered, 'but I'm weally not feeling tho good. But I will do the interview. I pwomise. I always keep my word, don't I, Leanne? By the way, could you make a reservation for me and Max for Rhubarb tonight?'

'Of course, Minnie,' Leanne said instantly. 'What time?'

Minnie yawned. 'Say nine. And call Witchery to say we'll be along later.'

'But it's nearly nine now,' Leanne pointed out. Thea eyed her sympathetically. What was it Gran said about how there was always someone worse off than you?

'Well, ten, then.'

'You couldn't do the interview before you go out for dinner?' Thea tried. 'It will only take half an hour.'

'Sorry.' Minnie shrugged and smiled winsomely. 'We'll just have to take a raincheck. How about next time I'm in London? We're going to be in London some time soon, aren't we, Leanne?'

'You are, Minnie,' Leanne said. Minnie walked out of the room and with a mouthed, 'Sorry', Leanne followed her.

34

Thea broke the news to Dean from the bedroom of the Balmoral suite, while the rest of the team dismantled the unused lights and cameras, packed away the candelabra and folded up the billowy, white sheets.

'I fly people in from all over the world to interview Minnie Maltravers and she blew you out. Are you taking the piss, Thea?'

'She didn't feel well,' Thea said. 'We tried, Dean, honestly. We tried everything. But she just wouldn't play ball. She says she'll do it in London.'

'*When* will she do it in London?'

'I don't know. Some time next week, her PA says. Hopefully.' The last word was whispered.

'She'd fucking better, Thea. Because this is a joke. Sort it out. Or else.'

Her spirits didn't improve when, at around eleven, their taxi pulled up outside the Hootsmon Hotel. From the website, Thea had hoped for a cutting-edge joint epitomizing minimalist, funky cool. What she got was a shabby unchic building on the outskirts of town with a lobby full of wilting flower arrangements and a blazing fire in the grate, despite the fact it was a warm May night. As they bundled through the door, they were greeted by the strains of 'Hi ho, silver lining' blaring through ancient fire doors.

'It's a wedding,' said the elderly lady at reception, who looked as if she'd wandered out of an Agatha Christie series. 'I do hope they warned you. It might be just a wee bit noisy.'

Luke groaned and smote his forehead with his fist. George rubbed his hands in glee.

The receptionist glared at him over the top of her glasses, then turned to Thea. 'Your shower's a bit temperamental,' she warned her, handing over a brass key attached to a wooden plank so hefty it could double as a murder weapon, 'but otherwise it's a very nice room.'

'Is there a mini bar in the room?' George was asking the receptionist.

'No sir. This is a small, family-run establishment. No mini bars. However, the bar is open for the party, but I should respectfully ask you to make it clear you are not an invited guest and to pay for all your drinks.'

'Absolutely.' George smiled, a huge grin spreading across his face. 'Anyone care to join me for a nightcap?'

'All right,' Rhys said gamely. Luke, Alexa and Thea shook their heads.

'I, for one, am looking forward to my bed,' Luke said.

Four hours later, Thea was woken by a text bleeping. She rolled over and stared at the clock radio: 3.02 blinked the neon digits. In the dawn light filtering through the curtains, she fumbled for her phone.

Heard about the cock-up. Really sorry. Call me if you want to talk. Sure we can sort something. Jake x

She flung the phone across the room. Bloody incompetent dwarf. He should have known something like this was going to happen. He should have somehow stopped it. It was her own stupid fault for thinking someone so young, so inexperienced, someone who should have been working as an extra in *The Hobbit* could deliver her a scoop.

She lay back on her lumpy polyester pillow and closed her eyes, but thoughts of the aborted interview rampaged round her head like a mad bull. It was no good. She wasn't going back to sleep. The plane was leaving at eight, they had to be at the airport at six. From downstairs, she could hear a faint wheeze of bagpipes. She might as well go and see what was happening rather than fester here. Cursing, she pulled on her jeans and sweatshirt and headed down the corridor to the creaking lift.

The wedding party was still in full swing. Bodies were draped across sofas, in armchairs, on the floor. Thea stepped over them and headed towards the library where a hard-core posse of three men in kilts were reeling vigorously with Alexa and another young woman in an unfortunate yellow dress. A CD player in the corner rattled out 'Scotland the Brave' as they clapped and stamped.

'All right,' bellowed one of the reddest-faced men. 'Gentlemen. Right hands joined over ladies' shoulder. Left hands joined in front. Walk forwards four steps, that's right . . .'

'*Haii, caramba!*' cried Alexa spotting her. 'Come and join us, Thea. Everybody salsa!'

'You're not in Guatemala now.'

'Oh shit. Nor I am. *Arriba, arriba!*' She clicked a pair of imaginary castanets.

'I thought you were going to bed?' Thea couldn't help smiling.

'I was talked out of it.'

'How nice to see you,' said a voice behind her. A flushed but slightly more cheerful-looking Luke was leaning back in an armchair, nursing what looked like a large glass of Scotch.

'I thought you wanted to go to bed. Am I the only one old-fashioned enough to think a few hour's kip might be in order?'

'Looks like it. The rest of us decided it would be rude not to toast the happy couple.'

'Where are they?'

'They left for their honeymoon at midnight.' He laughed.

'Right.' Thea looked at the devastation. 'Where's Rhys?'

'Head down the toilet. These young ones are such lightweights.'

'George?'

'In bed with the matron of honour.'

'The *matron*? You mean the maid.'

'I mean the matron; the bride's elder married sister. Her husband's over there.' He nodded in the direction of a chaise lounge, where a man with a ginger beard lay comatose.

'Oh, good Lord,' Thea started to laugh.

'It's good to see you smile again.' He nodded towards the bar. No one was tending it. 'Fancy a tipple?'

'Yup, I think this calls for a large . . . Oh, I don't know, let's make it a pina colada.' She smiled at him, as he held a glass up to an optic, which dispensed a measure of whisky.

'That's a bit miserable,' Luke said. 'Let's double it. No, sorry, triple it.' He handed her the glass brimming with neat alcohol and raised his. 'Cheers, then.'

'Cheers.' They clinked. Memories of other bars, other late nights, other large whiskies flooded Thea's mind. She swallowed hard.

'Good luck to the happy couple,' Luke said. 'May they have better luck than I have.' He nodded towards a pair of French doors. 'Shall we go outside? Snatch a breath of air?'

'Why not?'

Luke opened the door and she followed him outside on to a terrace. The Hootsmon was on a hill. The craggy spires of Edinburgh lay spread out beneath them in the midsummer dawn like a city in a fairy tale. They leant against the parapet.

'Christ, I thought we'd never be alone,' Luke said.

Despite the whisky, Thea's throat was suddenly dry. 'It's been a busy day.'

'I'll say.' He grinned. 'Busy week. Manic. I've enjoyed it, though. I miss my old life on the road, bumbling from place to place not knowing where you're going to lay your head that night.' He paused. 'But I realize my full-time roving reporter days are over. Getting too old.'

You're only as old as the person you feel, Thea thought with sudden viciousness, but she said, 'You're hardly old. You're what – forty-five?'

'Fifty-one.' Her white lie cheered him enormously. 'That's not that old these days, is it?'

331

'Of course not. John Simpson's sixty-three or something and he's still going strong.'

It was the wrong thing to say, she realized. Luke loathed his BBC rival. He scowled.

'Well, hardly going strong, Thea. I mean, those reports he did recently from South Africa were pretty weak.'

'You're right,' she agreed hastily. 'What I meant was he's still working as much as ever and no one's talking about replacing him.'

'What do you mean? Are they thinking about replacing me?'

God, she shouldn't have taken such a big slug of whisky. 'No, no, of course not, Luke. You *are* the *SevenThirty News*. It would be unthinkable without you at its helm.'

'Hmm.' Luke frowned, then looked at her again. 'Just like old times, isn't it? You. Me. A hotel. On location.'

'Um . . .'

'Anyone in your life right now?' he asked, staring straight ahead towards the mossy green mound of Arthur's Seat. Before she could reply, he continued, 'I can't *believe* you're still single. An attractive woman like you.'

'I'm happy this way.' She shrugged. 'You know that.'

A great weariness came over her, a weariness that had nothing to do with the dawn hour and everything to do with the fact she was sick of pretending, sick of having to act as if she was indifferent to Luke when just standing next to him she was aware of her body tingling and the fact that she was wearing boring black M&S knickers.

'What do you think of your wife's new column?' she

said, desperate to steer the conversation in a different direction.

'Sorry?'

'You know, in *Wicked* magazine.'

'What column?'

'Oh. I guess you haven't seen it. You were in Guatemala. It's nothing,' Thea said hastily. 'Ask Poppy about it.'

He turned to look at her. 'I don't ask Poppy about anything any more. Our marriage is a farce, Thea. The worst mistake of my life.'

She gulped.

'I've really missed you, you know,' Luke said softly, taking her face in his hands.

'I . . .' she said, looking up at him. Her body felt as if it had been turned inside out and her ears buzzed with deafness. A voice just behind her broke through the static.

'Minnie Maltravers is the hor-se's arse!'

They jumped away from each other as if goaded by electric prods.

'She's the meanest! She sucks the horse's penis.'

'Bloody hell, George. You gave us a shock.' Luke was quite red in the face.

'Her left tit hangs down to her belly,' George warbled to the tune of 'My Bonnie Lies Over the Ocean'. 'Her right tit lies down to her knee.'

'George,' Thea said firmly, 'perhaps you should cool it.'

'If her left tit did equal her right tit, she'd get lots of weenie from me.' He slumped on an iron chair, wiping away tears of mirth.

Thea and Luke looked at each other. They smiled.

'It *is* just like old times,' Luke said.

Then, as if in slow motion, he leant towards her, put his hand on her arm and whispered in her ear, 'Things might be quieter back in my room.'

35

Without Brigita, Saturdays were the day Poppy dedicated to chores like the shopping. She strapped Clara in the buggy and set off to Tesco's, stopping at the cash machine outside to extract the enormous wodge of cash she needed to pay Brigita at the end of every day. Briefly, she thought of Luke, probably in Scotland now, cosying up to Minnie. When he'd called to say that was his next port of call, Poppy realized her heart had acquired some kind of double glazing. The sadness that hit her was a niggly draught rather than the freezing-cold blast she'd endured for so long.

Pondering on this, she took Luke's card out of her wallet when a thought struck her. She put it back and took out her HSBC card which she hadn't used since she had moved in with Luke. The bank had sent her a new card recently, but it was as yet unused. What was the point when Poppy knew her old account contained £19.11? But that should have changed. She slipped it in, keyed in her PIN and clicked on 'balance'.

There is £419.11 in your account

All right, it wasn't exactly enough to retire on. But next week, with her pay rise, there would be £1,019.11. Then

£1,519.11. Then ... Poppy wasn't very good at maths, but she got the point. Having been totally reliant on Luke she now had a little something of her own. She felt light-headed as if she'd jumped out of a steamy bath.

'Mummeee, come on.'

'OK, darling.'

She pushed the buggy round Tesco's, realizing, too late, she'd forgotten her list. Now, what was it Brigita had wanted her to buy? Ready Brek for Clara, tick. Organic frozen peas, tick. Potatoes, tick. Brigita was a great one for making trains out of mashed potato and diced vegetables, meals that even Gordon Ramsay might have found a bit of a hassle, but which Clara adored.

'Mummeee?'

'Yes, darling?' Poppy stopped at the magazine rack. Daisy McNeil was on the cover of bloody *Elle*. And where was *Wicked*? Down at the bottom where no one taller than Clara was going to see it. Glancing over her shoulder, she picked up the three copies and lined them up on the top shelf. She stood back, admiring her handiwork. Maybe she'd go into Martin's next door and do the same and then in the afternoon she could go down to WH Smith's at Paddington ...

'Mummeee? Need to do a wee.'

'Oh. Hang on a minute, schnooks. I'll just get you out of here.' Rapidly, she headed towards the checkout, when a voice said:

'Hello!'

'Oh, hello.' It was the unfriendly mum she'd last bumped into that bleak January day when she'd felt so low.

'How are you?' said the mum, sounding distinctly warmer than last time.

'I'm fine.'

Her child had snot running down his face in thick rivulets. Poppy looked at him disdainfully. Why were other people's children never anywhere near as gorgeous as one's own?

'I saw you in *Wicked* last week. How ... well, how wicked.' The woman laughed. 'I mean, not that I buy it or anything, but I picked it up at the hairdressers and I thought: "I *know* that woman." What fun. Have you been doing it for long?'

'Yeah, a while now,' Poppy said airily.

'I had no idea.' She had terrible split ends. They always said no one over forty should even dream of having long hair. 'Listen, I was hoping I'd see you around,' she continued. 'Some of us local mums have coffee every Thursday at eleven at Starbucks. If you'd like to join us.'

'Sorry,' Poppy said. 'I *work* on Thursdays.'

'Mummeee!' came a very distressed wail.

Poppy looked at Tesco's newly mopped floor marred by a small yellow puddle. 'Oh, Clara,' she exclaimed, 'never mind. Let's get you home quickly, shall we? Bye, nice to see you,' she added airily over her shoulder and outside resisted the temptation to punch the air like a contestant in some TV reality show.

Back home, Clara refused to touch her spaghetti Bolognese.

'But it's your favourite!' Poppy exclaimed, horrified that the old dependable had fallen out of fashion as brutally as last season's vogue for acid yellows.

'No like.' Clara pushed her bowl away.

'Come on, darling. Just a little bite. Have one for Daddy.'

'Where is Daddy?'

'He's in Scotland with a famous lady.'

'What's Scotland?'

'It's a country far away. OK. One for Daddy. Good girl. One for Granny Louise.' Poppy's phone rang. She was too busy flying the spoon, like an aeroplane, into Clara's mouth to look at the caller ID.

'Hello?'

'Poppy.'

He didn't say who he was; he didn't need to. 'Toby!' she squawked.

'Hey. How's it going?'

'Wanna biscuit! Gimme biscuit! No Mummy, no Bolognese.'

'Christ, what the hell's that noise? Are you torturing a chipmunk?'

'Nothing. Just a second.' Poppy got up, ran to the cupboard, got out a Jaffa Cake and shoved it in Clara's hands, then switched her phone to mute.

'Now, just eat that while Mummy has a little talk on the phone.'

For a second, Clara looked shocked at her victory, then she began cramming the biscuit into her mouth as if she had just been released from a Japanese POW camp. Poppy switched the phone back on.

'Sorry about that. How are you?'

'Oh, you know, busy. But, listen, it's my birthday so I wondered if you fancied dinner tonight.'

Poppy jolted as if she'd accidentally touched a hot iron. 'I'd love to.' Provided Brigita can babysit. But she wasn't going to bore Toby with such mundanities.

He named a Thai restaurant in Bayswater, and they arranged to meet at eight; she hung up, heart skittering. Toby had asked her on a date. For his birthday. Immediately, Poppy reproved herself. It wasn't a date, she was a married woman. But married women could have male friends; they weren't living in Afghanistan. Clara would be asleep tonight. Why should Poppy stay in in front of *American Idol* when every other woman of her age in the Western world would be sitting, laughing somewhere, out with friends? When Luke was in Scotland, hanging out with glamorous Thea and Minnie Maltravers.

Of course Brigita was available. She arrived just after Poppy had tucked Clara up in bed. Having checked and double checked herself in the cheval mirror, she decided to walk to the restaurant, even though it involved a slightly scary journey through the nearby council estate and a urine-soaked underpass, because then she could buy Toby a present on the way. She almost ran to the bridge that led over the canal. Even though it was a May night, it was chilly and the people she passed looked grey and worried. Poppy felt sorry for them; their heads were bent as they walked into the wind, unlike Poppy who stood erect and faced the elements full on.

She racked her brains thinking what to buy Toby. Nothing too expensive, that would obviously be a mistake. She ran into Whiteley's mall and headed straight to Books Etc where she had spent so many long hours browsing while Clara slept in her pram. She'd get him

London from the Air, a book of beautiful aerial photos of the city she loved flicking through. As she handed over her card, full of pride that she was paying for this herself, she grabbed a pen from the desk and wrote on the inside flap: To Toby from Poppy on his birthday.

Nicely understated, she thought, then glanced at the clock in a panic. It was quarter past eight. Heart pittering, because, despite her time in the fashion industry, she hated being late, she hurried down messy Queensway with its foot traffic of women in burkas pushing buggies with six-year-olds asleep in them, American tourists wondering if they were in Notting Hill and teenagers coming out of the ice rink. The restaurant was in a quiet side road. Pushing the door open, Poppy saw Toby straight away, sitting at a corner table. Waving.

'Finally! Now we can order.'

He stood up, smiling. Nine other people looked at her. It wasn't a date. It was his birthday party. And one of the guests was Daisy McNeil.

Poppy felt dizzy. Some of it was shock, some of it was because she hadn't eaten much that day. She opened her bag and got out the book.

'This is for you,' she said. 'It's one of my favourites.'

'Oh thanks,' said Toby. Without looking at it, he deposited it on top of a pile of presents on the floor. Poppy noted it contained two Jo Malone bags, one Hermès bag and one Gucci. Her face flamed. Why hadn't she been more lavish?

'Now you sit there,' Toby gestured to a space between a tall man in a hacking jacket with a green silk scarf round his neck and a dark guy in a cream polo neck and matching jeans. 'This is Freddie and this is Andreas. Freddie, Andreas, Poppy.'

'Madam?' asked a waiter. 'What would you like to drink?'

She looked wildly to see what the others had. 'A beer,' she said rapidly, pointing at the dark guy's glass.

'Ooh, how macho,' Freddie of the hacking jacket purred. Poppy fought the urge to beat him over the head with her handbag. 'One of the boys are we, darling?'

'Hardly,' exclaimed Andreas, the dark guy. 'A beautiful girl like her.'

Everyone was chatting merrily. Poppy's eyes raked the other women. A virtually emaciated Asian girl was on one side of Toby, laughing at his every word. On the other was a Scandinavian-looking blonde who stared moodily into a glass of champagne.

Poppy tried to work out which one was playing the game best, but Toby didn't seem particularly bothered by either of them, holding court to the entire table. It's cool, Poppy told herself. You're a young woman out having dinner with friends. It's what young women do on a Saturday night. You're in a hip London restaurant. And anyway you're married. But the words on the menu still swam in front of her eyes.

'So how do you know Toby?' Andreas was asking.

'Oh, just from here and there.' Poppy shrugged.

'Poppy has a column in a magazine,' Freddie reproved him. 'It's hilarious, it's called "The Bimbo Bites Back" and she really lays in to people. So you'd better watch yourself, Andy-Pandy.'

'I'm not that nasty.' Poppy flushed. She debated telling him she didn't actually write it, but decided against it.

'I think you're vile. That's why I love it.'

'It's great, Poppy,' said Daisy from Andreas's left. 'I thought you were all washed-up after you got married. That's what the agency said, anyway. I mean it's so difficult to work after you've had kids. Your boobs are ruined and everything. So hats off to you for reinventing yourself.'

'Thanks, Daisy.'

'I have to tell you. I can't keep it a secret any longer. I've just got my first *Vogue* cover. Isn't that great? They're going to profile me as one of the new breed of super-models.'

'Well, make sure Poppy doesn't write it up,' Freddie tittered.

'I wouldn't worry,' Poppy said with her sweetest smile, 'Daisy wouldn't be able to read it.' Then she stopped, shocked. Where the hell had that come from?

'Miaow!' Freddie howled. Toby, who'd been listening, threw back his beautiful head and roared. After a second, Daisy giggled too.

'Sorry, I didn't mean it like that. I . . .'

'That's OK, Poppy. I knew you were only joking.'

After that, the dynamic changed. Poppy worked like a court jester, to entertain Freddie and Andreas. She could feel pearls of sweat forming on her forehead, as she cracked bad jokes and made spirited conversation. She could see Toby straining to be part of their gang, but the two women on either side of him were battling to gain his attention. She realized the more she ignored him, the more he watched her. Poppy began to enjoy herself; she felt part of the action, which was more than she ever did at one of Luke's stuffy affairs. The food was delicious and the alcohol kept flowing. The only thing she didn't like was the way groups kept getting up and disappearing to the loos. When they came back, they'd be even noisier than before, pushing their untouched food around their plates. Poppy knew what was going on and it made her uneasy.

'Going to join us?' Freddie asked when he and Daisy got up.

Poppy thought of Clara, asleep in her fairy sleeping-bag. She thought of how shocked Luke would be. She thought of the movie they'd been shown at school of the pink-and-white cheeked middle-class girl slumped on a dank bathroom floor clutching a needle.

'No thanks.' She smiled.

'Come on.' He nodded at the passion-fruit soufflé, which had just been placed under her nose. 'Stop you eating so much.'

Poppy felt slapped.

'I like a woman who enjoys her food,' Andreas said, with a wink.

Ears still ringing, she was just standing up to join Freddie in his bathroom visit, when from behind them, Toby said, 'Shift your fat arse, Freddie. I want to talk to Poppy now.'

Her heart helter-skeltered, as Freddie stood up and Toby slipped into his seat.

'I thought I'd never get a chance,' he said in a low voice, so only she could hear. 'Are you having fun?'

'Um . . .'

He laughed at her expression. 'Say no more. I'm sorry, sweetheart. Most of these people are arseholes.'

'Then why have you invited them to your birthday dinner?' Poppy found the world a stranger and stranger place.

'Work really. They're contacts you know. My job's all about keeping people sweet. Freddie helps style a lot of my male clients and Andreas is . . . well, he knows a lot of people I have to deal with too.'

'And the girls?' Poppy said, glancing at a giggling Daisy.

'Well, the girls are gorgeous. They come with me to a lot of events my clients attend and they keep my clients very happy.' He lowered his voice again. 'But none of them are as gorgeous as you.'

'Oh.' Poppy felt her phone vibrating in her pocket. 'Excuse me a second,' she said pulling it out, her cheeks hot. Probably Luke. She wondered what she'd tell him she was doing. But no, it was Brigita.

'Is everything OK?' she gasped, sticking a finger in her ear so she could hear.

'I don't think so. Clara she is puking everywhere. Very sick. Like *Exorcist*. She wants Mummy. You must come home.'

Shock crashed Poppy into an invisible wall. 'Oh my God. I'll be right back.' She hung up. 'I'm sorry, but I have to go,' she said to the table at large.

'Cinderella!' Freddie giggled. 'It's not gone midnight yet. Does your carriage await?'

'My little girl's not well.'

'God, kids,' Daisy snorted. 'Eating too many pies? *Like her mum*,' she added under her breath.

Face flaming, head held high, Poppy tapped Toby on

the shoulder. 'I'm sorry, but I have to go,' she said again. 'Thank you for a lovely evening.'

'I'll see you to a taxi.' Toby stood up.

Outside, they spotted a cab straight away. Poppy got in, heart thudding. 'Thank you,' she said distractedly. 'Have fun.'

'I won't without you,' Toby said in a low voice. He bent forward and kissed her softly on the lips. For a second, inhaling his musky smell, Poppy felt a sherbert fizzle in her veins but anxiety almost immediately erased it.

'Why is it that whenever I'm with you, someone somewhere always starts vomiting?'

Poppy was sure there was a witty retort to this, but she just smiled and shrugged. 'Maida Vale,' she told the driver. 'As quick as you can, please. My baby's sick.'

36

By the time Poppy ran up the stairs to Clara's room, the drama was all over.

'I tidy up vomit, she is fast asleep now,' Brigita explained, as Clara rolled over and squawked 'Mummy', before rolling back on to her front, her bottom poking up in the air.

'But is she OK?' Poppy stroked her soft blonde curls.

'I take her temperature. Is normal. I think is just one of these children things.'

She certainly looked fine. 'You could have called me, to tell me she was better,' Poppy said crossly. 'I was really worried.'

'Me too, but this is children for you. I think it's best you are home.' Brigita gave Poppy a look she didn't like very much. 'Better the safe than the sorry, this is what I say. Anyway, now you're back I'll be off. I will see you Monday.'

So Poppy crawled into bed alone. Already rewriting history, she thought of her new friends in the restaurant, laughing and joking without her, before moving on to a nightclub. There'd been talk of Mahiki or Boujis. She forgot that she'd felt slightly awkward among them and instead brooded that she should be with them, dancing and flirting. But instead, yet again, here she was stuck alone in her marital bed with a two-year-old next door. It wasn't fair. She'd missed out on her youth and now she'd been given a chance to snatch some of it back, domestic responsibilities still got in the way.

Then she reprimanded herself for thinking of adored Clara as a domestic responsibility. A second later, she squirmed at her naivety in thinking she was going on a date with Toby. After all, he'd never actually described it as such. How everyone must have laughed at that silly book she'd given him and at her having to leave so suddenly. Then she thought of Luke in Scotland, whom she had deliberately not called and guilt crept over her. All right, she was angry at how often he left her alone and – now she analysed it – a little jealous of his freedom. But she'd known Luke travelled when she married him. He was out earning money to support her and Clara while she'd been out flirting with another man. There was no getting away from it, she'd behaved badly.

Mother and daughter spent the following morning curled up on the sofa, watching the *Jungle Book*. As Clara roared with laughter at the antics of Mowgli and Baloo, Poppy's heart ached with love. She was furious with herself for resenting Clara's sickness. She was a terrible mother, a terrible person.

The doorbell rang.

'Mr Postman!' Clara cried.

'No, darling, it's Sunday.' Poppy was baffled. She went to the front door and opened it to be greeted by a huge bunch of poppies.

'Miss Poppy,' said a bored-sounding man from behind them.

'That's me.'

'For you.' He thrust the flowers at her, then ran back down the steps to his van. Poppy put the bunch down and looked at the accompanying card. Her heart was thudding. She was pretty sure she knew who they were from, but you could always get these things wrong.

Poppies make drugs and you're certainly my narcotic. See you soon, beautiful. T xxx

Poppy inhaled sharply. She read the message again, then again and was saved from another perusal by the phone ringing.

'Hello?' she said, breathily sure it was him.

'Darling, it's me!' Honk, honk. 'Oh, get out of my way, you arsehole.'

'Hi, Mum. How was Marseilles?'

Her mother's voice was like bleach down a clogged drain. 'A dump. I shan't be returning there in a hurry.'

'Oh. So you didn't see . . . ?' Poppy couldn't remember his name. 'Your friend?'

'We had a drink. His sister was staying with him, so we were unable to go out for dinner as we'd arranged. But he says he'll be in England soon and we'll meet then.'

'Oh, really? Well, that's good.' The front door opened and Luke stood there, looking weary, a suitcase at his feet. 'Oh, hello!' she squawked shoving the card from the flowers into her pocket. 'Mum, I've got to go. Luke's just got back. We'll talk later.' Ignoring the squawks of protest, she hung up. 'How was Minnie?' she said to her husband.

'I wouldn't really know. She blew us out.'

'Daddeeee!' called Clara, running into the hallway. Luke dropped on to his knees.

'Hello, my sugarplum. I missed you. Daddy's bought you a doll from Guatemala and – um – a hairy cow from Scotland.'

'Gimme.'

'In a minute.' Luke grabbed his daughter and flung her in the air. She giggled rapturously.

'She blew you out?'

'Yup. Interview all set up, lights, camera and Minnie decides she's a bit tired and she'll do the interview another day, thank you.'

'Oh you poor thing.' Even though Poppy had spent the whole week growing angrier and angrier with Luke for being such a lousy husband, her soft heart still overflowed with sympathy for him. She began walking to the kitchen. 'Would you like a coffee?'

'I hear you've got a column,' Luke said behind her.

Poppy's hand stopped on its way to the kettle. 'Yes. You know about that,' she said brightly.

'No I don't.'

'Yes, you do! I told you.'

'You didn't tell me anything.'

'I'm sure I did.' Poppy began fumbling through the cupboards for the Lavazza that he preferred. 'The column for *Wicked* magazine,' she continued, her back still to her husband. 'I *thought* you weren't listening when I told you.'

'You didn't tell me.'

'I *did*.' Poppy was a terrible liar. Her face was carnation, her body as rigid as a frozen sausage. Luke snorted.

'Can I see it then?'

Reluctantly, Poppy picked up her well-thumbed copy from the kitchen table. She'd meant to hide it before he got back. Luke flicked through it aghast.

'The Bimbo Bites Back?' He spat out each word like a piece of rotten meat.

'They gave it that name, not me.'

'Well, so I should hope. But Christ, it's not exactly dignified.' He read in silence, trying to frown, though Dr Mazza's handiwork prevented that. 'Poppy,' he said after a moment, 'you can't do this.'

'Why not? You wanted me to get a job. Now I have one.'

'I wanted you to get a proper job. Not waffle to a ghost writer about how badly some film star dresses and what a bitch Hannah is. Christ, she'll go nuclear over this.'

Poppy's insides shrivelled. Not knowing how to respond, she buried her face in her daughter's neck. 'Darling, shall we look at the hairy cow Dad's bought you?'

Luke spent the afternoon at his desk, catching up on paperwork. Poppy and Clara watched a *Balamory* DVD. She heated up a frozen risotto for dinner and they were in bed before ten, lying side by side, doing their best not to touch, both breathing deeply even though they were wide awake. Even though they knew they had to discuss the column again, both decided they were feeling too fragile and too guilty about their respective indiscretions to face it now.

The week passed. Poppy texted Toby to thank him for the flowers but heard nothing back. She attended a few more parties but didn't see him. She had lunch with Barbara, who told her she'd always known she'd make a brilliant comeback and then presented her with a long list of interested clients, wanting to know if Poppy would like to endorse their products. Poppy took it home to mull over trying to feel excited, but too much of her mind was focused on Luke and the ever growing hole in their marriage and on Toby and why he hadn't been in touch.

On Thursday at eleven sharp, Migsy rang.

'Hey, Poppy. How are you? Did you get paid all right? Good! So what have you been up to this week?'

Poppy reeled off a list of the famous faces she'd seen and the places she'd been.

'Fabulous. You really do sound like the ultimate girl-about-town, the sort all our readers aspire to be. But we'll need to give the column a little bit more edge, Poppy, if it's going to be as good as last week's. What did you think of Danielle Minton, up close and personal? I tell you, I always used to think there was nothing wrong with Botox until I saw her.'

Poppy squirmed awkwardly. 'Migsy, you know I don't want to say anything mean.'

'It's not mean! It's *funny*. Come on, Poppy, everyone says your observations are a breath of fresh air. You can't tell me you didn't think Danielle looked just like Tutankhamun.'

'She did a bit,' Poppy agreed unwillingly.

'And what has little Clara been up to?'

Now she was on safer ground. 'Oh, she's being a nightmare with food at the moment. Won't eat a thing but Jaffa Cakes, and at the weekend she weed all over Tesco's newly cleaned floor. I was mortified.'

Migsy laughed. 'Ah, how lovely. Our readers will really

relate to that. And what do you think of this whole Minnie Maltravers thing? After all, your hubby's just been in Guatemala, hasn't he, doing reports on her charity work.'

'Yes,' Poppy said as proudly as the day she'd won best-kept locker at Brettenden Hall. 'And then . . .'

'And then?'

'Nothing.'

'And then what?'

'This won't go in the magazine, will it? This is strictly between you and me.'

'*Of course.*'

'Well, Luke was pulled out of Guatemala and had to go straight to Edinburgh to interview her. The idea was he'd do the interview in the afternoon and fly back in the morning, but Minnie kept them waiting for six hours and then, when she finally decided she was ready to do the interview, her phone rang, and then she decided she was too tired and would rather go out for dinner.'

'Really?' Migsy sounded bored. 'How annoying for Luke.'

'Yes.' Poppy was driven by that age-old desire to impress Migsy. 'He was furious. He'd flown halfway round the globe for nothing. He thinks she's a total flake.'

'Is he going to interview her again?'

'Well, he hopes so but he doesn't know. He hates her, he calls her Moaning Minnie. Said she was nothing like as gorgeous close up, you could see the scars round her eyes.'

'Poor Luke,' Migsy said. She sounded as bored as if Poppy had tried to explain EU agricultural policy to her. 'Listen, Poppy, I'd better go, got to do a phone interview with Kate Thornton about what she keeps on her bedside table. We'll speak same time next week. Have fun, take care.'

'You too,' Poppy said and only after she'd hung up did she realize she'd forgotten to remind Migsy to email her the column in advance. Oh well, she'd call her back later. She had an appointment to have her highlights done. She wondered if Toby would like them.

Story of a split-up: the update. Hannah Creighton, 46, was devastated nearly three years ago when her husband, newsreader Luke Norton, walked out on her and their three children Tilly, 16, Issy, 15 and Jonty, 10, for a 22-year-old model known as the 'Bimbo'. Now, in the latest of her hilarious reports from the divorce frontline, Hannah describes her feelings when the bimbo was revealed last week to be magazine columnist Poppy Norton.

So now you all know. The Bimbo, who callously stole my husband, has a name. She's called Poppy Norton, she's 24, she has a two-year-old daughter called Clara who likes *Teletubbies* and she goes to lots of parties. Oh. And she used to be a model. In other words, I think you'll agree, she is a woman of substance.

I've never actually met Poppy, but when I opened a trashy magazine in the dentist's waiting room to find a big picture of her over a new column, rabbiting on about some parties she'd been to, what clothes she liked, what their little daughter enjoyed watching on television I felt as if I'd received a physical blow. I know my feelings were illogical – I don't want Luke back – but seeing these inane ramblings made me feel as if a bucket of cold water had been thrown over me. This fluffy little thing was the woman my husband had left his three beautiful children for? Amazingly, none of us have ever met Luke's second wife: with touching loyalty the children decided they had no interest in getting to know her. But now my heart ached to think of Jonty, Tilly and Issy being thrown over for this piece of trailer trash. At the same time I couldn't deny it: Poppy was prettier than I was, even in my heyday, and obviously she was much, much younger. Fair enough, Luke, why bother with a woman with a degree, a cookery diploma and a sterling record of helping out at the PTA when you could have a cookie-cut member of a girls' band.

But my overriding emotion on reading Poppy's column was one of pity. Reading between the lines, I got no sense of a happy home, of a supportive husband; instead I perceived a lonely, young woman trying to fill her days with parties and shopping. Or perhaps I'm imagining that. It can't help that even on the day of our decree absolute, Luke was sending me texts saying: 'I miss you. I love you so much. Please tell me you love me.'

It doesn't help that Viagra ordered from the internet still regularly arrives in the post for him, more than two years after he moved out. That friends and colleagues keep me informed of spotting my ex canoodling with other women, be it at home and abroad.

It all shows how far I have come since that dark day nearly three years ago when I found out that Luke was carrying on with this piece of jail bait. At the time, losing my husband was like someone dying, but without being able to mourn. Now, however, I see that it was in fact the start of a new life. By throwing Luke out I have regained my self-esteem. My new boyfriend is gorgeous. I'm having great sex – I'd virtually given up with my husband. I've been inundated with opportunities to appear on television, to write a novel, to work for magazines.

Still, it hasn't all been easy. I was sort of used to being a single mum, with Luke away so much on assignments, but since he left home and I've been obliged to earn a crust, there's been no choice but to send the children to boarding school. Don't get me wrong, we're not talking Dotheboys Hall here, but it still breaks all our hearts to be separated in this way.

But the fact I have survived has given me much to think about, not least when Luke emailed me recently asking if I fancied dinner. A whole new future began to open up to me. Instead of being the dowdy wife at home looking after the children, I realized I could now be the glamorous woman having a flirtatious dinner with the legendary Luke Norton.

For the briefest of seconds I wondered if I would fall for his charm again. Then I remembered I was busy that night washing my hair and that I was going to be busy every night for the rest of my life. It looks like poor Poppy's busy filling her diary too. I wish her luck.

37

After two years dreaming about him, brooding on past times, wondering if it would ever happen again and telling herself how well shot of Luke she was, Thea almost couldn't believe it. Dawn had broken over Edinburgh and she and Luke were in bed together. Naked. They'd had sex. All the feelings she'd tried to dismiss for so long were now rampaging like a herd of wildebeest. Like a junkie picking up the needle after years of sobriety, she was back at stage one. She was a Lukeoholic. Adored him. Had missed him as much as she might have missed one of her limbs. She wanted to open her window and shout it to Scotland, but fortunately it was locked and the key was nowhere to be seen, so instead she made do by whispering.

'That was good.'

'Sorry?' Before she could repeat herself, Luke rolled off the bed and grabbed a worn towel from the ugly purple chair in the corner. 'I'm going to jump in the shower. We've got to leave for the airport soon, haven't we? Be careful leaving my room, we don't want anyone to spot us.'

He headed into the en-suite. Thea sat up. Déjà vu drenched her like a sudden freak shower. She'd been here before with Luke, in other hotel rooms all over the world: a shared half hour of intimacy, followed by terse reminders to make sure no one saw them. Every time, in the past, she'd hoped next time would be different, but it never was. Even after a two-year break, the pattern was the same.

Slow-burning humiliation crept over her like a vile rash. Hastily, she got off the bed and pulled on her clothes, discarded all over the floor. Opening the door, she peered one way down the corridor, then the other, then satisfied the coast was clear, made the dash for her room. Just time to shower and change before she had to be downstairs for checkout.

All the way back to London, while Luke slept in the seat beside her, she berated herself: how she could have been such an idiot to have succumbed to him yet again? But at the same time, another voice in her head told her that the sex had been good. Really good. Even exhausted and drunk and pissed off with life in general, Luke still knew how to press all Thea's buttons and she was pretty sure she knew how to press his back. Why, why, why had she sent that stupid email to Hannah? If she hadn't, he and Poppy would almost certainly have fizzled out and they might have been together by now.

The next few days were even more miserable than Thea could have anticipated. The Luke relapse had temporarily distracted her from her work worries, but once she was back in the office there was no escape. Dean was furious; Roxanne was incandescent. Thea decided the only thing to do was keep pestering Leanne like a toddler wanting sweeties until she finally buckled and arranged a new interview time.

'Hey,' said Alexa, stopping by her desk on Thursday morning. 'How's it going? Any word from Jake?'

'He texted a grovelling apology. Not that that will save me from garrotting him next time I see him.'

'Ah, poor Jake! Don't be mean. He's such a sweetheart.'

That sounded heartfelt. Thea looked at her.

'Excuse me? Do I sense a spark between you and Mr Kaplan?'

'Nah. Not my type at all. Too small. But a lot of other women fancied him. He was quite the talk of the Marriott Guatemala City.'

'Really?' Thea was unconvinced. She began dialling Leanne's number for the third time that morning, but with about as much confidence as an eight-month pregnant woman hoping to get out of childbirth.

'Hello?'

'Oh hi, Leanne!' Thea said, startled she'd picked up so quickly. 'It's Thea Mackharven, here. How are you?'

'Uh. Yeah, good.'

'Are you in Barbados?'

'I can't tell you that,' Leanne said. 'Minnie would kill me. Somewhere hot, though. Minnie decided she needed a bit of sunshine to get over her cold. Little Cristiano's been playing on the beach, it's beautiful to see.'

'How lovely for you all,' Thea gushed. 'I take it you got my messages.'

'Thea, I'd love to help you, but Minnie's feeling a bit fragile this week. She *will* do the interview, I promise, but I can't give you an exact date. I'm sorry.'

'It's OK, I understand. Just call me as soon as you have something. Take care, Leanne. Enjoy the sun. Have a lovely day.'

Thea hung up and bawled. 'Shiiiiit!' Her phone rang again. 'Hello,' she snapped into it.

'Thea?'

'Yes.'

'It's Jake. I'm back. Fancy a drink tonight?'

Luke sat at his desk watching Thea. She looked good with her hair in a ponytail; it showed off her cheekbones. He'd enjoyed his session with her in Edinburgh, not that he could remember that much about it, addled as he had been by jet lag and booze. They'd have a repeat performance some time soon, he thought, watching her chatting to Alexa. He'd leave her waiting a few more days, then next week he'd ask her for dinner.

More than ever, Luke felt in need of reassurance that somebody still wanted him. There'd always been plenty of women around to validate him, prove that he was one of the most desirable men on the planet. But not any more. There'd been an embarrassing moment in Guatemala when he'd made a pass at the interpreter and she'd laughed and told him he was the same age as her grandfather, and another in Scotland, just before Thea appeared on the scene, when one of the girls at the wedding had called him a 'dirty old man'. Then there'd been the nasty discovery of Poppy's column. He knew they had to have another discussion or – who was he kidding? – fight about it, but he simply didn't know if he could summon up the energy.

His phone rang. It was his eldest daughter, Tilly. See-ing her name, Luke felt a flash of joy, mixed with unease as he thought about today's attack by Hannah. What must it be like to have your school friends reading about your parents in this undignified fashion? Whenever he put this to Hannah, she simply snorted and said he should have thought about that before impregnating a bimbo, which didn't seem exactly fair, but he could never think of a comeback. He was sure Tilly would be calling to berate him about something but still he smiled as he picked up.

'Hi, darling.'

'Hi, Dad. How are you? Wow. I've just been reading Poppy's column in *Wicked*. It's sooo, like, book. All my friends think she's ledge.'

'Oh,' said Luke. He had no idea what his daughter meant but she sounded approving. 'Good. Good.'

'I was just wondering, Dad. Do you think we could meet Poppy some time? Only, I think we've been mean to her and we ought to make it up.'

'Have you asked your mum about this?'

A brief pause.

'You know what Mum's like. She'd only say no, but it's up to you, not her.'

'I'll see what I can do,' Luke said, not sure whether to be pleased or depressed that his wife's unwelcome celeb-rity seemed to be bringing him back in touch with his daughters. 'And how are you, kitten? Working hard?'

'Yeah, yeah, Dad.'

Luke saw his call-waiting light flashing. Loren, Rox-anne's secretary. 'Sweetheart, it's an important call on the other line. I'd better get it. Lovely to hear from you, my pumpkin. Speak soon . . . Hi, Loren.'

'Hi, Luke. Roxanne was wondering if you had a spare moment after work tonight?'

Now that sounded interesting. Roxanne probably still hadn't got over him. Probably desperate to see if she could rekindle their flame. He'd have to think about it . . .

'Luke?'

'Yes, I'm free.'

'She'll see you in her office straight after the show.'

Thea didn't really want a drink with Jake, but as long as the slenderest of threads connected him to Minnie she had no choice. So at the end of the day she took the Tube to Camden, where Jake was waiting for her in the same pub as before. He was tanned and had a bit of stubble. It suited him. The talk of the Marriott Guatemala City was still pushing it, though.

'I'm really, really sorry,' he said, before she'd even sat down.

'Thanks,' Thea replied and then with great effort, 'I know it's not your fault.'

'Yeah, but I still feel responsible. Getting your hopes up.'

'You can't do anything about Minnie. No one can. She's a law unto herself. But you tried and I appreciated it.' Thea hoped the gods were looking down on such a display of graciousness. 'Anyway,' she said, 'how was the trip for you?'

'Knackering. But good. Luke's reports were brilliant.

We received a huge surge in donations off the back of them. So I'm for ever in your debt.'

'Good,' said Thea. 'You can buy me a drink, then.'

While he was at the bar, she noticed the pub was filling up. A man was setting himself up on a dais with a microphone and noisy gangs were gathering round each table.

'What's going on?' she asked Jake as he returned with the wine. A whole bottle, which seemed a bit presumptuous as she wasn't going to stick around that long.

'It's pub quiz night. I'd forgotten. It's a good laugh, though. Want to have a go?'

'Don't be silly!'

He laughed. 'Why not? The prize is two hundred and fifty pounds. We could donate it to Guatemala Children.'

'I don't do pub quizzes.'

'What a waste. Your general knowledge must be incredible. I bet you know your capital cities. Australia?'

'Canberra,' Thea said, giving him a withering glance.

'Very good. Most people say Sydney. Brazil?'

'Brasilia, of course. Did you think I was going to say Rio?'

He laughed. 'You're a natural nerd. Come on, Thea, let's do it. Why not? What have you got to rush off to?'

He was right.

'Go on, get a sheet then.'

It was a surprisingly enjoyable hour. She and Jake squabbled over what colour zero was on a roulette wheel (she said red, he said green but she insisted) and what the official language of the United States was (she said it had none, he said English but in the end they went with her answer).

'Right, pop music now,' said the compère. 'Tonight we're doing the eighties.'

'Yay!' bellowed Thea. 'My decade.'

Jake grinned. 'Well, at least one of us will know what he's talking about.'

She glared at him with mock froideur. 'No need to be cheeky, youngster. Just because you're jealous I don't wear nappies at night and sleep in a cot.'

'What was the name of the band consisting of Andy McCluskey and Paul Humphreys?'

'OMD! OMD!' Thea yelled. She was on her third glass of wine and more than a little drunk, she realized. Jake laughed and spread out his hands in ignorance.

'Who had a hit in 1982 with "John Wayne is Big Leggy"?'

'Easy! Haysi Fantayzee.' Thea started singing. 'John Wayne in lovers lane making whoopee . . .'

'Nineteen eighty-two.' Jake shook his head as if she'd referred to the glorious age of the steam engine. She slapped his hand.

'All right, so how old are you?'

'I'm twenty-eight.' He cleared his throat and squared up like one of the Mitchell brothers in *EastEnders*. 'Got a problem with that?'

Thea was wondering if she did, when her phone started ringing.

'Oh fuck off,' she told it. 'I'm having fun here.' But the lure of a BlackBerry was too strong for her to resist. She glanced at the screen. Number withheld.

'Sorry,' she said to Jake. 'I'd better get it. Hello?'

'Is that Thea?' It was an American voice. Female, tremulous, a slight lisp. Thea could only just hear her over the surrounding noise and banter.

'Yes?'

'It's Minnie Maltravers here.'

'Come in, Luke,' Roxanne said. Luke eyed her approvingly. He loved those neat little suits she favoured, that hinted at so much underneath. He was sure he could glimpse a bulge of suspender under the skirt. Yes, he'd definitely been too hasty ending things. He sat down, smiling.

'What can I do for you, Roxanne?'

'I wanted to play you this,' she said, putting a digital voice recorder on her desk. Luke looked at it, confused.

'OK.'

She pressed play. The sound of a phone ringing, then: 'Hello?' A man's voice. Slightly wavery. Refined.

'Hello.' It was Roxanne's voice, although for some reason she'd affected a terrible Cockney accent. 'Is that the Bishop of Bellchester?'

'Yes, my dear, how can I help you?'

'I'm calling from the Frontline Club in Paddington. We have a coat here that we think you must have left behind.'

'The Frontline Club? I don't know it I'm afraid, my dear.'

'But you were here quite recently with Luke Norton.'

'Luke Norton? I'm sorry you have the wrong man. I haven't seen Luke in years.'

365

'Oh, I'm so sorry. We must've made a mistake. I do apologize, guv'nor.'

'Not to worry, my dear. I hope you find the coat's owner.'

'I 'ope so too. Thank you for your help m'Lord.'

Click.

'What do you say to that, Luke?'

'I . . .'

'Who did you spend £179.80 in the Frontline Club on? Falsifying expenses is a sackable offence you know. You're in serious trouble, Luke.' Her desk phone rang. 'Excuse me one second. Hello? . . . Oh! Hello.' She listened intently, nodding. 'Yes, yes, I see. Well, if she's going to call Thea directly, then wonderful. Excellent. Thank you for letting me know.'

She hung up.

'Well.'

She stared at Luke.

'I'm going to give you one more chance it seems. That was Minnie Maltravers' assistant. She's going to do the interview. Tomorrow. In the studio. And she'll only talk to you.'

38

The office was in uproar. Minnie was due to arrive in an hour and the interview was going to take place face-to-face live at seven forty-eight, just after the commercial break. The network had been flagging it all day: 'Tonight Minnie Maltravers speaks exclusively to the *SevenThirty News* about *that* adoption.'

Minnie's people had sent over a new list of demands that made Barbra Streisand sound like a hermit.

'She wants her dressing room decorated with white roses and white curtains, it's got to have an MP3 and DVD player,' Alexa read incredulously from an email. 'There are to be two boxes of Pop Tarts, a box of Fruit Loops and a "bowl of fresh tuna salad, with Hellmann's mayo, eggs, relish and tuna (albacore, solid, white, in spring water)". The only acceptable brand of water is Volvic.' This is even madder than in Scotland. Are you sure this isn't a joke?'

'I wish,' said an ashen-faced Thea. She'd been up all night again, negotiating terms with Leanne, eventually triumphing by insisting that Minnie be not allowed to see the questions in advance. To keep going, she'd had eight espressos, making her as fidgety as a grasshopper at a disco.

Her phone rang. 'Luke?' she said tersely. She was keeping her tone as professional as possible.

'I was wondering if we could have a quick word. I'm in the canteen.'

'OK.'

He'd be wanting to discuss the wording of one of the questions. Thea hurried out of the newsroom and along the corridor with its big window looking into the studio. With less than an hour to go before the programme started, lighting men stood on ladders working out the most flattering angle to illuminate Minnie's still flawless features. In a special make-up room hastily constructed at the back of the studio, scented with Jo Malone pomegranate noir candles, Minnie's second-favourite make-up artist (the favourite had given birth that morning and had resisted all Thea's very best pleas and bribes to come) mixed colours in a palette as if she was Picasso. Carlo the hairdresser, flown in again first class from New York and put up in the Lanesborough, fiddled with tongs and straightening irons. She pushed open the door of the canteen. Luke was sitting at a table in the far corner, frowning over the list of questions and nursing a cup of tea.

'You must know those by heart now,' she teased him. Since the weekend she'd been feeling distinctly ill-at-ease with him, but she'd decided the only way to play it was to carry on as normal.

'Yup,' he said. Under his make-up he looked white. Thea stared at him. She'd never seen him like this before.

'Are you OK?'

'Fine. Yes.'

'What did you want to see me for?'

'I . . .' He sat back in his chair. 'Christ, Thea, do you think it's going to be all right?'

Thea was astonished. Confident, controlled Luke Norton didn't ask things like that. 'Of course it is,' she said. 'Minnie's on her way in right now, I've just spoken to Leanne and you are going to have the world exclusive with her. It'll be a triumph.'

'But suppose it's not.' He looked at her beseechingly. 'So much is resting on this, Thea. I know I'm out of favour with Dean and Roxanne.' Before Thea could interrupt, he held up a hand. 'It's not just the presenting side of things, there . . . well, I'm in trouble about something else too. And the school fees keep going up and Hannah's asking for more alimony and it's all . . .' He exhaled. 'Tonight, has to be a success.'

'And it will be,' Thea said, trying to hide her unease. Seeing Luke nervous was like seeing the prime minister on the loo. It ruined your image of him.

'Thea, I'm sorry I've been running a bit hot and cold recently. I . . . It was an amazing night we had in Scotland, but you can understand why I backed off. You're such an incredible woman but . . . I *am* married and . . .'

'I understand,' she said quickly.

'But my marriage is on the rocks. I can't fool myself any longer. And . . . I don't want to be presumptuous but it would be wonderful to think the . . . connection we've always had was still as strong as ever.'

Thea felt as if she'd been spring cleaned. It was all coming right. So suddenly. They'd got the interview and Luke loved her.

'Thea?'

369

'Luke, I—' Her phone rang. 'Hello? Leanne? Oh. OK. Great. We're all ready for her.' She hung up. 'I've got to run, Luke. Minnie's coming in now.'

'Shall we have a drink after the show?'

She smiled at him. 'After the show would be great.'

After much discussion it had been agreed that the interview with Minnie wouldn't be the lead item on the show. Even Dean agreed that would be far too much against the serious spirit the *SevenThirty News* still paid lip service to and would garner them a pasting from the critics. Instead, they'd get the day's main headlines dispatched before the first advert break, devote the next two sections to the Minnie interview, then allocate five minutes to other news at the end. So, as Luke read the headlines about freak storms devastating America, disastrous sales figures for Marks & Spencer and another suicide bombing in Tel Aviv, Minnie sat in make-up, surrounded by bodyguards, having her powder touched up and her curls tweaked.

'Is everything OK this time?' Thea said in a low voice to Leanne.

'Yup. It really is. Minnie's astrologer told her she should do the interview today, so there's no way she'll back out.'

'Great.' Thea still wasn't wholly convinced. She looked at the clock. 'She needs to be in the studio in five minutes when the adverts start.'

'No problem, Thea.'

And sure enough, five minutes later Minnie emerged from make-up in a demure dove-grey trouser suit and was ushered to her seat. For the second time in a week, she shook hands graciously with Luke. Virtually genuflecting, Rhys ran forward to clip her microphone to her collar, the make-up artist appeared with a powder puff, Carlo did a last-minute tug with some hot tongs.

It was going to happen. It was actually going to happen! Thea dashed up to the gallery. 'And lights, camera!' Jayne was counting down. Dean and Roxanne Fox stood behind her. 'Over to you, Luke.'

Luke looked into the camera and gave his trademark boyish grin.

'Good evening and welcome back to the *Seven Thirty News*. Tonight, we are delighted to be bringing you an exclusive interview with Minnie Maltravers, legendary supermodel and icon.'

'Cameras to Minnie,' Abe, the director, intoned and the nation saw Minnie smile graciously at Luke through flirtatiously lowered eyelids. Thea exhaled with relief. It was happening. Finally happening.

'Minnie,' Luke was saying, leaning forward, 'you recently adopted a nine-month-old baby boy from Guatemala, in what most of us would see as an act of charity. Yet your actions seem to have sparked fury round the world. Do you understand why you have upset so many people?'

Minnie shook her head. 'I acted in good faith,' she lisped. 'All I wanted was to be a mom and give a child a better life, but I've been greeted with so much aggression.'

'But can't you understand why?' Luke said. 'You have a court order for anger-management issues, and many people who have spent years trying to adopt feel that you have been given preferential treatment over them.'

'Well, if they do, that's their problem,' Minnie snapped, mouth closing like a zip on a purse.

Luke raised an eyebrow. 'Really?'

'Tell him to be less aggressive,' Dean flapped.

'Luke, calm down,' Thea said into his earpiece. 'Don't give her such a hard time straight off.'

'Yeah,' Minnie replied. 'I'm sorry for other people if they can't adopt for whatever reason, but I don't see why I should suffer for it. Social workers checked me and my husband out extensively and they decided we would make excellent parents for my little Cristiano.'

'And the fact you opened a health clinic and a school in his village had nothing to do with it?'

Minnie's cat-like eyes narrowed.

'Why are you being so critical? Surely it's a good thing to open a school and a clinic? I don't understand why this is getting me such a hard time.'

'I don't know.' Luke shrugged. 'You tell me.'

'Tell him to cool it,' Dean hissed.

Roxanne shook her head. 'He's doing a good job. Asking what everyone wants to hear. If she gets angry it'll make great TV.'

'I just wanted a baby,' Minnie said, in her tweetie-pie voice. 'What's so wrong with that?' *Wasso wong wid dat?* 'Did I commit a crime?'

'Of course not,' Luke said, smiling appeasingly. 'People just wonder why – having wanted this baby so much – you have barely seen him for nearly a month.'

Minnie stood up, her face thunderous.

'How do you know I haven't spent time with him? *How do you know?* I don't have to put up with this crap.'

Jayne's hands flew to her mouth. 'Oh my God, she's going to walk.'

'Get him to calm her down,' Dean flapped.

'Luke, Luke. Apologize!' Thea hissed into the microphone. 'Please!'

'I'm so sorry,' Luke said, leaning forward and patting her on the arm. 'Don't take offence. None was intended. I'm just putting the questions to you that the public has been asking for the past few weeks in the knowledge you want to refute them, to set the record straight.'

Minnie smiled warily, clearly only partially appeased.

'OK,' she whispered.

'He's doing a great job,' Roxanne said happily. 'He's got the balance of obsequious and cheeky just right. Well done, Luke, back on form.'

'Yeah,' Dean admitted reluctantly, 'it's good.'

'Ad break,' Jayne intoned.

'All right,' Luke said. 'We'll be back after the break with Minnie Maltravers speaking exclusively to the *SevenThirty News* about her adoption battle.'

In the post mortems, no one could quite work out how it happened. But somehow before cutting to the adverts there was the briefest of pauses. For the rest of his life, Luke would wonder if one of the engineers had landed him in it, someone he'd once been rude or offhand to. All he knew was he was unusually nervous, worn down by Hannah's humiliations, his children's demands, Poppy's new social life, the fact this interview was either going to be his renaissance or his swan-song and that somehow, despite all his years of experience, he didn't realize he was still on air when he muttered into his microphone.

'Stupid cunt.'

A nation heard it and gasped. Virtually immediately, a clip started running on YouTube, while Channel 6 switched to a commercial for a new eco-friendly washing-up liquid.

39

Poppy missed this historic moment in British television because she was in the basement of a nightclub in Mayfair, a canapé in one hand and a glass of champagne in the other, toasting the launch of a new designer suitcase. She'd been glad to get out of the house: Clara had been tetchy all day, Brigita said her molars were coming through, and whenever Poppy had tried to kiss or cuddle her, she'd flung herself on her nanny, shouting, 'Go 'way.'

Glenda had been in a funny mood too. When Poppy had asked how everything was, instead of the usual cheerful recital of her family's goings-on, she'd snapped 'Fine' and virtually pushed past Poppy with her feather duster.

'What's up with her?' Poppy wondered aloud, as the kitchen door slammed.

'She's pissed off,' Brigita observed. 'I think you forget her birthday.'

Poppy's hand flew to her mouth. 'Shit! It was last week, wasn't it? Oh my God, how could I have been so stupid?'

'You're busy, Mummy.'

'Not that busy.' Poppy ran into the kitchen. 'Glenda, Glenda, I'm so sorry about your birthday. I've just been . . . distracted. I'll make it up to you.'

Glenda shrugged. ''S OK, Poppy. I am not a child. Birthdays mean nothing to me.' From the pinkness of her cheeks, it was obvious they meant everything. She smiled at Poppy, but without any of her past warmth. 'Excuse me, darling, I go and do the bathroom now.'

All in all, it was a relief to get to the party. Things had changed so much since the column had started: she was no longer a virtually invisible observer, but someone people wanted to talk to. Although the only person Poppy was really interested in seeing was Toby. She hadn't heard from him since the flowers, but she had decided that was simply his style. Something inside her reassured her all would be well. Of course there was the more troubling question of Luke hanging over her, but she kept shoving that to the bottom of her priorities list, like the dentist's appointment she'd been putting off for years. She and Luke hadn't spoken properly since he'd got back from Scotland and even though Poppy knew tonight was his big night she'd had no desire to stay in and cheer him on. They would talk, she told herself. Soon. When his big interview was over and, she whispered this last bit to herself, 'When I know where I stand with Toby.'

Charlie tapped her on the shoulder.

'Hey, I saw the column! I didn't realize *you* were the Bimbo.'

A week ago, Poppy would have blushed, but now she smiled cheekily. 'Perhaps I'm not as dumb as I look.'

'Evidently not.' Charlie took a slice of foie gras wrapped in Parma ham from a passing tray, while Poppy grabbed champagne from another one. She'd been so nervous, she'd had three already but they didn't seem to be exerting their usual magical effect. 'I'm surprised you're not watching your husband's big interview.'

'I'm recording it. I've got a job too, you know.' Poppy

was taken aback by how sharp she sounded, but before she could apologize, she caught her breath. There was Toby, at the other end of the room, laughing with a woman so perfect she had to be an android. 'Excuse me a second,' she said hastily.

It was a moment or two before Toby noticed her, so engrossed was he in his conversation. Then he said, 'Oh hi!' He leant forward and kissed her on both cheeks. 'Great to see you. I've been thinking about you a lot.'

'Really?'

'Of course.' He surveyed her. 'You look gorgeous.' His attention moved to yet another woman who'd sidled up to him. 'Hey, Miranda! How are you? Miranda, this is Poppy.'

Miranda, who was petite and dark with an Audrey Hepburn quality that made Poppy feel like the Incredible Hulk, barely registered her. 'Hi. Toby darling, just wondering if you could help me out.'

'For you, anything.' He put his hand in his pocket. 'How much do you want?'

'Two please. Can I pay you later?'

Toby rolled his eyes. 'No, darling, you know the rules. Cash on delivery.'

'Oh, all right,' she said, fumbling in her handbag. Poppy watched, a large penny rapidly dropping. Toby caught her eye.

'Do you want some?'

'I, er, no thanks.'

'Sure? I'm going to have a quick line in a second. Give me the energy to keep going. Come with me.'

'You don't need drugs to have a good time.' 'It was

just the once and I was hooked.' But Poppy was young; she wanted to be like everyone else for a change. Drugs couldn't really be as bad as everyone said. Meena was fine, Toby was fine, or actually . . . he wasn't fine, he was yawning slightly and moving away from her.

'I'll see you later,' he said.

'No! Wait! I'll come with you.'

Heart thudding, she followed him to the doors of the gents. 'Just a sec,' he said sticking his head round the door, then he stuck it back out again. 'Quick, in here.' Briskly, he pushed her into a cubicle and locked the door. There was paper all over the floor. Poppy only hoped it hadn't been used. Toby appeared not to have even noticed, he was too busy running his fingers over the top of the cistern.

'Bugger,' he said, 'they've covered it in Vaseline. Oh well. Too bad.' He pulled a little white envelope out of his pocket. Squatting down, he flipped down the toilet lid and shook some white powder on to it. It looked just like Persil automatic, Poppy thought, as he began chopping it with a black Amex card.

'Fat or thin?' he said, turning to her.

Poppy had no idea what he was talking about. 'I suppose I could do with losing a few pounds,' she said modestly.

He roared with laughter. 'No, silly. I meant the lines.'

He might as well have been speaking Turkmenistani. 'I'm easy.' She shrugged nonchalantly.

'I know that!' Toby grinned. 'But I still don't know if you want fat or thin.' Seeing her hurt face, he sighed. 'OK. Two skinnies coming up.' He chopped some more, then rapidly rolled up a bank note, stuck it up his right nostril and snorted. Poppy watched and learnt.

'Oh, that's good,' he breathed. 'Diego's done it again.' He handed the note to Poppy. 'Here you go, sweetheart.'

It was slightly sticky and warm with Toby's snot. Gingerly, Poppy stuck it into a nostril and inhaled like a truffling pig. Most of the white stuff spluttered all over the place. Embarrassed, she tried again and felt a burning in her nostrils. She glanced at Toby, mortified by her lack of expertise but he was busy dabbing up the remains with a wet index finger and rubbing it on his gums.

'Happy?' he asked.

'Oh, yes,' Poppy lied. He took her face in his hands and she thought he was going to kiss her, but instead he tilted her head backwards and examined her nostrils as if she were a prize racehorse.

'Little lump there,' he said, flicking it away. 'Am I OK?'

'Uh, yes.'

'Good.' He pushed open the cubicle door. Poppy grinned sheepishly at a man adjusting his combover in the mirror. Equally sheepishly, he grinned back.

'Shall we?' Toby said, pushing open the door. They headed back to the party. 'Have a glass of champagne,' he whispered in her ear. 'Hi, Markus! How are you?' He pumped hands with a blond man in a leather jacket. 'Have you met Poppy?'

'Hi.' Poppy smiled. The ends of her teeth were numb, but her brain was as clear as a pane of glass. She downed her glass in one, unable to taste it. 'I like your tie.'

'Thank you,' Markus said. He had a German accent.

'I thought about wearing a tie,' Poppy said. 'I think

they can look really sexy on women. Sort of strong and androgynous. If you're Annie Lennox or whoever. But then I wondered if it might make me look a prat so I chose this.'

'You look very nice,' Markus said. Toby had already been collared by another annoyingly pretty girl.

'Do you think so? Thank you. These shoes are killing me, actually, but never mind. You have to suffer to be beautiful, don't you? I read that somewhere. I've started to make much more of an effort now I've got a column and going to parties is my job.'

'You've got a column?' Markus had stepped back a couple of inches. Poppy wondered if she'd showered him with spit.

'Yes.' She didn't know what came over her as she added, 'In *The Times.*'

'*The Times?*'

'Yes.'

'The London *Times?*' Markus sounded as if she'd just announced she was the new Messiah. Pompous arse.

'That's where we are, aren't we? Good old Larn-dun.' Poppy said the last in a Cockney accent, then giggled. 'Wha-evver, mate. Innit.' Her heart pounded, adrenalin swooped round her veins like a rollercoaster. She felt fantastic.

'Excuse me a minute,' said Markus backing away.

Boring git. She turned her attention to the dance floor where only a few people were dancing in a desultory fashion. Poppy felt the urge to show them how it was done. To the strains of Rihanna, she stepped out on the floor. 'Wa-hoo!' she cried. Christ, she was a brilliant dancer. Her limbs were feather light, as she swirled across the floor. She felt acutely conscious of the outline of her body within the folds of her dress. She could feel Toby watching her and she felt as if she too was observing herself from a distance. Her mouth felt as if it had been pebbledashed, so she snatched another drink from a tray and downed it in two gulps. She glanced at Toby again, but once more he was talking to a pretty girl.

'Hey, Toby!'

'Hey, Poppy!' He sounded pleasant but a bit distracted.

'Have you got any more of the . . . you know?'

'Sure.' He reached in his pocket and handed her a tiny envelope.

'I . . . can you come with me?'

Toby laughed. 'You're a big girl.'

She put her arm on his. 'Please.'

He rolled his eyes. 'Oh, all right then.'

This time the cubicle reeked of warm diarrhoea. Poppy didn't care. As soon as the door was bolted behind them, she jumped on him.

'Hey! Steady on.' For a moment he seemed stiff, then he pulled her to him and they kissed and kissed. Poppy's insides were molten, though her anaesthetized mouth found it hard to feel the shape of his lips. She was starting to grapple with his belt buckle when there was a rap on the door.

'Hey, what's going on in there?'

Toby gave a bark of laughter. 'It's OK, mate. Not what you think. We're having a good old-fashioned snog.'

'No ladies in the gents.'

'All right, all right.' Gently, Toby disentangled himself

as if Poppy were a piece of barbed wire. 'Sorry, my darling, but we're going to have to cool it.'

'Can we go back to yours?' she asked.

He looked at her for a moment, seeming to hesitate. 'Yours might be a better idea.'

'No! Remember I'm married.'

'Oh yeah.' He looked at her again, then smiled and shook his head. 'OK, gorgeous. You've won. Come on. Let's find a cab.'

40

As Britain was being exhorted to buy Andrex, L'Oreal conditioner, Huggies and Flash dishwasher tablets, Minnie Maltravers was in the back of her black limousine ('must have a male driver') and on her way back to the Mandarin Oriental where the first thing she would do was sack a mightily relieved Leanne, who would retrain as a rebirthing guru and relocate to Hawaii. The *Seven Thirty News* studio was in meltdown.

'How the *fuck* did this happen?' Dean bellowed. 'Didn't Luke realize we were still on air?'

'Evidently not,' Thea said quietly.

'Look on the bright side,' Alexa chirruped in. '*Everyone's* going to be talking about the *Seven Thirty News.*'

'Yeah, but bugger that for now! We're going to get fucking hammered by the Broadcasting Standards Commission for using expletives before the watershed. Fuck me! What a stupid wanker. Quick, get him off the set! And put Emma in his place.'

So the *Seven Thirty News*'s audience, which had grown by two million during the break, thanks to viewers frantically texting friends and family, urging them to watch this car crash, were welcomed back by a rather wild-eyed but smug Emma.

'Good evening. This is the *Seven Thirty News*. We're sorry, but we've had to cut short the interview with

Minnie Maltravers because she has left the studio. Apologies to everyone. Now to tonight's other stories. The Catholic Church tonight announced . . .'

At his desk, Luke was wiping the sweat from his brow.

'I'm sorry, Dean, I'm really sorry,' he said as they all crowded round him. 'It was a genuine mistake. I didn't know I was still live.'

'A man of your experience, Luke. How could you?'

Rhys, who – ever professional even during this storm – was scouring the newspaper websites for the following day's stories exclaimed:

'Oh, Christ. Take a look at this.'

Everyone gathered round his computer, its screen filled with the *Daily Post* website.

Exclusive: How Minnie Wasted 'The Cad's' Time

It's the story everyone's been fighting for: Minnie Maltravers's account of her recent adoption of Cristiano Morales. But last night it was revealed that Ms Maltravers promised an interview to veteran war reporter Luke Norton of the *SevenThirty News* only to keep him waiting 6 hours before cancelling. According to his wife, model Poppy Norton, 24, Mr Norton and a team from the *SevenThirty News* flew to Edinburgh to interview Maltravers only to have to turn back after waiting 6 hours for the notoriously tardy supermodel, because she 'didn't feel well'.

'Luke was furious,' revealed Mrs Norton, in her new column for *Wicked* magazine. 'He flew to Edinburgh from Guatemala City. He was meant to do the interview in the afternoon and fly back the next morning. Minnie kept them waiting for 6 hours and when she finally decided she was ready to do the interview, her phone rang and then she decided she was too tired and would rather go out for dinner. So the next morning the whole team flew back empty-handed. Luke thought she was a total flake. He calls her "Moaning Minnie" and said she was nothing like as beautiful in the flesh as he'd expected, with scars visible round her eyes.'

There was a dumbfounded silence. Naturally, Dean was the first to break it.

'The Bimbo put this in her column?'

Luke looked round aghast. 'It's news to me. I promise you.'

'You didn't tell her to keep her mouth shut.' Dean began to laugh. 'This is priceless.'

Roxanne came into the room. 'I think it's best if you don't come in for the next couple of days, don't you Luke?'

'Are you suspending me?'

Roxanne shrugged. 'If you like, yes. We'll need to talk to the governors and work out how best to deal with this. It's been a bloody disaster.'

It wasn't until Luke was in a taxi on the way home that he looked at his phone. Forty-three new messages. Mainly from friends laughing. Tilly saying: 'Dad, have you gone mad?' And then somehow jammed in the middle of it all, Poppy saying, 'I'm staying at Meena's tonight, I've spoken to Brigita, she'll stay the night and get Clara up in the morning, so you need have no worries there.'

Luke gazed at the phone, as a ventriloquist might at a dummy who had spoken back to him. Where was his wife? She'd betrayed his confidences in public and then – on the worst professional night of his life – disappeared to her friend's house as if nothing had happened.

The car pulled up outside his flat. A small group of men in parkas standing round the gatepost leapt to attention. Who the hell were they? As Luke climbed out of the cab, their camera motors began buzzing like insects.

'Luke, hey, Luke! Where's the bimbo?'

'Excuse me.' Luke pushed through them. A couple tried to block his way. 'Hey, what do you think you're doing? This is my property. Get out! You're trespassing.'

'Ah, fuck off, you stupid cunt.'

'Stupid cunt,' they all jeered. 'What a rude word, Luke.'

'Fuck off!' Luke shouted, putting his key in the lock. He twiddled and turned it but it wouldn't open. Someone had bolted the door from the inside. Furiously, he jabbed the doorbell.

'Brigita, let me in!'

It seemed an age before she opened up.

'Sorry, Daddy,' she said, as he stumbled into the hall. 'Those men keep banging on the door, so I triple lock it. Come in and tell me: why were you so bloody rude to Minnie?'

It was nearly midnight by the time the dust semi-settled. There was a long debrief with the head of PR, trying to work out how to present this disaster to the world tomorrow. By the time it ended Thea's phone was jammed with texts and messages. None of them seemed to appreciate the trouble she was in; they all thought it was the most brilliant joke.

Funniest thing I've seen in years. Dunc says it will be a MySpace classic, Rachel. x

Irritated, Thea deleted it. Sodding Dunc.

'Darling,' said her mother, sounding the cheeriest Thea had heard in ages. 'I am shocked. I told you that Luke Norton was a dreadful man. Too handsome for his own good.'

Gloomily Thea hung up. For the fifth time, she dialled Luke's number. One moment they'd been about to relight a smouldering romance, the next he'd been kicked out of the building. But he still could have called her back. She got voicemail.

Thea looked at the next text.

Oh bugger. I bet you're wishing you never met me. Fancy an apologetic drink? Jake

Thea did. Not least because when Luke called she wanted him to hear the background noise of a lively bar, rather than her fridge humming and a distant ambulance wailing in Brixton. She replied rapidly,

Only if we're talking right now.

The reply came almost instantly.

When else?

They met in Soho House, which was the only place Thea could think of that would be open so late.

'I haven't been here in ages,' Jake said, looking round the dim room with its arrangements of low leather sofas and chairs, occupied by slightly past their prime media executives.

'The scene of too many mispent nights in my youth,' Thea said. In fact the last time she'd been there was on BAFTA night. 'I've kind of gone off it.'

'Ah, don't give me all this "my youth" stuff again. You're hardly ready for a Zimmer frame.'

'I think I aged about a trillion years tonight.' She finished her wine and refilled the glass from the bottle in front of them. 'Thank God tomorrow's my day off. I'd better check the daytime TV schedules and start to organize my life round them; develop a crush on Jeremy Kyle.'

'You won't lose your job over this!'

'I wouldn't be surprised.' Another big gulp. 'Luke will for sure. They've had the knives out for him for a while now.' She thought about Luke. He still hadn't returned any of her calls, but he was probably in bed by now. He'd as good as said he was leaving Poppy for her. They'd talk in the morning, she decided. Right now she'd enjoy herself with Jake and hope, rather unrealistically, that news of their flirtatious late-night drink would get back to the man she loved, further fuelling his passion.

'It'll be a shame if Luke gets the sack,' Jake said. 'I like him. We had some good laughs in Guatemala though he is a bit of a liability, isn't he? I mean, I see where all that cad stuff comes from.'

Thea looked at him sharply.

'What do you mean?'

'Well, he was leching all over one of the interpreters and flirting with everyone in sight. We were all having a bit of a laugh about it. He was trying to be subtle, but he wasn't subtle enough.' Jake glanced at Thea. 'Are you OK?'

Thea felt as if cement was solidifying in her limbs. 'Yeah, I'm fine.'

'You sure?' He leant forward and took her hand in his. She snatched it away. 'Listen, I know tonight's been a disaster in some ways, but think of all the publicity the programme will get as a result. No one's going to blame you. It'll just mean even more bad press for Minnie.'

'It's got nothing to do with tonight's show,' said Thea. 'I just . . . I just don't feel very well.'

Jake's face creased in concern. 'Is there anything I can get you?'

'You can get me another bottle of wine.'

'Is that a good idea if you're feeling ill?'

'Oh don't be such a granny,' she snapped.

Jake stood up. 'Look, Thea, I'm sorry if you don't feel well. But I'm not going to stick around to have my head bitten off. If you need a friend, great. If you want to be alone, that's fine too.'

She could almost hear the gears crunching in her head, as she computed it all. Luke had been leching over everyone in Guatemala. Luke was never going to change. He'd said those things tonight because . . . well, because he could. But he didn't mean them. He never would. In the words of the poet Roxette, it must have been love. But now it was over. Sod Luke Norton. As her thoughts juddered to a disillusioned halt, she did a mental hand-break turn.

'I'm sorry,' she said. 'I'm a bitch. Please sit down.'

'OK,' Jake looked firm, 'but only if you promise to behave.'

'I can't promise, but I'll do my best.'

She took a gulp of wine. She smiled at Jake. He smiled back. Hey, he was eight years younger than her. Hey, he was short. Hey, he was a charity worker. Hey, she should know better. But . . .

She leant forward. 'Let's not get another bottle here. Why don't we have a nightcap at mine?'

41

Poppy couldn't sleep. Even though it was a balmy summer night, it was cold in Toby's flat and she pulled the bedclothes over her naked body, teeth chattering, an unpleasant metallic taste in her mouth. Her head was beginning to throb as if it was pressed under a huge weight like a wild flower. Beside her Toby lay, snuffling faintly, one hand thrown back over his head. After they'd had sex, he'd swallowed a little blue pill. 'It'll help bring me down,' he said. 'Want one?' But Poppy had refused. Mistake, she thought now, peering at her watch in the half light. Nearly three.

Lying back, images of the past few hours ran through her head like a bad music video. She and Toby coming out of the party, where some flashbulbs went off in her face. Hailing a cab, heading to Whitechapel where he lived, kissing madly in the back. Stumbling up the stairs to his flat, which wasn't the white loft space she'd envisaged but a floor of a tiny terraced house, furnished by Ikea. A lot more kissing on the sofa. Poppy squirmed in a mixture of joy and agony as she recalled those kisses, soft ones on her lips, firm ones on the tops of her thighs, hungry ones on her breasts. Somehow, they'd stumbled into the bedroom, where Toby had waved vaguely at the clothes scattered on the floor and the unmade bed, before he pushed her down on it and . . .

Actually, it hadn't been that good. Inexperienced as she was, even Poppy knew that. It had been a bit perfunctory and Toby had come before she was even remotely ready. Even more than last time, Poppy felt guilty about Luke. But he treated me so badly, she justified herself to Migsy, as she watched the shadow of Toby's body moving on top of her on the ceiling. He was never around. We had nothing in common. Basically, I married too young. And I was so unhappy, though I never told anyone. Of course I have no regrets because I have Clara. But Toby is my soul mate. We were meant to be together . . .

Anxiously, she curled into him. In his sleep, he rolled towards her and cupped her bottom with his hand. She lay awake for hours, listening to the water pipes announcing morning. As the sun gushed in through the curtains, she pushed herself up on her elbow and traced Toby's eagle-beak profile with her finger. He stirred again; she froze. She listened, as his breathing, which had been slow and rhythmical, grew shorter and sharper. Poppy began to suspect that Toby was not asleep any more, that he was faking it. Hurriedly, she rolled on to her side. If he didn't want to talk to her just yet, then she wasn't going to spoil things. She shut her eyes and willed sleep to come.

'Hi.'

Instantly, she flipped over. 'Hi!'

He shook his head slightly and winced, regretting it, then suddenly sat up. 'Shit, it's nearly eight. I need to get going. Do you want to have a shower?'

'No, no. You go first.'

'No, no.' He shook his head. 'I insist.'

Poppy showered feeling a bit shaky. Why did he sound so cold? She lathered her body in his Clarins shower gel, admiring his taste – far nicer than Luke's boring old Imperial Leather – then wrapped herself in a towel, dressed and made her way into the dining area, where he was standing up eating cornflakes from a bowl. A cupboard was open behind him, revealing three cans of chopped tomatoes, two tubes of Berocca, a packet of penne and a tube of Pringles. By the kettle was a variety of teas. rosehip, Earl Grey, peppermint, echinacea. For a second, Poppy felt all gooey. There was something about a man's choice of groceries that made him somehow vulnerable. She wouldn't have taken Toby for a tea man and it made her want to throw her arms round him, but the look on his face made it quite clear that wasn't an option.

'Do you want some breakfast?' he said unwillingly. Poppy knew it was time to get out of there.

'I'm fine, thanks,' she said, ignoring her loudly rumbling tummy. 'Better be going. See how my little girl is.'

'Christ. I'd forgotten you had a child.' He rubbed his eyes blearily. 'How old is she?'

'Just turned two.'

'Nice.' He smiled weakly and headed towards the door. 'I could call you a cab,' he said unenthusiastically. 'If you want to get the Tube, turn right then second left and you'll see it.'

'I'll get the Tube,' Poppy said hastily.

It was only a couple of weeks since she'd returned from Meena's in her party clothes. Then it had felt glamorous in an Amy Winehouse kind of way; this time it just felt cheap and shabby. Poppy didn't know how Meena could do this all the time. The happiness she'd felt last night at being wanted again was rapidly being replaced by renewed guilt that she had actually been unfaithful to her husband.

But I was so miserable, she kept repeating to herself, but somehow that excuse didn't work. As she approached her front gate she was snatched from her thoughts by the sight of a group of men in anoraks. Some were smoking, some were talking into phones, some were chatting. As she approached, they all jumped to attention, pointing their cameras at her.

'Oi, Poppy!' They shouted over the guillotine snapping of the cameras. 'Hey, bimbo!' 'Where have you been?' 'How's your stupid cunt of a husband?'

'Sorry?' Poppy tried to push through them, but the flashes were in her face, bang, bang, bang, blinding her. 'Go away!' she snapped, surprisingly ferociously, fumbling in her bag for her keys, which slipped between her fingers on to the pavement. She bent down to retrieve them.

'Hey! There's a ladder in her tights!'

Neighbours' heads appeared at windows. Passers-by stopped and stared. Somehow Poppy managed to get her key into the lock and almost fell into the hallway and Luke's arms.

'Oh. So you're home at last?'

'Sorry!' she said, taken aback at his furious face. 'I texted you. I had to stay at Meena's. She was sick. I was worried about her.'

'And what about me? Why didn't you call me? I've left about ten messages.'

Despite his tone, Poppy felt a glow of vindication. So he'd missed her. Now he knew what it felt like.

'What *about* you?' Then she remembered. 'Oh, yes. How did the Minnie interview go?'

'You don't know?'

'No. I was going to catch it on Sky Plus. Shall I watch it now?'

'It was a bloody disaster,' Luke said. 'A disaster not helped by you telling the world how we'd already had one bloody disaster in Scotland.'

'What do you mean?' Actually Poppy suddenly had a very good idea what he meant. Shit. Perhaps she'd told Migsy too much again.

'I don't believe it,' Luke shouted. 'First Hannah betraying me in print. Now you. What is it? What is it with my wives?'

'I didn't betray you. What do you mean?'

He brandished a copy of *Wicked* at her. '"My husband went to Scotland to interview Minnie but she wouldn't talk to him." Why didn't you tell me, Poppy? That was confidential. I'm in big, big trouble now. I've been suspended.'

'What does that mean?'

'It means I'll almost certainly be sacked.' He smote his chest, like a bad actor performing a Shakespearean soliloquy. 'What have you done?'

'I'm sorry,' said Poppy, taking her phone out of her bag and plugging it in to its charger. Immediately, it began ringing.

'That'll be all my messages,' Luke said, as Poppy held it to her ear. She expected it to be her husband's berating tones, but instead she got Barbara's throaty voice.

'Poppy.' She laughed like a braying donkey. 'Well, what a storm you and your husband have stirred up. The phones haven't stopped ringing all morning. Call me, babe. This is going to lead to big things.'

The doorbell dringed again.

'I've had enough!' Luke yelled. 'I'm going to disconnect it.'

An hour later, everything had become clear. With Luke in bed, eyemask on and earplugs in, Poppy had watched the recording. She'd also talked to an amused Meena, a delighted Barbara and an ecstatic Migsy.

'I have to tell you, Poppy, everyone at *Wicked*'s thrilled. I knew you'd make a great columnist, but we could never have foreseen this. We're going to give you two pages next week. How's Luke reacting to the whole scandal?'

'Um. I'm not sure I should go into details.'

'But you have to! Our readers will be dying to know. I imagine he's a bit embarrassed, isn't he?'

'Yes, he is. And cross. He's been suspended.'

'Oh, poor man. But Minnie was being very difficult, wasn't she?'

'Oh yes, she's a nightmare,' Poppy agreed.

They talked on in this vein for a few more minutes.

'Who was that?' snapped Luke from the doorway as she hung up. Poppy jumped like a cricket.

'Just the magazine wanting to know how I was getting on.'

'You're *not* still doing that column for them, are you?'

His tone made something explode in Poppy's head.

'Yes, I am! Why the hell shouldn't I?' Tears filled her eyes. 'Luke, I'm sorry. I told them some things about Minnie, but I didn't think they'd print them. It was stupid of me, but it won't happen again.'

'Why couldn't you get a proper job?'

'I didn't know what else I could do.' Her throat was burning, she felt an embarrassing lump of snot about to dribble out of her nose. 'This is the way I am. I never pretended to be anything else. I'm not a genius. I don't have any qualifications. I'm not a thrusting business-woman. I don't bake great cakes like Hannah. I'm not clever like Thea and Roxanne and those other women in your office. I'm just me. Poppy. If you didn't like it, you shouldn't have married me.'

'I didn't want to marry you,' Luke shouted. 'I only did it because . . . well, because you were pregnant and I'd made a mess of my real life and I thought I should. But as soon as we did it I knew I'd made a mistake.'

And there it was. The long-unspoken, avoided truth.

'I see,' Poppy said slowly into the cavernous silence that followed.

Luke ran his fingers through his hair. 'Sweetheart, I'm sorry. Hey, I didn't mean it like that. I *did* want to marry you, it was just . . . well, it wasn't ideal.'

'I suppose not,' Poppy said. She turned on her heel and went upstairs. In the bedroom, she sat on the bed, just staring at the wall, too numb to fully come to terms with what she'd always known at some level.

Luke doesn't love me. Well, never mind. Toby does. Luke doesn't love me. Well, never mind . . .

She wished she could be surer about the Toby bit. Her

phone rang. This would be him now! 'Hello?' she said nervously.

'Darling, it's me.'

'Oh, hi, Mum.'

'Luke's in trouble isn't he?' Before Poppy could reply, Louise continued. 'And I am *so* upset. I've just found out Jean-Claude was in town and he didn't call me.'

'Sorry?'

'I knew he was coming to London and I waited for his call, but nothing, even though I must have left at least five messages on his mobile. And then I tried his hotel and they said he'd checked out that morning, the bastard! Men, Poppy! They're all the bloody same.'

'I . . .'

'I feel so let down. I was sure this one was different.'

Luke stuck his head around the door.

'Mum, I'm really sorry, but if he behaved like that, you've got to think he wasn't worthy of you.' Poppy had said it all a trillion times before. 'Listen, I have to go. Luke needs me.'

'The idiot. Swearing on live television. What's going to become of you now, Poppy?'

'I have to go. We'll speak later.' Poppy hung up. 'What is it?'

'I've had a call from work. They want me to go in.'

'Oh. Is that good or bad news?'

'Take a wild guess.'

Even after the conversation they'd just had, Poppy still couldn't help but feel for him. She held out her arms.

'Honey, come here. It will all be all right.'

'It bloody won't,' Luke said, not moving. He paused

for a moment. 'I'll be back later,' he said, then turned and left the room.

So that was how it was. Poppy breathed deeply, trying to comprehend her new situation. Had Luke really told her it was all over? Did she care? Poppy wasn't sure. It was almost as if she could feel a shell growing round her heart, the shell she'd long yearned to acquire, to protect her from the outside world.

Through the window she could hear the photographers jostling and laughing. Suddenly she couldn't take the claustrophobia any more. She opened her bedside drawer and started leafing through the pile of invitations. Then she picked up her phone.

'Meena? Are you feeling better? Good. Because there's a party tonight that sounds like fun.'

42

Luke knew how the conversation was going to go. But that didn't make it any more bearable.

'I'm sorry,' Roxanne said. 'I wish it could be different. But the board of governors and I met this morning and we all agree it's too many things. First the swearing on air before the watershed, then your wife's article, then the Bishop of Bellchester stuff. Add that to your ex-wife's column and it's all just too much for the channel. You'll receive a very generous settlement, Luke, and we'll tell the world it was mutual.'

'They'll know it wasn't.'

'That won't be our fault.' She stood up, holding out a slender hand. 'You've been a wonderful anchorman, Luke. I hope we can all retain fond memories of the times we spent together.'

He could barely remember how he left the building, only that he was escorted by security and ushered to a waiting car.

'Where to, sir?' asked the driver.

Luke couldn't think. After their frank exchange, he simply couldn't face going home to Poppy and the paparazzi. He thought of Hannah. Whenever he'd had hiccups in the past, she'd always been there for him with a slice of home-baked cake, a drink and usually a fine blow job. What had he been thinking of to throw all that away?

He took his phone out of his pocket and before he could stop himself dialled her number.

'Hello. This is Hannah. I'm away, horse riding in India this week. Back on Monday. Leave me a message . . .'

Luke hung up. Who could he possibly turn to? He needed a friend. Then he remembered. God, only last night he'd been promising her some kind of future; he'd been so bloody nervous. Well, she'd still be there for him this morning. He scrolled down his list of contacts, until he reached the Ts.

In Stockwell, Thea, in pyjamas, was sitting at her kitchen table, spooning jam on to a croissant. She and Jake had spent all morning in bed. They'd had sex three times. It had been good. It had been very good. Lovely, in fact, which was the kind of word Thea usually used to describe a Laura Ashley tissue box given to her by Aunt Morna at Christmas. Jake had told her again and again how gorgeous she was, how much he had the hots for her and, strangely, she believed him. Even now when it felt as if a troupe of tap-dancing mice had decided to perform *Chicago* inside her head, she still felt bizarrely cheery.

'How did this happen?' she demanded. 'You know I don't fancy you.'

Jake grinned and picked up the kettle which had just boiled. 'Your behaviour last night made that quite obvious, Ms Mackharven.'

'Hmm.' She frowned. 'I was drunk.'

'So was I. That's what I'm going to tell the police anyway. You took advantage of me.'

'Oh, shut up.' She giggled. 'Can I have a cup of tea, please?'

'How do you like it?'

'How do you think? Milk, no sugar. Obviously.' She yawned. 'Shit, I suppose I'd better pop down to the shops in a minute and get the papers. What happened last night has to be a huge story.' But for once in her life Thea didn't feel like rushing off somewhere. Still, she hadn't had a total lobotomy, so she bent over and plucked her phone from her bag. She'd turned it off last night when the kissing had intensified. Instantly, it began ringing.

'Messages, messages,' she said, hitting the red button. 'I'll listen to them later. Shit, I've got about fifty texts as well.' Before she could start scrolling through them, the phone started ringing again. She looked at the screen and her expression changed.

'Oh. It's Luke. I'd better take it.'

Jake looked at her.

'I'd better,' she repeated more defensively, clicking the green button. 'Hi. What's happened?'

'Don't you know?'

Thea had a pretty good idea. 'No.'

'They've given me the boot. After ten years.'

'Oh Luke, I'm so sorry.' Jake drew a knife across his throat. Thea shook her head and turned her back on him. She didn't like the idea of anyone mocking Luke.

'Can I come over?'

Thea froze. 'I . . . Well, I'm a bit . . .'

'It's fine,' Luke snapped. 'Don't worry. Forget I asked.'

Thea looked at Jake, with his little tuft of hair and pointy face, then she thought of Luke and his film-star features. Luke, her friend, her sometimes lover. She'd always been there for him and now he really needed her.

She couldn't turn him away. All right, so maybe he'd used her a bit in the past, but this time it would be different.

'No, wait! That's fine. I'm not busy. Do you want my address?'

'I can remember where you live,' Luke said. 'I'll be with you very shortly.'

She hung up and smiled apologetically at Jake.

'Sorry, but Luke really needs to see me.'

'Are you saying you want me to go?'

'Well,' Thea shrugged, 'I mean, I don't know if you want to be around while we have the post mortem.'

Jake inhaled. 'OK,' he said. 'Though I don't think that's the kindest way to treat someone you've spent the night with.'

Thea felt wounded. 'Jake! I had a great night. We had a laugh.' She knew that was inadequate, that it had been a bit more than a laugh. But. But . . . 'But Luke's been sacked. He's my *friend*. He needs me.'

'Just your friend? Are you sure?'

The way he looked at her made her flustered. 'Luke and I go way back,' she said defensively. 'He's done a lot for me over the years. The least I can do now is something for him.'

Jake was pulling on his denim jacket emblazoned with a vintage CND badge. He was such a student, Thea thought, doing her best to distance herself from him.

'OK,' he said. 'I hear you.'

'Jake, don't be like that.' Thea put her hand on his arm. 'I had a great night, I really did. I . . .' She cringed at her pleading tone. This wasn't her style but still . . . 'Please. Can we stay friends?'

'Maybe,' Jake shrugged. 'If you can spare the time from tending to Luke.'

A car was drawing up outside. God, Luke must have already been on his way when he called. He knew she'd be there for him. A tiny bit of her felt irritated at his presumptuousness, but she decided not to dwell on that.

'OK,' she said briskly. 'Well. See you around, I guess.'

She opened the front door. Jake looked at her for a moment, then shook his head with something like disgust.

'See you around,' he said.

As soon as the door was shut, Thea hurried to the window. Luke was climbing out of a Volvo. Bugger! Jake came out of the front door and the two men clocked each other. They shook hands. Luke was shaking his head. Jake was obviously commiserating. They might have been exchanging cordial words, but their body language was as hostile as a stand off between a sheriff and some cattle rustlers. Thea watched them. Luke so tall and handsome, Jake so small and ... not ugly, but definitely nothing special. But before she had time to consider the choice she'd made, the men were saying goodbye to each other. Jake was heading up the road and Luke was approaching her front door.

Buzzzzzz.

Fuck! Thea dashed into the bedroom. No time for her Frizz-Ease. She pulled a brush through her hair, applied a slash of lipgloss, pulled off her pyjamas and dragged her jeans out of the laundry basket.

Buzzzzz.

'Hi,' she panted.

'Hi.' A pause and then, 'Can I come up?'

'Of course.'

As she pulled a sweatshirt over her head, she heard Luke hurrying up the stairs. She ran to the door and opened it. She wasn't to know it, but Luke's words when he entered the room were almost identical to the ones he'd used to Poppy three years before.

'I've left Poppy. I'm coming to live with you.'

43

Tonight's party was in a private room in Claridge's.

'What's it for?' asked Abdul, the cab driver.

'I can't remember,' Poppy said.

'But there'll be free drinks?' Meena asked anxiously.

'Of course there will.'

'You sure it's right you going out tonight?' Meena asked with unusual sensitivity. 'I mean, doesn't Luke need you at home what with all this malarkey?'

'No, he's fine,' Poppy said staring out of the window. She couldn't admit the conversation she'd just had to Meena, who would almost certainly say she never liked him and Poppy didn't need to be reminded so brutally that her marriage had been a mistake before it even started. Instead, she focused on Toby. There'd not been a word from him all day and her optimism was fast fading. But perhaps he knew she'd be there tonight.

Entering the room, she looked round for him. Never mind. It was still early. Automatically, she reached out for a glass of champagne. Meena had rushed over to talk to Claudia Winkleman whom she'd bonded with at the last party after admiring her boots in the ladies. For a second, Poppy felt isolated, then to her relief, she saw Charlie heading towards her. She waved enthusiastically.

'Hey!' He kissed her on both cheeks. 'I'm surprised

you're out tonight what with all this kerfuffle around your husband.'

'The show must go on,' she said just as she spotted Toby in the middle of a lively group. Suddenly it felt as though too much blood was pumping round her body. 'Um, sorry, Charlie, I . . . need the loo.'

Charlie sighed, following her eyes. 'Still running after that boy?'

'No!' Poppy flushed.

Charlie put his arm gently round her shoulder. 'Listen, sweetpea, I know you think I'm a boring old fart, but please just listen to some advice from your uncle Charlie. Don't pursue Toby. He's bad news.'

'I'm not pursuing him,' she protested, though her nose was growing red. 'I'm married.'

'Not very happily, perhaps?'

The way Charlie looked at her made her want to burst into tears, to tell him what a disaster her marriage was. But Poppy wasn't going to do that. She was tough now.

She tilted her chin. 'I'm perfectly happy.'

'Then why aren't you at home with Luke?' He said it very gently, not at all critically.

'He'd gone out,' Poppy snapped. Then a thought occurred to her. 'This isn't going to go in your paper, is it?'

Charlie sighed. 'If I were a better journalist, then yes, it would. But I've been doing this job for too long and I'm growing soft.'

Someone tapped her on the shoulder. She turned round to see a fat, blond man in glasses, with a sweaty forehead.

'Poppy. Hi. Giles Ford, *Observer*. Just wondering what your feelings were on this "stupid cunt" debacle.'

'No comment.' Poppy smiled.

'You know your husband's lost his job?'

For a second, she froze. He hadn't even been in touch to tell her. But then she smiled again.

'No comment. Excuse me.'

Draining her glass, she moved rapidly across the room towards Toby, who was talking to a woman who bore a striking resemblance to a giraffe.

'Hello,' she said boldly.

'Hi,' he said, smiling. 'How great to see you.'

'Thanks for last night,' she said loudly, to be sure the giraffe would hear. 'It was amazing.'

'Er.' A look of alarm passed over Toby's face. He put his hand on Poppy's arm. 'Sweetheart, I'll be right with you, yeah?'

Suddenly, Charlie was at her side again. 'Poppy, my dear, just come with me a second.'

'Why?'

'I want to show you something.' He smiled at Toby. 'You don't mind, do you?'

'Not at all,' Toby said. There was no mistaking the eagerness in his voice. Charlie put his hand into the small of Poppy's back and gently steered her through the crowd into an empty side room. She looked round.

'What are you doing?'

'I wanted us to talk in private.' He cleared his throat. 'Listen, honey. I don't know what's going on in your home life. But I do know it's not the greatest move being here tonight. You and your husband are all over the papers for the wrong reason and you being out alone is giving out a pretty strong message.'

'I don't care,' Poppy said unsteadily.

'I think you might care tomorrow. You're drunk, Poppy. In fact you always are when I see you. It worries me. Remember I've been there.'

Poppy was outraged. Charlie had been a sleazy alcoholic. Her situation was quite different.

'I know what I'm doing. I'm just having fun.'

'I know that's what you think. But believe me, it's all going to end in tears.'

His tone was so kind, so understanding, that before she could stop herself, Poppy had thrown her arms round him and was trying to kiss him. Charlie jumped backwards as if she was about to garrott him with a length of barbed wire.

'No!' he yelled.

'What?'

Charlie held out his arms as if pacifying a raging bull. 'Sorry, darling,' he said in appeasing tones. 'Not that you're not beautiful and everything. But this *really* isn't a good idea.'

'Don't you . . . don't you like me?'

'I think you're great,' Charlie said. 'But, look. I'm old enough to be your father.'

'So's my husband,' Poppy said dolefully.

'I think that might be part of the problem.'

Poppy was mortified. She didn't even find Charlie attractive; she didn't know what had come over her. 'I'm sorry.'

Charlie smiled and patted her on the arm. 'Don't worry,

you're drunk. But I really do think it's time to go now. I can help you get a cab if you want.'

'Don't worry,' she mumbled. 'I'll be fine.'

'Have you got some family you could go to? Perhaps a week at your parents?'

Poppy laughed. 'I don't have parents. Just a mum. And I don't think I'll get much help there. She'll be pleased my life's such a disaster.'

'Oh, I don't think so.'

'No, she will. She's had a horrible time of it herself and she can't help but be sort of pleased when bad things happen to other people.'

'What happened to her?'

'Oh, she got pregnant by some bloke she met in St Tropez when she was very young and then he just disappeared and she had to bring me up all by herself and . . . she didn't make the best job of it. So she sort of hates all men.'

'St Tropez?'

'Yes.' There was a strange look on Charlie's face, but Poppy didn't really care. 'Look, thanks for being so nice. You're right, I'll go home.'

She stumbled out of the room, Charlie following.

'Hey, Poppy,' a man said. 'What do you think of all this "stupid cunt" stuff then?'

'It's my husband who's the stupid cunt,' she snapped as the room tilted on its axis and everything went black.

Thea woke first. It took a moment to register what was going on, but then it hit her like a knock-out punch.

Luke. Luke was lying in bed beside her. Again. Luke,

the man she'd loved for so long who, for the first time ever, had come to her without being invited. Who'd undressed her and tried to have sex with her, sex which Thea – still sore from her night with Jake – had managed to avoid by giving him a fine blow job. After which, he fell asleep.

Thea looked at him, surprised at how emotionless she felt. But then she'd been here so often, she knew what to expect. Whatever passionate words he might have uttered In the heat of the moment, as sure as night followed day and guilt followed the purchase of a bumper pack of Skittles, Luke would wake up, squawk, pull on his clothes and run out of the door, home to the Bimbo.

As usual, Thea would have to act with total nonchalance, breezily waving him off as if there was nothing humiliating about these recurring one-night stands. The only difference between this time and the others was that it would probably be the last, given he'd lost his job and they wouldn't be coming across each other at work any more. Though they still might bump into each other down at the Job Centre or working behind the tills at Maccy-Ds.

He was stirring. Hastily, she jumped out of bed and pulled her dressing gown round her. She didn't want to be rejected naked. She wished there was time to dash into the bathroom and put some more make-up on but he was opening his eyes.

'Hello.'

'Hi,' she said, as if he were cold-calling about double glazing.

'How are you doing?'

'Fine.'

There was an awkward pause. 'Are you OK?' he asked.

'I'm fine. Just about to make some tea. Would you like some?'

'Love some. Milk, two sugars. And maybe I could use the bathroom?'

'Of course.' There was another pause.

'Um, you don't have a towel, do you?'

'Absolutely!' Thea opened a drawer and pulled one out. She handed it to him and he wrapped it round himself while still under the duvet, like a participant in some silly party game.

'I'll go and make the tea,' she said hastily.

While he was in the bathroom, she dressed rapidly and – unable to get at her collection in the bathroom cabinet – put make-up on from the bag in her handbag. She was still applying mascara when he emerged.

'Would you like something to eat?'

'Maybe in a minute. I thought I'd have a bath. Wash away some of the cobwebs.' He walked over to Thea who was standing by the window. 'That was very nice just now. Very nice,' he whispered in her ear.

'It was,' she whispered back. All right, so it wasn't strictly the truth but Luke was saying it to her, which was more than he'd ever bothered before.

While he was in the bath, she looked in the fridge. As usual, nothing but a carton of eggs a month past their sell-by date and some bacon. Thank God, she hadn't offered them to Jake, Thea thought, cracking four into a bowl and sniffing. They didn't make her gag, so they should be OK. It was early evening now, not an ideal time to be whipping up breakfast, but that was the kind of thing that would bother her mother. By the time Luke emerged, looking like an advert for a deluxe hotel chain with his hair all wet and a white towel wrapped round him, his snack was on the table.

'Oh,' he said.

'Is everything all right?'

'Yeah, it's just . . .' His lip curled so he looked like a sulky toddler. 'I don't really like scrambled eggs. I like them boiled.'

'Oh, sorry.'

'That's OK. You can have mine,' he said generously. 'Do you have any ketchup?'

'Afraid not.'

'Oh, shit. A bacon sandwich is no good without ketchup.'

Thea felt a faint prickle of annoyance. 'I could go downstairs to the shop and get some,' she tried.

'No, no, don't bother!' He smiled up at her. 'This is just what the doctor ordered. Poppy couldn't cook something like this to save her life.'

Poppy. Whose name hadn't been mentioned since he'd announced he'd left her. 'Um, have you seen her?'

'I have.' A big sigh. 'It's over, Thea. Like I told you. It was all a stupid, terrible mistake.'

'Right,' she said, waiting for joy to engulf her. This was exactly what she'd always wanted. But nothing happened except a prickle of worry about how she'd treated Jake. Could they remain friends after this? She didn't see how.

'I'd better call the office,' she said. 'See what's going on.'

Luke looked at her. 'You mean you're going to carry on working for those bastards?'

She looked back at him aghast. 'Well, yes. I mean, who else am I going to work for?'

'I thought you were going to resign. Out of solidarity with me.'

'I can't resign. What would I do?'

'I don't know. What am *I* going to do? I suppose I'd better set up some meetings. Talk to my agent. I should be able to find some work presenting. I can get the book finished. I could work in your spare room if you shifted some of the boxes in there. What are they anyway? Haven't you unpacked from New York yet?'

'Um. Not completely, no.' Thea's mind was elsewhere. She couldn't believe what she was hearing. 'What about Maida Vale?' she asked.

He shrugged. 'I'll let Poppy live there for now, I suppose. We'll have to sit down and talk about what we want to do.'

'You can't end it with Poppy just like that. You have to give it a try, surely?'

He shook his head. 'Our marriage was a joke from day one. If it wasn't for Clara . . .' His voice petered away. 'Well, I'll have to arrange to see her.' He held out his mug. 'Could I have another cup of tea? Less milk in it this time, please.'

What a Stupid C***

HANNAH CREIGHTON, ex-wife of the *Seven Thirty News* chief anchorman, Luke Norton, thought her heart would break when he left her three years ago for ex-model Poppy Price. But now in the light of his disastrous interview with Minnie Maltravers, in an article that will be a tonic to all jilted wives, she reflects how you must be careful what you wish for.

I wish I could say I'd been watching when my ex-husband made a prize fool of himself on national television last week. But instead I was tucked up under the 1000-thread-count linen sheets of a new boutique hotel in Udaipur, India, with my wonderful new boyfriend. We were woken by my phone bleeping. A text had arrived, followed by another, another and another.

Like any mother, my first thought was: could anything have happened to my three children, who, I assumed, were all safe in their marvellous boarding schools. To my eternal relief, the news was not about them but about how Luke, the man I shared my life with for 15 years, had committed career suicide.

What was going on in Luke's head when he insulted Minnie Maltravers? That's what everyone has been wanting to know and of course I can't tell them. But having lived with the man for so long, I *can* tell you that a ferocious temper and a fondness for expletives have always been a feature of life with Luke Norton.

I also know, from experience, that Luke is a control freak, one who likes to have everything his way. Having already been messed about once by Minnie Maltravers (a fact we know thanks to the deliciously indiscreet second Mrs Norton) he would not have been able to cope with a second botched encounter, not least because after a long and illustrious career, everyone knew that Luke's days in the anchorman's chair were already numbered with his gorgeous young rival, Marco Jensen, taking up more and more air time. Luke must have been nervous, knowing this was his last chance to prove himself, not to mention furious that his biggest story in years concerned a model – someone the great foreign correspondent would definitely have considered beneath his contempt.

So, all in all, I have a pretty strong suspicion why Luke might have committed career hari-kari in such a spectacular fashion.

Naturally, as his ex-wife, I was in two minds about his behaviour. Having sacrificed my career in order to bring up his children, Luke's alimony is extremely important to me. There are school fees to pay, the family home to maintain and to see all that threatened because of a crude word would be more than I could bear. However, a quick call to my lawyer reassured me that Luke's pay-off, along with his pension from the *SevenThirty News* would leave my family safely cushioned.

That vulgar little worry laid to rest, I was then free to reflect on something else: how happy I am not to be married to Luke any more. Having always loathed the young Mrs Norton, who, until recently, I would only refer to as the Bimbo, for the first time I genuinely felt for her.

The thought of moody Luke returning from the office that night made me both quake in my boots and laugh with almost hysterical relief. I realized in other circumstances I would have been the sponge soaking up his rage. Instead I could roll over into the arms of my lover and go back to sleep for eight more blissful hours before another bout of inventive sex. It made me almost delirious with relief.

Of course there are things I loved and still love about Luke, but as our marriage fades into history, I also realize how unhappy he made me, how difficult it was to live with such an egotist and what a joy it is to be free of his tantrums and hissy fits. For the first time in my life, I can honestly wish Poppy well in coping with the dark days and nights that will follow. I even hope she's more up to the task than I would have been.

44

It was faintly surreal. Luke didn't seem to be in any hurry to go anywhere. Too shy suddenly to ask what his intentions were, Thea asked if he'd like to watch the *Seven Thirty News*.

'And see that little pillock Jensen sitting in my seat? No thanks.'

Later they shared a takeaway from Thea's favourite Indian down the road.

'Do you like it?' Thea asked, apprehensively. She'd always dreamt of doing this with Luke.

'It's OK, a bit heavy handed on the spices. You haven't been to India, have you? Until you have I'm not sure you can understand what a real curry is all about.'

'Oh. Right. Well I think it's pretty tasty.' She pressed a button on her iPod so the strains of Bob Dylan singing 'Lay Lady Lay' floated across her dinner table. Had a more romantic song ever been written?

'Oh Christ, do we have to listen to this? I can't stand Dylan, he's so nasal and whiny. Can't we just eat in silence?'

'OK,' Thea said. How could she never have known this about Luke before? But she'd never exposed him to her music, always letting him do the choosing.

After dinner, she wasn't quite sure what to do. Normally when a friend came over you caught up and gossiped, but Luke wasn't exactly a friend. Thea realised she didn't know what he was. Her lover? An occasional shag? Her boyfriend? None of them was quite right.

'Would you like to watch a DVD?' she asked.

He studied her extensive film library. 'Mmm. Nothing here I really feel like. Have you got any good westerns?'

'No. They're boys' films.'

'I always thought you *were* an honorary boy,' Luke said, almost absently. He yawned. 'Whatever. Not sure I'm up to a film, anyway. Let's go to bed.'

They took prim turns to use the bathroom.

'Do you mind if I use your toothbrush?' Luke asked, sticking his head out from behind the door.

'Not at all,' Thea said politely. She went in after him, to find a rather nasty stink in the air. Breathing through her mouth, she touched up her make-up. It'd have to be full slap in bed tonight. Luke staying the whole night. It was what she'd always wanted. Tomorrow was Sunday, they could wake up, have sex, lie in bed all morning with the papers and a cafetière, before going for a walk by the river. Her fantasy was coming true.

She wondered what to do about undressing. Normally she slept in pyjamas, but that seemed a bit coy; going into the bedroom and stripping naked seemed a bit full on. She wondered what Luke had done. She came out and found him, lying under the covers, hands behind his head, staring into the air.

'I'd better buy a few things tomorrow if I'm going to stay here for a while.'

She should have booked the victory parade, arranged a flypast from the RAF. But instead, again she had that odd sensation of let down.

'So you *want* to stay?'

'If you don't mind.'

'Of course not,' she said, hastily pulling her top over her head and whipping off her jeans. In her bra and knickers she climbed into bed. Luke and she lay very still, side by side, like effigies on a tomb. Then his hand landed on her thigh.

Oh my God, she thought, as he eased her knickers off and climbed on top of her. I've turned into a woman who has sex with her bra on. She wanted to call Rachel and share this thought, but instead she dutifully moaned and groaned, until finally he juddered on top of her and was still.

They woke early.

'God, your mattress is uncomfortable,' he said. 'It's far too soft. And what was that noise in the night?'

'The drunks who use the pub across the road always have a fight on a Saturday night. It's traditional.'

'I don't know how you can stand living here. I mean, it's above a shop.'

'You wouldn't say that if you were struck by an urge for a scratchcard and a pack of UHT milk.' But Luke didn't smile.

Thea suggested they went out for brunch to a café she loved in Brixton, but he demurred. 'We don't want everyone staring at us.'

Thea went down to the shop for the papers and they sat in the living room reading them together over toast and coffee. There were profiles of him in all of them, many overflowing with inaccuracies and unkindnesses from journalists who'd long been jealous of Luke's personal and professional successes and everyone had picked up on Poppy's off-the-cuff remark to the *Sunday Mirror* about how it was her husband who was the 'stupid cunt'.

'She's deliberately trying to destroy me. I'll never work again,' Luke groaned. He'd been very unamused to discover that his agent was on holiday in the Maldives and unwilling to discuss a game plan until his return a week on Monday.

'Of course you will, Luke,' Thea said loyally. 'You're a star in your field.'

'I do have something of a reputation, don't I?'

'Of course. People will be knocking the door down wanting to hire you. Not that they know you're here,' she added jovially.

'They've got my mobile number,' Luke said tersely, then his face changed. 'Fucking hell, I don't *believe* it!'

A disloyal image of Victor Meldrew flashed into Thea's brain. 'What is it?' she asked sweetly.

'Hannah's in the sodding *Sunday Prophet*. God, even from India she manages to have a go at me.'

'Your poor children,' said Thea softly. Luke turned and looked at her.

'Sorry?'

'Nothing. Let me see the story.'

Luke threw the paper across the room. 'No, I can't bear to look at this any more.'

'Could be a lot worse,' Thea said brightly.

'I don't see how.'

Thea decided the best plan was to ignore him. 'So what shall we do today? We could go for a walk.'

Luke merely grimaced.

'I told you we can't go out. We'd be recognized. Anyway, my leg hurts. That shrapnel wound I got in Afghanistan is giving me gyp.'

'Oh. Right. How about the cinema?' This was another fantasy as well-nurtured as a rich dowager's pet Siamese: the two of them sitting in the back row of the Clapham Picture House, feeding each other spoonfuls of Ben & Jerry's, while subtitles flickered on the screen. 'There's this great new film set in pre-war Hungary.'

'Oh God, no. I'm not in the mood for a film.' He picked up the TV listings. 'The cricket's on at two. I'll watch that.'

So Thea spent the first day of her new life with her great love, sitting in her living room, the curtains half drawn, while Luke shouted, 'C'mon you bastards!' at the screen.

She was restless, constantly glancing at the corner of window revealing a perfect blue sky. Outside, she knew people were lying on patches of grass, drinking bottles of iced tea, laughing, making the most of the precarious English summer. She wanted to join them. But there would be plenty of time for all that, she appeased herself. It was an exceptional time for Luke, after all. Surreptitiously, she picked up the papers and began going through them, ticking potential stories that might tickle Dean's fancy. Because, whatever Luke said, she was going to work tomorrow. After all, no one had called to say she couldn't.

'Oh, howzat! Nice one, Kev.'

Thea's phone rang. Relieved at any distraction, she grabbed it not even looking to see who was calling.

'Hello?'

'Hi. It's Jake.'

'Oh. Hi.' She looked nervously at Luke but his attention was fully fixed on the TV. Thea moved into the bedroom. 'How are you doing?'

'Fine. Just wondering what you were up to tonight.'

Unexpected relief rushed over her. 'I thought you weren't speaking to me.'

Jake sounded gruff. 'Yeah, sorry. I overreacted. I'd like to see you, Thea, if you're free.'

Shit. She didn't know what to reply. She was fond of Jake. She wanted to let him down gently.

'I can't, I'm afraid,' she said. 'Sorry. My . . . mum's coming to stay the night. We're going to have a quiet dinner.'

'Oh.' A pause. 'Well, never mind. When are you about then?'

'Um. I haven't got my diary, but I'll get back to you.' Thea winced. She sounded like an officious secretary, but how else was she supposed to manage this situation?

'Thea?' She jumped at the sound of Luke's voice.

'Yes?' she said, putting her hand over the phone.

'Haven't you got any beers in the fridge?'

'Um, no. Sorry.'

'Bugger. I'm really in the mood for a beer.'

'I could go to the shop in a minute. Get you some.'

'OK,' Luke said and lumbered back into the living room.

'Was that Luke?' Jake asked.

'No!' she yelped like a puppy being torn from its mother. 'No! It was one of my brothers.'

'Oh, your brothers are there too?'

'Yes. Didn't I say? Jake, I'd better go. They're waiting for me.'

'OK,' he said sounding distinctly cold now.

'I'll call you tomorrow when I'm at work and have my diary.'

'Whatever,' he said. As she hung up, feeling as though a granite boulder was in her stomach, Thea heard Luke's phone ring in the other room and him reluctantly answer: 'Hello, Poppy.'

Poppy couldn't remember getting home from the party at Claridge's but Brigita told her Charlie had driven her.

'What a kind man. He help you inside and tell me to look after you. You were bloody shitfaced. I'm sorry, Poppy, it wasn't good.'

'I know, Brigita. I'm sorry too.'

'Don't let it happen again, please. I know going to parties is your job now but in my country women do not behave like this.'

'I know, I'm sorry.'

Brigita tutted. 'That Mr Charlie he is a hero. I give him a cup of tea. He asks if you have any photos of your mother. I say I don't think so.'

'Really?' Did Charlie want to be matched up with Louise? It seemed unlikely. But Poppy had more important things to worry about for the moment.

With Brigita's reprimand ringing in her ears, Poppy stayed in on Saturday night. She planned to have a couple of drinks in front of the telly. Having recently started this habit she couldn't believe she hadn't embraced it years ago. But there was no booze in the house, so frustrated, she'd gone to bed early and woke on Sunday feeling unusually clear-headed. Miraculously, Clara was still asleep, so she lay staring at the chink of light peeking round the edge of the curtain, wondering if Luke was coming home. He'd texted her saying he was staying with friends and thinking about what to do next.

The fact her husband couldn't even bring himself to speak to her angered her so much she resolved not to reply. Luke must despise her, she thought, to make so little effort. She was sick of making all the running. She knew she'd been an idiot to tell Migsy about Minnie, but Luke had done her a greater wrong by marrying her when he didn't love her.

Her thoughts turned to Toby. He was no better. He'd been so cold towards her on Friday night, she had got the message. All the stories Meena had shared with her over the years about one-night stands, stories which had sounded like jolly escapades, took on a new, harsher resonance. Meena had always made it sound like a bit of a lark, but a lot of it must have hurt like hell. Of course Poppy had been treated badly before, but that was years ago when she was a schoolgirl. Because her experience of single life had been so brief she hadn't really understood how brutal it could be, how strangely men could behave.

But even though Toby had hurt her, Poppy couldn't honestly say he'd broken her heart. She'd been strongly attracted to him, but she barely knew him. She'd just been flattered that he'd obviously felt the same way about her. All the same, it wounded her that he seemed to be able to take or leave her just as Meena could let a Mars Bar sit in the fridge for days without touching it.

'Mummeee!'

'Hi, darling,' Poppy rolled over, relieved to see her daughter's pink morning face staring into hers. 'Come into bed with me.'

They were lying together, flicking through old magazines, discussing the colours they liked best, when Poppy's phone rang.

'Heeeey!' Why did Meena always sound so damn perky? 'God, Poppy you're really famous now.'

'What do you mean?'

'It's all over the Sunday papers – my husband's a stupid cunt.' Meena giggled. 'Of course they've asterisked out the C word but you don't exactly have to be Stephen Hawking to guess what it might be. I hope my mum doesn't see it. She's on at me a lot right now asking if you're a suitable friend.' When Poppy didn't reply, Meena continued a little more apprehensively. 'Luke must be pissed off.'

'I don't know what Luke is.' Poppy's voice was hollow. 'I haven't seen him.'

'You haven't seen him? What? You mean he's left?'

'It looks like it.'

'Oh. Do you want me to come over?'

'Yes, please.' There was a pause, then Poppy said, 'Meena, I'm so sad. I've fucked everything up and now I'm going to be a single mum.'

'Hey, hey! Don't worry. What's wrong with being a single mum? You and Clara, you'll be like Kate Moss and little Lila Grace. It'll be cool.'

'What, you mean I'll just go out and party all the time and never see my daughter?' Poppy wanted a drink to steady her nerves, but it wasn't even lunch time yet.

'Of course you'll see your daughter. You'll just sue the arse off any photographer who prints her picture and that way you'll get rich. Anyway, don't fret, Pops. I'll be over as soon as I've had a shower and got dressed. Take me – what? – three hours?'

Poppy looked out of the window. Yesterday the photographers had vanished, but overnight they had re-appeared and were standing around examining lenses, drinking coffee and bitching about how up themselves *EastEnders*' actors were. Horrified, Poppy stepped back behind the curtains. There was no way she was going to face them. Instead, she went into Luke's office and turned on the computer and went online. Once acquainted with the latest coverage, she covered her face with her hands.

'What have I done?'

'My favourite colour is pink, red, purple, orange, blue,' Clara said at her feet.

Although, childishly, she'd been trying not to call Luke, her resistance crumbled. Somewhat to her surprise, he answered.

'Where are you?' she asked. In the background she could hear the noise of a television. No other clues.

'Just staying with a friend from work.'

'Anyone I know?' Poppy asked blandly.

'No, nobody,' Luke snapped, then more contritely, 'How's Clara?'

'She's fine. Clara come and talk to Daddy.'

'No, Daddy, go 'way!' said Clara, who was disembowelling a toy raccoon.

'Sorry.' Poppy paused. 'So when are you coming back?' Into the silence, she asked, 'Hello? Are you still there?'

'I'm still here,' he said eventually.

'Luke, I know we've really messed things up but we do need to at least talk. For Clara's sake.'

'I know.'

'So when are we going to do that?'

'I'm not sure. Give me a few days to think about things.'

'All right,' said Poppy. She was about to hang up, when Luke added, 'You wouldn't wa.t me anyway. Now I'm unemployed. I'm not the rich, successful man you married any more.'

'I didn't marry you for your job. I married you because I loved you.' Poppy hung up feeling as if she'd been stung. She thought she was becoming immune to pain but obviously not.

'Mummy, why you crying? Don't cry.'

45

Several days passed. Miraculously, Thea was told that she wouldn't be blamed for the Minnie débâcle.

'If Luke can't keep his potty mouth shut that's his fault, not mine,' said Dean. 'And, anyway, it brought in amazing viewing figures. So just fuck off and try to find some more tantrummy divas to throw water over Marco or tell Emma she shouldn't wear such low-cut tops.'

Luke showed no sign of moving out of Thea's flat. While she was at work, he went out and bought a toothbrush and shaving gear, some socks and underwear, a pair of trousers, a couple of shirts. He hung them in the wardrobe squashing Thea's clothes and at the end of the day, he chucked them in the laundry basket. On Thursday morning, he got cross.

'I don't have any clean pants,' he complained, as Thea pulled on her jacket and picked up her keys.

'Sorry?'

'I've run out of clean boxer shorts. Didn't you wash any?'

Thea was aghast. 'Er, no. Didn't you?'

For a second Luke looked vaguely embarrassed. But only for a second.

'I don't know how to work your washing machine.'

Thea took a deep breath. She'd been doing a lot of this lately. 'Luke, you've been to Kashmir and Somalia and

Afghanistan and East Timor. You can work out how to use a washing machine.'

'What temperature would you wash underwear at?'

'Sixty degrees to be on the safe side. Now I have to go. I'll be late for work.'

'Just show me,' he said, trying to negotiate, as if she was the head of some Taliban faction needing to be talked in to giving an interview.

'I'm going to be late. I'm on thin ice at work already.' Wrong thing to say.

'At least some of us have work to go to. Show me. Please.'

So Thea explained to Luke how to fill the ball, put it in the drum and turn the dial to the required temperature. 'Then when it's all finished you get it out and hang it up in the bathroom.' Before he could ask for guidelines on that, she continued, 'I'm meeting my friend Rachel for a drink after work so I'll be back quite late.'

'What will I do for dinner?' Luke sounded as if she'd told him he had to do a duty tour of 'Nam.

'I don't know. Get something from the shops? I've got to go now.'

It was a relief to swap the increasingly claustrophobic flat for the sweaty, unreliable Tube and even more of a relief to arrive at the office. The passing of Luke, like the passing of everyone in the media, had been swift and silent. Already, you could barely remember the days when Luke had reigned supreme. And Marco, although Thea would only have admitted it after having all her fingernails ripped out, was doing a much better job as chief anchor than she might have predicted.

'It's annoying, isn't it?' Lana said, as they sat watching the show from their desks in the newsroom.

'He's not nearly as slimy as he used to be,' Thea agreed grudgingly. 'It's as if he's suddenly grown up.'

'Luke always seemed a bit bored, as if the job was slightly beneath him. You can tell Marco's absolutely loving it. By the way how *is* Luke?'

Thea froze. The idea of the office finding out he was living with her horrified her, like a teenager might be terrorized by getting a pimple on the morning of the prom.

'I've no idea,' she said after a tiny beat.

'Oh? I thought you might have heard from him.' Lana's face was a picture of innocence. 'You were such good friends. Oh well, he's probably too busy shagging his new piece of totty, whoever she may be.'

'Mmm. God, look at the time. I must call a contact.'

Lana lowered her voice. 'The rumour is he's moved in with some other young woman. You've got to hand it to the old greaseball, he never gives up.'

Just then, to her relief, her phone rang. 'Sorry,' she mouthed insincerely. 'Hey, Rach, do not even *think* about telling me you've gone into labour and won't make it to the pub.'

'What? Oof. Just felt a twinge. Yikes! What was that?'

'Rachel! Are you OK?'

'Ha, had you! Don't worry, the baby's under strict instructions to stay in. I've got more important issues to attend to than the birth of my own child.'

'Get its priorities straight from the start,' Thea agreed. 'Mummy's friends will always take precedence.'

'Absolutely. Anyway, I was calling to say all's in order and I'll see you at half eight.'

'In the vegan Indian?'

'No, bugger that, in the Prince Alfred. As of a month's time I'm never going to go out again, so I might as well enjoy my last days in the boozer while I still can.'

On her way to the pub, Thea felt liberated like the man in the final scene of *Midnight Express*. This was her first evening off, as she couldn't help thinking of it, since Luke moved in. She had had to put up with six whole evenings of cricket and bad Westerns with Luke hogging the remote control. Evenings that she would usually have spent wallowing in a Jo Malone bath with a face pack on and Bob playing on her podcast were now ruined by Luke rattling the door handle saying, 'Are you going to be long? I need a pee.' Evenings when she had to rinse Luke's shaving hairs from the basin before she brushed her teeth and where sex had been transformed overnight from a source of unspeakable bliss into another chore that had to be performed, whether she was in the mood or not.

Thea hadn't thought it would be like this, but then she hadn't thought anything much, she realized. Her dreams about Luke had never featured any sort of domesticity, because domesticity just didn't float her boat. She'd some-how imagined them moving from hotel room to hotel room, with staff to make the beds and bring them meals under silver domes, with the buzz of the story they'd covered that day to drive their conversation.

Home was somewhere to be alone. She realized how

much she relished her evenings of silence after the chaos of the office, her weekends with a packet of Skittles and a fat detective novel. She remembered that all her adult relationships had come to an end when her boyfriends had wanted to go round Ikea with her and have dinner parties. Why did she think things were going to be any different with Luke?

And then there was Jake. She hadn't heard from him and she didn't blame him. Every day, she thought about calling him. Emailing at least. But every day she restrained herself. She liked Jake, liked him quite a lot. She'd had good sex with him. But she was with Luke now and they had to make things work. After so many years of wanting him, it was too humiliating to admit she might have changed her mind.

'What can I get you?' she asked her friend, who was slumped on a banquette. Then she noticed the wine nestling in an ice bucket and the two glasses.

'Rachel! What's happened?'

'Oh, don't you start. I couldn't stand it any longer. I'm only going to have a glass. Or two. I mean, the bastard's cooked now, so what difference can it make? Anyway, what about you? What about Luke? Is it going any better?'

'Not really.' Thea filled her glass. 'It's so weird, we've been all over the world together in intense situations, under huge pressure, being shot at, but living in a flat in Stockwell seems to be pushing us to the limit.'

'It's not quite as glamorous is it?'

'Excuse me? Are you saying my flat's not glamorous?' They both giggled, thinking of the slightly peeling paintwork. Then Thea sighed. 'You're right, it's not. Luke keeps complaining that it's studenty. I suppose he's used to something more . . . homely. But I hate all that. And he's used to someone cooking him dinner every evening and doing his washing and he simply can't handle the fact that I don't do that sort of thing.'

'Maybe you're going to have to start.' Rachel shrugged. 'I mean, I do all that for Dunc.'

'But I *can't*,' Thea said. 'It's just not me.'

'It wasn't me either, but you learn.'

'But . . .' Watching her friend's philosophical expression, Thea had the sense that she'd spent her whole life playing a game but with the wrong rule book. 'But did suffragettes throw themselves under horses so we could end up doing the washing and cleaning and cooking as well as having jobs?'

'And doing the childcare.' Rachel patted her enormous bump, somewhat apprehensively. 'At least you don't want any part of that.'

'Are you having second thoughts?'

'I was wondering about calling Angelina Jolie and seeing if she fancied adding a newborn Caucasian to her brood. But I doubt my baby will be pretty enough for her and Brad.' Rachel took a gulp of wine. 'Yeah, Thea, of course I'm having doubts. I'm shit scared what the future's going to bring. I used to think: why do women make this big deal about juggling? I'd just hire a nanny and everything would go on as before. But even though I haven't met the bastard yet I already love him so much I'm not sure I can go off to the office all day and leave him behind.' Rachel's face was both dreamy and troubled. 'I wish I could rely more on Dunc.'

'He's still saying he'll never change a nappy?'

'No, well, not quite. But he's insisting we do a sort of contract that he's allowed out three nights a week with the lads.'

'Allowed! You're not a bloody character in a Bernard Manning sketch. Does he think you'll be waiting for him with a rolling pin?'

'No. But . . .' Rachel sighed. 'It's hard, Thea. I can't tell him, but I do wish he'd go out less. It's funny. I wanted a baby so much I didn't really care how Dunc fitted in to it all, but now . . . I *need* him. I'm like some pathetic Mills & Boon heroine. And the bastard will need him too.'

Prickles of guilt tingled on Thea's spine. Why had she never thought about Luke like this before? However dire both his wives, they must have needed him too. Why had she been so arrogant to think she could set her sights at him?

'Are you OK?' Rachel was saying. 'You look a bit weird. Probably bored by me and my silly troubles. What are *you* going to do? You've got what you always wanted and now you're not so sure about it.'

'I probably just have to give it time,' Thea said, but she didn't sound convinced. 'It's a big adjustment, but we'll get there.'

'So Luke has said he's staying for good?'

'Not in so many words, but he's showing no sign of leaving.'

'Well, if he *is* staying then make sure he does it all

properly. Don't let things drift like Dunc and me. You ought to get married.'

'Yeah. I guess.' Thea's reaction was so lukewarm, Rachel put down her glass and stared at her.

'You've fallen out of love with Luke, haven't you?'

'No!'

'You have. It's like me and the bastard. It was all a lovely dream and now it's become reality it's no fun any more. You . . .' But before Rachel could say any more true, disquieting things, Dunc walked through the door.

'All right, my ladies?' He patted Rachel on the head in the way one might a pet cat. To Thea's annoyance she simpered up at him. 'How are you doing? Any more twinges?'

'No, I'm fine. Must go to the loo though. I have to pee about sixteen million times a day,' she explained as she stood up laboriously. Thea wondered how long it would be before she was forced to listen to an in-depth description of the contents of the bastard's nappy.

'Can I get you a drink?' Dunc asked as his partner waddled away.

'No, I'm all right.' She nodded at the bottle. 'You might want to get yourself a glass.'

'I don't really like white,' Dunc said, as a voice behind them cried, 'Thea!'

Thea turned round. A very attractive woman, with red hair in a shaggy, feathery cut was standing there. She wore an expensive-looking shearling gilet and had a wide, painted mouth. Fear coursed through Thea's veins like electricity.

'Hannah! How are you?' She jumped up and kissed

Luke's first wife on both cheeks. She and Hannah had always had a relationship that was about as genuine as an orgasm in a porn film. 'You look great.' Annoyingly, she really did; far, far greater than when she'd been with Luke.

'Thanks.' Hannah Creighton, formerly Norton, smirked. 'Been road testing some new creams for *Elle*. It's fabulous. They're sending me to a spa in the Maldives next month. The joys of single life: not having to worry about feeding Luke, or attending dull as shit functions with him. I can just cover my face in Crème de la Mer and go to bed at seven and then bugger off for a month if it suits me.' She smiled. 'Sorry, getting ahead of myself. So how are you, Thea? I'd heard you were back from the States. Enjoying life at the *SevenThirty*. Must be eventful, huh?'

'I'm really well. How are the children?' Thea didn't want any dwelling on her private life.

'The children?' Hannah looked as blank as if she'd asked her about weather patterns in Paraguay. 'Oh. Them. Well, they love their boarding schools and of course every other weekend Luke takes them so I suddenly have all this me-time. It's wonderful.' Her eyes rested on Dunc. 'Hello, I'm Hannah Creighton.'

'Duncan. I was just getting some drinks. Would you like one?'

Please, no! thought Thea. Fortunately, Hannah shook her head. 'No, thank you, Duncan. I'm meeting someone.' Dunc moved off to the bar. Hannah stared after him, appreciatively.

'Gosh, Thea, look at him. He's gorgeous.'

'Do you think?' Thea stared after Dunc, wondering why she was the only one who couldn't see it.

'Absolutely. Look at those buns! I'm so pleased for you. I used to worry about you not finding someone because you were so wrapped up in your job. Miss Moneypenny.'

'Sorry?'

Hannah grinned with distinct malice. 'That's what Luke always called you. His faithful aide. Always there for him.' As Thea sat, too stunned to even begin to form a retort, Hannah continued, 'Well, we all move on. So Poppy kicked him out. Do you know who he's living with now?'

'No,' said Thea, sounding like a choirboy who'd sat on a drawing pin.

'Nor do I. He's keeping very schtum. But the girls will tell me.' Hannah's laugh sounded uncannily like Vincent Price in Thea's ancient copy of Michael Jackson's *Thriller*. 'Poor thing, whoever she is. She'll be in for a rude shock. I've never felt more liberated since I left Luke, I . . . Oh, hello!'

A man laid his hand on Hannah's shoulder. He had wispy grey hair in a bad combover and wore a rust-coloured raincoat that was shiny with age. He was an obvious all-day drinker, who only saw daylight since the smoking ban had forced him to nip outside for a twice hourly cigarette. Thea's stomach squelched the way it always did when approached by a down and out. Was he going to harass Hannah for spare change? But instead, he was holding out his hand.

'Hello, I'm Jay, Hannah's boyfriend.'

'I . . . uh . . . I'm Thea.'

'Come on, Jay,' Hannah snapped. The end of her nose had turned an unfetching pink. Thea realized she was mortified. 'Nice to see you,' she said briskly to Thea. 'We should catch up properly soon. Have lunch.'

'Lovely,' Thea muttered, just as Dunc returned with his wine glass.

'Lovely to meet *you*, Duncan. Look after this lady, she's very special.'

'Er, yeah.'

She moved off, just as Rachel reappeared.

'Was that who I thought it was?'

'It was,' said Thea. She felt as if she'd just been drenched by a bus driving way too fast through a puddle.

'Shit. What did she say to you?'

'She thought I was Thea's boyfriend.' Dunc chortled as if this was as ridiculous a prospect as finding a Burger King open on Mars.

With an enormous effort of will, Thea got a grip on her tilting self. 'More importantly though, have you seen *her* boyfriend?' To her relief, her voice sounded normal. She nodded towards the corner where Hannah and Jay were sitting. He was nursing a pint, she had a glass of wine. They weren't exactly indulging in hilarious repartee, more looking as if they were mulling over a suicide pact.

'Christ, I'd imagined some Enrique Iglesias stud. Are you sure that's her boyfriend, not her granddad?'

'That's what happens to women on the verge of fifty,' said Dunc with infuriating smugness. 'Doesn't matter how much Botox you've had, how much jogging you do. You've still got to scrape the bottom of the barrel just to find someone to go for a drink with.'

'What a ridiculously sexist thing to say,' Thea snapped. But the evidence lay before them. Her head swam as she tried to take in all this new information. She was Luke's Miss Moneypenny – while Hannah's stud was a sad old man in a raincoat. Could it be that all Hannah's other boasts about being so ridiculously happy were just as shaky? Was everyone lying? Thea was beginning to think it might be time to start telling the truth.

46

Thea slept badly that night. The Miss Moneypenny remark taunted her like a playground bully, forcing her eyes open, even as Luke slept silently beside her. Hannah was right. Even if she wasn't a desk-bound secretary, she'd still been his stooge, sitting up straighter every time he entered the office, yearningly watching his departing figure, smiling indulgently when faced with his flings, masking her inner torment. She'd always kidded herself she and Luke were equals, when in fact he'd been laughing at her. She'd thought she'd played it cool, but now she realized he'd always known about her devotion and had been happy to abuse it.

All the doubts that had been building about being with Luke exploded like a giant, pus-filled spot. In the red glow of the digital clock, Thea looked at the man she'd been in love with for so long and shook her head. Disgust at so many wasted years consumed her. Years when she could have learnt another language, studied astrophysics, written poetry, cultivated a garden. Well, OK, maybe not the garden, but she could have become editor of the *Seven Thirty News* rather than sticking in a producer's role so she got to spend more time with Luke. Years which she could have spent forming relationships with sensible, down-to-earth men. Even if they did look like Hobbits. Thea knew there was no point following that line of thought.

She didn't want to waste any more time; she had to end things as soon as possible. She'd do it subtly she decided, as the dawn chorus began. She'd already broken up one family through her thoughtless selfishness, so she'd try to mend another by pushing him back in Poppy's direction, so poor little Clara would have a father again.

They had a silent breakfast over the papers. At the end, Thea asked, 'Are you going to see Clara soon?'

She expected the usual 'I don't know,' but instead Luke replied, without looking up from the *Guardian*. 'I texted Poppy this morning, while you were in the shower. I'm going over there tomorrow afternoon.'

'Good.'

'I'll bring back some of my stuff.'

Thea looked up in alarm. 'How much stuff? There's not a lot of room here.'

'Just a few boxes of books. I need them if I'm going to get on with researching mine. I told you the publishers want it out sooner than later, now I'm controversial.' He waggled his fingers in the form of quote marks. Thea hated people who did that. How had she never noticed before? 'You'll have to meet Clara at some point, I suppose. Though she might be a bit wary of you initally. Maybe Brigita could chaperone her.'

'Brigita?'

'Her nanny. And then maybe meet the other kids. If Hannah's OK with it.'

Thea's head jerked up.

'Hannah?'

'Well, yeah. I might as well tell her sooner rather than later. I guess she might be a bit weird about us, seeing as she knows you and everything. But my sense is she'll prefer you to Poppy because you're not young, blonde and gorgeous.'

'Oh. Right.'

'And you're obviously not a bimbo.' A thought struck Luke. 'God, I wonder what she'll call *you* in the column? Should be interesting.'

'Luke,' said Thea after a cautious pause, 'have you told anyone else about . . . ?' She wanted to say 'us' but it seemed the wrong choice of word. 'About the fact you're living here?'

'Not yet,' he said. 'Like I say, I'll tell the children first, then Hannah. Then we can make it official.'

Poppy was keeping herself busy. She was going out virtually every night. Days were full now too: if she wasn't sleeping off the night before, she was having treatments or meetings with various companies who wanted her to endorse their products. Without officially agreeing to anything, Brigita was working five days a week and big chunks of the weekend and her wages were so high Poppy was barely breaking even, despite the money she was making. She thanked heaven that the joint account still seemed to be working, while trying not to worry about how she'd manage when it was inevitably stopped. She knew if she divorced Luke she would get some kind of settlement, but the idea of pursuing a Heather Mills type vendetta appalled her. So long as he gave Clara something, Poppy didn't want to take a penny.

Finally, Luke rang. They had a terse conversation when he said he'd come over on Saturday to see Clara.

On Saturday Clara was very grouchy, even by her own high standards.

'Daddy's coming to see you,' Poppy told her over breakfast. When there was no reply, she asked, 'Darling, are you going to eat your cereal?'

'No.' Clara pushed her plate away.

'Has it got too much milk in it?' That was usually the crime.

'Uf.'

'Or maybe there's not enough?'

'Oog.'

'Just have a bite. One for Mummy.'

'Nowagh!' Clara began howling. Poppy tried to keep her cool.

'A bite for Brigita.'

'Go 'way, Mummy.' Clara continued to weep bitterly. 'I wanna sleep.'

'Really?' Poppy felt a flicker of alarm. Farting loudly in public places, getting water all over the bathroom floor and refusing all green vegetables were part of Clara's repertoire. Sleep was not. 'Don't you want to watch CBeebies?'

'Nooo!'

So she put Clara back in her cot and had an unexpectedly peaceful morning in a scented bath. Wrapped in a towel, she went to check on her daughter. An hour later she crept in again. Clara was still asleep, her blonde hair sweaty and tousled. Poppy felt her forehead. She was definitely hotter than normal, so she let her carry on sleeping until lunchtime. Then Clara woke up, quickly drank two beakers of water, ate a small piece of bread, screamed the house down when Poppy tried and failed to take her temperature and went back to sleep.

Poppy was wondering if she should call NHS Direct when the doorbell rang. Opening the door, she caught her breath. She'd forgotten how handsome Luke was, she'd also forgotten how old. He looked much more tired than she remembered: greyer, looser somehow, as if the stuffing had been taken out of him.

'Hello.'

'Hi. Where's my fairy monkey?'

'She's asleep. I think she's got some kind of a bug.'

Luke looked as if he'd been slapped in the face. 'Can't I see her?'

'Of course you can. But I don't think she's going to be much company.'

'I've missed her so much.'

Poppy bit her lip. 'She's missed you too. Come in.'

Clara was still fast asleep. Her breathing was laboured, her cheeks were very red.

'Is she OK?'

'Like I say, I think she's got a bit of a bug. She wouldn't let me take her temperature. When she wakes up I'll give her some Calpol.' Poppy looked at her husband. 'What do you want to do?'

'Just sit by her for a while. When she wakes up I'll read to her.'

'I'll go out then. How long do you want?'

'A couple of hours,' Luke shrugged.

'Fine. I'll come back at four. Call me if you think she's getting worse.'

She could have gone shopping, looking for a necklace to set off the yellow and green top she planned to wear that night, but her heart wasn't in it, so instead she walked down to the canal, where she sat on a bench and watched a family of ducks drift by. Tears splashed down her face. Seeing Clara with Luke made her realize how horribly she'd messed up. Another child was going to grow up without a father, with a mother who had to work every second of the day just to survive. Poppy thought she'd broken the cycle by marrying Luke, but it seemed there was no escaping her destiny.

She thought ahead to the evening. She was meant to be going to a party in Regent's Park to celebrate the opening of a new art gallery. For once Meena couldn't come with her, ordered back to Wembley to celebrate her brother's birthday. A month ago, there was no way Poppy would have gone on her own, but now the prospect didn't bother her. She was more concerned about whether she should leave Clara if she was ill.

It sounded like a very glamorous event and Poppy liked galleries. If the people were boring, she'd look at the art. But that was beside the point. She had to go because this was her job now, rather than just a way of earning pin money. She couldn't just duck in and out at will; she had to think about how to support herself and Clara. Still, Clara's health came first. Brigita was coming at six; she'd take her advice on what was the best thing to do.

She returned home on the dot of four to find Luke

holding a very rumpled-looking Clara in his arms, her arms shielding her eyes.

'Is bright, bright, Mummy. Wanna go back to bed.'

Poppy held out her arms. Luke passed her to her. 'Sweetpea, are you OK?'

'Bright!'

'Have you had a drink?'

'She had a beaker of water,' said Luke. 'And I gave her some Calpol at three. You'll call the doctor if she gets worse?'

'Of course!'

He knelt down and kissed Clara. 'Darling, Daddy has to go now, but I'll see you soon.'

A look of devastation crossed Clara's face. 'Don't go, Daddy.'

'I have to.'

She flung herself at him, screaming, wrapping her arms round his legs. Luke tried to prise her off. Poppy swallowed back the tears.

'Darling, Daddy has to go, but he'll be back very soon. I promise.'

'Noooooo!'

'I love you.' Over the bawling, he spoke to Poppy. 'You and I need to talk properly.'

'I know.'

'Maybe one day next week. We could have lunch.' He grinned ruefully. 'I'm free every day.'

'I'm quite busy next week. A lot of meetings and some modelling jobs. I'll look at my diary and let you know what I can do.'

'OK.' Luke knelt down and kissed his sobbing child.

'My angel, I love you. I'll see you very soon. We'll go to the zoo.'

Clara screamed for the next hour. Poppy tried to feed her, but she threw all her supper on the floor. It was a huge relief when Brigita arrived.

'Do you think she's OK? Should I go out tonight?'

Brigita frowned. 'She has temperature and a little rash. I think maybe she is having the poxy.'

'The what?'

'The chicken's poxy. Is very common in children. And not serious.'

'I should stay at home,' Poppy said.

'No, no, Mummy. Dinna you fret. This is not serious condition. You go out. Enjoy. Brigita can cope.'

'Are you sure?' Poppy was torn. She felt she should be at home, but what – realistically – could she do? She thought of the episode on Toby's birthday. Little children were always getting sick and then getting better in the time it took to run a bath.

'I am completely sure,' Brigita said. 'If Clara gets worse I will call you. Now go and get dressed. Don't wear the black dress, it makes yer knees look funny.'

The party was in a marquee in the middle of Regent's Park. Poppy had to run the gamut of photographers to leave the flat and then another gamut when she arrived. Walking under the long awning that led to the main marquee, she saw Toby standing at the cloakroom. For a second she froze. She turned to an expressionless waiter, took a glass of champagne from his tray and downed it in one. Then she stalked up to Toby.

'Hello,' she said coolly.

'Oh! Hi!' He bent down and kissed her on both cheeks. 'How nice to see you.'

'And you,' she said haughtily. She hadn't meant to check in her denim jacket or her bag but she wanted to keep Toby talking, so she handed them over to the young French woman behind the desk. Her emotions were see-sawing. She'd dismissed Toby as dodgy, as a lightweight, but seeing him again she still felt the urge to prove herself to him, to see him grovel for his dilettantish behaviour.

'How have you been?' she said.

'Really well. Look. I . . . I'm sorry, I've been meaning to call you, but it's all been frantic. For you too, I'm guessing.'

'Yes, it's been really busy.'

'Shall we?' he said, flicking his head towards the main marquee where the party was buzzing away.

Poppy followed him in. It was quickly apparent that this was a more upmarket do than normal. The glamour models and boyband members who normally made up the numbers had been replaced by beaky-nosed men and women with accents so cut-glass they could double as trifle bowls. As usual, Toby seemed completely at ease, moving from group to group, shaking hands, laughing. Ill at ease, Poppy followed him like a shadow. She'd dismissed Toby as a stupid fling, but seeing him again she couldn't deny the attraction that crackled between them like a force field, nor the fury she felt at how he'd treated her.

She focused her attention on a young man in a green Nehru jacket with a name Poppy knew would sprain her tongue if she tried to repeat it back to him.

'How do you know Toby?'

'Oh, just from round and about,' she said airily.

'So you must know Inge too?'

A shard of unease pierced Poppy's breastbone. 'Um, no,' she said with a forced smile.

The man looked horrified. 'Oh Christ! Have I put my foot in it? I'm always doing that.'

Poppy gave a hollow laugh. 'Goodness, Toby's not my boyfriend. He's just a . . . mate.'

'Thank God. I thought I'd really gone and goofed. Mind you, it wouldn't have completely surprised me if they'd split up. Their relationship's always been pretty volatile but since he moved into her place in Shoreditch it seemed to be on stronger ground. The thing is she's away so much for work and a lot of temptation comes his way and . . . Are you OK?'

Thea was the happiest she'd been in weeks. Luke had left late that morning to visit Clara and after that he was taking Tilly and Isabelle to the theatre. She'd got her old Saturday back: a swim at the scuzzy local pool, a film at the Ritzy in Brixton with a family pack of Skittles. Now, as the sun started to go down, she turned Bob up loud on the stereo and ran a scalding Jo Malone bath. This was the life.

'All by myself,' she warbled as she climbed into the scalding water, 'and it's blooooody great!'

But it wasn't really funny. She had to give Luke his marching orders. Maybe tonight when he got back. No, he'd still have to sleep there; it would be ludicrous. She'd tell him in the morning, giving him all day to make alternative arrangements. Hopefully seeing his children that day would have pricked his conscience enough to make him realize he had to go home.

She reached for her phone in preparation for a long chat with Rachel, just three days off her due date. But as she called her number, Luke's phone began blaring in the other room, some stupid hip-hop tune he'd allowed one of his children to programme in. Bugger. He'd obviously left it behind. Not Thea's problem. She dialled her friend.

'Hi, I can't come to the phone right now.'

So much for that. Thea left a message asking if she'd gone into labour, then dunked her head under the water. When she came up for air, Luke's phone was still ringing. Voicemail calling back. It would ring twice more, then give up.

But the phone kept ringing. And ringing. And ringing.

'Oh for Christ's sake,' Thea bawled when the hideous tune had repeated itself for ten minutes. 'I'm coming!' Crossly, she hauled herself out of the bath and, wrapped in a towel, padded across the flat. She'd turn the bloody thing off. But then looking at the caller ID she saw 'Brigita'. One of Luke's floozies, she thought drily, but then she remembered: Clara's nanny. She switched the voice to voicemail but within seconds 'Brigita' started calling again. Surely Luke hadn't been so tacky as to have a fling with her too? She would put nothing past him. Crossly, she answered, 'Hello?'

'Luke? Where is Luke?'

'He's not here. He's at the theatre.'

'Oh no.' There was no mistaking the terror in Brigita's voice.

Dread shot down Thea's spine. 'What is it? What's wrong?'

'I am at the hospital with Clara. She's reight poorly. She get a rash, so I take her in and the doctors say they think is meningitis. And I can't find Poppy. Or Luke. Help me. Please. Help.'

47

Desperate to find Luke, Thea called the theatre.

'I'm sorry,' said an adenoidal-sounding woman. 'The interval has just finished and we can't page members of the audience until the play's over.'

'When will that be?'

'Another two hours. It's *Hamlet*, you know. Very long.'

'That's no good!' Thea screamed. 'His daughter is in hospital. She may be dying. You have to page him *now*.'

The woman sighed dramatically. 'For a dying child I'll make an exception.'

As Luke was being tannoyed to gasps from the packed auditorium, Thea called Brigita to try to find Poppy.

'She was going to a party, but she don't answer her phone.' Brigita wept.

'What party was it?' Silly bimbo, what a thing to do when your child is sick.

'I don't know.' Brigita struggled for something that might help. 'She wear a dress, not jeans, so I think it's a posh one.'

'That doesn't narrow it down.' Thea chewed her lip. Years of journalistic experience had made her an expert at tracking things down. 'How did she get there?'

'In a minicab.'

'Do you know the name of the firm?'

'Yeah. Cooper's. She always uses them.'

'I'll call Cooper's,' Thea said.

Poppy had been drinking steadily. The lights in the room flashed in and out of focus as she reeled round the gallery. She was aware of people staring at her as she stalked towards Toby, but she didn't care.

'Toby, who's Inge?'

A quick but definite look of unease passed over his face. 'Who told you about Inge?'

'That guy over there. He says you're living in her flat in Shoreditch.'

A heavy sigh. 'I thought you knew.'

'How would I know? I think you forgot to tell me. Here's my flat, by the way don't use the beauty flash balm in the bathroom because it's my girlfriend's.'

'Um. She's my fiancée actually.' He high-fived a passing Indian man. 'Rav, I'll be with you in a minute. Sorry, Poppy, I thought you realized.'

'She won't be your fiancée when she finds out about us.'

Toby looked incredulous. 'There *is* no us. We just shared some good times.'

'There was more to it than that,' she argued. 'You slept with me.'

He shook his head. 'Oh Christ, I thought you of all people would understand. After all, you're married, I thought you had more to lose than me.'

Poppy felt like one of Clara's towers when she pulled out the bottom brick. She realized she'd still obscurely been hoping that Toby was her white knight who would gallop in just before the credits to save her. As all her dreams crashed down, she knew no one was going to rescue her, that she was on her own. She couldn't be angry with him. She could only be angry with herself.

'Poppy, come back!'

But she had disappeared into the crowd.

The man at Cooper's minicabs was enjoying his power kick.

'What you are asking for is classified information, darling.' He sucked his teeth. 'You could be a stalker or anything, innit?'

'This woman's child is seriously ill in hospital. If I don't find her she may not get there in time.'

A long pause, then, 'I'll radio Abdul.' Another wait, this time so long Thea was about to hang up and try again when he finally came back on. 'He took her to the Sanition Gallery in Regent's Park.'

Thea couldn't find a number for the gallery, most probably because, as a temporary structure, it didn't have one. Cursing, she called Brigita again.

'How's she doing?'

'She's not good. She's on a life-support machine. If she doesn't respond they say they may have to amputate her leg to stop the infection.'

'Oh, fuck,' Thea said. 'I'm getting in my car.'

It took forty minutes to get to Regent's Park, not bad by London standards but an age in the circumstances. Thea cursed at every traffic light, wished unpleasant venereal diseases on giggling couples who ambled lovingly across every zebra crossing. Even when she arrived, she had to drive round four times before she found somewhere to park. Having finally manoeuvred the car into a space intended for a baby buggy, she jumped out and sprinted through the metal gates into the park, past gangs of friends enjoying picnics in the twilight, towards the big, white marquee.

'Sorry,' said a security guard sticking a burly arm in front of her.

'Invitation please.'

'I forgot it.'

Scornfully, he eyed the make-up-less face, the still damp hair, the threadbare jeans and dirty sweatshirt. 'No ticket, no entry, love.'

'No, you don't understand! You have to let me in. My . . . my *friend's* at a party in there, but her daughter's really sick in hospital. I have to let her know.'

'Yeah, yeah, now I've heard it all.'

'Do you think I'd try to gatecrash your stupid party dressed like this?'

He shrugged. 'People do the strangest things to be in the same room as Kate Moss.' He turned his back to her.

'For Christ's sake,' Thea cried, 'a child is dying here.'

He turned back. 'You're sick trying that.'

Suddenly Thea understood how people found the strength to lift cars and rescue bodies trapped beneath. Dipping her head, she charged at the bouncer, ducking beneath his arms.

'Oi! You stupid cow! Come back.' He started running after her, but Thea was inside the marquee. A band was playing and the dance floor was crowded. Thea virtually dived into the middle of it, then started weaving her way in and out of the dancers. 'Excuse me,' she said as Elle Macpherson screeched in pain at her squashed foot. 'Excuse me.'

And there Poppy was, in the middle of the floor, moving woodenly to the beat. For a second, Thea stopped and watched. She was so pretty, but she looked so lost. Once again, much as she would have liked to despise Poppy Norton, the only emotion Thea felt was pity.

But there was no time for such thoughts now. Thea squeezed past a skinny man in a sarong and shook Poppy on the shoulder.

'Poppy, hey Poppy!'

Poppy looked at her, her eyes as blank as the bullets in a movie gun.

'It's me. Thea. I . . . Luke's friend.'

Poppy bristled. 'What the hell do you want?'

'It's about Clara. She's really ill. In hospital. Meningitis. You have to get there quickly.'

Poppy's face, already pale, turned white.

'Clara?'

'Yes, Clara. Come on. We have to go.'

Poppy didn't move. 'Why didn't Brigita call me? She promised she'd call.'

'She did. You weren't answering.' Thea began dragging her across the dance floor. 'Come on. We have to go.'

'My phone's in the bag in the cloakroom.' Poppy stopped dead and looked into Thea's eyes. 'What a stupid cow I am. How the hell could I have done that?'

'It doesn't matter,' Thea said.

'It does. I left it there so I could keep on talking to Toby. I'm an idiot.'

457

'Come on!' Thea was virtually manhandling her. They stepped out of the marquee.

'There she is!' yelled the bouncer, as he spotted Thea. 'Oi. You cheeky cow.'

'Oh bugger off,' Thea snapped over her shoulder, as she pulled a still semi-frozen Poppy across the sun-scorched grass. 'Come *on*. I'm going to drive you to the hospital.' She stepped out of the gates she'd come in by, pointing her keys in the direction where she'd left her car.

No beep.

'What the fuck?' Thea knew immediately what had happened. She'd slammed the door without locking it, as if she were a character in a movie. But unlocked cars in central London didn't stick around for long. Still, she'd worry about that later.

'We'll get a taxi,' she said, looking round. Nothing with a light on. 'Come on. We'll have to run down to Baker Street and find one.'

'Poppy?' said a man's voice behind them. Thea looked round. A middle-aged blond guy in a suit was grinning at them, as he locked the doors of his Skoda. 'You're not leaving the party already, are you? I've only just got here.'

'Charlie!' Poppy exclaimed and burst into tears.

'Are you OK?'

'No, I'm not. Clara's in hospital and we can't find a taxi.'

Charlie's sack-of-potatoes face crumpled. 'Don't worry,' he said. 'I'll take you there.'

From the front seat of Charlie's car, Poppy twisted round to interrogate Thea.

'What about Luke?'

'He should be there by now. I can't call him because he left his mobile behind.' She pulled it out of her bag. 'I'll try Brigita again though.'

'How could I have done this?' Poppy gibbered. 'I'm a bad mother, a bad, bad mother.'

'No you're not,' Charlie said. 'You only went to a party.'

'But Clara was sick. I should have known.' She turned back to Thea.

'Thank you for coming to find me,' she said. 'It was so sweet of you.' Before Thea could work out how to reply to this, they were pulling up outside the hospital.

48

It was noon the following day but to Poppy and Luke time had stopped. They were living in a stifling new world of linoleum floors, the sound of wailing in corridors, hushed voices, an overwhelming odour of bleach and fear, and cold toast arriving at odd hours. In the harsh glare of the hospital strip lighting, Clara looked even more beautiful and more fragile than when she was newly born. Eyes shut, a tube in her nose, a needle at the end of another tube in her arm, the only sound in the room was the flashing and beeping of the monitor and of Poppy sobbing softly.

'It's all right,' said Luke, putting his hand on her arm. 'She's getting antibiotics through the drip and they're going to make her better. They caught it just in time.'

'Suppose they hadn't?' Poppy stroked her daughter's forehead. She'd been there all night, a night that had seen Clara endure a lumbar puncture and a couple of terrifying hours on a life-support machine. She would keep her vigil until her child was completely cured.

'Oh my darling, I'm sorry. I'm so, so sorry I wasn't with you,' she whispered again. She looked at Luke. 'Brigita did a great job getting her to hospital.'

'I know.'

'And Thea did a great job tracking us both down.'

'She did.' Then Luke said wryly, 'I'm not surprised. She's a brilliant journalist.'

'She was so sweet to me,' Poppy said. 'I thought she was a cow before, but last night she was a star.' A pause and then she said, 'But . . . how did she know Clara was ill?' In all the uproar, it hadn't crossed her mind to ask.

Luke said nothing.

'Of course, Brigita tried to track you down through the office.' Poppy smiled at her powers of deduction. 'She was probably in such a state she forgot you weren't there any more.'

'That's right,' Luke said, to the sound of a commotion outside the door.

'Poppy, darling. Poppy, are you in here? With my gorgeous Clarabelle?' Louise burst into the room, followed by Gary. 'Oh Christ!' she yelled at the sight of her granddaughter. 'So it's true!' She flung herself on Gary and began weeping noisily. 'Oh my God, oh my God. What am I going to do?'

'What's happened?' Gary asked, looking over Louise's heaving shoulders at Poppy.

'She'll have to stay in a few days, but they say she's going to be fine.'

'Oh my God! I've been crucified with worry! Crucified!'

'But I told you she was on the mend, Mum.'

'I had to see for myself.' Louise shook her head. 'Thank God Gary had come over to watch the golf and could drive me here because I was in no fit state to go anywhere.'

'Well done, Gary,' Poppy said.

He nodded curtly.

'I've never been in such agony in my life.'

'Clara must have had it tough too,' Gary said. For the first time in the past twelve hours, the faintest of smiles crossed Luke's face. There was a knock on the door. 'Come in,' he said, expecting one of the doctors. But instead, Charlie's head appeared. He too, looked as if he'd had a sleepless night.

'Hey, guys. Sorry to disturb. I just wanted to check everything was OK now.'

'You're not going to print this in the paper are you?' said Luke with narrowed eyes.

'Luke! Of course he's not.' Poppy was furious. 'Clara's on the mend now. Thank you so much Charlie for all your help last night.' She stepped forward and hugged him.

'It was my greatest pleasure,' Charlie said, just as Louise gave a little stifled scream.

'Charles Grimes?'

Charlie stiffened.

'Yes,' he said uneasily.

Under her fake tan, Louise had turned white.

'You know who I am, don't you?'

Poppy looked at them both, baffled.

'Or do you need some reminding?' Louise was asking. 'Ronnie's bar in St Tropez. Early eighties. "Owner of a Lonely Heart" by Yes. Me with a big floppy bow in my hair. A studio flat above the Chinese restaurant. Six glorious weeks until you disappeared into the ether and left me up the duff.'

Charlie looked at the floor.

'I know. I worked it out the other day. Lulu Price.'

'The very same.' Louise turned to Poppy. Her mouth was strangely twisted. 'I sincerely hope there's nothing going on between you and this man because he's your father.'

49

Clara stayed in hospital for a week. Horrified by how close she'd come to losing her, Poppy scarcely moved from her bedside. Thanks to Luke's very public summons in the theatre, the papers were full of the story of the Cad and the Bimbo's mercy dash to hospital, but within a few days Paris Hilton found a new boyfriend and the world moved on to other stories.

Poppy and Luke spent more time with each other than at any other point in their short marriage and when Clara was sleeping, they talked far more than they ever had before

'We both know it's not working,' she said. 'I married you for all the wrong reasons. I wasn't ready to be a wife. I needed someone to protect me. And you only married me because I was pregnant.' As Luke tried to protest she held up her hand to silence him. 'You did. That was very noble of you, but it wasn't fair. I did a bad thing and all I can do to remedy it is to set you free; let you go back to your old life.'

'I don't think that's an option.'

'I'll move out of the flat,' Poppy continued. 'Find somewhere to live with Clara. You can see her whenever you like.'

Luke shook his head. 'I'll move out. I mean, I already have. You two should carry on living there.'

'Thank you. But you can't afford to keep us there. You

don't have a job. You need to cut back on your spending.'

'I can't just abandon you and Clara,' said Luke.

'We can move somewhere much smaller. Less grand. We'll be just fine.'

Luke's throat caught. Poppy had lost so much weight the past few days. It bothered him that someone so much younger than him could be coming to such mature conclusions about their lives.

He reached out and traced the soft curve of her jawline. 'Are you sure about this, Poppy? Maybe we should give it another try. For Clara's sake at least.'

She shook her head. 'It wouldn't work. Really. We should end it now before Clara's old enough to understand.'

Luke knew she was right. In some ways he was relieved to be released. But still, he felt a desperate sadness at the way he'd messed up so many lives.

'You're a pretty amazing woman, you know. You've brought Clara up pretty much all by yourself and she's turned out so well.'

'I don't know about that. Being a mum is so hard. You never think you've got it right. Any good work is almost certainly down to Brigita, not me.'

'It's down to you. You've done brilliantly.'

Her eyes shone with tears. 'Why didn't you tell me that before?'

'I've only really understood it now.' Luke looked choked, as Clara stirred, then opened her eyes.

'Hi, darling,' they both cooed.

'Mummy,' she said indignantly, 'Daddy. I want chocolate.'

*

465

On the third day, Charlie came to visit. Poppy was still reeling from Louise's revelation, though naturally not as much as Louise herself, who, after pointing the finger at the man who had ruined her life, had staggered straight from her granddaughter's hospital bed to the pub across the road, where she had ordered Gary to buy her the largest gin and tonic available, followed by another and then another.

'I'm so spooked,' Poppy told him, as they sat on a hard chair in the canteen, clutching polystyrene cups of tea. The nurses had sworn they'd page her if Clara woke up.

'You're not half as spooked as I was. There was I constantly thinking "Bloody hell, I'm so old, this bright young girl about town's young enough to be my daughter" and all the time you *were* my daughter. And I had a granddaughter as well.'

The memory of the time she'd tried to kiss him hovered over them both like a vulture, but neither referred to it and they never, ever would.

'But you guessed,' Poppy said.

'I was starting to. Something you said about your mum in the South of France in the eighties got me thinking.'

'And then that time you dropped me off, you had a good snoop. Brigita told me.'

'Did she? Oh, sorry. It was wrong of me, but I just had to know. Of course you didn't have any photos of your mum, but then I did a little googling and worked it all out.'

'Were you going to tell me?'

'Of course. When I went to Regent's Park I was hoping to make a date with you then to take you out somewhere quiet and break it to you. I was bloody nervous. Terrified you'd reject me. But then fate got in the way.'

'Didn't you ever think of looking for me before?' Poppy asked. 'When I was a child?' A bit of her couldn't help being angry. She'd always wanted to know where her father was, why he hadn't bothered to hunt her down.

Charlie spread out his hands. 'Of course I did. I thought about it all the time. But remember: after I left your mother I was drying out for six months. Completely out of touch with the outside world. When I came out a letter from Louise was waiting saying she'd had the baby, but she wanted nothing more to do with me. I didn't even know if you were a boy or a girl. Of course I wrote to her a few times but I didn't get any reply, so in the end I gave up. Decided to make a new life for myself.' He shrugged self-deprecatingly. 'Not that I got far on that front, as you can see.'

'You have your photo in the paper every day.'

Charlie smiled. 'I thought you'd know by now that having your picture in the paper doesn't mean a thing. The reality is I'm a forty-five-year-old man, living in a one-bedroom flat in Crouch End with a silly job and a series of girlfriends who always dump me when they realize how rubbish my prospects are.' He looked at her ruefully. 'At least I have a kind of family now.'

Poppy hugged him. 'You do. And I couldn't be happier. We're going to see a lot, lot more of you, Clara and I.'

'And what are *you* going to do?' Charlie asked.

Now it was Poppy's turn to shrug. 'I don't know. Carry on with the column I guess. What else can I do? Especially now I'm a single mother.'

'What do you mean you're a single mother? You're still married to Luke. You've just had a bit of a blip.'

'I'm a single mother,' Poppy said.

Charlie reached for his daughter's hand. 'Why don't you give it another try? More than anyone, I should know that you have to work at things.'

Resolutely, Poppy shook her head. 'If Hannah doesn't want Luke, that's up to her. But I can't hold on to him. I'll never really be able to make him happy.'

'I'm not sure anyone can do that.'

'I'm not going to drink any more. You were right. It was getting just a tiny bit out of hand.'

'It's in the genes. I hate to say it, but I don't think you should be touching the booze at all.'

'Really?'

Charlie shook his head. 'Mineral water from now on.'

'Tonic water's better. Put a slice of lemon in it and you can almost fool yourself about the gin.'

Charlie squeezed her hand again and they sat in silence, neither quite able to believe they had found the other.

Thea was in the office, trying to find a nun who would come in to have a go at the Prime Minister about his stance on abortion, when her landline rang.

'Is that Thea?' said a soft, fresh female voice.

'Speaking. Is that Sister Mary?'

There was a laugh that sounded as if it had been permeated with fabric conditioner. 'I wouldn't be surprised if that's how I end up. But no, it's Poppy. Poppy Norton.'

'Oh! How are you? How's Clara?' She must have found out about Luke and was calling to berate her.

'She's doing really well. We can take her home to-morrow. We had a lucky escape. I just wanted to thank you for coming to find me that night. If you hadn't I don't know . . .'

Thea swallowed. 'Clara would have been OK, anyway,' she said gruffly.

'That's not the point. The point was I got there. I owe you one. Though I'm not sure what that could be.'

'Don't worry. I did what anyone would have done.'

'Goodbye, Thea.'

'Goodbye.'

Thea found it hard to concentrate on Sister Mary, she felt so guilty. She couldn't put it off any longer, she'd talk to Luke that night.

She got home just after nine. She wasn't expecting to see him; he'd been more or less permanently at the hospital, just coming back to sleep and shower. But this evening, the front door wasn't double locked and he was sitting in front of the television, the usual large whisky in his hand. It was a hot summer night and a breeze fanned in, carrying reggae noises from the barbecue down the street.

'How's Clara?' she asked.

'Going home tomorrow.' Luke looked straight in her eyes. 'And so am I.'

'You're going back to Poppy!' It came out as a yelp. Understandably, Luke mistook her relief for hurt.

'I'm sorry, Thea,' he said, standing up, 'but I've just

made too many mistakes. I can't keep moving on from woman to woman every time things get a bit rough. I've got to go home.'

'All right,' Thea said.

Luke was surprised. He knew he was doing a shitty thing, finally making Miss Moneypenny's dream of domestic bliss come true only to shatter it within weeks. Poor Thea. A future of cats that she called her babies and evening classes beckoned. But he'd wasted enough time the past few years living a lie and he just couldn't do it any more.

'What do you mean – all right?'

'I mean all right.' Thea shrugged and headed towards the kitchen. 'I'm going to have a glass of wine. Would you like one?'

Luke followed her. 'Don't you want to know why I'm ending it?'

'Minnie Maltravers called and said she just couldn't live without you.'

'Don't be silly,' Luke snapped, as Thea turned round from the fridge, a strange, slightly pitying smile on her face.

'Listen, Luke, don't worry. It wasn't working out. You and I have had some great times over the years, but it's been all about hotel rooms and exotic locations and adventures. It's not about life in a small two-bedroom flat in Stockwell and arguing about who runs down to the shop to buy some Paul Newman salad dressing. That's not how you like to live your life and it's not how I like to live mine. You're better off with Poppy. She can take care of you.'

He should have felt relief at being let off the hook so easily. But instead Luke was annoyed: first Poppy, now Thea letting him go with about as much regret as if he were a dodgy builder.

'I'm not going back to Poppy,' he corrected her, glad that at least in one way, he could have the upper hand. 'I'm going back to Hannah.'

It gave him some satisfaction to see Thea's startled expression.

'Hannah? *She* won't have you.'

A tiny chuckle escaped Luke's lips.

'Have you asked her? Because I have: she's ecstatic I'm coming back.'

Another flash of anger at all the years she'd wasted consumed Thea. But there was no point showing her frustration. Luke would think it was to do with losing him. So all she said was, 'That's the best thing that could happen. After all, I forwarded Hannah that email from Poppy. So it's right you leave me and go back to her. Poetic justice if you like.'

Luke stared at her in amazement.

'*You* sent the email.'

Thea flushed and shrugged. 'Yeah.'

'You silly bitch. You sent the email.' Luke turned and stared out of the window. 'Do you know how much pain you've caused, Thea? Do you have any inkling of the damage you've done? That email broke up my family. It ruined people's lives.'

'I know. I'm sorry.' It sounded so inadequate. It *was* so inadequate. Thea would have to live with the guilt for the rest of her life. Perhaps it was because she'd never had a father herself that it had taken her so long to realize how essential they were to a family, how wrong it was to try and dislodge them.

'You're right,' Luke said. 'I *am* better off with Hannah.' He picked up his suitcase. 'The sooner I get round there the better. Goodbye, Thea.'

'Goodbye, Luke.' She'd thought she'd be happy, but as the door slammed shut, a big tear rolled down Thea's cheek, followed by another, then another, as the dream she'd nurtured for so many years finally died a long-overdue death.

Why Divorce Can Never be the Answer

A few weeks ago, there was a bit of a to-do in the press when it was revealed that I had been reunited with my ex-husband, Luke Norton, former anchorman of the *SevenThirty News* and contestant on this year's *Strictly Come Dancing*. I suppose some of the uproar was inevitable.

Since Luke and I divorced three years ago, after I discovered his affair with Poppy Price, 25, I have chronicled in some detail the pain he put me through, not to mention that of our three children. I called him a cad and Poppy a bimbo, I mocked him for his habit of buying Viagra on the internet and told the world I was better off without him.

And indeed, in many ways, life without Luke was a revelation. I revived my old journalistic career, former friendships sprang back to life, I travelled the world and rediscovered much of my old zest for life: a zest that had been buried by the crushing demands of motherhood. But for all my apparent jauntiness in the face of this calamity, I could not kill the ache in my heart, the ache any woman whose family has collapsed will recognize, the feeling that I should somehow have fought harder to save my marriage.

When I discovered my husband's affair, after an email from his lover was mysteriously sent to my inbox, I reacted out of pique, pride and fury. After years of turning a blind eye to alleged indiscretions, the mousey housewife suddenly turned.

473

Without giving Luke a chance to explain himself, I kicked him out, into the arms of his pregnant lover. When he begged me to take him back I refused to listen, and instead served him with divorce papers. Friends told me I had done the right thing, that I had refused to be a 'little woman', a doormat. For a long time I believed them.

But as time passed, I began to think differently. Although I was still angry with Luke, I missed him and so did the children. I began to understand that his infidelities might have been abhorrent, but they were not unpardonable. I saw that in the years Luke and I had been together I had transformed from the sparky career woman he married into a drudge, whose only topics of conversation were who'd made the best jam at the school fête and our next-door neighbour's au pair's nose ring. I'd piled on the pounds and slopped round the house in dirty old fleeces and Ugg boots. Could I really blame him for sometimes feeling a little bored?

When I pondered on the parlous state of our once great nation, I realized I had been guilty of failing to practise what I preached. The lawlessness on our streets, the incivility that governs virtually all our everyday interactions all comes down to broken homes. Luke and I were two grown adults who should have known better, but we'd refused to hack our way through the thorny copses that block all our marital paths, instead choosing to go for the short-term easy way out.

I began to berate myself: why hadn't Luke and I worked harder to mend things? And Luke was obviously thinking the same thing. The calls, emails and texts kept coming as he pleaded with me to meet him for dinner, to at least talk on the phone. He sent me flowers and jewellery, but pride made me send them back and continue to boast to the outside world about how happy I was, when inwardly my heart was breaking.

Of course, I had not been lonely during this time, but I realized that charming as my new lover was, he was no substitute for the bond Luke and I had shared together, built over nearly two decades of huge life experiences such as having children, installing an Aga and being presented to the Queen at a Buckingham Palace garden party.

Naturally, when Luke approached me about a reunion we had to factor in the question of his new young wife and their small daughter. Was it fair to break up a new family in order to mend an old one? I was torn, but Luke persuaded me it was all for the best. Poppy and he had married only because I had pushed them together and – as I predicted – virtually instantly discovered their relationship was based on nothing but fleeting sexual attraction. He continues to see their daughter regularly and Poppy is bravely forging a new life for herself as a TV presenter and single mother. I wish her well.

But back to Luke and me. I can honestly say the day he returned to our house and our bed was the happiest of our lives – happier even than our wedding day, because this time we really understood what we meant to each other. We have learnt the hard way what the true meaning of love, trust and family is. We've been tested, and, despite everything, we have passed the test. We are stronger now than we have ever been and I don't regret the decision to take him back for one second. Success isn't about never making a mistake; it's about trying, failing and trying again. Too many women throw everything away because their husband turns out not to be perfect. They don't understand that, for men, sex is, just that – sex.

Heaven knows, I am hardly a saint. Luke knows he is in the last-chance saloon. If he strays again then woe betide his *cojones*! But I trust that he won't. He knows now what he has to lose. He values me and the children far more than he did before, and when I see the love in his eyes every morning, I know that whatever happens, it's been worth it.

50

It was a bleak Sunday morning in mid September and Poppy was trying to get Clara out of the door en route to Tesco's.

'Don't wanner wear this hat! It's not pink.'

Poppy's pride in her daughter's brilliant vocabulary was eclipsed by exasperation.

'It's purple and it's a very pretty hat,' she said levelly.

'Want a pink hat. Want to wear a pink haaaat.'

'Darling, you don't have a pink hat.'

'Buy me one.'

'Oh for heaven's sake,' Poppy said, as Clara flung herself to the floor, screaming as if her limbs were being torn off by slavering wolves. Poppy could barely hear her phone ringing.

'Hello?' she said, grabbing it, a finger jabbed in her other ear.

'Wanner . . . pink oooone.'

'Christ. Where are you? Bedlam?'

'Your granddaughter wants to wear a pink hat.'

'I see,' Charlie said sagely. 'Well, just to add to your joys, have you seen the *Sunday Prophet* yet?'

'Are you trying to warn me about something?'

'Only the latest instalment from your dear friend. Do you want me to read it to you?'

'No, don't worry, I'll read it online.' Poppy stepped

over Clara's writhing body, sat down at her computer and clicked in newly expert fashion. 'Are you still there?' she asked as the page she was looking for shimmered into view. 'How are things anyway?'

'Not bad, not bad at all. I was wondering if you needed any babysitting in the next few days.'

'Any excuse to hang out with Miss Pinky,' Poppy teased him as the article came into focus. 'Don't worry, I'm not going out at night much any more and Brigita's covering the few times that I am, but it'd be good if you'd come round on Monday night anyway. It's Clara's first day at nursery and I'm bound to be a gibbering wreck. I'm so nervous.'

'She'll be fine.'

'What if she hates it and begs me not to leave her?'

'She won't do that,' Charlie said with the misplaced confidence of one who knew nothing about the ways of small children. 'Have you found the article yet?'

'Yup, just wait a second while I read it.' She skimmed it quickly, then laughed.

'Well done, Hannah. She's turned a potentially embarrassing situation to her advantage.'

'Is any of it true?'

'They're happy enough, as far as I can tell,' Poppy said. 'Hannah's got Luke by the short and curlies. Since she's the main breadwinner now, he's been allocated chauffeur duties, going up and down the motorway to pick the kids up from their various schools. Plus he has to pose for pictures to go with all the articles she's writing about their marvellous family life.'

'Will he ever get another job?' Charlie wondered.

'I don't think he's in any hurry to. His book's coming out in February and Hannah's insisted he does a load of publicity for it. "I was the real-life cad" that sort of thing. And then he told me he's going to write an autobiography that involves a year's research with lots of travel.'

'I can see why he'd want to get away, but what about Clara?'

'It's OK. Clara and I will go out and join him in a couple of the safer parts of the world. I'm looking forward to it. I think when I see some of the places he's worked in I'll finally know what makes Luke tick.'

'Does that mean a reunion's on the cards?' Charlie sounded alarmed.

Poppy laughed. Seeing the tantrum had passed, she pulled Clara off the floor, kissed her on the nose and for the second time that morning opened the front door of their new flat in Shepherd's Bush. 'Definitely, definitely not. Come on, darling. We're going to buy you the CBeebies magazine now. Or would you like *Angelina*?'

'Both of them!'

'Well . . . maybe.' As they set off down the road, hand in hand, Poppy switched her attention back to Charlie. 'I've been through all the emotions with Luke. Passionate love. Bewilderment. Sadness. Hatred. And now when I talk to him I feel . . . I don't know, sort of content. I made a mistake marrying him, but Clara came out of it so I didn't exactly come off badly.'

'That's the spirit.'

'And she ended my modelling career, for which thank God. And she started my new career as a columnist, because if I hadn't had a child to witter on about the readers wouldn't have wanted to know. And . . . I suppose that's what takes us to where we are today.'

'With your new job?'

'I'm so nervous, Charlie. Do you think I'll be OK?'

'You'll be brilliant. A TV guide to places to spend a lost afternoon. I can't think of anything you're more suited to.'

'On a channel with about five viewers.'

'There'll be more than five once word gets around someone as beautiful as you's presenting it.'

'It's all thanks to your introductions that I've got it. I'm so grateful to you.'

'It was nothing.' There was a pause then Charlie said, 'I love you, Poppy.'

'I love you too, Charlie. By the way. When you come round would you mind bringing a tool kit? Only my kitchen tap is dripping.' Poppy stopped short. 'Sorry, excuse me a second. I've seen someone I know. I'll speak to you later.'

Holding Clara's hand, she hurried across the road.

'Hi! Oh my God. Congratulations! I had no idea.'

Standing behind a splendid Silver Cross pram, Thea blushed. The short man at her side laughed.

'Is it a girl or a boy?' Poppy cooed, peering in. 'Oh God, I'm stupid, of course it's a boy, look at all that blue. It used to drive me nuts little old ladies saying "Bless him" when Clara was in a bright pink dress and had a ribbon in her hair. I . . .'

'Um. It's not mine,' Thea said.

'Sorry?'

'It's not mine. It belongs to my friend, Rachel. I'm

taking it for a walk, while its parents are looking at wedding rings.'

'Oh. Right.' Poppy peered at the squashed-faced sleeping bundle to hide her embarrassment. 'Of course. It was only a couple of months ago you took me to hospital and you didn't exactly look pregnant then. Ah, bless him, isn't he gorgeous though?'

'He's all right,' Thea conceded with a grudging pride. 'I'm his godmother.'

There was a pause. Poppy turned to the man. 'Sorry, I'm Poppy. My ex-husband used to work with Thea.'

'Yes, I know him a little. We did some work together in Guatemala. I'm Jake.'

'Hi.' A beat. 'So are you still at the *SevenThirty News*?' she said to Thea.

'I am. Just been promoted to programme editor.' Thea looked over her shoulder, as if the slightly tatty urban street might be bugged. 'Though I'm not sure how long I'll be staying.'

'Have you got another job lined up?'

Thea smiled and shrugged. 'No. But I'm beginning to think it might be time for a change. Jake's going to head up a charity operation in Brazil and I'm wondering about going with him. Doing some freelancing out there. I used to have some financial obligations you see, but now I don't and—'

Clara pulled at Poppy's hand. 'Mummee. Want my CBeebies. And *Angelina*.'

'Clara, don't be rude. Mummy's talking.'

'It's OK,' Thea said. 'We need to keep moving or this one will kick off.'

Poppy shifted awkwardly from foot to foot. 'Well, nice to see you, Thea. Good luck with it all.' She thought about saying keep in touch but that would have been ludicrous.

'Thanks,' Thea said. 'And the same to you.' She and Jake carried on pushing the buggy down the suddenly sunlit street. Poppy watched them for a second then, as Clara tugged impatiently on her arm, she headed off in the opposite direction.

JULIA LLEWELLYN

THE LOVE TRAINER

Men are like puppies – they need training. Otherwise:

1 They wee on the floor
2 They stay out late and scratch at the door to be let in
3 They whine when you say No
4 They think they can get away with murder by gazing mournfully into your eyes.

Katie Wallace had her heart broken once, and she's not going to let it happen again. What's more, she doesn't want it to happen to anyone else if she can help it. After discovering a talent for advice, Katy becomes a unique service provider – a Love Trainer, capable of answering all of the following:

1 Should I call him even though he hasn't called me?
2 Why hasn't he called even though I've texted, left two messages on his mobile and one on his landline?
3 When he turns up drunk in the middle of the night wanting a shag, do I say yes or no?
4 Is he worth the effort if I'm not even sure I want to marry him?

But can you really coach a man like you would a dog? Or is Katy about to learn that when it comes to training, the work needs to start much closer to home…

JULIA LLEWELLYN

IF I WERE YOU

My name is Natasha
I have a successful career
A gorgeous penthouse flat
Trouble is, I'm in love with a man who already has a girlfriend

My name is Sophie
I have a man I love
He's gorgeous and we've been together four years
Trouble is, he won't propose

Natasha and Sophie have been best friends since their first day at school. Natasha was always the more intelligent and Sophie the more beautiful, but it never came between them … until now. Suddenly the tiny, niggling, inescapable fact of their envy for each other's life is trying to surface and a number of casualties are getting caught in the crossfire. Is a fading love worth clinging to at all costs? Is marriage the be-all and end-all? And can an affair ever be fulfilling?

Natasha and Sophie need to learn that they might be hunting for happiness in all the wrong places …

JULIA LLEWELLYN

AMY'S HONEYMOON

A five-star honeymoon in Rome…

What more could a girl want?

In Amy's case, a husband might come in handy…but, with the cost of a cancelled wedding to mop up and no chance of a refund on the honeymoon, she's jetting off to bask in the Italian sunshine on her own.

Except no one seems willing to leave her alone. If it's not nosy hotel guests, it's famous movie stars desperate to exchange suites. How's a girl supposed to wallow in misery when, under protest, she's dragged off to shop till she drops, or to film premieres or intimate picnics à deux?

But why was the wedding called off? Where is the absent groom? And can movie stars really fall in love with the girl next door? You'd be mad to miss out on this Roman holiday …

'A hilarious new novel' *Evening Standard*

JULIA LLEWELLYN

If you enjoyed this book, there are several ways you can read more by the same author and make sure you get the inside track on all Penguin books.

Order any of the following titles direct:

9780141010458 THE LOVE TRAINER   £6.99

'A promising debut novel' *Daily Express*

9780141018256 IF I WERE YOU   £7.99

'An enjoyable, fun bit of chick-lit' *OK!*

9780141018263 AMY'S HONEYMOON   £6.99

'A perfect summer read' *Easy Living*

Simply call Penguin c/o Bookpost on **01624 677237** and have your credit/debit card ready. Alternatively e-mail your order to **bookshop@enterprise.net**. Postage and package is free in mainland UK. Overseas customers must add £2 per book. Prices and availability subject to change without notice.

Visit www.penguin.com and find out first about forthcoming titles, read exclusive material and author interviews, and enter exciting competitions. You can also browse through thousands of Penguin books and buy online.

IT'S NEVER BEEN EASIER TO READ MORE WITH PENGUIN

Frustrated by the quality of books available at Exeter station for his journey back to London one day in 1935, Allen Lane decided to do something about it. The Penguin paperback was born that day, and with it first-class writing became available to a mass audience for the very first time. This book is a direct descendant of those original Penguins and Lane's momentous vision. What will you read next?

He just wanted a decent book to read ...

Not too much to ask, is it? It was in 1935 when Allen Lane, Managing Director of Bodley Head Publishers, stood on a platform at Exeter railway station looking for something good to read on his journey back to London. His choice was limited to popular magazines and poor-quality paperbacks – the same choice faced every day by the vast majority of readers, few of whom could afford hardbacks. Lane's disappointment and subsequent anger at the range of books generally available led him to found a company – and change the world.

'We believed in the existence in this country of a vast reading public for intelligent books at a low price, and staked everything on it'
Sir Allen Lane, 1902–1970, founder of Penguin Books

The quality paperback had arrived – and not just in bookshops. Lane was adamant that his Penguins should appear in chain stores and tobacconists, and should cost no more than a packet of cigarettes.

Reading habits (and cigarette prices) have changed since 1935, but Penguin still believes in publishing the best books for everybody to enjoy. We still believe that good design costs no more than bad design, and we still believe that quality books published passionately and responsibly make the world a better place.

So wherever you see the little bird – whether it's on a piece of prize-winning literary fiction or a celebrity autobiography, political tour de force or historical masterpiece, a serial-killer thriller, reference book, world classic or a piece of pure escapism – you can bet that it represents the very best that the genre has to offer.

Whatever you like to read – trust Penguin.